DEAR BEN

The Secret Life of Benjamin Franklin

Michael Koski

Edited by Joan Lane and Sophie Cox BA (Oxon)

Copyright © 2024 Michael Koski
All rights reserved
First Edition

Fulton Books
Meadville, PA

Published by Fulton Books 2024

"Dear Ben: The Secret Life of Benjamin Franklin" is a work of fiction. Although based on historical records, liberties have been taken with names, dates, and places for the sake of storytelling. Where little is known of certain figures, i.e. Margaret Stevenson, the author has filled in the record from his imagination. Several characters are pure invention.

Copyright 2022 Michael Koski
WGA Registration 2184950
U.S. Copyright Office TX 2-339-892

ISBN 979-8-88982-969-0 (paperback)
ISBN 979-8-88982-972-0 (hardcover)
ISBN 979-8-88982-971-3 (digital)

Printed in the United States of America

For Steven Shipp Hannegan,
ever a port in the storm.

PART ONE

Runaway

CHAPTER ONE

Long Ago, Far Away

BOSTON   1701

Heavy wet snow pelts the windows as Abiah Franklin enters the kitchen with little Ebenezer tucked under her arm. Cold air creeps under the back door, but a good fire in the hearth warms the kitchen enough for the baby's bath. The saltbox-style house is too small for her family of six children, her husband, Josiah, and Josiah's brother, Uncle Benjamin; it groans under the strain. But the cramped quarters will have to do until Josiah's candle business prospers enough to afford the larger house in town she dreams about.

Raising so many children on so little has worn Abiah down. She appears older than her thirty-four years. She is haggard-looking, her hair thinning and gray, her skin deeply lined and sallow. Josiah, who had had six children in a previous marriage, is a pious man who takes the words in the Bible, '*be fruitful and multiply*', as an Eleventh Commandment. Five of those six children still live with him and Abiah, making a total of fourteen souls living under their roof.

With her free hand, she tests the temperature of the water in a tin wash tub on the kitchen table, takes a kettle off the grate and adds a dash of hot water. She disrobes the baby and lowers him gently into the shallow, tepid water. He squeals with delight, slapping his hands on the water, splashing it onto Abiah's calico apron. It pleases her that Ebenezer is the first of her four boys to enjoy his bath. She hears a loud 'crash', then a boy's scream from the front room. She props the baby carefully against the side of the tub.

"Don't move. Stay there," she commands him and rushes out of the kitchen. She finds a table on its side in the parlor and broken porcelain scattered over the floor. Her sons, John and Peter, tussle amidst the jagged shards. John has his arm firmly around Peter's neck.

"John! Stop that! You're choking him," she shouts.

"I didn't break nothin', Ma! *He* did it!" John says, releasing his grip on the other boy's neck.

"I didn't do it, Ma! *He* broke it!" Peter says, gasping for air.

"I don't care who broke it! I'm gonna have your father whip the tar outta the both of ya when he gets home!"

"I swear Peter knocked over the table!"

"You swear, my foot. How many times have I told you not to roughhouse in the parlor? That was my mama's favorite pitcher. Now, right that table and clean up this mess."

"John did it on purpose, Ma," Peter argues, rubbing his sore neck.

"Doesn't matter. You're both gettin' a thrashing when yer Pa gets home."

The boys help their mother pick up pieces of porcelain.

"Careful, now. Save the pieces. Don't cut yourself! John, get the broom off the back porch…"

Her eyes widen, remembering Ebenezer in the tub. She drops the broken pieces in her hands and runs to the kitchen, where the baby has slipped under the water. He lies motionless, his tiny hands thrust heavenward. Abiah screams, a piercing wail of agony the boys will remember all their lives.

LONDON   WINTER 1790

Snowflakes settle silently on the Thames as day fades to evening. Lights glow in the windows of a fine brick house on Savoy Hill, perched above the Embankment. Inside the house, in a wood-paneled library, a dapper gentleman is seated at his desk, writing a letter by candlelight. A fire glows in a fireplace across the room. Atop the creamy paper on which he writes, the name 'William Franklin, Esq.' is engraved. William wears a velvet smoking jacket and cravat, his salt-and-pepper hair pulled back into a ponytail. He writes without spectacles, his vision remarkable for a man of sixty-eight years. His quill pen scratches along the surface of the thick paper.

'*My Dearest Sally,*' he begins, '*Word around town is that the old man lingers on...* ' Snow falls outside the bow window behind him, as his pen dips into the inkwell, '*...though it is said he sleeps most of the time, like the old dog our father is. Local wags would also have it that Mrs. Hewson, neé Polly Stevenson, has come to you for an extended stay. Quelle dommage! I don't envy you that nasty woman's company.*'

A light tap at the door and a butler in uniform enters the room. He carries a small silver tray, bearing a dram of whiskey in a crystal glass.

"Your libation, sir."

William looks up from his letter. "Thank you."

The butler sets the drink on the desk and crosses to the fireplace. He picks up a poker and stokes the fire. "On a day like today, one wishes one had a cozy Franklin stove in the room, doesn't one?" he offers cheerily.

"Does one?" William replies icily.

"Supper will be served in one-half hour, sir." The butler replaces the poker in its stand and walks to the door. He brushes a speck of lint off his lapel with his fingertips. "What shall I tell Mrs. Franklin, sir?" he inquires.

"I won't be long. I'm writing to my sister in America."

"I shall advise the cook." The butler leaves, closing the door firmly behind him.

William resumes writing. '*Speaking of the Stevensons, I saw dear old Peter at a party in Mayfair last week. He must be nigh on eighty and still in service, but quite dotty. He seemed not to know me.*' William swirls the spirits in his glass, takes a sip, '*...or pretended not to.*'

Virginia

April 1790

With the stately portico of Monticello looming behind them, a dozen African-American slaves load travel bags into a line of three waiting coaches as day breaks. Some carry lanterns in the near-dark, a few young men calm the skittish horses queued up and ready to pull the coaches. Thomas Jefferson emerges from the house. He is a youthful looking forty-seven, wears a great coat, breeches, boots, and carries a leather valise. He surveys the proceedings, nodding his approval as he inspects the horses.

A few moments later, an attractive African-American woman appears on the front stair. She is in her late twenties, her attire that of a housemaid, but fancier than the others. She carries a man's wide-brimmed leather hat.

"You forgot your hat," she calls out.

Jefferson turns back to look at her and smiles. She descends the steps, walks to meet him, and offers the hat to him. "Your hat."

Much taller than she, Jefferson bends at the waist as she places the hat on his head. He stands, reaching up to adjust the brim. "Why, thank you."

"Never know… might rain up North."

"You never know," he says, touching her shoulder.

She smiles. His handsome face and wavy dark hair often make her smile. She returns to the porch of the house.

He calls after her. "Keep the fires burning!"

She looks back, smiles again, and gives him a small wave.

Jefferson is helped into the first carriage by a coachman. "How are the roads to Philadelphia this morning?" he inquires.

"Three days, maybe four, Mr. Jefferson."

"We'd best make haste, then."

CHAPTER TWO

Night Visitor

PHILADELPHIA   APRIL 1790

Approaching from the countryside to the west, Philadelphia reveals itself at the last moment, when a few church steeples, one with a clock tower beneath it, rise above the trees. The clock in the tower begins to chime the hour; it is six in the evening. Cornfields sway in the wind, heat lightning shimmers to the east, distant thunder rumbles.

On Market Street in town, a light burns in a third-story window of an imposing brick and timber mansion. Across the cobbled street, a weathervane topped with a headless rooster spins in the wind atop the neighbor's barn. Benjamin Franklin, at eighty-four, his eyesight failing, has yet to notice the cockerel is missing its head.

He lies in his bed, with eyes closed, and appears to sleep fitfully. He is gaunt, his skin sallow, and his thin hair matted. Feverish, he drifts in and out of delirium. Curtains flutter in and out the open window near his bed.

Polly Stevenson opens the bedroom door and tiptoes in. She is fifty-one, brunette, slender, and still girlishly pretty. She looks at Franklin, appearing concerned, places her hand on his forehead, and smiles slightly. She picks up a teacup and empty glass from the bedside table and quietly retreats, closing the door behind her.

The terrace behind the house is bathed in twilight, its brick pavers covered with fallen leaves. No one sees a whirlwind cross the terrace, madly stirring and twirling the leaves. The French doors to the library are flung open, then closed in the wind.

On the walk in front of the house, a half-dozen neighbors have gathered under a street lamp. They speak to one another in a near-whisper.

"Feels like rain comin' soon," a man says.

"Looks like it to me, too," another man says. He points to an upper story of the house. "I hear tell he's near the end."

"Oh, I don't know, Hector. He's a tough old bird," a woman argues.

A second woman pulls her coat tight around herself. "I think I might just stay a while."

"I'll stay here with ya, Melba," the first woman offers.

"Well, don't get wet. I'm goin' on home. Can't do any good here," Hector says as he walks away.

In the bedroom upstairs, a gust of wind blows out the candle on the table next to Franklin. The room grows dark, illuminated only by the light of the streetlamp outside. He struggles with a nightmare, beads of perspiration form on his forehead. He sees an infant boy, lying still under soapy water, drowned. Franklin tosses and turns, moans, then awakens abruptly from his dream. He gasps for air and speaks aloud in a weak voice.

"I'm still alive. Why me? Why do I live on to useless old age, when others must die so young?" His eyes dart about the near-dark room. "My brother, drowned at just sixteen months! I am grown too old. My thoughts meander. I hear something. I hear the wind. Wait! Do I hear voices? A horse on the cobbles? Nay, they say the hearing is the last to go as we die…"

He closes his eyes and attempts to shout. "Bobby!"

In the kitchen downstairs, Bobby, Franklin's manservant, a slave, sings softly as he prepares a tea tray. Nobody knows with certainty, but Bobby, who is graying at the temples, may be in his late forties. He has been in service with the Franklin family most of his life and rarely strays further from the house than the farmers' market at the end of the street. He has an easy smile, a twinkle in his eye, and a kind word for everybody he meets. Now, he makes certain he is alone, reaches into the back of a cupboard, retrieves a wine bottle, and slips it into the deep pocket of his apron.

DEAR BEN

Sally Franklin Bache and Polly Stevenson pass each other in the narrow hallway leading from the dining room to the parlor. Polly carries a silver tray laden with a tea service. Sally is Benjamin Franklin's only daughter and lives with her husband, Richard, and their children in the big house on Market Street, as she always has. A famous clergyman, visiting the house recently, described Sally as 'gross and homely,' but she is not that. Although plain and a little plump, with graying blonde hair, her face is pleasing and unlined at forty-seven.

A breeze, a cool mist, appears to brush between the two women. They do not see it, but feel something. They both stop.

Sally looks at Polly indignantly. "Excuse me! Did you just push me?"

"What?"

"You pushed me."

"No, I didn't push you. The tray's heavy. My elbow may have touched you," Polly offers defensively, in her crisp accent.

"I do wish you'd be more careful," Sally says sharply.

"I felt a draft. Did you open a window?"

"No, I didn't open any windows."

"Well, something made me shiver. There must be a door ajar…" Polly suggests.

Bobby carries his tea tray and a small oil lamp as he meets Sally and Polly in the hallway.

"Evenin', ladies. Pardon, Missus Bache, Miss Polly." He gestures toward the stairway. "I'm goin' up those stairs."

"How is he?" Sally asks, surveying Bobby's tray.

"Oh, 'bout the same."

"He was sleeping when I looked in on him," Polly offers. "His fever's down."

"Time for his tea now. I got his medicine, too." Bobby squeezes past the women.

"Well don't give him too much… and <u>no</u> spirits! Hear me?"

"No Ma'am. No spirits. 'Course not."

"Tell him I'll be up shortly," Sally instructs.

"I will do that, Ma'am," Bobby tells her, and starts up the stairs.

Sally casts a stern eye on Polly's silver tray, which bears a porcelain tea pot, cups, saucers and plates. "I don't think that tea service is the right choice for grand company, do you?"

"I think it's lovely. You may recall that my mother sent it to you as a wedding present."

"Did she? I forgot. Never used it much. Well, carry on," Sally says curtly as she continues on her way.

A few moments later, Bobby reaches the landing one flight up, sits, sets down the lamp and his tray, takes the bottle from his pocket, and has a nip or two.

Upstairs, Franklin's eyes are still closed as he tugs at the bed sheets covering him, looking for warmth and comfort. A figure hovers nearby, hidden in shadow. She watches Franklin twist and turn for a moment, then whispers to him, "*Je suis ici, mon amour.*"

Franklin becomes still. He thinks aloud. "Was that a woman's voice? She whispered something. Was it in French?" He speaks out in a raspy voice. "Am I in Paris? My mind is playing tricks!" He tries again to shout. "Bobby!" Franklin opens his eyes, his frail hand grasping the bedspread. "There's somebody in this room," he says under his breath. "Who goes there?"

The pale figure steps out of the shadows and sits in a chair near his bed. It is an apparition of Madame Hélène Brillon, his lover during the time he lived in France. In her late forties, her beauty is remarkable. She is poised and bejeweled, wearing a white satin opera cloak. Her ebony hair is worn up, there is a silver streak in her forelock.

"Bon soir, cher Papa."

Half asleep, half awake, Franklin raises himself on one elbow. "Hélène? Is that you?"

He sits up, reaches out towards her. "Why are you here?"

"I escort you to the other side."

He looks startled. "Now? But I'm not ready. I don't look my best... and I have many things yet to do."

"Come. It is your time."

"What of Henri?"

DEAR BEN

"The Pox took my poor Henri two years ago. News travels slowly in this time of anarchy. Come. I will be your guide, as I promised you those many years ago."

She extends a delicate, very white hand to Franklin. He reaches for it, then pulls back. They hear Bobby singing in the hall outside the bedroom door. Bobby unlatches the door.

"You have company," Madame Brillon says, rising from the chair. "I go now. I return before daybreak. You must make ready! *À tout à l'heure.*" She recedes into the shadows and vanishes.

"Hélène! Don't go… Bobby!" he croaks, as Bobby opens the door and enters the room.

"Here I am! Here I am! What's all this noise about? Mercy, it's dark in here. Wind must-a blowed your candle out." Bobby sets the tray on a side table and turns up the lamp.

Franklin appears agitated and pulls his blanket up around his neck. "Did you see her? Did you see the lady? She's come for me!"

"I ain't seen nobody. They's a chill comin' in that window."

"She spoke to me. She said I haven't much time. Only tonight…"

Bobby goes to the window and closes it. "This big ol' house creak so bad in the wind, a person hear voices that ain't there, sometime." He takes the wine bottle from his pocket and places it on a bureau.

"She was in this room… I can smell her perfume!"

Bobby squeezes out a cloth in a basin on the dresser. "Next time I smell a lady in here, I let you know." He hums a tune as he wipes Franklin's brow.

"I must have had another bad dream. I get so confused… I didn't know where I was or *if* I was."

Bobby's gentle touch calms Franklin. "You're 't home, Dr. Ben. Right here on Market Street, safe and sound."

Franklin leans back against his pillows. "Did you bring the laudanum?"

"Yes, sir, like you ask." Bobby takes a vial from his pocket and sets it on the bedside table. He prepares Franklin's medicine in a small glass.

"Between the stones and the gout, a man could go mad. The opiate makes an idiot of me, but dulls the knife in my gut." He winces in pain as he adjusts a portable writing desk on the bed. Papers fall to the floor.

"I bring some of that wine you like, too. I hid a bottle back of the pie safe."

"Bless you. Madeira is the last of my pleasures. I made the mistake of growing ancient… an experience of little merit, I can assure you."

"I remember that when the time come."

"No, you won't. Old age sneaks up on you like a bandit, stealing all that is dear to you. At least I lived to see Washington made president."

Bobby helps Franklin to sit up and take his medicine.

"How are my girls getting on?"

"Oh, they gettin' on, you know, like women do sometime… pullin' each other's hair out."

Bobby pours wine into a teacup. "Your papers is on the floor."

The house trembles with a nearby lightning strike and a clap of thunder, startling Bobby. He recoils, stepping on Franklin's papers.

"My maps. Give them to me."

Bobby picks up the papers and replaces them on the writing desk.

"I promised Jefferson I'd make some notes for him about those maps. We used them to define our boundaries when we signed the Treaty of Paris, but I can't think straight to write, damn it. Has he come yet?"

"Not yet, but the ladies sure makin' a fuss gettin' ready."

"'Tis a privilege to have the man under this roof. He is the most brilliant and honorable statesman of our time."

"What about yourself?"

"Me? Brilliant? I suppose so. Honorable? No." He takes a long sip from the teacup. "I would have kissed the King's arse for a plantation in Ohio. Has my son-in-law turned up yet?"

"Mr. Bache not home yet, no sir."

"Of course not. No point coming home while there's a good tavern open. How about my grandsons?"

"Young Mr. Bache down at his print shop, I think." Bobby sings softly as he reaches behind Franklin and fluffs his pillows.

"Benny will make a success of that business, you'll see. He's more steady on his feet than his father ever was."

"He don't drink like his papa. That help."

"What news of Temple?"

"Young Mr. Franklin rode off 'bout a hour ago. Don't know where to."

"Poor Temple. He's a lost soul over here. My keenest wish is that he never sees his father again, but William issues his siren call from across the sea. Bobby, would you do me a favor?"

"What is it?"

"Help me to get up for a few minutes and tidy this bed for me. I should like to die in fresh linens."

"Nobody's dyin' around here anytime soon." Bobby helps him to rise from his bed.

Franklin steps into slippers, then shuffles with effort across the room, pulling his nightshirt close about him as he goes. "Nothing is easy for a dying man." He looks at the fireplace at the far end of the room. "Fire's burned down to nothing, Bobby."

"One thing at a time…" Bobby takes linens from a press, shakes out a sheet, and goes about changing the bed. "When I think about crossin' over, Dr. Ben, it scare me more than the storm do."

"Nothing to fear. We go where we've been before. We just don't remember it." Franklin leans a shoulder against the wall. "Lay out my blue velvet suit, will you? I should like to be buried in it. It is of historical significance, you know." He points to the ceiling "I hear a good rain starting." Franklin goes to the window and peers out. "There are people down there in the street!"

"Mm, hm. They come and they go, all day long."

Franklin sounds annoyed. "It's a damned deathwatch, is what it is."

"They's just bein' neighborly."

"Neighborly, hell. Bobby, fetch me the bedpan. The way the wind is blowing, I can hit Melba Perkins square on her bonnet."

Bobby shakes his head. "I don't know I'd upset those folk. I remember one night they was downright hostile. You was away that time, livin' in England."

"Yes. I was over there trying to keep the King from falling on his own sword. Poor Deborah was alone in the house that night, as I recall."

"No, sir, I was there, too."

CHAPTER THREE

Blazes

PHILADELPHIA   OCTOBER 1765

Evening falls as Deborah Franklin lights candles in the parlor of the house on Market Street. A stone hits and glances off a window; she looks out. She hears fallen leaves crunching under the boots of two dozen or more men gathering in the street outside. They look menacing. Some wear disguises or war paint and carry torches. The leader wears a bandana over his face and barks instructions to the gang as they take positions around the house.

"Christ! What new hell is this?" she wonders aloud. Deborah doesn't see her neighbor across Market Street, an old woman made curious by the commotion outside, part her curtains and look out. Frightened by what she sees, she jerks the curtains closed and retreats.

Deborah is fifty-seven, full of face, and a bit plump in her cotton housedress. Her hair is streaked with gray and worn pinned up. She has piercing blue eyes, a razor-sharp tongue, and is known for her fiery temper.

'If only Ben was home,' she thinks. But he is not home, nor has he been home for the past year. Another stone hits a window, cracking the pane of glass. Alarmed, she blows out candles, rushes to the kitchen and out the back door.

Deborah runs across the back yard to the servants' quarters and pounds on the door. "Jake! It's me! Open up!" Moments later, a powerfully built African-American man opens the door a crack and looks out. He is middle-aged, shirtless, and wears overalls. His back bears the scars of mistreatment by a previous owner. His skin is as dark as night.

That of his pretty wife, Aggie, who peeks over his shoulder, is the color of cocoa. "What is it, Ma'am?" Jake asks groggily, pulling up the braces on his pants.

"We got us a bad situation! Ride as fast as you can over to Cousin Josie's place and tell him to round up some men and get over here straight away!" Deborah instructs him urgently. "There are men out front who intend to do some damage, looks like to me! Go now!" She turns and hurries back to the house.

Jake grabs a shirt, runs to the barn, and slides open the big wooden door. He finds a saddle, throws it on a horse, mounts it, and rides off. When he reaches Josiah Read's house on the edge of town minutes later, he finds Josiah in his yard raking and burning leaves in the gathering dark. Jake tells him anxiously of his cousin's plight.

"Jesus! It don't take much for men to go plain crazy!" Josiah says. He drops his rake and runs to the carriage house. "Follow me out to the McCrae place," Josiah yells to Jake as he hastily saddles up his horse. Sandy-haired and fit in his fifties, he and Jake gallop off down the Post Road, heading for farm country.

The farms close to town have seen little trouble from the Iroquois in recent years, but the farmers remain armed and ready for a fight. Jake follows Josiah into the rutted drive of Henry McCrae's white-washed farmhouse.

"Wait here," he commands Jake. Josiah dismounts, tucking in his shirt as he runs to the side porch and up the steps. The house is dark. He pounds on the door, and a moment later, a light is turned on inside.

"Henry! It's me, Josiah! Open up!"

Henry McCrae opens the door a crack. His hair is tousled, the belt on his trousers hangs open. "Josiah? What the hell do you want at this hour? I was just goin' to bed."

"Grab your rifle! Cousin Deborah's got big trouble. They's a gang 'bout to burn down her and Ben's house!" He points to Jake waiting on horseback. "Deborah yelled for old Jake, here, to come and get me. We need yer help!"

Henry cinches his belt and takes a jacket off a hook by the door. "Gimme a couple of minutes to saddle up."

"Hurry! We'll go on down to the Gooding place."

"I'll stop and get Waterman. We'll catch up. We'll find out who stirred everybody up and hang the sons of bitches!" he shouts as he runs to the barn.

Before long, Josiah has raised an army of twenty recruits, who whip their horses as they ride toward the lights of town, all with rifles in scabbards strapped to their saddles.

The gang leader outside the Franklin house calls to Deborah, who hides in the darkened library, peeking out a window. "Come outta that house, Deborah Franklin, or you are gonna die in the flames!" Yet another stone strikes a window.

Frantic, Deborah runs to the front hall closet, where she finds two rifles, shot and powder. With trembling hands, she loads the rifles and rushes with them up a stairway. Breathless, she arrives at the door of Bobby's bedroom in the attic. Bobby is asleep in his tiny garret room. An oil lamp burns next to the bed, a schoolbook, a primer, lies open on the floor next to him.

Deborah raps sharply at his door. "Bobby! Get up! Quick, now!"

Bobby stirs and rouses himself awake. "Missus Franklin? That you?" He turns up the lamp.

"Yes! It's me! Open up!"

Wearing only underdrawers, Bobby jumps out of bed, unlatches and opens the door.

"What is it, ma'am? What's goin' on?" he asks, his eyes blinking.

Deborah pushes past him and looks out the dormer window. She sees the orange glow of torches being lit. "Put your pants on, will ya?" She opens the window as Bobby buttons his trousers and puts on a shirt. They hear the din of angry voices below. "Our neighbors have gone crazy! They'd like to burn our house down over that stupid Stamp Act."

"What Stamp Act?" Bobby asks, tying the laces of his boots.

"It's a new English tax. They think Ben was behind it. Get over here and take this rifle," she says, offering a weapon to Bobby. "If anybody shoots this way, you shoot right back." She thrusts the rifle into Bobby's reluctant arms.

Bobby attempts to return the rifle. "But ma'am, I ain't never fired one 'a these!"

Deborah plants the rifle firmly in his arms. "You'll get the hang of it. Every man loves to shoot his gun."

"I might kill somebody! How 'bout I go out back and practice?"

"How about you do as I tell you? I sent Jake to get Cousin Josie and some men to help us. 'Til they come, we're alone in the house. Thank Jesus Sally's up north at her brother's place."

The gang leader sees Deborah in the dormer window and shouts up to her. "We ain't sayin' it again! You come outta that house or you are gonna burn up with it!"

Deborah leans out the window and displays her rifle to the gang below. "And ye will burn in hell! Big brave man, hidin' behind your old lady's kerchief! I know who you are! Now get away from my house!"

Bobby stands next to her, nervously peering out the window.

The gang leader grows impatient. "You come down from there, damn it! We aim to teach your husband a lesson! We trusted him and he betrayed us! Him and his masters in Parliament is robbin' us!" The leader's cohorts howl like wild men, brandishing their torches and firearms.

"And what have I done to offend you that you would take my home from me?" Deborah yells out the window, her heart pounding. "I am waitin' on ye to name my crime!"

Another gang member, his face slathered in red and black war paint, shouts up to her. "This ain't about you, Miz Franklin, or that colored boy up there with ye!"

"I do not fear ye and I will not stir!" Deborah shouts in return, her resolve stiffened. "We are armed and we got help on the way! If it's war ye want, I will give ye a good one!"

"Big talk! You and the colored boy is all you got!" the painted man taunts.

"I said… get off my land before I blast that paint off your face!"

Bobby's rifle fires. With a loud report, he hits something metallic. Deborah ducks under the window. The gang disperses and runs for cover, shouting and cursing as they flee. Deborah stands and fires a second shot over their heads. A few men turn and throw lighted torches toward the house, which land in the street, flaring out harmlessly.

A minute later, buggies and pedestrians scatter as Josiah's militia thunders down Market Street and into the fray outside the Franklin house, whooping like Indians on the war path.

Henry McCrae horse-whips gang members as he encircles them. "'At's it! Keep on runnin'! We're gonna follow you men and burn *your* houses down! How d'ya like that!"

Josiah's band of farmers dismount and chase after gang members on foot for several blocks, cracking their whips overhead and screaming threats as they run.

Deborah looks at Bobby wide-eyed. "Damn, Bobby! What'd you hit?"

Bobby stands dumbfounded. "Don't rightly know! I was aimed at the moon!"

"Well, Josie's got that rabble on the run."

"That rabble was our neighbors!" Bobby exclaims, gingerly laying down his rifle.

"Yeah. Our neighbors. Think about that, will ya?" Deborah says, pushing stray strands of hair off her face. "I'm gonna get some beers poured for Cousin Josie. You keep watch here. If any of those bastards tramples my camellias, shoot his fekkin' boots off!" she orders as she dashes out the door and down the stairs.

The leader and a gang member cower behind a tree across the street from the Franklin house. "I warned you not to fool with the bitch. She is one hellcat," the gang member whispers.

The leader removes the bandana covering his face. He is Noah Portman, an elder of the Episcopal Church, who regularly sits in a pew behind Deborah on Sundays. "I ain't done with that woman yet," he says.

"Well, I am. I'm goin' home," the other man says and retreats into the darkness.

CHAPTER FOUR

Strange Bedfellows

PHILADELPHIA   APRIL 1790

Franklin stares out of the bedroom window, as if expecting someone. After a long moment: "My Deborah had spirit, didn't she?"

Bobby smooths the bed sheets. "You could say that, yes, sir."

Franklin turns back from the window. "Neighbors… Citizens. A mob is a monstrous thing, Bobby… all head and no brains."

"Let's get you back to bed now."

Franklin leans against the window frame, weaving a bit. "Such a mob has mocked and spat upon my friends, the King and Queen of France, in the streets of Paris."

Franklin holds his abdomen, wincing in pain as Bobby walks him back to his bed. "The fury of a mob is a fearsome thing," Franklin says, as he sits on the edge of the bed. He tilts his head, as if listening. "Can you hear them, Bobby?" He closes his eyes, imagining '*The Terror.*'

PALACE OF VERSAILLES   OCTOBER 1789

It is late at night as a mob of hundreds of scruffy-looking revolutionaries, most in their twenties and thirties, push open the gilded gates of the palace. An elaborate horse-drawn coach, closely surrounded by a gang of ragged men and women armed with clubs and rifles, emerges through the gates. Two of their own are at the reins, perched in the coachmen's seat.

The mob pounds on the doors, screaming insults and threats at the coach's passengers as it moves. "Swine! Perverts! Thieves! Murderers!" they shout at the rolling coach.

King Louis XVI and Queen Marie Antoinette and their family are seated inside, peering out of the windows, terrified. They see the twisted, angry faces of the men and women around them, hear their screams. They try to cover the eyes and ears of their children. The Royal Guard has abandoned them. They know their fate.

Bobby interrupts Franklin's reverie. "They was your friends?"

"Yes, and friends to this country as well." Franklin opens his eyes. "I have a picture here somewhere." He points to a side table. "Open that drawer. Take out the blue velvet box."

Bobby removes the box from the drawer and opens it. Inside he finds a cameo portrait of King Louis XVI, with his long, curly hair. "Mercy! That one ugly queen," Bobby notes.

"That is a portrait of Louis, the King. He gave it to me as a farewell gift at the end of my nine years' service in France."

"They's diamonds all around the picture." The stones sparkle as Bobby examines the cameo under the lamp light.

"408, if you were to count them. I should leave it to Polly. She met the King when she came to visit me in Paris after her husband died."

Bobby nestles the cameo back in the velvet box. "Now Miss Polly come all the way from England to see you."

"She knows I am near the end."

"She tell me you doin' better now." Bobby returns the box to the drawer in the table."

"Nay. My body is like an old run-down house. 'Tis much cheaper for the owner to tear it down and start over than to make the needed repairs."

Bobby folds soiled linens into a basket. "We could pray on that, if you like," he offers softly.

"Pray? No, thank you." Franklin chuckles. "I think of my French friend, the great poet, Voltaire, on his deathbed. A priest asked him to pray and renounce Satan. Voltaire replied, '*Zees is no time to make new enemies, you fool.*'" Franklin gestures to the window near his bed. "Open it again, will you? Nothing like the scent of a spring rain."

Bobby sets down the basket and opens the window a few inches.

Franklin speaks through a cough. "I like to sleep with an open window. There was a night I shared a bed with John Adams many years ago. Stranger bedfellows there never were. You know who John Adams is?"

"I heard the name," Bobby replies.

"He's the Vice President of these United States. A prickly sort of man... has little use for me. We were on a mission to meet with the Commander of the British troops on the eve of the Revolution. There was an early snowstorm..."

NEW YORK   SEPTEMBER 1776

John Adams, built like a teapot, with a hawkish face, is forty-one. Franklin is trim and youthful at seventy. They scurry from a horse-drawn carriage to the entrance of a coaching inn. Welcoming lights glow in the windows. A sign over the door reads: '*Fox and Hounds. Publik House.*' They wrap their cloaks tightly around themselves against the billowing snow. Their coachman leans into the wind as he follows the two men with their bags.

Inside, a few guests huddle around a fireplace in the tavern. The proprietor, a man in his sixties with a fringe of white hair, stands behind a reception desk, with the collar of his woolen coat pulled up against the chill.

Adams brushes snow off his shoulders and approaches the desk. "Adams and Franklin here. We have two rooms reserved. May we have our keys, please?" he asks. Franklin helps their bag-laden young coachman through the front door, then stands next to Adams at the desk. He wipes melting snowflakes off his spectacles with a kerchief.

"I'm sorry, gentlemen, but I have only one room left," the proprietor says apologetically.

Adams looks at him indignantly. "You can't mean that, my man. We wrote to you and confirmed more than two weeks ago. You must have two rooms left."

"I did, but you're late. I let one go."

"That's plain unscrupulous!"

The proprietor takes a defensive stance. "It's good business. I made a lot of money off that room. So, do you want the room I have left, or no?"

Adams looks as though he is about to climb over the desk and pummel the man. "Very well. Give me the key. Where will *you* sleep, Franklin?"

The proprietor takes a room key off a hook on a board behind the desk and extends the hand holding the key to Adams. Franklin and Adams grab for it.

"We will share the room, of course," Franklin says as they grapple over the key.

"We will not!" Adams argues.

The proprietor withdraws his hand and the key.

"Then let's toss a coin for it," Franklin suggests.

"And where will the loser sleep?"

"You will recall that our Lord slept in a manger," Franklin offers innocently.

"All right, we'll share it, damn you!"

The proprietor places the key on the desk and Adams pockets it. The two men pick up their bags and climb the stairway behind the desk.

The proprietor calls after them. "I will collect the tariff from you gentlemen in the morning! Breakfast is at 7:00. Your man will be comfortable enough in the coachmen's quarters over the stables. 'Tis an extra charge, you know."

Adams glares at him from the landing, continues on up the stairs and unlocks the door to their compact room. Franklin steps in, drops his bag, and lights candles, illuminating a double bed, dresser, and one straight-backed chair sitting in a corner. A screen in the opposite corner conceals a commode chair and chamber pot.

Adams throws his leather satchel on the bed, opens it, unpacks his nightshirt, and smooths it out. Franklin goes to the window, opens it, breathes deeply and stretches his arms.

"Close that damn window and get into bed!" Adams orders. "We're both going to catch our deaths."

Franklin continues stretching. He can almost touch the ceiling with his fingertips. "Balderdash! I've a theory that fresh air is the best preventative."

"You and your theories. And you will stay on your side of the bed, you reprobate." Adams steps behind the screen and changes into his nightshirt. "I will not be a victim of your depravity."

Franklin pulls his nightgown out of his bag and shakes out the wrinkles. "Adams, did I ever tell you that my dear English friend, Billy Strahan, who has six children, told me the best sex he ever had was at boarding school?" he inquires as he changes into his sleeping attire.

Adams steps out from behind the screen and turns down the bed. "Revolting, you scapegrace!"

Franklin sorts through his bag. "I've often thought about dear old Strahan."

"I'm warning you, you… you pederast," Adams says menacingly, while fluffing his pillow.

"One can't be a pederast with another old man, you nincompoop."

Adams folds a cloak on the bed as a barrier between them. "Don't you dare cross this line of demarcation! How did you meet the Admiral we're going to see, anyway?" He takes a hand towel from his bag, and goes to the pitcher and washbasin on the dresser. He pours water into the basin and dabs his face.

"Through his sister, Caroline. She got word around London that she wished an assignation with me."

"And you sought her out?"

"I flattered myself into thinking she might have an ember beneath her skirts for me… but all we played at was chess." He finds a flask and silver cup in his valise and pours himself a drink.

Adams is curious. "I trust she was a comely woman?"

"Why take up such a tedious enterprise with an ugly woman, my man? Would you care for a drink?" Franklin offers the flask.

"No, I would not," Adams replies, pushing it away.

"Would do you some good. One evening her brother dropped in. We chatted. He made himself out to be an advocate of the restoration of harmony between our two countries."

"That would be Admiral Howe?"

"No. *General* Howe, his brother. He suggested I draft a plan for reconciliation, which they would present to the proper ministers."

Adams jumps into bed and pulls the quilt up to his neck. "Close the damn window now and come to bed." He looks at Franklin suspiciously. "So? Did you?"

Franklin watches snow fall outside by the light of a lamp mounted over the inn's entrance. "Why not?" He takes a sip of his drink. "I'd been offering a path to peace to the government for ten years with nothing to show for my efforts. The General's idea was to have Caroline copy my brief in her own hand, so my part in it would be secret." Franklin sets his drink on a bedside table and resumes his exercises, twisting at the waist.

"You should have avoided complicity in the scheme. Probity is always the best course of action."

"What? Tell the truth? That's a technique unknown in diplomacy and politics." Franklin lies on the floor, pumping his legs in the air.

"I would have handled the matter quite differently."

"Yes… with a torrent of words. Your mouth is a hot, moist, factory of specious argument."

"You have long envied my Harvard education, you rustic ignorant."

Franklin is indignant. "May I remind you that I, too, hold a degree from that institution, as well as from several others?"

"All of them given, not earned!" Adams argues.

Franklin concedes the point, breathing heavily as he pedals air. "Anyway, before long, the very lordly Lord Chatham turned up at my humble lodgings and offered to present my points of concerns to the Lords as his own bill. He wished to avert a war, you see."

"You tricked the poor man."

Franklin rises, finds a bed pan under the bed and carries it behind the dressing screen. Adams sneaks a sip of Franklin's drink. "Well, yes. I was present in the chamber for the debate on the bill," Franklin says from behind the screen. "Chatham's oratory was eloquent…"

Westminster,   London 1775

Gilded, fluted columns support a lofty ceiling in the House of Lords. Walls painted celadon above carved wood wainscoting are punctuated by gothic windows, shedding late afternoon sunlight on a group of elderly Peers seated in the Members' Gallery. They wear powdered wigs, robes of state, and other paraphernalia associated with their noble rank. All seem distracted, somewhat bored by the proceedings. The gallery is separated from the chamber's floor by a wooden rail, burnished by centuries of use.

Lord Chatham stands on the opposite side of the rail, addressing the assembly. Franklin is seated nearby in a small visitors' gallery, like a jury box. He appears retiring and is simply dressed.

His Lordship, on the other hand, stands tall and regal-looking, splendidly dressed. His red frockcoat is decorated with an intricate pattern woven of gold thread. His silver hair is pulled severely back into a ponytail and tied with velvet ribbon.

Chatham speaks with authority in a melodic baritone as he addresses the Lords. "This great country of ours," he intones, "may be mistress of the world, but she must also be seen as the guardian of liberty, not as the oppressor of it! Now our fellow countrymen across the Atlantic ask to be freed of unwise tariffs and unwarranted taxation. It is in our best interests, my Lords, that we grant what is asked of us!"

Franklin sees an ancient Peer doze off on his neighbor's shoulder, who pushes him away. The napping Peer awakens with a snort, prompting a few snickers.

Chatham continues, pacing the floor as he speaks: "I propose that Parliament may fairly regulate Imperial trade, but only colonial assemblies shall impose taxes. If we do not accede to this point, we beg for war between our two nations! I do not predict a happy outcome. Once that noble china tea pot, the British Empire, is torn asunder, the separate parts can never retain the value that existed in the whole!"

The ancient Peer leans close to his elderly neighbor. "What did he say?" he asks.

"Something about a pee pot hit by thunder," his neighbor tells him.

"Ah..." The ancient Peer nods his head.

Franklin appears pleased by Chatham's speech until Lord Sandwich, his face bright pink with rosacea, springs to his feet, commencing a tirade in a squeaky tenor voice. "Do not be deceived, my Lords! These timid words are not those of an English Peer! I tell you they flow from the pen of an American… and I fancy I see him in this very room!" He turns to Franklin, stabbing a fleshy finger toward the visitors' gallery. "And there he sits! The most bitter and mischievous enemy this country has ever known!"

Lord Chatham is stunned by the unsparing invective. "I have not surrendered the floor, sir!"

"No! You have surrendered our colonies to the rebels with a wag of your loose tongue! J'accuse!" Sandwich fumes.

"This is an unprecedented outrage, my Lords!"

Sandwich steps down from the Members' Gallery and turns to address the Lords. "As First Lord of the Admiralty, I know whereof I speak. A show of force, a resounding blow, is what is called for to restore order among the belligerents!"

Chatham moves to within inches of Sandwich's bushy sideburns. "The plan I espouse is my own, though I happily consulted with our distinguished visitor… who has so injuriously been reflected upon by His Lordship!" He shoulders past Sandwich to stand close to the gallery rail. "No man is better versed in the entirety of American affairs. Ranked with Newton for his brilliance, no man is held in higher esteem in all of Europe for his knowledge, than is Dr. Franklin!"

Sandwich brushes past Chatham, his face gone to crimson. "This ruinous bill must be rejected forthwith, my Lords! Let us show our contempt for it and for the traitor in our midst! Without further consideration, let us come to a vote!"

Coaching Inn, New York   1776

Adams appears to have fallen asleep, snoring loudly.

"I know you are awake, you old fraud," Franklin says as he replaces the bedpan under the bed. "I needn't tell you how the vote went."

Adams opens one eye. "You deserved the tongue-lashing you received from Lord Sandwich."

"I prayed that my many years of hard work were about to bear fruit, but it was not to be," Franklin says, digging through his valise.

Adams raises himself on one elbow. "Why subject yourself to further humiliation at the hands of these pirates?" he asks.

"Because we may yet witness a turning point in history."

"The Howes were playing a game with you… playing the fool for intelligence. *Un jouer au fou.*'" Adams says tartly.

Franklin takes a book from his valise. "You mean *'Un jeu de dupes.'* At any rate, the thing was dead in the crib."

"Clearly, somebody had tipped your hand to Lord Sandwich. It is likely the peace feeler proffered to us is yet another of the Admiral's games," Adams suggests.

"You think we *'Cherchez le goose'*, as you might say?"

"Precisely. His olive branch is a ploy to lead you to renounce our Declaration of Independence. I am here to prevent that."

"There has never been a good war, John… or a bad peace."

"Tell me… what really kept you in England for so many years? Certainly not affairs of state."

Franklin closes the window, sets his book and drink on the bedside table, and climbs into bed.

"Your feet, Franklin! Your feet!" Adams moves to the far side of the bed.

"I think I'll read for a while. Do you mind?"

"I do mind. You had little measurable success while you were over in England. Did you not miss your wife and daughter? All those years…" Adams snuffs out his candle as Franklin takes a sip of his drink, then opens his book. "And please blow out that candle, will you? And you haven't answered my question."

"A satisfactory answer to your query eludes me. But let me ask you this… where did you learn to speak French?" Franklin reluctantly closes his book and blows out his candle. The room goes dark, but for the dim glow of the entry light outside.

"I memorized funeral orations in that language as a young man," Adams replies.

"I should have guessed." Franklin lets go a powerful fart.

Adams sits up abruptly. "Jesus, Franklin! Open that damn window!"

CHAPTER FIVE

Parlor Games

PHILADELPHIA   APRIL 1790

The parlor of the house on Market Street is a generous room, wood-paneled and painted the color of rich cream. Four paned windows framed by toile linen curtains face the street. Mahogany chests of fine quality, upholstered chairs and settees, and a Franklin stove glowing in the hearth, offer a high level of comfort. A sprinkle of rain taps at the windows.

Sally Bache sits at the center table, reading a letter by the first candle of the evening. The letter is from her half-brother, William, in London. She hears his voice in her head as she reads.

'Mrs. Hewson, nee Polly Stevenson, has come to you for an extended stay. Quelle dommage! I don't envy you that nasty woman's company!'

Polly walks into the room, fussing with her hair. She wears a fancy, low-cut silk gown. "Anything I can do to help?" she inquires.

Sally puts down the letter, turns to Polly. "Well, if it ain't ol' Jezebel herself!" she exclaims, looking her up and down.

"Do you like it? I bought it in Paris." Polly performs a pirouette, the skirt billowing as she spins.

"I see Paris, all right. Downright immodest, is what it is! Go get a shawl and cover yourself."

"It was all the fashion when I was there, Sally."

"Must have been a long time ago. Looks like the moths ate half of it. Is that paint on your face, or did you lay your cheeks on the hot stove?"

Polly re-arranges Forsythia branches in a vase on a sideboard. "A bit of rouge, silly. You might join the living and try some yourself."

Sally looks away pensively, her tone softens. "There *was* a time I wore powder and had pretty dresses. Once, I rode with the Governor in his coach to a fancy ball. People waved at me as we rode by. Everybody knew who I was. Imagine…" she says wistfully, a half-smile on her face.

"Well, you're still pretty. I wonder if we shouldn't open a bottle of wine. It's so late in the day."

Sally's smile vanishes. "Mr. Jefferson is coming to *tea,* not supper," she retorts. After a pause, she thinks back: "Then I married Richard Bache and had babies… one after another! Bang, bang, bang!"

"Papa would serve wine, I'm sure."

"He's not your 'Papa'!"

Polly glances at the letter on the table. Sally quickly folds it and sticks it in her pocket. "It's a letter from my brother in London," she says sharply. "None of your affair."

"Of course not. Shall I light the rest of the candles? I do wish you'd let me help you."

"I don't need your help. I raised seven children without anybody's help."

"Where *is* Mr. Bache tonight?" Polly wonders, arranging teacups on the table.

"Out," Sally snaps, and rises from the table.

Polly looks up from her task, turning to Sally. "Sally, I've come all this way to…"

Sally walks to the window and looks out. "If you've come to sniff after an inheritance, you'd best forget about it. Everything will go to Temple. He's Pa's favorite."

"I've come to be near the only father I ever knew."

Sally turns from the window with arms crossed. "That's fine, but keep out of my way," she says curtly. "You're like those people out there on the street, just waitin' on Papa to die. Well, don't expect much. I'm goin' to change my dress," she says coldly and leaves the room.

Franklin's Bedroom

Franklin sits on the edge of his bed, lost in thought. Candles near the bed flicker in a breeze from an open window. Bobby stands at the far end of the room, stirring embers in the fireplace with a poker. He takes a log from a basket on the hearth and tosses it on the fire, watching it flare up for a moment.

Franklin calls out to him. "Listen to the rain come down, Bobby. Can you smell it?"

"Rain blowin' in here pretty good now." He sets down the poker, crosses the room, and closes the window.

"You say you've seen the boys?" One of Franklin's slippers falls to the floor.

"No, sir. I ain't seen 'em in a while now." Bobby picks up the slipper and replaces it on Franklin's dangling foot.

"Where in hell do you suppose they are?"

Near Philadelphia   April 1790

Tree branches bend and groan in a blustery wind, and heavy rain washes over a sign reading: *'H. Bradley, Public House. Fine Ales.'* Inside the tavern, the middle-aged proprietor closes windows against the storm and wipes water off windowsills with his apron.

Benny Bache and Temple Franklin ride into the drive, guiding their horses through deep puddles to the stable next to the inn. Grateful for a respite from the rain, they dismount and leave their horses with a young groom, making a dash for the front door. A roaring fire in the hearth greets them as they enter a warm and inviting establishment, even with its mismatched furniture and paucity of lamplight. A handful of patrons who have braved the inclement weather are scattered about the large room, talking and drinking.

Benny and Temple stamp mud from their boots, remove their sodden greatcoats, shake water off their hats, and hang them on hooks near the door. Both men are in their twenties, both are handsome. Benny's dark hair is tousled, his cravat untied, while Temple is carefully groomed, his blonde hair smooth and slicked back.

"I don't know about you, but this rain makes me terrible thirsty," Temple says, surveying the premises.

"You're crazy. Makes me cold. Hot coffee for me," Benny says.

They spot an empty booth: a pair of wooden settles with a table between. They slide in and take seats.

"Come now, lad. One little drink can't hurt ye," Temple teases.

"When have I ever been out with you and had one drink?"

"Allow me to ponder that."

"We should get back to Grandfather's house. I don't think he's long for this world."

"Nonsense. He'll rally again. He always does," Temple replies optimistically.

An attractive and shapely barmaid, freckle-faced and no more than sixteen years of age, sashays to the table. "You boys drinkin', or just come in outta the rain?" she inquires. "If you ain't drinkin', I gotta charge rent for that bench you're sittin' on."

Benny laughs and orders coffee.

"Don't listen to him. A pitcher of stout and two tankards," Temple says, flashing the girl a dazzling smile. "And don't dawdle, *ma Cherie*."

"Yes, sir. Straight away, sir," she says, returning his smile and flipping the back of her red hair.

Temple watches the barmaid walk away. "The evening has promise, eh, my friend?" He turns sideways, putting his feet up on the bench. "Benny, when the old man does pass, I've made up my mind to go back to France."

"Not me. I'm happy here. I have my business… my family."

"This backward village annoys me no end! I'll sail to London first and visit my father. I would like to get to know him."

"Don't tell Grandfather that," Benny advises.

Temple takes a small pipe from his shirt pocket. "And I miss the women of Paris."

"What? Their *savoir faire?* Their *je ne sais pas quoi?*"

"Mostly, their bosoms."

Benny wags a finger. "Naughty, naughty! So, what keeps you? What are you waiting for?"

"I can't leave Grandfather. He's looked after me since I was a young child," Temple says, searching through his pockets. "Damn. I forgot my tobacco." He jumps down from his seat. "I'm going to the bar for a pouch."

Temple leaves the table as the barmaid arrives with their drinks. They smile and flirt as they pass one another. "That your brother?" she asks Benny as she pours ale into their tankards.

"Nearly. We grew up together. We're cousins, actually." he replies.

"Nice boy. Good lookin'. You ain't so bad either. I'd like to see more of you gents around here," she winks as she wipes off her tray and moves on to another table.

Midway into the tavern, Temple pays the bartender for his tobacco. He turns to see Richard Bache, Benny's father, seated in a far corner with a disheveled-looking woman. The woman is twenty years younger than Bache, buxom, and overweight. They appear amorous. Temple looks away quickly and returns to the table.

"Your father's here," he says as he slides back into the booth.

Benny is wide-eyed. "Is he? Where?"

Temple packs his pipe with tobacco. "He's sitting in back with some woman draped over him."

"Let me guess. *Not* my mother. The rotten bastard!" He gulps down his beer. "I'm going to say 'hello' to the old man."

"No. Don't. I wouldn't do that…"

Benny rises from his seat, with his half-empty tankard in hand. "Sit tight."

He finds his father and the lady slumped on a high-backed bench in a dim corner. His father's face is nuzzled into the woman's substantial shoulder; she caresses his neck with a chubby hand, whispering in his ear. She is heavily made up, her hair frizzed, her clothing unkempt. An open whiskey bottle, empty shot glasses, a pitcher of ale, and two mugs sit on a pine plank table before them. They don't notice Benny's approach.

"'Evening, Pa."

Bache sits up, surprised to see his son. "Benny! Hallo!" He disentangles himself from the woman's arms.

"Where have you been? Church services again?"

"Yes, exactly. Vespers. Down at the church. We thought we'd stop for a tipple afterwards… the rain and all."

Benny moves closer to the table. "She doesn't look like a church lady."

"What's vespers?" the woman asks, a blank look on her doughy face.

Bache moves away from the woman. "Son, meet an old friend of mine, Miss Jane Parker." He gestures toward Benny. "Jane, this is my son, Benjamin. Benjamin Bache."

Benny smirks. "I hope you're not paying the bitch by the pound. She'll break the bank!"

Miss Parker's mouth moves like a goldfish, but makes no sound.

Bache, enraged, stands unsteadily on his feet, weaving from side-to-side. "Why, you little bugger! You apologize to Miss Parker, and to me!"

"Oh, sit down, you old sot, before you fall down." Benny tosses the beer from his tankard into his father's crotch. "Oh look! You pissed in your pants again! Well, goodnight, Pa... Miss Porker," he says as he retreats from the table.

Bache looks down at his trousers in disbelief, his mouth agape.

Benny rushes back to his own table, reaches in his pocket for coins, and throws them on the table.

"How'd it go?" Temple asks as he drags on his pipe.

"Let's get out of here before he catches me."

"Where to?"

"Anywhere we can get good and drunk."

Temple empties his tankard and joins Benny, as he retrieves his hat and coat and hurries out the door.

Franklin's Bedroom

Bobby picks up a hairbrush and comb from the dresser.

"Turns out that Adams did catch a cold that night," Franklin chortles.

Bobby sits next to him on the edge of his bed. "Let's see if we can make you look nice for company. Your hair's a mess." He brushes what is left of Franklin's long, gray hair. "You and Mr. Adams catch that goose you was after?"

"Wasn't any goose. Admiral Howe carried with him a bona fide offer for peace." Franklin reaches into his memory. "The next day, we joined him at his headquarters on the island."

STATEN ISLAND, NEW YORK   SEPTEMBER 1776

A chilly morning, the sky is leaden and gray. Franklin, John Adams, and their young male secretary huddle together in a rowboat, bundled against a biting wind. Four British sailors row the craft toward the shore of the island, their oars moving in unison. They land, disembark, and follow the sailors to a compound of simple frame military buildings, all painted as gray as the sea. Inside, they are led to a mess hall, where Admiral Howe is to join them. The room is spare, utilitarian, a Union Jack hangs on a white-washed wall.

Franklin and Adams adjust to their surroundings as an aide takes their greatcoats. A charming attempt has been made to decorate the room with tree branches propped in the corners and greenery spread on the floor. After a moment, Admiral Howe enters the room with a purposeful stride. He is in his fifties, tall and commanding, though dressed informally. He greets Franklin's party cordially and introduces his adjutant, who trails behind.

The Admiral invites his guests to be seated at the dining table, where they are to be served a hot meal. "I appreciate you gentlemen having made the long journey to meet with me. I do hope you brought your appetites with you," Howe says, taking his seat at the head of the table. Franklin and Adams sit on his right and left.

Two British sailors in white uniforms appear and serve the table, offering platters of roasted meats, vegetables, and fresh bread. Early in the day for such a heavy repast, Franklin thinks, but most welcome. He takes generous portions of beef, ham, duck, and trimmings.

The American secretary and British adjutant take notes of the conversation while they dine.

"I see, Your Lordship, that thanks to the bounty of this region, you are well-provisioned," Adams comments as he fills his plate.

"Yes. We want for nothing," the Admiral concurs.

"One does hope that the poor farmers hereabouts are compensated for your requisitions," Adams says bluntly.

DEAR BEN

"Of course, His Lordship pays the farmers, John. May I inquire after your lovely sister, Caroline, Your Lordship?" Franklin asks with his mouth full, hoping to change the subject.

"She is very well. She prays for a quick cessation of hostilities, so that you can return to England and to her game board."

Franklin smiles broadly, drinks from his wine glass. "It would be my great pleasure. Let us strive to answer the dear lady's prayer."

"That, my friend, is the point of our visit today." The Admiral helps himself to a slice of ham. "I have hope that face-to-face, we can yet work out our differences and bring this terrible war to a prompt conclusion."

Adams pulls a kerchief from his pocket with a flourish. "Your proposed truce calls for union within the Empire. An impossibility, since we have already declared our independence from Great Britain." He blows his nose with a loud *'honk.'*

The Admiral is undaunted. "Under the Crown, henceforth, you will be granted real authority for your legislatures, power to tax, control over the plantations, and so forth."

A third sailor in dress uniform circles the table, filling wine glasses. Adams demurs, placing a hand atop his goblet. "You cannot give us that which we have taken for ourselves."

Howe's eyes bore through Adams. He wipes his mouth with his serviette. "We will win this war, Mr. Adams. Where do you intend to hide at its conclusion?"

Franklin lays down his knife and fork, attempting to snuff out a lighted fuse. "John alludes, Your Lordship, to the damage already done, which cannot be undone. Towns have been burnt, savages induced to massacre peaceful farmers, slaves to murder their masters in their beds. A treaty which requires allegiance to the Crown will not find favor in the Congress."

The Admiral turns to Franklin. "Ben, you of all people know that we British are kith and kin with you Americans. When an American falls, England feels it."

'My Lord, we will do our utmost to spare Your Lordship that mortification."

"Perhaps you can send home for authority to negotiate a treaty with us as a separate, sovereign state," Adams suggests pertly, before blowing his nose again.

"Yes! There's our solution!" Franklin raises his goblet.

The Admiral does not join Franklin in his toast. "There is scant hope that such a request would succeed."

Franklin sips his wine. "Let us not be hasty, Your Lordship. Perhaps if we draft a resolution…"

The Admiral interrupts Franklin. "By the time your resolution reaches His Majesty's Government, the war will be over. My brother and I will see to that. I regret that you gentlemen have come so far for naught, but I thank you again for making the journey."

Franklin conceals his disappointment. "It was our great pleasure. We have come due to the high esteem in which we hold Your Lordship."

Adams glares at Franklin across the table. The men continue eating, in silence.

CHAPTER SIX

Slave Trade

Franklin's Bedroom   1790

Franklin winces as Bobby brushes through a tangle in his hair. "So, war came, as it always does. Lord Howe's scheme included pardons for us rebels… except for Adams, I later learned."

"That so?" Bobby says, pulling strands of hair from the brush.

"They planned to hang Adams."

Bobby pauses in thought. "You ever answer Mr. Adams' question 'bout bein' away from your family so long? Or you leave him hangin'?" He falls back on the bed, laughing.

Franklin wheezes and laughs, holding his stomach. "You mustn't make a dying man laugh. It's inappropriate!"

Franklin and Bobby collect themselves. "Wonder where I put that pretty robe you bring back from France? The blue one?" Bobby sits up, rises from the bed, and starts across the room.

Franklin coughs a ragged cough. "I've been thinking about some unfinished business, Bobby. Another of my errors I wish to make right."

Bobby opens a mahogany wardrobe and sorts through hanging garments. "It got to be in here somewhere."

"When I die, all my properties will go to Sally and her husband."

"Well, they your close kin, ain't they?" Bobby calls over his shoulder.

"There's one condition attached to my bequest: Bache must make a free man of you before he inherits one penny."

Bobby continues his search. "Free me? Oh, I don't know about that."

"I would have done away with slavery by article of the Constitution, but we would have lost the South."

"Sometime, I wonder how it right for white folk to own black folk… but I'm happier when I don't think 'bout that." Bobby takes a shirt from the wardrobe and studies it.

"It isn't right, but we've had slavery since the beginning of time. Think of the Egyptians and the Jews in the Bible. I have come to think of it as the most heinous of crimes."

Bobby shakes his head. "It too late for me. Too late now."

"Nonsense. You're in the prime of your life." Franklin watches a moth flap against the window, wondering if he will outlive it.

"I got a cozy room here, dry and warm in winter. I ain't never missed a meal, and your family been decent to me. I am blessed, far as I can see." Bobby hangs the shirt on a hook on the wardrobe door. "Aggie outta wash this one," he murmurs to himself.

"That's all well and good, but…"

"The preacher at church say that *'man who is born of woman will live but a short time and be full of misery.'* I think to stay here and skip over some a that misery."

"That's hogwash. The poor preacher must suffer with piles. We are born to be happy and to be of service," Franklin argues.

"Your offer very kind, but I don't have nothin' to start out with, either."

"You have time, Bobby, the only currency we have of real value."

Bobby finds the blue robe in the wardrobe. "Here it is," he says, holding it up. "Where would I go if I was to leave this house?"

"You might stay right here if you chose to, but if you venture out, you will find your rightful place in the world."

"My place? I am too ignorant." Bobby walks back to the bed. He lays the silk damask robe carefully over the back of a chair. "Let's put this on you. First, take your teeth out and I clean 'em up for you."

Franklin pays no attention. "We are all born ignorant, Bobby, but we must work hard to remain stupid. Stupid you are not. And my teeth are fine where they are."

"Well, I think about it."

Heavy rain pounds on the roof. Franklin looks up. "This rain will surely send my busy-body neighbors outside running for cover."

Bobby peers out the window. "No, it ain't. They got umbrellas."

Franklin sighs. "You may not be aware of it, Bobby, but I knew servitude myself as a boy."

Bobby turns to Franklin with a puzzled look. "How's that so?"

"I was an indentured apprentice in my older brother's print shop. I learned the trade, but James was a passionate man…" He listens to the rain for a moment. "I was obligated to work eight years at no pay. I was a kind of slave, printing advertisements for the slave trade."

BOSTON   OCTOBER 1723

A window sign reads: '*Boston Courier printed here. James Franklin, prop.*' A bell on the door jingles as patrons come and go from the busy print shop. Inside, a young Benjamin Franklin, seventeen, works at a press. He is of medium height, has sparkling blue eyes set in a pleasant face, and a swimmer's build, with a powerful torso. He pulls a flyer off the press and looks it over. The flyer reads: '*FOR SALE. Two very likely Negroes, boy appx. 13, and girl, appx. 11. Inquire of printer herein.*'

An older journeyman walks by. Franklin stops him, holding up the flyer. "What do you think, Luke?"

Luke scans it carefully. "'Tis fine work boy. Very clean and clear."

"Clear, maybe, but I don't know about clean. They're just children."

"What's the difference? They's Africans, ain't they?" Luke shrugs and walks on.

The doorbell jingles again as James Franklin, twenty-six, enters the shop with a newspaper in hand. His eyes are dark with fury. He slams the door shut behind him and goes directly to Benjamin, slapping him – hard – on both sides of his head.

Benjamin cowers, raising his hands to protect himself. He turns to face James. "Damn you, James! What's wrong with you? That hurts!"

James waves the newspaper in his brother's face. "Are you tryin' to fekkin' ruin me, boy? Look here at today's edition of my paper!" He points to a column of print. "You wrote that Miles Clark *died* at the Athenaeum Tavern, when it should have said he *dined* there! The owner is furious! The whole town is laughing at me!" He pushes Franklin, who loses his footing, falls against the wall, and slides down to the floor. Several workers stop what they are doing to watch. "Can't you ever get it right, you imbecile? I'm bloody sick of your careless mistakes!" James yells, kicking his brother in the thigh.

Benjamin sees a hammer on the floor beside him and picks it up, rising slowly to his feet. He looks from the hammer to his brother, whose face is twisted in anger, then silently sets down the hammer, takes off his apron and walks out of the shop.

James follows him to the door, shaking his fist. "Don't think you're walkin' out on me, you saucy little bastard! I own you! Get your ass back here! Your day ain't over yet!"

Franklin's Bedroom

Franklin's eyes are brimming. "When I determined to kill my brother, I thought it best to leave." He wipes away a tear at the memory, then chuckles. "It was rumored 'twas the creamed spinach that did in poor Mr. Clark."

Bobby sits on the chair next to the bed and speaks quietly. "I know some folk who like to kill a white man. You know… just on a matter of principle."

"Do you? I am loathe to think what's coming in this country. At any rate, my father took sides with my brother, as I had not fulfilled my indentures. So, I left in secret. A friend arranged passage for me on a ship bound for New York, telling the captain I was running from a naughty girl with child."

Bobby leans back in his chair. "Was you?"

"Not yet. My life can be measured in voyages, when I think of it. Eight crossings of the Atlantic, I made… nearly two years at sea."

Boston   Late September 1723

Late evening, the autumn air is crisp. A ship's bell rings. Young Franklin scurries across the shipyard, dodging crates and barrels stacked on the wharf as he goes. He carries a satchel over his shoulder and pulls a trunk behind him, heading for the dock where a square-rigger cargo ship makes ready to sail. Inside the trunk are most of Franklin's worldly possessions, including his best clothes and a few treasured books. The ship's bell rings again. Franklin hails an elderly porter, a stevedore past his prime, who loads the trunk onto a push cart and follows him to the vessel.

A mate aboard ship looks at his pocket watch, sees Franklin approaching, and shouts to him: "Run, boy! Ye'd best step lively lest that whore's daddy come after ye! We have a fair wind and a bright moon and Cap'n will be raisin' anchor soon!"

Franklin climbs the gangway and boards the ship, the porter struggling behind with his chattels.

"Follow me lad," the Mate says. "I'll show ya to yer quarters. We'll be shovin' off soon, the high tide's in." He leads Franklin through a door to a narrow, dimly lit corridor between cabins on deck. Franklin trips over a bulkhead and bangs his head on cross beams. Twice.

"Watch yer head, lad. 'Tis tight quarters in here," he warns Franklin, too late.

The mate opens the door to a tiny cabin with one up-and-down bunk and a small table with a wash basin sunk into it. "Yer lucky you'll have this luxury accommodation all to yerself," he says, grinning. "I can get three or four crew in here, as a rule."

The porter, wheezing, catches up and delivers Franklin's trunk, shoving it into the cramped cabin. Franklin fishes in his pocket for a shilling, of which he has very few, and gives one to the old man. The Mate and porter leave him to adjust to his home at sea. *'Thank God I have a porthole',* he thinks to himself, throwing his satchel on the bunk.

The ship groans and lurches; dockhands yell *'farewells'* to mates aboard. Franklin makes his way onto the open deck, banging his head once on the way. He walks to the stern of the ship to watch the sail-away. The jib is raised and the ship slides forward, picking up speed as the foresail and mainsail are raised to a cacophony of shouting and cursing from the crew. He has never before witnessed the parting of the land and the sea.

Only three days later, thanks to favorable winds, Franklin disembarks in New York harbor, three hundred miles from Boston. He leaves his trunk and satchel in the care of a freight office and makes his way to H. Bradford & Co., the only printer he has heard of in the town. He introduces himself to Mr. Bradford, a gentleman of about seventy, offering his services.

"I'm sorry, lad, but I have little work at this time and have plenty of staff to handle what I do have," Bradford says apologetically. Franklin's eyes are downcast. "It might be of some use to ye, though, that my son, who is also in this trade, has just lost a man and could use a good typesetter. Aquila Rose, the fellow's name was. Died, he did. A poet, he was, so they say, and a right good worker. Peculiar name, eh? 'Aquila Rose'?"

"That it is, sir. Is your son's shop nearby? I will seek him out."

"Not far. Only one hundred miles… in Philadelphia."

Franklin is stunned by the distance and dejected, but determined. "I shall return to the port and book myself on a ship bound hither," he says.

"You may a find an overland route, taking inland waterways, cheaper and more expedient," Bradford proffers. "Cross the bay here to Perth Amboy in New Jersey, then take the road to Burlington, that's fifty miles, and where craft plying the Delaware River can carry ye to Philadelphia. Myself, I ride a horse, but I wouldn't recommend it."

Franklin thanks Mr. Bradford for his courtesy and returns to the freight office at the port, where he makes arrangements for his belongings to follow him around to Philadelphia by sea. He stuffs his pockets with a clean shirt, socks, and under-drawers, before parting with his baggage. That afternoon, he locates a sloop about to set sail for the voyage across New York Bay, and signs on as one of its two passengers. The tiny ship has seen better days. Its sails are tattered and most of the paint above the water line has peeled off. *Not to worry*, Franklin thinks, 'tis but a brief sail to the New Jersey side.

Franklin has miscalculated. Shortly after entering the bay, the sloop runs into a sudden squall. Hurricane-like winds tear her ancient sails to shreds and blow the ship off course, thrusting the vessel back toward Long Island. High surf causes the ship to pitch violently, and the other passenger, a drunken Dutchman, loses his footing and falls overboard. Franklin manages to grab the man by his collar and pull him out of the heaving water. The dunking sobers the Dutchman a little, and Franklin and the boatman settle the man in a skiff, where he promptly falls asleep.

A rocky beach and forbidding surf make a landing on the island impossible, so the boatman drops anchor and turns the ship into the wind, where they ride out the storm overnight. Franklin and the boatman crawl into the skiff with the Dutchman for protection from the wind and try to sleep, but spray blowing over the ship douses them until they are nearly as wet as the Dutchman. The cold is numbing. The two strangers huddle together and shiver in the tiny boat until morning, when the wind dies down and the boatman is able to turn the ship once again toward their destination. Thirty hours after setting out, having had no nourishment or water, save a bottle of cheap rum, they reach the New Jersey shore.

New Jersey

A dismal, overcast morning. A steady rain falls as Franklin trudges along a rutted country lane outside Perth Amboy, stepping over runnels with his muddy boots. His cap is pulled down and his woolen jacket closed tight. They help to shed water for a time, but by noon he is soaked to the skin and exhausted. He meets only one rider along the road, a man on horseback who slows his pace and regards Franklin suspiciously as he passes. Franklin considers a run for the woods off to his right, but thinks better of it and the man continues on his way.

As the long day begins to grow dark, he sees a small inn on the side of the road. It is as dreary as the weather, but welcoming nonetheless. Upon entering, he is met by a tall, gaunt innkeeper in his middle years, whose countenance matches the day outside.

Franklin doffs his cap. "Have you a room available, sir, for a weary traveler?" he inquires, aware of his wretched appearance.

The innkeeper studies him suspiciously. "I might. Who would be asking?"

"Name's Franklin, sir. On my way to the fair city of Philadelphia."

The innkeeper is unsmiling. "And where, pray tell, did you leave your horse?"

"I am on foot, sir. I plan to book passage on the river at Burlington for the balance of the journey. I am very tired and in need of a rest."

"I'd say you have run away from service in a great house, boy. Is that not so?"

"A great house? No, sir. Not at all. I am a printer, sir."

"Well, I will grant you a room, but I won't be surprised when the sheriff comes looking for ye."

Mean as the accommodation is, Franklin is grateful for a bed and a fire by which he dries his coat and boots, and sleeps soundly. He leaves quietly, early in the morning, carrying his boots to the door, fearing the dour old innkeeper might send for the authorities.

He walks all day in better weather, stopping only briefly a few times to relieve himself in a thicket of trees. By evening, he has reached an inn just eight miles from Burlington which presents a more hopeful prospect than the previous night's lodging. *'Brown's Inn'*, reads a sign at the roadside, inviting Franklin to enter. The proprietor is one Dr. Brown, who offers Franklin a warm welcome and a comfortable bed for the night. The doctor is an affable sort, a man of letters and well-read. He and Franklin quickly fall into a conversation about books and share a supper of hot stew and crusty bread, served by the doctor's cook in the dining room. Brown enjoys Franklin's erudite company, while the younger man is grateful for the blazing fire in the hearth.

"It was most amazing to me," Franklin says, washing down his stew with a sip of dark ale, "that the drunken Dutchman took a book from his pocket as he emerged from the sea, and asked me to dry it out. The fool was nearly drowned, and his first concern was for a book!"

"Was it the Bible?"

"Nay. One might think so, but 'twas 'The Pilgrim's Progress,' one of my favorites, set entirely in Dutch and beautifully engraved."

Dr. Brown laughs. "'Tis indeed a blessing that such a fine volume was saved from Davy Jones's locker, but perhaps not the old sot."

Franklin joins him in laughter. "You are quite right. I realized that the book must have been translated into every European language, and perhaps the Arabic and Oriental tongues as well. Interesting…" The candles burn low as Franklin listens, spellbound, to the doctor's engrossing stories of his extensive travels in England and on the Continent in his younger years. Franklin wonders if there is any truth to the doctor's tales of his fantastic adventures in the Levant, as recounted after several tankards of ale.

The next morning, Franklin sets out for Burlington at daybreak, before Dr. Brown has arisen. He reaches the town in the early afternoon and stops to buy bread at a bakehouse owned by an elderly lady, Mrs.

Dean, whose apron and gray hair are dusted with flour. He proceeds to the wharf, where he is dismayed to learn that there will be no river traffic going his way until Tuesday. He returns to town and the bakehouse, thinking the old baker may have some sage advice for him. Mrs. Dean shakes flour from her apron and advises Franklin there is nothing to be done but to wait the three days. Taken with his sad eyes, she offers him lodging in her house at no charge, which he gladly accepts. At dinner that evening, Mrs. Dean learns that Franklin is a printer and endearingly suggests that he establish himself in Burlington, unaware as she is of the costly equipment required for such an enterprise.

Though hardly in need of a stroll, Franklin walks along the riverside after dinner, pondering his prospects. As luck would have it, a boat appears on the river, filled with several passengers. When it docks to disembark a few passengers, he learns that the rest are bound for Philadelphia. They invite him to come along, which he does without hesitation.

There being no wind to speak of to fill the sails, Franklin joins the men in rowing the craft. They establish a smooth rhythm. A man on board plays a Jew's harp, until he nods off in the gloom and mist gathering over the river. As long as the light holds, a woman works at her knitting. Another woman sings softly to the little girl sitting on her lap, who dances to the tune with her delicate hands. Darkness falls, and by midnight the crew surmises they have passed Philadelphia, the city being dark at night those days, and they row into a creek for shelter. It is an exceedingly cold night for early October. The men spot a decrepit split-rail fence on the shore and break it up for firewood.

Franklin sidles over as near to the fire as he can get, warming his hands, turning them front to back. He looks over the camp where his comrades whisper to one another as they seek comfort. A man and woman next to him curl up with their boy-child between them. A few men stretch out on benches on the boat, their coats pulled up over their noses. The two crew members huddle in the prow, covered in blankets from their kits, passing a flask between them. One of them bellows a few notes of a bawdy shanty song, but is hushed by a Reverend Eckstrom, a pastor of the Lutheran sect. Franklin lies back on the cold ground and wishes he had said good-bye to Mrs. Dean, the kindly baker. She must be wondering whatever became of him. He also wishes he had never left home.

Thus, the frigid night passes until daybreak, when the men get their bearings and row back downstream to Philadelphia. They land at the Market Street wharf on Sunday morning.

CHAPTER SEVEN

Providence

PHILADELPHIA   OCTOBER 1723

Later that day, Franklin walks down dusty, rutted Market Street, making way for passing horse-drawn carriages and dodging the droppings they leave behind. He is a sight. His appearance is scruffy, he is dirty and disheveled from his travels, his pockets are stuffed with socks and underwear. He looks every inch a bumpkin as he gawks at the unfamiliar surroundings, with but a few coins in his purse. He cannot help but wonder: *Who was Aquila Rose?*

He discovers a bakery on Fourth Street, where he purchases three puffy rolls, one of which he eats, two of which he stuffs under each arm. Before long, he passes Deborah Read, who is sweeping the steps outside her front door. She is blonde, fresh-faced, also seventeen. They catch each other's eye. Franklin slows his pace and they study one another. He doffs his filthy cap. She looks away and scurries inside the house.

FRANKLIN'S BEDROOM   1790

"Then I spied her, Bobby. Miss Deborah Read. She was a pretty thing to my eye, but she looked at me with contempt. No matter. I decided to return another day."

Bobby wraps a light blanket around Franklin's shoulders.

"I was acquainted with the boatman out of New York," Franklin says, tugging at the blanket, "only a very brief time. But Dr. Brown, the innkeeper, and I corresponded as long as he lived."

Bobby sits again in the chair next to the bed. "Don't mind my askin', how you go from bein' a slave to bein' a rich man? Miss Polly say you more famous than the man in the moon!"

Franklin pulls the blanket close about him. "Polly is prone to exaggeration. Pour me some more of that 'tea', will you?"

Bobby pours Madeira into Franklin's teacup.

"I've been very particular in describing my journey from Boston to you, as well as my first entry into this city, so you may compare in your mind such unlikely beginnings and the figure I have made since then."

"With respect, sir, you been lucky all the time. I ain't never had no luck."

Franklin sips his wine. "I don't believe in luck, Bobby. To succeed, one must jump as quickly at opportunities as we do to conclusions."

"Maybe luck and opportunity the same thing."

"Twins, perhaps, but not identical."

PHILADELPHIA   OCTOBER 1723

Young Franklin kneels on the bank of the Delaware River, rinsing out socks and under-drawers. He hangs them on a tree on the river's edge to dry. A fisherman stands downstream with his fishing line in the water. He wears a light jacket and a cap on his head. A pair of Franklin's under-drawers slip away in the current and drift downstream.

The fisherman hooks the shorts with his fishing pole, holds them aloft, and calls over to Franklin: "These belong to you? They look to be your size!"

Franklin shouts downstream: "That they are!"

They walk toward one another.

"I am very grateful to you, sir," Franklin says. "I hope that wasn't your best catch of the day!"

The fisherman unhooks the shorts, squeezes water from them, and hands them to Franklin. He displays an empty creel. "Sad to say, 'tis my one and only. But the day is young." He looks Franklin up and down. "You look to be a runaway, lad."

"That I am, sir."

"From what do you run, boy?"

Franklin looks at the sandy ground under his feet. "Mayhem," he says.

"I see. What brings you to our fair city?"

"Providence."

"Are you passing through?" The fisherman takes a tiny pipe from his jacket pocket and lights it.

"I thought to stay, if I can find work and lodging."

"Have you a trade?"

Franklin's face brightens. "I'm a printer, sir, and a good one, if I may be so bold as to say."

"Well, there are only two print shops in town, Bradford's and Keimer's. I will direct you to both. Perhaps one of them could use a good man."

"I've heard of Bradford. I met his father in New York." He extends his hand to the fisherman. "Name's Franklin, sir. Benjamin Franklin."

They shake hands.

"Charlie Fothergill. As for accommodation, Mrs. Read on Market Street often has a cheap room to let, since her husband died. She's a testy old crow, but she has a daughter about your age. Not a bad looking wench at that. When your wash on yonder tree has dried, I will lead you there." He turns and walks back to his fishing-hole.

Franklin calls after him, "You, sir, like the Apostles of old, are a fisher of men!"

FRANKLIN HOUSE, PHILADELPHIA   APRIL 1790

The last of the day's light lingers outside the kitchen windows. Polly stands next to a scarred pine table, watching as Aggie, now seventy-one, slides baking pans out from a brick oven and sets them on the table. Polly helps Aggie lift tea cakes from the pans and arrange them on fancy china plates. She pulls a kerchief from the sleeve of her dress, wipes a tear from her eye and blows her nose.

"I'm not used to being spoken to in such harsh terms, Aggie."

"Course you ain't. Don't you pay Missus Bache no mind. She real worried about her Pa, that's all."

"We are *all* worried. But I didn't travel across the ocean to be humiliated and abused by her." She blows her nose again.

"That the difference 'tween you and me. I only gotta cross the yard to get abused."

Jake opens the kitchen door and enters. He is seventy-three and gray-haired, but still cuts an impressive figure. "Evenin' ladies."

"Hello, Jake," Polly says, returning her kerchief to its hiding place.

"It just how she is, Miss Polly," Aggie says soothingly. "Her words bite you sometime. She like her Mama that way. Don't you be bothered none." She lifts two plates filled with cakes and offers them to Polly. "Maybe you like to put these on the sideboard in the parlor? I get the bread outta the oven."

"Of course. And thank you for your comforting words, Aggie." Polly accepts the plates and leaves the kitchen.

Jake runs a hand across Aggie's back. "Miss Polly got troubles?"

"Mm-hm. I tell ya, the fur is gonna fly 'fore this night is over."

Franklin's Bedroom

Bobby offers the silk robe he found in the wardrobe to Franklin. "How 'bout you try this on? Mr. Jefferson be along any time now."

"I followed that fisherman on the path back to town, which led to the path I have followed all my life," Franklin says, accepting the robe.

Bobby walks to a corner of the room where a screen conceals a potty chair. He removes a chamber pot from under the chair and covers it with a towel. "You not gonna tell me that the 'ol crow' was that blonde girl's mother?" he calls from behind the screen.

"One and the same." Franklin inserts one arm into a sleeve of the robe with difficulty. "I found work at Keimer's shop. Bradford, it turns out, had already hired a hand… And soon I took a room in the Read house, courting Deborah from the first day."

Bobby walks to the door, opens it, sets the chamber pot in the hall, and closes the door. He fetches a replacement pot from a cupboard. "Sound like luck to me."

Franklin watches Bobby at his chore while he attempts to get his other arm into the robe. "I've often wondered, Bobby, does it bother you to carry my night soil?"

"How you like to carry mine?"

"No, I think not."

"There's your answer." Bobby stops at the window and looks out. "Rain's lettin' up now."

"My first job at Keimer's was to print an elegy for Aquila Rose."

"I wish you'd give me those teeth."

"No. Don't want to."

Bobby returns to the chair behind the screen, places the clean pot under it, and kneels to wipe the floor around it with a rag.

"The Keimer print shop was a wreck of a place, but I patched things up as best I could and business improved." Franklin stands, with both arms in the robe. He smooths the front and attempts to tie the sash around his waist. "It wasn't long before opportunity swaggered through the door." He loses his balance, grips the wall, and slides down it to the floor. "The lady…" Franklin groans. He grips his abdomen, grimacing in pain, and topples over onto his side.

Bobby calls again from behind the screen. "What you say come through that door?"

Franklin doesn't answer. Bobby looks around the screen, sees Franklin on the floor, and rushes over to him, a horrified look on his face. "Dr. Ben? Dr. Ben!" He kneels next to the old man, frantically looking for signs of life.

PART TWO

Jefferson Calls

CHAPTER EIGHT

Miss Read

PHILADELPHIA				APRIL 1790

Franklin lies on his side, motionless, on the bedroom floor, but he is breathing steadily and his eyes are open. Bobby rolls the old man onto his back, then strains to help him up and onto the bed. Franklin perches precariously on its edge. Neither man speaks as Bobby wets a cloth in the basin on the dresser and wipes Franklin's brow.

Bobby breaks the silence. "Why you go and scare me like that? You hurt anything?"

"No... I felt a little dizzy, that's all."

"Don't you be gettin' up all by you self. Miss Sally don't want you outta that bed no how," Bobby scolds, as he props pillows behind Franklin's back.

"Oh, stop fretting so. I was just looking for dust balls. No harm done. Shall I carry on with my story?"

"If you like," Bobby says, calming himself.

"Where's my teacup?"

Bobby finds the teacup and places it in Franklin's hand.

"Did I mention that Bradford the elder turned up at his son's shop, having come on horseback from New York and preceding me by two days?"

Bobby shakes his head *'no'*.

Franklin takes a deep breath. "Bradford was surprised that his son had already replaced his lost man, Aquila Rose, as was I. To right matters, he offered to accompany me to Keimer's shop, newly established in the town, to meet the proprietor." Franklin takes a sip of his wine and collects his thoughts. "Bradford's gesture was hardly magnanimous, as he was on a spy mission. He failed to reveal his identity to Keimer and pried trade secrets from the old boy. I forgave Bradford his subterfuge, however, as Keimer took me on. Then, as I said, opportunity strolled into the shop one afternoon.

Philadelphia   1724

A window sign reads: *'H. Keimer & Son, Printer'.* Young Franklin is inside, repairing an ancient press. Sir William Keith, the Governor of Pennsylvania, enters the shop. He serves at the behest of the Penn family, Proprietaries of the colony, and owners of vast royal land-grant plantations therein. Keith is a dandy, over-dressed for daytime. His yellow hair is worn long, falling over the satin collar of his frock coat, which is nipped in at his waist. He fluffs a silk foulard spilling from his breast pocket as he walks. His visit is unexpected.

Franklin looks up from his work and wipes his greasy hands with a rag. "Governor Keith! I have your job finished. I was going to bring it to your office in a short while."

"Then I've saved you a trip, haven't I? Is the old man about?"

"Mr. Keimer has gone to lunch."

"Good. I must speak with you privately." Governor Keith approaches Franklin, getting uncomfortably close. "I've had my eye on you, young man."

Franklin recoils. "You have?"

"Indeed, I have."

Franklin walks around a printing press to put some distance between them.

"I have a proposition for you."

Franklin is bug-eyed. "You do?"

The Governor circles the machine, moving closer to Franklin. "Yes, but you must keep what I tell you in the strictest confidence."

Franklin takes a step back. "But of course, Your Excellency."

Keith points to a quiet corner of the shop. "Let us retire thither and I will tell you of my plan."

Franklin looks toward the dingy corner, takes a deep breath, and follows the Governor.

Franklin's Bedroom   1790

"Are you listening, Bobby?"

"Mm-hmm," Bobby murmurs, as he tidies the bed.

"Fothergill, the fisherman, had suggested I seek out a fellow my age by the name of James Ralph, a writer of poetry. We soon became fast friends."

A Green Park in Philadelphia   1724

On the Sunday following the Governor's visit, Franklin and James Ralph, a classically handsome twenty-year-old, lie on a blanket on the grass. Both are shirtless, enjoying the warm afternoon sun, and both are reading books. Ralph is on his stomach, with the ebony ringlets of his hair nearly brushing the pages of his book.

Franklin lies perpendicular to him, using Ralph's muscular back as a pillow.

"So, James, what do you think of the Governor's proposition?" Franklin asks, peering over the top of his book.

"Well, old man, I'd think long and hard on that one." He pushes Franklin away, rolls onto his back, holds up his book, and reads aloud. "I wish I had written this: *'Tis better to reign in hell than to serve in heaven.'* How true. Guess who wrote it."

Franklin's eyes don't stray from his book. "John Milton wrote those words. He also wrote: *'The mind is its own place, and in itself can make heav'n of hell, and hell of heav'n.'*"

Ralph looks annoyed. "How did you know that?"

"I read… in English, Latin, French, Italian and Spanish."

"You worm! I am presently serving in a supposed 'heaven' called marriage. Mary's parents detest me. They think me a ne'er-do-well."

"Because you are one. Milton also said, *'They serve who only stand and wait.'* So, what are you waiting for? Take a break from Mary's miserable family and come with me."

Ralph sits up. "What? To England?"

Franklin rolls onto his stomach, his head on his hand. "Yes, to England. I'll convince Governor Keith to pay for your passage as well. I've got to do this, James. I have an offer of Keith's help in opening my own shop… and that won't happen every day. I'd love your company on the journey."

"Mary would have a fit… and I can't leave my children," he says as he puts on his shirt.

Franklin sits up next to Ralph. "We won't be gone long. C'mon, Jemmy."

"What about *your* girl?"

"I'm working on that…"

A few evenings later, Franklin leads Deborah Read up a narrow, winding stairway in her mother's house. They are both eighteen. They walk on tip-toe, carrying their shoes. He carries a lighted candle, they arrive in the attic. He spreads his coat on the floor, sits, and pulls her down to him.

Deborah looks nervously toward the stairway and whispers, "We've got to be quiet. She'll hear us up here."

He answers in a near-whisper. "She hasn't yet." He kisses her gently on her neck. "I must tell you something. I'm going to take a little trip… on business."

Deborah brushes her blonde hair off her forehead with her hand. "Where to?"

"England."

Her eyes open wide. "Little trip? I will never see you again!"

"I won't be gone long, I swear. A month or two at most." He kisses her lips.

She rests her head on his shoulder. "Aren't you afraid, Ben? Crossing the sea? It's so dangerous."

"Nay. I'm going to ask your mother for your hand. Tomorrow. What do you think of that?"

Deborah raises her head. "Are you proposing to me?"

"That I am. We'll marry as soon as I return. What do you say?"

She rests her chin on her knee. "I need time to think."

"Don't think! Just say 'yes'." He raises her chin with his finger, and unbuttons the top of her dress. She isn't wearing undergarments. He caresses her full, firm breasts. Deborah delights in his touch and loves seeing the young man's eyes ignite with pleasure. He kisses her on the mouth as he gently pushes her shoulders to the floor, removes his shirt, and moves on top of her.

They hear Mrs. Read's footsteps at the bottom of the stairway. They freeze. Franklin snuffs out the candle. Mrs. Read climbs a few steps, then pauses, listening. A few moments later, she turns around and descends the stairs. They hear the 'click' of her leather heels receding down the hallway.

The next evening, Mrs. Read leans against the wooden sink in her kitchen, with her arms folded across her ample bosom. Her graying hair is loosely pulled back, with stray strands of it falling over her eyes. Shadows from a candle flickering on the sideboard dance across her craggy face, making her look older than her thirty-nine years. Deborah and Franklin sit at the table, drinking tea. Their young faces glow in the light of a candle burning on the table.

Mrs. Read stares at Franklin for a long moment, then: "How long do you expect to be over there, boy?"

"Not long. Just a few months."

"Pshaw! You'll be three months in each direction, boy. That is, if the sea don't swallow ya up. I figure my Deborah here has as much school learnin' as any woman needs. She's a pretty thing, too, far as that goes. She's a fine catch in this village."

Deborah blushes. "Mama, please."

"I couldn't agree more," Franklin says, sipping his tea.

"But…" Mrs. Read wipes the table with a rag. "The way I see it, you ain't the man to catch her. Not yet, anyhow. Now, if all that you say about makin' a business for yourself comes to pass, I might be of another mind."

"Mrs. Read, I fully intend to prove myself worthy of your blessing."

"When do you sail?" she asks.

"In a fortnight."

"Well, we will have to wait and see what comes to pass, if anything. Deborah, you say 'goodnight' to Mr. Franklin and put out that light. We don't own a candle works." Mrs. Read squeezes out the rag in a basin in the sink. "I do wish you a safe journey, boy, and calmer seas than what we had when we come over here when she was a baby." She points to Deborah. "Still has nightmares over it, don't ya, Deb? Well, come along now." Mrs. Read picks up the candle from the sideboard and leaves the room without looking back.

Franklin calls after her, "Goodnight, Mrs. Read."

Deborah stands and begins to clear the tea. "Good night, Mama. I'll be up in a minute!"

Franklin rises and helps to clear the table. He and Deborah don't speak for a few moments. He places his hand on her forearm. She turns to him. They embrace and kiss, then she pushes him away firmly.

"She might come back," she warns.

He takes both her hands in his. "No matter what your mother says, I am going to marry you."

Deborah looks up at Franklin and smiles sweetly. "I *will* wait for you, Ben."

He squeezes her hand. "I'm going to take that as an affirmation."

She pulls her hand away, turns to the tin basin in the sink, and rinses out tea cups. "But I *won't* wait forever," she adds. "Do you hear me?"

They hear Mrs. Read shouting from her bedroom upstairs. "Deborah! You come along now!"

CHAPTER NINE

Pals

Port of Philadelphia   1724

Two weeks later, James Ralph stands on deck, leaning against the railing of a packet boat as its sails are unfurled. Gilded letters on the stern read, *'Annie French, Liverpool.'* Ralph watches intently as the shoreline of Pennsylvania recedes.

Franklin approaches him from behind and places a hand on his friend's shoulder. "'Tis a sight, is it not? Watching terra firma vanish, I mean."

"Mm." Ralph doesn't look at Franklin.

"A pound for your thoughts, Jemmy."

"I wonder if I will ever gaze upon those shores again."

Franklin moves closer to him. "There's the poet in ye! *'If I shall ever gaze upon these shores… and lie in clover with a dozen lusty…'*"

Ralph smacks Franklin on the back of his head. "Don't be crass, laddie."

"Ouch!" Franklin rubs his head. "Are you fearful of the sea?"

"No. I just have a feeling."

Franklin turns and leans back against the railing. "I did expect to find Mary at the port to see you off."

"She's not speaking to me. She's gone to her mother with the children."

"She'll come 'round. We'll be home again in no time. We will secure the Governor's letters of credit from his solicitors in London, buy what we need for my new shop, and be on our way."

"I hope so," Ralph says. He looks at Franklin, with an anxious look on his face. "I think I'll go to the cabin and sort out my gear."

"You do that. I'm going to explore the ship. See if there's anybody aboard worth meeting. I'll fetch you for dinner." Franklin watches Ralph walk away, envious of the feline way in which he moves his perfectly shaped frame.

Later that evening, Franklin struggles to find his sea legs as he navigates a narrow corridor. His shoulders hit the wall a few times as he walks. He approaches the cabin door and knocks lightly. "Jemmy. It's me," he says. There is no response.

Franklin finds the door is unlatched, opens it, and enters the cabin. Ralph lies on his bunk with his face to the wall, wearing the same clothing he had worn hours before. There is a pail on the floor next to the bed. "You awake?" Franklin asks, shaking Ralph's shoulder. "It's suppertime! Get up now. *Levez-vous.*"

Ralph groans, waves Franklin away with his free hand and keeps his face to the wall.

"'Tis a nice roast the cooks have prepared tonight, I'm told," Franklin says cheerily.

Ralph groans again and points to the pail.

"Oh, I see. You poor man. If you change your mind, I'll be in the dining saloon."

Ralph emits a deep, pitiful groan. Franklin backs out of the cabin, closing the door behind him. He pauses for a moment, thinking. Thomas Denham, a middle-aged gentleman, graying at the temples and of cheerful countenance, passes by. He stops and looks at Franklin.

"Evening, son. Something vexing you?" Denham inquires.

"No. Well, yes." Franklin points to his cabin. "My friend in there is too unwell to come to supper. Seasick."

Denham shakes his head. "Poor fellow… and his journey has just begun."

"Doesn't bode well, does it?" Franklin sighs.

"No. He may get over it, and then again, he may not. I'm dining alone. Come sup with me, lad."

"Oh, I couldn't impose…"

"I would enjoy the company." He offers his hand. "Tom Denham. Dry Goods."

They shake hands. "Ben Franklin. Printer... or hope to be."

"Good. You can tell me over dinner how you plan to make yourself a printer, and I shall regale you with tales of buttons and yard goods." He steps aside and gestures for Franklin to lead the way to the dining room. They proceed down the narrow hall in single file, weaving with the roll of the ship.

LONDON   1725

A law office occupies the ground floor of a brick building in Covent Garden. A shiny brass plaque next to the door reads: *'Fearon and Weiss, Solicitors'*. In the far recesses of the office, Franklin, now nineteen, stands before a massive mahogany desk. Micah Fearon, a lawyer in his mid-sixties, sits behind the desk; piles of documents are spread over its leather top. Fearon appears to be a tall man, even when seated. His graying hair is neatly trimmed, with bushy sideburns brushing against his ears. His clothing is bespoke by a fine tailoring house.

Franklin is intimidated in the solicitor's presence. He stands holding his cap in his hands, shifting from one foot to the other as he speaks. "I apologize, sir, for being such a nuisance," he says, "but I had hoped something might have come for me on last week's packet boat."

Fearon looks up from a stack of papers. "No, son, nothing's come for ye, to be sure."

"Dammit! Oh, beg pardon sir... I've been waiting such a long time."

"There's another packet boat due to land at Harwich in about ten days. Perhaps then," Fearon offers in a consoling tone.

Franklin chews a fingernail. "I'm in desperate need of those letters of credit. My friend and I have nothing left."

The lawyer pushes back his chair and crosses his arms. "May I tell you something about Sir William, whom I have known for many years, long before he was appointed Governor?"

"Yes, please."

"He's not a bad sort, but people like him intend to be helpful and make promises they can ill-afford to keep. They are careless, not ill-intentioned."

"Oh, I see."

"Have you thought about finding employment? Have you any skills?"

"Yes, I do. Perhaps I'd best look for work."

"I would," Fearon says and returns to his papers.

Franklin looks at him briefly and realizes he has been dismissed. "Thank you," he says. Fearon gives a little wave with the back of his hand, but doesn't look up from his work as Franklin takes his leave.

Several months later, heads turn as James Ralph and a lady friend stroll arm-in-arm through Leicester Square. She is a floozy: her clothing is vulgar and cheap, her coal-black hair is unkempt, and she is heavily rouged. Pushcart jewelry adorns her wrists and neck and 'clanks' with her every move. They come upon a workshop, where a sign painted on the window reads: *'Watts & Co. Printers'*. Ralph is aware that Franklin has worked at Watts for some time. He and the girl stop, shade their eyes, and peer into the window. They see Franklin inside, tinkering with a new machine with another pressman. Ralph points out Franklin to the girl and taps on the window. Franklin looks up from his task. Ralph and the girl smile and wave. Franklin gives a half-hearted wave with two fingers in return. Ralph and his lady friend giggle and walk on as Franklin shakes his head and returns to his work.

PHILADELPHIA   APRIL 1790

Bobby finishes fussing with the bed and places soiled linens in a basket near the bedroom door. Franklin recalls those days in London. "I might as well have been waiting for the Second Coming," he says. "My blunder turned out to be a blessing, however, as I learned the tricks of my trade at the hands of a master printer. Friend James was too busy sowing his wild oats to bother with employment, and was soon in my debt. After more than a year, I lost patience with him."

LONDON   1726

The sign painted on the front of a café in Soho reads: *Turkish coffees, China teas, Fresh baked goods'*. Franklin and James Ralph are seated at a table in the window. Ralph is engrossed in a book he is reading.

Franklin looks at his friend, who appears well-rested and the picture of robust good health. Franklin, on the other hand, is a little threadbare and his skin is pale from long days working indoors. After a moment: "It's been seventeen months, Jemmy. Those instructions for Micah Fearon from the Governor are not forthcoming."

Ralph may not have heard. He looks up from his book. "It says here that Shakespeare, in all his works, asks only three questions: *'Who are we? Why are we? Why are we here?'*"

"I thought *'To be or not to be'* was the question," Franklin says smugly.

"It's the very same thing, don't you see?" Ralph replies excitedly.

"*'Why are we here?'* That resonates. It's time to go home."

"How do you propose to do that? We haven't any money." Ralph looks about the coffee house. "Where is that boy with our coffee?" he asks impatiently.

Franklin shrugs his shoulders. "I had a fortuitous meeting in Covent Garden yesterday. Do you remember a Quaker gentleman, a Mr. Denham, who sailed with us on the Annie French?"

"Yes. A nice enough chap."

"He's been over here buying for his dry goods store back home."

A waiter wearing a long white apron arrives at the table and serves their coffee.

"Oh?" Ralph says, adding a spoonful of sugar to his cup.

"We dined on board several times and got on well. He's asked me to join him in the venture… to become a partner with him." Franklin lifts his cup, sips his coffee.

"You don't say! Like Governor Keith?" Ralph smirks.

"I accepted his offer. Passage home for both of us is part of our agreement."

Ralph is surprised. "Both of us?"

"Yes! You as well. Now kiss me and tell me how brilliant I am and how blessed you are to know me." Franklin offers his cheek in jest. There is an awkward pause in the conversation. "You don't look very happy."

Ralph takes a small pipe from his vest pocket and packs it with tobacco. "I've decided to stay in London."

Franklin's eyes widen. "You can't be serious."

"You know I detested the crossing. I couldn't face another voyage."

"But what about Mary? What of your children?"

"I've met a girl. I'm in love with her. Mary will be better off without me," Ralph sighs.

Franklin sets down his cup. "Are you mad? You need to think this through."

Ralph attempts to light his pipe, but Franklin grabs it out of his hand. "You know I hate the smell of that. What of your debt to me? You owe me near fifty pounds!"

Ralph looks sheepish. "I promise I will send you the money… somehow."

"Like Governor Keith?" Franklin says ironically. He rises from the table and takes his coat from a coat rack on the wall next to him.

Ralph looks pleadingly at Franklin. "You will say good-bye to Mary for me, won't you? Explain things?"

"I will not. I am too ashamed of you."

"Don't pass judgement, Ben. You are not in an unhappy marriage."

Franklin puts on his coat. "I find your decision shocking. I would never deny the mother of my children… *Never.* You may pay for my coffee."

"I haven't any money," Ralph says, with downcast eyes.

Franklin fishes coins out of his pocket. "A fitting end!" he says, his voice raised. He slams the coins down on the table and storms out of the coffee house. Franklin hurries down the street, pulling the collar of his coat up about his neck. He elbows his way through the crowd of passers-by, melting into it. His eyes are blazing, brimming over with disappointment.

CHAPTER TEN

Shopkeeper

FRANKLIN'S BEDROOM   APRIL 1790

Bobby sees a moth flailing on the window sill. "You ever see Mr. Ralph again?" He whacks the moth with the towel in his hand.

"Yes… years later. Again he asked me to send his regards to Mary and the children, but I never did." He sighs deeply. "I loved him, you know… One of my first big mistakes."

"Maybe you should lay youself down now."

Franklin ignores Bobby. "I sailed on the 23rd of July, 1726, landing in Philadelphia on October 11th. I found many changes. Sir William was no longer Governor, for one."

PHILADELPHIA   1726

A cool, overcast morning on a day in autumn. Mrs. Read and Franklin are speaking through her front door, which is open a few inches. She wears a woolen robe over her flannel nightgown, her coarse gray hair is loose and falling to her shoulders. Franklin's warm jacket is buttoned up to his neck.

"I am sorry, but I ain't got a room to let, Mr. Franklin," she laments. "House is full. Nice to see you back safe from your journey, though."

Franklin kicks at a pebble on her doorstep with his boot, looking dejected. "I'm sorry, too. I was happy living here."

"Anyhow, Deborah's not here. She moved out. I suppose you didn't know that."

Franklin looks up. "No, I didn't know."

"I was just having a cup… You can join me if you like."

"I would like that, yes."

Mrs. Read opens the door wider and leads Franklin to the kitchen. He sits at the table while she heats a kettle of water on the fire. "You don't look any worse for the wear, I must say," she says, pushing stray strands of hair from her face. "But what did you expect? She never got but one letter from you."

"I was remiss…"

"Then Mr. Rogers come along. Seemed four-square enough. Handsome devil… cheek bones like a Greek god, he had. More hair than you, too. They was married in no time."

Franklin looks at his boots. "I see."

"I told you she was a good catch, didn't I, Mr. Franklin?"

"Indeed she is… was."

Mrs. Read takes biscuits from a crockery jar and arranges them on a plate. "They wasn't married but a few months when some creditors who was after him come down from New York. They chased him all the way to Barbados. Don't rightly know why."

"His debts must have been considerable."

"Yes. Then we heard he caught somethin' dreadful down there and passed. Can't be confirmed, you understand." She sets the plate on the table. "Help yourself."

Franklin nods. "The distance…"

"Yes. Too far away. But until his corpse washes up on some shore, my Deborah is Mrs. John Rogers," she says as she pours tea. "It's one helluva thing."

"A difficult situation, that…" Franklin concurs.

"If Deb marries somebody else and Rogers turns up again, alive that is, she'd go to prison. Hard labor, at that." Mrs. Reed cackles: "If he *rolls* up, she's home free!" She finds a piece of paper and pen on the sideboard and joins Franklin at the table. "Well, what will you do now that your printin' business is a bust?"

"I have a partner in a store on Water Street. I'm going to try my hand at shopkeeping. Dry goods."

Mrs. Read jots something on the paper. "You might think about a smithy when the store fails. We can always use a good blacksmith.

DEAR BEN

Deborah's got a little cottage over on Mason Street." She hands Franklin the paper. "Here's the number. I'm sure she'd like to see ya… regardless."

Franklin sips his tea while he looks at the paper.

Later that day, Franklin stands outside a modest frame cottage. The house is removed from the street by a tiny front yard, defined by a low picket fence. Franklin opens the gate, approaches the front door, and knocks lightly.

Inside the cottage, Deborah hears the knock at the door, parts the parlor curtains slightly, and peeks out the window. She sees Franklin and quickly retreats, pressing herself against the wall. He knocks again, more forcefully. Again she doesn't move. He listens at the door for a minute, hears nothing, then turns and walks away, dodging carriage traffic in the street.

PHILADELPHIA   APRIL 1790

It is early evening as a half-dozen neighbors gathered on the walk beneath Franklin's bedroom windows hear Thomas Jefferson's coach-and-four clatter up Market Street. Two ladies lower their umbrellas as the grand rig arrives in front of the Franklin house, its horses wild-eyed and whinnying. Jefferson's equipage is impressive, with polished tack, a driver atop, and a coachman in the rear, both of whom wear Jefferson's Monticello Estate livery in deep blue.

"It's Jefferson!" Franklin's near neighbor, Lucas McLeod, exclaims excitedly as the coach comes to a stop. The coachman jumps down and opens Jefferson's door.

Jefferson alights to polite applause from the gathering on the walk. Although a light rain falls, he doffs his hat, tucks a package he carries under his arm, and shakes a few hands. A stout, middle-aged woman curtsies to him. He smiles and touches her arm with his forefinger. "No need for that, ma'am. As Dr. Franklin has said, '*We've given you a democracy… if you can keep it!*'"

"How *is* Dr. Franklin?" she inquires. "We are all very concerned…"

"He is on the mend, I trust,"

"What news do you bring us from France, Mr. Secretary?" McLeod inquires.

"You must read Dr. Franklin's newspaper, my friend," Jefferson replies.

Curtains are pulled closed in the parlor as Sally Bache opens the front door. Jefferson gives a wave to the neighbors, and enters the house. The front door closes firmly behind him.

Franklin's Bedroom

Franklin's face brightens. He sits upright against his pillows. "Bobby! He's come! Did you hear the people?"

"Yeah, I heard."

"How do I look? He'll be along soon. Am I presentable?"

Bobby steps back and studies Franklin's appearance. He picks up a brush and fusses with the old man's sparse hair. "Only so much I can do, you know. I been wonderin.' You ever get your money from that Mr. Ralph?"

"Certainly not."

"Maybe you run outta luck that time."

Franklin sighs and a pensive look crosses his face. "So it seemed…"

Philadelphia   1727

A sign hanging over the entrance of a shop on Water Street reads: 'Denham & Co. Dry Goods'. A young clerk, sixteen or seventeen years of age, wearing his shop apron, waits outside the front door.

Franklin approaches, carrying his apron in his hand. "What are you doing out here?" he asks the clerk.

"The door is locked, Mr. Franklin."

Franklin looks at his pocket watch. "That's odd. Did you try the back?"

"Yes, sir. That's locked, too."

"Have you seen Mr. Denham?"

"No, sir."

Franklin peers in the shop window. "That's very strange. He's usually here at first light. I have a key here somewhere." Franklin produces a key from his pocket and unlocks the front door. He and the clerk enter the store.

The clerk calls out: "Mr. Denham?"

Franklin dons his apron. "Denham? Are you about?"

They wander through the store, shouting Denham's name, until Franklin steps behind a display counter and finds Mr. Denham lying on the floor. "Thomas! Are you all right?" He kneels on the floor next to Denham, puts his ear to Denham's chest and checks his wrist for a pulse. He turns to the clerk. "Go fetch Dr. Haskell, lad… Run boy, run!"

The clerk runs out of the shop as Franklin continues to examine Mr. Denham for a whisper of breath. He hears none, and stands staring incredulously at the figure lying on the floor.

Thomas Denham's sudden demise was unexpected, to say the least. Franklin's partner had not yet turned fifty and appeared to be in robust health. He was a kind, honest man and good company; Franklin knew he was going to miss him. To his credit, Denham had taught Franklin the intricacies of the business at a rapid pace, and he was confident he could continue operating the dry goods store on his own, although tinged with sadness.

A few weeks after Denham's death, Franklin is seated in his office in the rear of the store, pouring over ledgers. Denham was a clever merchant, but untrained in accounting and had left books and records that were wanting for clarity and challenging to decipher.

Franklin looks up when he hears a light knock on the office door. Alfred Denham, Thomas's nephew, a short man in his mid-twenties, stands there. He bears a family resemblance, wears business attire, and appears nervous.

Franklin closes a ledger book. "Alfred! Good morning! This is a surprise." Alfred enters the office. Franklin points to a chair against the wall. "Sit, sit. Please, take a seat."

Alfred sits in the chair. "Good morning, Benjamin," he says cautiously. "I trust you have been well?"

"Yes. Yes, thank you. May I again offer my condolences at the loss of your dear uncle. So unexpected. I am still in a state of shock."

"Yes, shock is the word." Alfred pauses. "My family has sent me to speak with you," he says, fidgeting with the lapel of his coat.

"Have they?"

"Yes. Now that Uncle has passed away, we won't have need of your services any longer."

"And what services might those be?"

"As we feel we are quite capable of managing the store's affairs on our own, your assistance will not, henceforth, be required."

Franklin gets up, moves around the desk, sits on its edge, and looks down on Alfred. "As I am your uncle's partner in the business, I am quite capable of managing without *your* assistance henceforth."

Alfred squirms in his chair. "As we find no trace of an agreement between Uncle and yourself creating such a partnership, we, his family, are his legal and rightful heirs and have assumed control of Denham and Company."

Franklin raises his voice. "Our partnership was a handshake agreement between two gentlemen, more sacred than any document!"

"An agreement which lives only in your imagination." Alfred summons his courage and sits up in his chair. "We are prepared to defend our position by any legal means necessary. It is, additionally, our wish that you remove yourself from the premises at your earliest convenience."

Franklin cannot believe his ears. "You are obviously not heir to your uncle's kind and generous nature, or his integrity. I will have my desk emptied by the week's end!" he fumes and returns to his seat behind the desk. He re-opens the ledger book.

"It may be best if you do so today," Alfred says bravely.

Franklin looks up again, seething. "Very well. Perhaps it is best I leave. The air in this room has been fouled by your presence."

Alfred rises, with a smug look on his face. "I shall return in a few hours to collect your keys."

"Ten minutes will do!" Franklin takes his keys from a desk drawer and hurls them at the wall. They hit with a loud *crack,* sending Alfred scurrying out of the office and out of the store.

Franklin's Bedroom   1790

Franklin sits on the edge of his bed, with a gloomy expression on his face. "That was a dark day. I had lost Deborah, was out of funds, and had no prospects. Open that window a little, will you Bobby? The rain's easing up. Have we any laudanum?"

"Mm-hm." Bobby opens the window a few inches. He takes a vial from his pocket and prepares laudanum for Franklin in a glass on the bedside table. "You know, my Mama always say it darkest just before the dawn," he offers, stirring the liquid in the glass.

Franklin breaks into a smile. "Yes, I've heard that somewhere…"

CHAPTER ELEVEN

The Fair Maiden

FRANKLIN HOUSE   APRIL 1790

Thomas Jefferson's greatcoat and hat hang on a rack next to the front door. Polly sets wine glasses on the center table in the parlor, where Sally sits demurely, with her back erect and her hands folded in her lap. She seems intimidated, overawed, by Jefferson's rugged good looks and erudite demeanor.

Jefferson stands next to the table, pulls a cork from a wine bottle he holds, and sniffs the cork. "Would you say your father has improved?" he asks Sally.

"Well, his fever is down," she replies politely.

"He was sleeping when I looked in a little while ago," Polly volunteers.

Sally shoots Polly a dark look.

Jefferson pours wine, twirls the wine in the glass, brings it to his nose, and sniffs it again. "We'll have a taste before I go up," he says, handing each lady a glass of wine. "Smell it, Sally. What does it remind you of?"

Sally sniffs her wine glass. "Mushrooms?"

"Nay," Jefferson scoffs. "'Tis the elixir of heaven. What say you, Polly?"

"It reminds me of France."

"It should! A fine vintage from our friend, Chevillot, in Beaune."

Sally tastes her wine. "I am told, Mr. Jefferson, that you saw my brother in France."

"Yes. He called on me in Paris."

"My father met with William in England on his way home. It didn't go well." Sally adds.

Jefferson sips his wine. "So I am told."

Sally looks over at Polly again. "I believe *somebody* drove a wedge between my father and his family."

The pointed remark makes Polly uncomfortable. She walks to the window with her glass in hand, pulls back the curtain, and looks outside. "The rain is easing up now," she comments.

Sally's eyes are trained on Polly. "Papa stayed in England for sixteen years. There must have been some reason, wouldn't you say, Mr. Jefferson?"

"I would say it was his work. Events of the day… circumstances," he surmises.

Polly turns to Jefferson. "I am in disbelief at the turmoil in Paris. What do you make of it, Mr. Secretary? It was so peaceful and lovely when I was there."

"You wouldn't say that now. The fighting is fierce." He takes a seat at the table. "Both the Bastille and the Treasury have been emptied by the rebels and the Royal Family is imprisoned in the near-derelict Tuileries Palace."

Polly returns to the table and sits down. "How very sad. Papa was terribly fond of the King and Queen."

"Still, I am an advocate of the revolutionary cause. The rebels follow in our footsteps, don't they?" Jefferson savors the bouquet and taste of the French wine.

"One might say the barbarians have crashed through the gates! That couldn't happen in America, could it?" Polly asks, sounding concerned.

"Of course not. We will have elections in this country," Jefferson assures her.

"My father wasted nine years over there in France, didn't he?" Sally snarls.

"Oh, I hardly think so. We may well have lost the war had he not been there to enlist the help of the French King." Jefferson lifts his glass. "Let us raise our glasses to Dear Ben. In practice, America's first Secretary of State!"

Polly raises her glass. Sally hesitates, then reluctantly joins in the toast. "Here, here! To Dear Papa Ben!" Polly exclaims.

Franklin's Bedroom

Bobby closes the window and wipes rain from the sill with a rag. "You told me how you got poor, but you still ain't told me how you got rich."

"Well, I went back to work for Keimer for a time, but we quarreled and I left him." Franklin points to a chair across the room. "Put me in that chair by the window. I'd like to sit up for Jefferson's visit."

Bobby guides Franklin from the bed to a straight-backed armchair. He helps Franklin lower himself into the chair.

Franklin catches his breath. "Then, I opened a print shop with a friend, Meredith, with funds borrowed from his father. We made a profit from the first day, but Meredith was a drunkard and rarely showed up. I bought him out and re-paid his father. That's how I got started. I've written a book about my life, it's all in there. You do read, don't you?"

"Yes, sir. Mr. Bache taught me how."

"Bravo! Then Bache accomplished *something*. There's a copy of my book around here somewhere... Read my book, Bobby."

Bobby thinks for a minute. "But... what's *not* in the book?" he asks.

Franklin doesn't reply. He turns to the window and stares out, soon lost in a reverie.

Near Philadelphia   1728

Franklin is seated at a round table with six friends in a crowded, smoky tavern. His friends are all men in their twenties, as is he. Heavy coats draped over the backs of their chairs suggest a cold night outside. Oak logs burn and crackle in the hearth of a massive fieldstone fireplace across the room. A few of his friends smoke pipes and all have near-empty pints of ale before them. Franklin's eyes follow the barmaid, Maureen, as she serves the table another round of drinks. She is nineteen years old and pretty, in a hard sort of way. She wears a daringly low-cut dress and knows how to display her attributes as she moves.

Laughter dies down from the men sitting around the table. "So, Franklin, how'd he get the second black eye, pray tell?" one of them asks, raising his voice above the din of the crowd.

Franklin takes a swig of his ale. "Well, when the congregation stood up to sing another hymn, he thought he'd help the lady out, so he stuffed her skirt back up her arse!" His friends roar with laughter. Franklin rises from the table, a bit tipsy. "A call of nature," he says, and weaves his way through tables to the rear exit, over which hangs a sign reading 'Privy.' Outside, a pair of outhouses stand at the back of the yard. He enters and uses one of them. When finished, he closes the door behind him. The barmaid is waiting for him just outside the door.

"Maureen! Are you waiting to use the privy?" he asks.

"No, I ain't heard from the piss fairy lately," she announces.

"You must be freezing in that costume," he says, surprised by her coarse remark.

"I'm not cold at all. I come out here to see you," she says coquettishly.

"You did?"

"I seen how you look at me every time you come in the tavern. I seen how your eyes follow me around the place, they do. You have a shine for me."

"I do? I didn't intend to be rude."

"I'd like to know you better. I think you're going to be somebody someday."

"I thank you for your vote of confidence."

"You're not like the others that come here," she says, pointing to the tavern behind them. "What's *rude*, though, is you never ask to see me. Has some woman put her hooks into you already?" she scolds.

"You might say I'm between acts."

She moves closer to Franklin and caresses his cheek. "Let's fix that right now." She kisses him on the lips.

He braces himself against the wall of the outhouse. "You're certain you're not cold?"

"I bet you got somethin' could make me warmer," she says as she slides her hand down the inside of his breeches.

Franklin closes his eyes. "Won't you be missed?" he whimpers.

"I got ten minutes or so," she replies.

Franklin opens his eyes, looks around the yard, and leads Maureen to a dark spot behind the outhouses. She lifts her skirts. He unbuttons his breeches, and takes her, standing up. Maureen's skill at love-making drives Franklin to a near-frenzy.

In the second outhouse, unknown to the lovers, a candle burns on a shelf above a man seated inside. The man's eyes grow wide as he listens to sounds of ecstasy while the couple moan and thrash against the wall of the outhouse he occupies. The candle quivers with the movement outside, then is extinguished.

Franklin's Bedroom April   1790

Franklin sees the last of the day's light fading to darkness. He turns from the window to Bobby. *"That's* not in the book and you will kindly keep it to yourself."

"I die with that one," Bobby assures him.

Franklin House, Parlor

Polly and Jefferson are seated at the center table with their glasses of wine.

Sally stands unsteadily nearby. "Whoo!" she says. "This wine has gone straight to my head. So like I said, Pa took my brother's son, Temple, and my little boy, Benny, off to Paris with him in '76. I never dreamed Benny would be sixteen before I saw him again."

Jefferson looks at her. "Your son enjoyed a fine education in Switzerland, as I recall."

"He did not. He loathed it there." Sally totters around the table. "His grandfather never once visited him. What did poor Benny do wrong? You just can't please the man."

"He was enormously pleased when you organized the ladies of the town to sew shirts for Washington's troops. He told me so."

Sally steadies herself with a hand on the back of a chair. "Was he? When I asked him to send over a bit of lace for me, he bristled. Why would he do that?"

"Genius is not readily explained, or understood, my dear." Jefferson stands and looks at his pocket watch. "I'd best go up now, ladies. The hour grows late."

Polly stands and picks up a candle from the table. "I'll take you up."

"No need. I'll find my way."

"Take this with you." She hands him the candle.

Jefferson walks to the stairway. "I won't be long," he says as he climbs the stairs.

"No... We don't want to tire him!" Sally calls after him. When Jefferson is out of sight, she turns to Polly. "He thinks my father walks on water."

Polly pours herself another glass of wine. "Well, he is no ordinary mortal."

Sally lowers herself onto a chair. "I guess we're about to find out," she says curtly.

Jefferson carries the lighted candle as he climbs the central stairway of the Franklin house. The steps creak underfoot as he goes. The big house has been rebuilt twice and is a maze of confusing corridors. He reaches a second-floor landing, and stops, suddenly. He sees a female figure in white moving down the dark hall ahead of him. Curious, he follows her, quietly, walking on his tiptoes.

Franklin's Bedroom

Bobby brings Franklin the glass containing a measure of laudanum.

Franklin drinks it down, then stares into the glass as the combination of alcohol and opium warms him. He rummages through his thoughts. "You know, choosing the woman you marry is the most important decision you will ever make. Do you lie with women, Bobby?"

"No, generally I tells 'em the truth," Bobby replies without hesitation.

Franklin smiles and sets the glass on the bedside table. "As I was saying, my business flourished and I managed to buy a local newspaper, 'The Gazette.' It turned out I hadn't seen the last of that barmaid."

Philadelphia   1728

A sign painted on the window of the modest frame building reads: *"B. Franklin, Printer. Philadelphia Gazette Printed Here."* It is a brisk spring day. Trees along the street are in bud and their branches sway in a stiff breeze. Maureen approaches the Franklin shop and peers into the window, fixing her hair in the reflection. She is scantily clad for town, especially on such a cool day. Her curly red hair is piled on top of her head and she has a lacy shawl draped over her shoulders. The skirt of her dress rustles in the wind. She sees Franklin inside, talking with two pressmen. Maureen taps on the window and gives him a cheery wave.

A shocked expression washes over Franklin's face, as he rushes outside. "Maureen! What brings you to town?" he inquires, closing the door firmly behind him.

"Ain't you happy to see me?" she asks, smiling broadly.

"Of course, but I'm very busy. Perhaps another time."

Her smile vanishes. "I need to talk to you. It is very important."

"All right, then. Come inside." Franklin opens the door and shows her into the shop. He ushers Maureen to his tiny office in the back. The pressmen's heads turn as they pass. He shows her to a seat at his desk, closes the office door, and takes a seat opposite her.

Maureen gets to the point. "I know I don't show hardly at all, but a baby, our baby, is comin' along. Trust me."

Franklin's face pales. "Trust you? How do I know this child is mine?"

"The time is right, ain't it? I'm not what you'd call a beginner at this."

"That goes without saying." Franklin concurs.

"If marriage is of no interest to ye, there's a doctor over Wilkes-Barre way who takes care of such things. Maybe I'll pay him a visit," she taunts.

'No, don't do that," Franklin argues.

"Well, I don't have the means to take care of a child, that's damn sure."

Franklin's tone softens. "Have the baby. When it's old enough for me to feed, bring the child to me... and I will care for it."

Maureen rises from the chair and moves around the office. She admires a picture hanging on the wall. "What about me?" she asks. "There's expenses a lady has and I sure as hell can't work when I get bigger." She picks up an empty vase from a shelf and turns it over.

Franklin looks annoyed. "I will pay you a monthly allowance for the rest of your days, provided, that is, you come nowhere near me or the child," he says.

Intrigued, Maureen smiles. "Boy or girl, you would take it?" She returns the vase to the shelf.

"Yes, but you must never come within a mile of us!"

Maureen's expression sours. "I do believe you threaten me, Mr. Franklin."

"Nay. I merely outline a course of action."

She caresses the back of his head. "You ask an awful lot of a mother, you know."

Franklin recoils from her touch. "On the contrary. I offer you salvation."

Maureen resumes her seat at the desk. "Now, tell me about this 'allowance' you're thinkin' about," she says, adjusting her shawl to reveal more cleavage.

Franklin House   1790

Thomas Jefferson follows the woman dressed in white, silently, at a distance. She is several steps ahead of him and disappears into a bedroom. He approaches the room and pauses to listen outside the door. After a moment, he looks in. He finds Aggie in the room. She wears a long white apron and a white bonnet on her head. She shakes out a bedsheet, startling Jefferson. He gasps.

Aggie turns to see him in the doorway. "Evenin,' Mr. Jefferson!"

"Aggie! What are you doing up here so late at night?"

"I tidy up Mr. Temple's room while he out." She goes about making up the bed, seeming to float around it.

Jefferson steps into the room. "This is Temple Franklin's room?"

"Yes, sir."

He picks up a book from a night table and flips through the pages. "What are young people reading these days?"

"Don't rightly know, sir. I can't read," Aggie replies.

Jefferson studies the cover of the book. "'History of the House of Hanover.' Hmm… The story of the English Kings. His father must have sent this. Don't let me interrupt your chores, Aggie. I thought I saw someone…"

"Nobody here but me," she says, tucking in a sheet.

Jefferson replaces the book on the table. "I see that. Well, it's nice to see you, Aggie."

"You, too, Mr. Jefferson. You been well?"

"Yes, very well, thank you." He retreats into the hallway, closing the door behind him.

CHAPTER TWELVE

Franky

Philadelphia   1731

Deborah Read, twenty-five years old, takes down laundry hanging on a clothes line in the backyard of her little cottage on a sunny, breezy, spring day. She wears a house dress with its pockets filled with clothes pegs. Her blonde hair blows in the wind as she folds linens into a basket. Franklin, also twenty-five, leads a little boy by the hand as they enter the yard from a side street, unseen by Deborah. She takes a bed sheet off the line to find Franklin and the boy hiding behind it. Startled, she shrieks.

"Hello, Deborah," Franklin grins.

She holds her hand over her chest. "Ben, you 'bout scared the daylights outta me!"

Franklin lifts the three-year-old boy into his arms. "I want you to meet someone. This is William."

"Cute little fellow," she says, touching the boy's cheek.

"William, say 'hello' to Miss Read."

Deborah pats the boy's head. He pulls away shyly. "This your nephew?"

Franklin offers a weak smile. "My son."

Deborah sets down her basket, doesn't speak, looks skyward, and fusses with her hair. After a moment she looks at Franklin. "I'd better put the kettle on."

Inside her cozy kitchen, Franklin and William sit at the table. Deborah lifts a kettle from the fire and makes tea. William squirms in his chair.

"We, the two of us, could make a proper home for the boy. He needs a mother."

"He's got a mother. What about her? Where is she?"

Franklin stares into his teacup. "Can't say as I know for certain."

Deborah takes a loaf of bread from a box near the sink and places it, along with a crock of butter, on the table. "You got yourself in a hell of a mess."

"I could make you comfortable, Deb. I'd build us a fine house. My business is doing well… better every day. We could look after your mother, too, when the time comes. You know I never forgot you."

Deborah joins them at the table, slices a piece of bread, butters it, and serves it to William, who ignores it. "Well, you can't live with me if we ain't married. Townspeople look at me like the Scarlet Woman in the Bible as it is," she says earnestly.

William grabs a teaspoon and bangs it loudly on the table. "William! Stop that!" Franklin commands, annoyed. "We'll get married in due course. I don't want to be responsible for Mr. Rogers' debts, or the consequences for you if he turns up alive. We'll wait a bit. See what happens."

"John Rogers is dead. I know he is… and I am alone here, *again*."

Franklin covers her hand with his. "I promise you, Deb, I will never leave you."

"You promise? Never?"

He leans closer to her and looks into her eyes. "I promise. 'Til death do us part."

Deborah stirs her tea. "I'll think about it," she says.

The boy picks up his slice of bread, licks the butter off it, and looks at his father, bewildered.

Franklin's bedroom   1790

"I built that house I promised her. She gave birth to our beautiful little boy, Franky, two years later. Franklin looks up at Bobby for affirmation. "Deb raised William as her own son, too, as best she knew how."

"Yes, sir, I believe she did," Bobby agrees.

Franklin House   1732

Deborah is seated in an upholstered chair in her bedroom, dappled with sunlight pouring in from a window next to her. The door to the room is ajar. The top of her dress is unbuttoned and a towel is draped over her shoulder. She looks down at the infant she suckles.

William, now four years old, pushes the door open a few inches wider. He watches her with the baby.

Deborah hears the door hinges squeak. She doesn't look up. "William? That you?"

The boy retreats, pulling the door closed sharply behind him.

A few years later, Deborah, with a basket on her arm, is looking through the root cellar. The light is dim, a candle burns in a holder on the wall. She selects a few potatoes and places them in her basket. William approaches the cellar, unseen and unheard. He watches her for a moment, then slams the door shut and throws the heavy wooden latch across the door to lock it.

"William? I know that's you!" Deborah sets down the basket and attempts to open the door. "William! Unlock the door this very minute!" She puts her shoulder to the door, but it won't give way.

William stands around the corner listening to her pleas, but doesn't respond.

"William! You little shit! Open this door now, you hear me?" Again, Deborah puts her shoulder to the door. "I'm going to slap you senseless when I get hold of you! Open the goddamn door!" She shouts and bangs on the wooden door until her fist turns red.

William looks pleased with himself as he listens to her pounding on the door, then walks away.

Franklin's Bedroom April   1790

Franklin smiles weakly. "You might say it was not a warm relationship."

"Maybe the boy jealous 'a the baby." Bobby walks to the chair by the window and offers Franklin his hand. "Come, let's get you back to bed."

"Jealous? I suppose he was." Franklin refuses Bobby's hand. "I want to sit here, thank you." His expression turns grim. "The next year, the visitor we most dreaded came to call."

Franklin House   1736

Francis 'Franky' Franklin lies in his bed in his upstairs bedroom, frightfully ill. He is not quite five years old. He is feverish, his eyes are closed, and his hair is matted. A blistery red rash has spread over his face and torso. Deborah sits on a stool on the far side of the bed, wiping Franky's brow with a wet cloth and singing softly to the boy. She is fatigued and disheveled, her face is contorted with worry. A doctor stands next to the boy. He is in his mid-fifties, portly, has thinning gray hair, and a round, pink face with spectacles perched on his nose. He works by candlelight. He is bleeding the boy; blood drips into a tin basin on the floor.

In the kitchen downstairs, Benjamin Franklin is seated at the kitchen table, with his face resting on his hands. He is in his shirtsleeves, his waistcoat is draped over the back of his chair. Aggie, Franklin's housemaid, lifts a kettle from the fire. She is about seventeen years old, wears a homespun dress and an apron. She takes a cup and saucer from an Irish dresser, pours a shot of whiskey from a flask in her apron pocket into the cup. She fills the cup with tea and sets it before Franklin. Aggie's husband, Jake, who is probably two years her senior, sits across the table from Franklin. Jake is a skilled and steady hand and relied upon to wear many hats in the Franklin household.

Franklin looks up with bloodshot eyes. "What is the hour, Jake?"

Jake finds his pocket watch. "It goin' on midnight."

"I made you a cup 'a my Mama's special tea, Mr. Ben. You drink some of it now. Make you feel better," Aggie says as she pours a cup of tea for Jake.

"I should go back upstairs," Franklin says in a hoarse whisper.

"Not much you can do right now," Aggie says, sympathetically. "Missus Franklin doin' all she can for the baby. The doctor bleeding him again."

"That doctor is bleeding the life out of the poor child. Why didn't I have him inoculated?" Franklin laments.

Aggie pours herself a cup of tea and joins the men at the table. "Missus Franklin say she afraid Franky might get the pox that way."

"Well, he got it anyway, didn't he?" Franklin takes a sip of his tea. "Better to have erred on the side of hope. Has he eaten anything?"

"I bring him some porridge, but doctor say it best he don't eat nothin' with the fever so high like it is."

"Perfect. If he can't bleed the boy to death, he'll starve him to extinction."

Aggie stirs her tea. "I hear doctor say he gonna try a new treatment he heared about."

Franklin's ears perk up. "What new treatment?"

"Them blisters already spread inside Franky's mouth, so the doctor say he gonna bleed the baby's tongue."

"His tongue? He will never speak again!" Franklin jumps up from the table, spilling his tea, and climbs the stairway to Franky's bedroom, two steps at a time.

He bursts into the room and sees the doctor heating his scalpel over the flame of a candle. "Stop!" he screams. "What, in the name of Christ, do you think you are doing?" Deborah and the doctor are startled by the intrusion.

"This is the most modern technique," the doctor replies. "We bleed the tongue and the evil humors are rushed from the throat this way."

"Are you mad? Have you ever seen an animal with a stuck tongue? It is horrific! Get out! You have done enough."

"The doctor is trying to help us!" Deborah pleads.

"He's a butcher!" Franklin screams at Deborah.

Franklin turns, his eyes blazing, to the doctor. "Can't you see you are murdering my child? Get out!" he shouts.

The doctor pulls himself up and looks at Franklin indignantly. "Well, *really*, Mr. Franklin! I have risked my own life to help you!" He stuffs his instruments into his bag and stomps out of the room, thundering down the stairs.

Deborah's eyes well up with tears. "*Please*, Ben…" They hear the kitchen door slam as the doctor leaves the house.

Franklin wraps a rag around the boy's wound. "Take that bloody pan out of my sight. Bring me some gauze and some alcohol… and fresh water. Be quick!"

"But I need to be here!"

"Do as I say. Go!"

Deborah wipes her tears with her apron, rises and hurries down the stairs, calling for Aggie. Franklin squeezes out a cloth in a bowl of water on the dresser and wipes the boy's forehead with the damp cloth. After a moment, Franky opens his swollen eyes.

"There's my little boy," Franklin whispers.

Franky's breathing is shallow and quick. He struggles to speak. "Am I going to die, Papa?"

"Of course not, son. You will be better in no time."

"Do you promise, Papa?"

Franklin holds the boy's small hand in his. "Oh, yes, I promise. You are an angel, and angels *can't* die. Angels never die," he tells Franky, with his voice cracking.

Franky smiles sweetly and closes his eyes.

Only a few days pass before the family gathers in the cemetery alongside the Anglican Church. A cool autumn breeze stirs leaves fallen between headstones, and a tiny white casket, covered with late-blooming garden flowers, waits to be lowered into a freshly dug grave.

A priest, wearing a cassock and stole, stands at the graveside, reading from a Book of Prayer. He struggles against a gust of wind with his 'combed-over' hair. He makes an effort to be heard. "Jesus said, '*In my Father's house, there are many mansions. I go to prepare a place for you,*" he intones.

Franklin, Deborah, Jake, Aggie and William stand near the casket. Deborah, wearing a long black coat and black hat with a veil, hugs herself for warmth. A group of neighbors, men and women of various ages, stand just behind them. All are dressed in black, their heads are bowed. Two sextons stand nearby, prepared for the grim chore ahead.

"So we in faith," the preacher continues, "know that little Franky has ascended, in the company of angels and archangels, to find his room in the celestial splendor of that great house."

Deborah sways as if she will swoon. Jake steadies her, cupping his hand under her elbow.

"Angels never die," Franklin whispers to a woman standing behind him, who smiles a taut smile in return.

The preacher looks over the gathering. "Jesus also said, '*Suffer the little children to come unto Me*', and '*He who would not receive the Kingdom of God as a little child shall never enter it.*'" He picks up a handful of dirt and sprinkles it on the casket. "'*Ashes to ashes, dust unto dust...*'"

Deborah wails as the sextons step forward to lower the casket into the grave on ropes. The preacher embraces her. "You must find solace in your faith now, daughter, and rest assured that your boy will be awaiting you when you approach the gates of heaven on a latter day."

William and the servants step back as neighbors try to comfort the sobbing Deborah. The preacher places an arm around Franklin's shoulder. "I share your grief, Mr. Franklin," he says, in a consoling tone.

Franklin chokes as he speaks. "How could it be, Reverend, that a good and merciful Creator should produce such exquisite machines to no other end or purpose but to be deposited in the dark chambers of the grave?"

"To be sure, there is no greater pain that a man can endure, no greater burden he must bear, than to lose a child," replies the preacher. "Do you have an envelope for me, perchance, Mr. Franklin?"

"He wasn't yet five years old! An envelope? Oh... yes." Franklin reaches into his waistcoat pocket and produces an envelope. He hands it to the preacher.

The preacher thumbs through the bank notes. "That's fine," he says, and turns to leave. Several of the neighbors follow him out of the cemetery.

Deborah stands at the side of the grave, wiping tears from her cheeks with a kerchief, staring at the casket in silence. Jake touches her shoulder in sympathy, Aggie hugs her, then they both walk slowly away.

William lingers near the grave.

Franklin watches the preacher wind his way through the gravestones for a moment, then turns to Deborah. "Come, Mother. William, help your mother," he says to his son.

Deborah doesn't look up. "Leave me. I'll be along."

Franklin goes to her side. "We should have had him inoculated."

"Don't you *ever* say that to me again!" Deborah snaps.

"I won't say it, but I will think it. Come, William." Franklin pats Deborah's back, then walks away. "Come, now," he calls over his shoulder.

After a few moments, William moves to stand next to her. "Well," he says coolly, "That was some bad luck."

Deborah doesn't move, doesn't speak.

"But, you'll get over it."

Deborah turns to him, with fire in her eyes. "I'll get over it? I'll get *over* it? What I *won't* get over is that the pox took him instead of you! Leave me!" she screeches.

William picks up a handful of dirt and throws it into the grave. "Ashes to ashes…" he says, then turns and walks away, kicking fallen leaves as he goes.

CHAPTER THIRTEEN

Duty Calls

Franklin's Bedroom   April 1790

The room has grown dark but for an oil lamp next to the bed and a candle flickering on a bureau. Franklin sits in the chair by the window. The glow from the fireplace at the end of the room is reflected in his spectacles. He removes them to wipe a tear from his cheek. "Franky's death," he says thoughtfully, "gnawed at me like a cancer. Not a day has passed that I don't think of him with a sigh. When nature gave us tears, she gave us good cause to weep."

Bobby sits on the edge of the bed. He blows his nose on the rag he holds in his hand. "That sure be true, Dr. Ben."

Franklin wipes his spectacles with his night shirt. "Jefferson appears to have gotten himself lost."

Bobby rises and heads toward the door. "I go look for him."

"No. Don't! *She* might come back! Let's find that brown suit we talked about."

Bobby goes to Franklin's wardrobe cabinet, pausing as he passes by the window.

"Thank God I had my business to distract me. I went about it ferociously and succeeded beyond anything I ever dreamed," Franklin tells him.

Bobby looks out the window. "Rain stopped. Folks is comin' back."

"I took on a brilliant and honest partner, David Hall, who enabled me to disengage from the business by the age of forty-two. I could not see the benefit of striving to earn more."

Bobby points to the street below. "There's a' opportunity for ya. Old Mrs. Cass down there sellin' lemonade."

"Nay! Don't tease me. Find that suit, will you?"

Bobby opens the doors of the wardrobe cabinet.

"Deborah, fortress that she was, kept watch over our accounts, which provided me time to pursue other interests: my inventions, correspondence abroad… But it was politics that caught my attention."

Bobby sorts through hanging garments. "I don't see no brown suit."

"I was elected to the Pennsylvania Assembly in '51, where I served for many years. Public service became my calling. You know, Bobby, I would rather have it said that *'He lived usefully'* than *'He died rich'.*"

Bobby glances over at Franklin. "Well, you ain't poor." He probes the depths of the wardrobe cabinet.

"Sally was born to us in '43. An affectionate little girl, she was. Good with needlework, enjoyed her books. She learned arithmetic and bookkeeping."

Bobby locates the brown suit. "Here it is."

"She never went to Latin school, as William did. In truth, she lacked wit."

Bobby holds up the suit. "This coat look small to me." After a beat: "I come to work in the house when Miss Sally was 'bout ten and I was maybe twelve or thirteen."

"Did you? The Crown had made me Deputy Postmaster for all the colonies by then. I made William Postmaster of Philadelphia, since he was out of work, as was usual."

Bobby brings the suit over to Franklin. "Let's try this on you. Now don't you go gettin' dizzy again."

Franklin leans forward in his chair as Bobby attempts to help him into the jacket of the suit. "I wasn't much of a father to Sally, poor girl… I travelled so much." He stops to think. "The Assembly in those days was constantly at odds with the Proprietors of the colony."

DEAR BEN

Assembly Hall, Philadelphia   1757

The cold and damp from three days of a steady spring rain have crept into a meeting room of the Assembly Hall, where eight men, members of the Defense Committee, are gathered around a conference table. They have kept their coats on and warm their hands with cups of hot tea.

The committee Chairman, a stout, white-haired gentleman, stands at the head of the table. He reads from an official-looking document: "This letter from the Governor of Pennsylvania vetoes our money bill, which proposed that the Proprietors pay a reasonable share of the cost of defending the Colony. As in the past, the Penn family argues their lands are not within our purview."

Franklin is seated midway along one side of the table. At fifty-one, he is one of the two or three youngest members of the committee, but he wears a weary expression on his face. He raises his hand to speak. "Mr. Chairman, we have heard this story many times before. Once again, the Penns issue instructions to their deputies, which are contrary to the needs of the people *and* to the service of the Crown. We are left exposed and vulnerable to our enemies. We've got to change tack… there must be another way!"

Nels Peterson, a brawny young farmer, newly elected to the Assembly, raises his hand. "Why not send one of our members to petition the King himself on this matter of taxation?" he suggests in a lilting Swedish accent. "Our request is in His Majesty's best interest and it seems a rational idea to me…"

Charles Blair, a wispy little man with a contrary demeanor, interrupts Peterson. "A waste of time and resources. The King's Privy Council is packed with cronies of the Penns. You wouldn't be heard."

"I'm not so sure, Charles." Bart Livingston, a Philadelphia lawyer, speaks up. "Nels makes a good point. I see merit in the scheme."

Horatio Morgan, the eldest member of the committee, points an arthritic finger at Franklin. He speaks in a raspy voice through yellow teeth. "Ben, *you* should go. You've negotiated a treaty with the Indians, and argued eloquently at Albany for the unification of the colonies…"

Blair interrupts him. "A treaty which failed, and a plan rejected by every province," he argues, folding his boney arms in a defensive posture.

"Franklin has lived in London, Charles. He knows people there," Morgan reminds him.

Blair looks up at the ceiling. "Utterly futile," he says curtly.

Franklin stirs his tea. "You have a right idea, Mr. Morgan, but I am not your man, for two reasons." Franklin nods toward Charles Blair. "One, I lack the skill in diplomacy so abundantly displayed here today, and two, Mrs. Franklin would never hear of it."

The Chairman looks at Franklin incredulously. "What the deuce does *she* have to say in the matter?" he asks.

Franklin House

A few days later, the spring sky again threatens rain. Deborah stands midway in her ample kitchen garden, turning over soil with a spade. She directs Aggie and Jake as they work in the garden near her. Sally Franklin, fourteen, stoops to pull weeds. "Jake!" Deborah shouts in his direction, "Plant that corn way back against the fence. As you're doin', you'll shade my green beans."

"Yes, ma'am," Jake complies.

Deborah looks to see what Aggie is doing. "Ground's still a little wet, eh, Aggie?"

"Yes, ma'am, but better than too dry, like last year."

Franklin steps out the kitchen door, crosses the back yard, and approaches the garden.

Sally looks up to see her father. "Hello, Papa! Have you come to help us?" She steps over furrows of turned soil to reach her father and give him a hug.

"Yes, sweet cake, in my fashion," he replies. Franklin calls to Deborah: "Mother! Come sit with me. I wish to talk with you for a minute." He motions toward a bench near the edge of the garden.

Deborah looks in his direction, but keeps working the soil. "What is it, Ben? Rain's comin' and I got lots to do before it gets here."

Franklin points again to the bench. "Come. Sit for a moment."

Deborah plants her spade in the earth and navigates through the freshly turned soil to join him.

"You are gonna wreck those good boots out here," she says, pointing to his feet as she sits next to him on the bench.

Franklin gathers his courage. "The Assembly has asked me to sail over to England and present a petition to the King for them," Franklin tells her, in a matter-of-fact tone.

"*'Sail over to England?'* You make it sound like a Sunday jaunt! You told 'em 'no', didn't ye?"

"I'm thinking I'd like to accommodate them." He bends to brush some mud from his boot.

"Well, stop thinking such foolish thoughts."

"It's a very brief assignment… just a few weeks," Franklin offers.

"That's what you said last time. 'Twas more than a year you were away… Or have you forgotten?"

Franklin sits up erect. "Due to unforeseen events!"

"Ye are *not* goin' to England. Ye have a daughter to raise and there's too much work around this big house. Ye spend enough time as it is with your crazy experiments and what not." Deborah shows Franklin the palms of her hands. "Look at these blisters I got, and it ain't even June yet," she huffs.

"I could take William with me…"

"Don't tempt me. I still say '*no*'." She wipes her hands on her apron.

"I truly think it my civic duty to go."

Deborah gets up from the bench. "You said you would never leave me."

"I am not leaving you. I am attending to provincial business for a short time."

"Ye will be stepping over my fekkin' corpse gettin' on any goddamn boat to England!" she shouts, defiantly.

He rises, turns toward the house, and takes a few steps away from her. She scoops up a clump of dirt and pitches it at Franklin, hitting him squarely on the back of the head.

"Damn it, woman! Have you gone mad?" He scrapes mud off his neck as it slides under his shirt collar.

Deborah stands with her feet spread apart, glaring at Franklin. "I said 'no'! No to London! You hear me?"

Franklin's bedroom   April 1790

Bobby attempts to fit Franklin's arm into the brown suit jacket but makes scant progress.

"Must've shrinked. Maybe we just put the vest on you."

Franklin pictures the bounty of Deborah's kitchen garden in his mind. Long ago, he had it dug up and turned into a French garden of flowers, manicured hedges, and garden benches, but the memory of her garden was not erased. "Deb wasn't keen on the idea of me going to England," he recalls.

Bobby holds up a waistcoat, looking it over. "She in a *real* bad mood that day. I remember you was gone a long time."

"I was away for five years."

"What happened over there?"

Franklin points to his desk across the room. "Fetch the black silk box on my writing table."

Bobby lays the waistcoat on the bed. He goes to the desk, finds the box, and brings it to Franklin. "Open it," Franklin requests.

Bobby opens the box to find a cameo portrait of a woman. "Pretty lady!" he exclaims.

"*She's* what happened over there."

Jefferson has found his way to Franklin's bedroom, and raps lightly on the door. "Ben?"

"He's here!" Franklin whispers, pulling himself up in the chair.

Bobby sets the cameo on a side table and goes to the door. He opens it a few inches and looks out. "Evenin', Mr. Jefferson."

"How is he?" Jefferson inquires.

Bobby places his hand on his own abdomen. "Some time he say his belly on fire, right about here, but I give him laudanum."

"Good man."

"He sure been lookin' forward to seein' you." Bobby opens the door wide. "Come in, come in. He been tellin' me stories."

"Careful! I can hear you!" Franklin calls from across the room. "Come sit by me, Tommy. Bobby, get Mr. Jefferson a chair." Bobby pulls up a chair for Jefferson, then closes the door and busies himself with chores across the room.

"Telling the tale, you know, is the next best thing to living again," Franklin says cheerily.

"Is it? How are you feeling?" Jefferson inquires, as he sits next to Franklin.

"Like hell. My body and I are soon to part ways… it is going one way and I another." After a beat: "I haven't quite finished with those maps, I'm sorry to say," Franklin sighs.

"Don't worry, I'm in town for a few more days, then on to New York."

"I have something else for you." He calls to Bobby, who is sweeping by the fireplace. "Bobby, find the letter on my desk with Mr. Jefferson's name on it."

Bobby puts down his broom and goes to the desk.

"I've been telling Bobby that he might like to see something of this country when I am gone, but he doesn't seem too eager."

"Would that be as a free man?"

"Yes."

"'Tis a bold move, for both of you."

Bobby brings Franklin a package wrapped in paper.

"I wrote this, Tommy, on my voyage home from France. It is a record of my last attempt before I left England to re-unite our two countries." Franklin hands him the package. "A failure of historic proportions. I've told Adams something of it."

Jefferson looks at the package. "Thank you, Ben. I will read it tonight and return it tomorrow."

Franklin takes a sip of his wine. "No, I want you to keep it. A memento."

"I shall treasure it," Jefferson says, holding the package close to his chest.

"My friend, James Ralph, liked to quote from King Lear: *'Men must endure, ripeness is everything.'* Well, son William endures, and I am over-ripe… Rotting."

"You, my friend, are as sharp as the proverbial tack."

"Nay. No longer." Franklin pauses in thought, then leans close to Jefferson. "Thomas, have a word with Temple, will you? Keep him from going to see his father. William is an evil man."

"If you wish."

"I told Bobby that I have written my memoirs, as far as I dare, that is. I wrote out of fear of being forgotten… of never having lived."

Jefferson is surprised by Franklin's words. "Forgotten? Impossible! You are the greatest man and the ornament of the age!"

Franklin is silent. Tears well up in his eyes. He attempts to stand, swoons, and teeters sideways. Jefferson catches him, Bobby rushes to his aid.

"Let's get him to bed," Jefferson urges.

Bobby helps him to lay Franklin back on his bed, and pulls a blanket over him. "He get dizzy sometime," Bobby explains.

"Is there a window open?"

"No, sir. Not no more."

"There's a chill in this room. Don't you feel it? Put another blanket on him… Stoke the fire." Jefferson goes to the door and turns back to Bobby. "I shall call again in the morning. I'll say goodnight to the ladies." Jefferson quietly closes the door behind him as he leaves the room.

LONDON   1790

William Franklin is seated at his desk on Savoy Hill, finishing the letter he is writing to his sister. Snow falls in the darkness outside the window of his study and the fire in the hearth has burned down. William's pen scratches across the creamy stationery. *'But then, Father never cared much for the women about him, did he? He sent my dear wife, Elizabeth, to an early grave, thanks to his indifference to my incarceration at the hands of traitors.'*

He picks up the crystal glass which sits on the desk next to his left hand, takes a sip of whiskey, then sets down the glass. *'When the inevitable happens, do come over here at your earliest convenience and bring Temple with you. I dearly long to see my boy. Together, dear Sally, we shall celebrate our inheritance and the end of my cruel exile. We have so much to look forward to!'*

DEAR BEN

 William lays down his pen, picks up his drink, and walks over to the fireplace. He stares into the flames and then, after a long moment, tosses the last of his drink onto the fire.
 The embers *sizzle*.

PART THREE

The Crossing

CHAPTER FOURTEEN

The *'Hanna B'*

PHILADELPHIA   APRIL 1790

Benjamin Franklin lies still in his bed. He appears to sleep peacefully, even though the storm outside has picked up and wind howls in the fireplace chimney.

Bobby picks up the cameo portrait he had set on the side table earlier and admires it by the light of the oil lamp. "*Very pretty,*" he says, under his breath, and returns the cameo to the table. He turns to the bed, watches the sleeping Franklin for a moment, then pulls the blanket up over the old man's shoulders.

He goes to the window and looks out. Four neighbors, two men and two women, are huddled together under a streetlamp on the walk below, maintaining their vigil in the wretched weather. Bobby shakes his head and pushes the window closed tight. He sees something reflected in the window glass: a white mist seems to quiver in a corner near the fireplace. He quickly turns to look; he finds nothing there. A flash of lightning and a loud crack of thunder outside startle him. He jumps back from the window.

Franklin opens his eyes. "Did something frighten you?"

"I thought you was sleepin'."

"Did you see the lady?"

"Why you keep talkin' about some lady who ain't here?"

"She's coming for me before long." After a pause: "Have you thought about my offer?"

Bobby fluffs Franklin's pillow. "Yes, sir, I been thinkin' 'bout it. Lift up you head. How you feelin'?"

"Like the devil. How about a jot of the Madeira?"

Bobby points to the cameo resting on the table as he pours wine in Franklin's cup. "So, who is the pretty lady in that picture?"

"Picture? Oh. That's Margaret Stevenson."

"Is she in your book?"

"No, no. She was Polly's Mama." Bobby helps Franklin to sit up.

"Did I let her down, Bobby?"

"Who?" He places Franklin's cup in his hand.

"Deborah. I broke my promise to her."

"Missus Franklin? She do okay. Now and again we tie her up in the barn and let her scream a while, otherwise she rub along fine."

Franklin looks at Bobby askance as he sips his wine. "I promised I wouldn't leave her… Ever. But I did. I sailed in 1757 with my son, William, and two of our hands, King and Peter."

"Peter was my uncle."

Franklin looks at Bobby thoughtfully. "Was he? I'd forgotten that. I bought him off my neighbor, McLeod. The days at sea are endless, so I devised experiments to amuse the boys and pass the time."

Bobby folds the quilt at the end of the bed. "Experiments?"

"As a lad, I wondered why a ship like mine, sailing from Philadelphia at the same time, but taking a longer route across the Atlantic, arrived in Portsmouth well ahead of us. What would you guess?"

"Better winds?"

"Not always."

MID-ATLANTIC   1757

A pleasant, sunny day. All the sails on a three-masted schooner are unfurled and filled with a steady wind. Franklin, his son, William, twenty-eight, and two of Franklin's slaves, King and Peter, are on deck. King and Peter are somewhere in their thirties, sturdily built, and tower over William. They lower bottles tied with rope into the white-capped waves, then, after a few minutes, raise them. As the bottles emerge from the sea, William measures the temperatures of the water samples, reads them aloud to Franklin, who records them in a ledger book.

"Father! This exercise is tedious and pointless," William shouts over the wind.

"Not so! Look at your readings." Franklin displays the ledger book to William. "The water temperature has risen steadily, has it not?"

"Yes, but…"

"We have proved my supposition that we are riding on a river of warm water flowing to the north-east, which propels us at a greater speed than a ship not sailing atop the stream. Let's keep at it a while longer."

William rolls his eyes and waits for further readings from King and Peter.

That evening, Franklin and William are seated at a long table in the dining saloon, with four other men and two women. King and Peter wear long, white aprons and serve the table. William is picking at his food, with a sour expression on his face. His father, on the other hand, is enjoying his food and wine and spirited conversation with his dinner companions.

FRANKLIN'S BEDROOM, PHILADELPHIA   1790

Franklin recalls the evening.

Bobby sits at the end of the bed with the folded quilt on his lap, listening.

"The passengers aboard our schooner, the '*Hanna B*,' which was returning to her home port of Portsmouth, were an interesting lot." Franklin looks up to the ceiling as he conjures up the memory. "Among them were the 4th Earl of Lindsay and his wife, the Countess, a lovely young creature with red hair, a scattering of freckles, and an exquisite bosom. They were travelling with two servants, a maid and butler, who attended to them. I suspected the Lindsays were accustomed to more sumptuous accommodation than our ship could provide, but they never complained. Most evenings they appeared content with the service of King and Peter at our table. They were returning from a tour of the Colonies, they said, out of fascination with the new world. I think Lindsay was more likely spying for Lord Granville, President of the King's Privy Council. An elderly barrister named Southern, two brothers, Carolina planters named Richard and Matthew Locke, and Richard's shrew of a wife, Agnes, rounded off our little group."

Mid-Atlantic   1757

Franklin sets down his fork and taps his wine glass with a knife to get the attention of his fellow diners. "If it is calm tomorrow, gentlemen, ladies," he announces, "I intend to bathe and scrub a shirt or two. Who will join me? William? What about you?"

William looks down at his plate and doesn't answer.

Lord Lindsay, seated on Franklin's right, offers a warning. "Ye'd best be mindful of sharks, Mr. Franklin."

"Ever mindful, your Lordship, but looking forward to a swim, nonetheless. I shan't venture far from the ladder."

William lifts his wine glass and looks at Peter. "Pour me another, eh, Peter?"

Peter comes around the table and fills William's glass.

"You may regret that in the morning," Franklin chides him.

"Why? There's nothing else to do on this tub. The food is so damned repetitious."

Mr. Southern looks up from his plate. "'Tis a limited larder at sea, son, that's for certain."

The Countess, who is seated next to her husband, looks over at Franklin. "You were saying last night, Mr. Franklin, that you have some celebrity in the field of electricity or some such thing."

"Ah, yes. I became interested in the subject when a visiting Scotsman gave a lecture on the topic several years ago."

"Our family seat is in Scotland," she offers with a smile.

"Is it? McBreen, was the man's name. He performed a few electrical demonstrations which intrigued me. I sent to England for some glass tubes which are used in the making of such experiments and perfected my understanding of the phenomenon."

Mrs. Locke speaks with a mouthful of food. "To what purpose, may I ask?"

King moves around the table removing plates, while Peter serves a pudding.

Franklin takes a sip of wine. "Only to amuse myself and my friends. But I determined that electricity and lightning are the same thing, which was not yet known. I wrote papers on my experiments and sent them to the Royal Society in London."

Richard Locke picks up his wife's napkin, which has fallen on the floor and hands it to her. "Had you any proof of your theory to offer the Society?" he inquires.

"Not that anyone had seen, save for William, here, and me. We flew a kite with a metal key attached into a storm one night and drew an electric charge from the clouds." Franklin leans back in his chair as King removes his plate.

Mr. Southern and the Locke brothers look at Franklin askance, the Lindsays smile at one another, skeptically.

William pushes his chair back from the table, ignoring the pudding in front of him. "Sounds preposterous, does it not?" he says.

"Preposterous, indeed," Matthew Locke concurs.

"So thought the Royal Society," Franklin admits. "Little notice was taken in England of my work for some time."

"And now?" Lindsay asks, pushing a blonde forelock off his forehead with his hand.

Franklin cuts into the piece of cake Peter has set before him. "The French are more advanced in philosophical matters than the English. Happily, a copy of my papers fell into the hands of scientists at the Court of Versailles."

PALACE OF VERSAILLES   NOVEMBER 1751

A group of courtiers mill about an elegant salon in the Palace. Their clothing and hairstyles are extravagant for daytime, fabulous jewelry on the women is not spared. Fires blaze in fireplaces at either end of the room. Although it is early afternoon, candles are lighted in chandeliers and in sconces on the mirrored walls. Uniformed footmen drift about the gathering, offering drinks and appetizers from silver salvers.

Outside, black storm clouds swirl in the sky, wind buffets the windows of the Palace and rain falls in sheets. Some of the courtiers gather at the windows, chattering in French as they watch five scientists, members of the French Academy, work outside in the rain and blustery wind. They are setting up an apparatus: it is a primitive wooden tower with a pointed metal rod at its peak. When completed to their satisfaction, the scientists rush inside to join the courtiers. Once inside, footmen serve glasses of wine to the soaking wet scientists, who mop their faces with the tea towels offered to them.

Within minutes, a flash of lightning strikes the metal rod with a loud *clap*, blowing the tower apart. A window in the salon shatters, silk draperies and rain blow into the room. A terrifying roar of thunder follows.

Ladies scream, a few courtiers drop to the floor, covering their heads with their hands. All are amazed and delighted, some applaud wildly.

A silver-haired scientist, who appears to be in charge, addresses the gathering. "And there, mesdames et messieurs," he says, beaming, "you see the 'Philadelphia Experiment' of Monsieur Benjamin Franklin! Ingenious, no?"

A gentleman lying on his back on the floor raises himself up onto his elbows. "Yes, but will Monsieur Franklin pay for His Majesty's broken window?" Fallen courtiers laugh as they pick themselves up.

"I do not see the point!" the Duchesse de Saint-Simon shouts over the laughter, adjusting her hairdo.

A diminutive scientist answers her. "If we had wired the rod to the ground, Duchesse, the strike would have proceeded harmlessly into the earth!" he says, garnering *'oohs'* and *'aahs'* from the courtiers.

The Duc de Richelieu rises from the floor. "I think these Americans enjoy blowing things up!" he says, laughing as he brushes off the seat of his satin breeches.

Mr. Southern listens to Franklin's tale with his elbow on the dining table and his head resting on his hand. "It was a lucky thing nobody was killed," he says.

'Yes, I suppose it was," Franklin chuckles. "The English made amends by inviting me to be the first American member of the Society… and bestowed the Copley Medal on me in 1753."

William tips back, finishes his glass of wine. "Father gives undue credence as to the value of that piece of tin."

Franklin looks at him indignantly. "Gold, I'll have you know, which has brought us friends around the world, some of whom you will meet in London, including Mr. Joseph Priestly. He has written a book on my work."

William rises from his chair. "Believe what you will, ladies and gentlemen. I am retiring to my cabin to read. Peter, fill me up for the walk. Good night." Peter fills his glass. William leaves the table, weaving with the roll of the ship and his fill of wine as he heads for the door.

Agnes Locke watches William make his exit. "What will the young man do whilst you are in England?" she inquires, with a pinched expression on her face.

Franklin sighs. "He intends to read law… and drive me to distraction."

CHAPTER FIFTEEN

The Widow

LONDON   JULY 1757

A fair day, unusually warm for London. Billy Strahan sits on the front steps of a town house on Craven Street in the West End, reading a newspaper. The street slopes gently down to the Thames in one direction and up to The Strand in the other, making it convenient both for the Royal Opera House and the government buildings at Whitehall. The house is of white stucco, three stories tall, with dormers in the roof. The front door and window frames are painted a mid-blue. The front of the house appears quite narrow, but it sits on a deep lot, with a small grassy yard and kitchen garden at the back, leading to a carriage house with an alleyway behind it.

Strahan's suit jacket lies folded on the step next to him, his cravat is undone. He is fifty-two, has wavy brown hair, bright green eyes and a ruddy complexion. He looks up from his newspaper when he hears the *click-click* of a walking stick on the pavement, as another gentleman approaches.

He sees Peter Collinson, a dapper fifty-five-year-old, walking toward him.

"Hallo?" Strahan says, with a question in his greeting.

"Hallo to you! Would you be waiting on Mr. Franklin?" Collinson inquires.

"I am indeed," Strahan concurs. He stands, extends a hand to Collinson, and they shake hands. "Billy Strahan. A boyhood friend."

"Peter Collinson... Corresponding friend. I have yet to meet the man in person."

"You're in for a treat. Jolly fellow. Have a seat," Strahan says, indicating the steps.

They both sit down after Strahan brushes away dust with his newspaper. Collinson, sandy-haired and blue-eyed, wears a tan suit with pocket kerchief, waistcoat, and a crisp high-collared shirt. He removes his jacket and folds it across his lap.

"I had word his party viewed Stonehenge in Salisbury Plain yesterday morning. They should be arriving in London quite soon," Collinson reports.

"So I heard as well."

"Should we ring the bell and go in?"

"Nay... I'm enjoying the sunshine." Strahan hands Collinson a page of the newspaper. "Here. I'll share with you."

Collinson looks at the paper's masthead. "The 'Chronicle'?"

"Be kind. I own it."

That same afternoon, Polly Stevenson, a pretty sixteen-year-old, and Mrs. Jolliker, the cook, prepare vegetables on a large plank table in the townhouse kitchen. Polly is a petite brunette, with soft brown eyes. Mrs. Jolliker is a middle-aged matron, broadly built beneath her apron. Her curly black hair peeks out from under a white bonnet. She speaks with an accent of indeterminate mid-European origin. No one is quite sure of her provenance, which she has thus far declined to specify.

"And why should I be excited? Just more mouths for me to feed," she says, not looking up from her task. "Two gentlemen, I am told, and two at the help's table."

Polly's voice is animated. "Well, *I am*. We haven't had any boarders from the Colonies in this house as long as I can remember," she says, chomping on a green bean.

"I pray they ain't savages, is all I can say. Save some a' them beans for the pot, child," Mrs. Jolliker scolds.

"Mr. Franklin is quite famous in philosophical circles, I've heard," Polly remarks.

"Still makes for a full house, famous or not. Our old gentlemen in the attic rooms ain't going to appreciate the added strain on the facilities." She points to a basket sitting on a pine cabinet across the room. "Hand me them carrots over there."

Polly crosses the room, returning with the basket of carrots. "His son is coming with him. I do hope he is handsome."

"Now, lass, don't be getting' ahead of yerself. Get busy on them leeks, now."

"Well, it wouldn't hurt anything if he *were* handsome."

Mrs. Jolliker commences peeling carrots. "You'll learn about 'handsome' one 'a these days, lass. I promise ya that."

Moments later, on the street outside, Strahan and Collinson jump to their feet as two carriages slow, then clatter to a halt, in front of the house. Benjamin Franklin alights from the first carriage; William Franklin follows him.

The senior Franklin blinks in the sunlight, and spots Mr. Strahan. "Billy! Aren't you a sight for these water-logged old eyes!" He and Strahan embrace warmly.

Strahan holds Franklin at arm's length, looks him up and down. "I wanted to be here when you arrived. You haven't changed a bit, you old coot! Life seems to agree with ye!"

"I couldn't be more pleased, Billy." Franklin turns to his son. "William, meet my old chum, Billy Strahan." He pulls William closer. "This is my boy… your namesake, by the way."

Strahan offers his hand to William. "'Tis an honor, son." They shake hands.

In the kitchen, Polly looks up from her chore and cocks an ear. "They're here! I hear voices outside!" She lays down her knife, takes off her apron and hurries out of the kitchen.

"Remember the leeks, child!" Mrs. Jolliker calls after her.

"I will, Mrs. Jolliker," Polly shouts over her shoulder, as she makes her way to the front parlor. She goes to a window facing Craven Street, pulls back the curtain and peeks out.

Polly sees King and Peter step down from the second carriage, and unload trunks and baggage on the walk. A porter emerges from the house to aid them with their task.

Franklin keeps an eye on the unloading of his luggage. "Mr. Strahan and I met when we were novices at the Watts & Co. printing house here. He's risen to lofty heights and now prints his own newspaper. Is that not so, Billy?"

Strahan laughs, holding up his hands. "The ink stains on my hands betray me."

Franklin extends a hand to Mr. Collinson. "And whom do I have the pleasure of meeting?"

"Peter Collinson, at your service."

Franklin smiles broadly. "Peter! Of course! Son, Peter is my contact at the Royal Society. Delighted to meet you at last!" They shake hands.

"And I you. I came to tell you that John Hanbury, the Virginia merchant, requested he be informed of your arrival. He has arranged an audience for you with Lord Granville. Hanbury is well connected, you know."

Franklin sees Polly behind the pulled-back curtain, peering out of the window. He points to her. "William, I think you have an admirer."

William looks up and smiles at Polly. She ducks out of sight.

Franklin turns back to Collinson. "Granville, you say? President of the Privy Council?"

"The same. He would like to see you at your earliest. Hanbury will take you there."

"What about tomorrow morning?"

"I shall inquire," Collinson assures him.

Strahan and Collinson help Franklin and William unload small packages from the carriage and place them on the front steps.

"So, how was your voyage, William?" Strahan asks.

"Long. Tedious. Malodorous people and hideous food," William replies in a monotone.

"Beast of an old ship, but the captain was clever about trimming the sails and we made good time once we got underway," Franklin offers. "We were detained in New York by the authorities for two weeks beforehand, though."

Collinson looks surprised. "Why was that?"

"Moving troops around, I suppose. The British are not making any friends lately, I must say. No matter! We have friends in London!"

William climbs the steps, following King and Peter into the townhouse.

"William and I are most grateful to you, Peter, for arranging lodging for us here." Franklin looks up at the house. "It appears to be a fine accommodation."

"Come and meet Mrs. Stevenson," Collinson says. "You will find her to be a very congenial landlady. Come along, Mr. Strahan."

The threesome, arms loaded with parcels, climbs the steps and enters the house. A woman, whom Franklin cannot clearly see as his eyes adjust to the light, strides purposefully into the foyer to greet her guests.

Outside London   Summer 1757

The next day, as Franklin had requested, he and another gentleman ride in a horse-drawn landau along a cobbled lane in Chiswick. Carefully pruned beech trees line the drive, which leads to a red brick Georgian mansion. The second passenger is John Hanbury, the colonial merchant mentioned by Peter Collinson the previous day. Franklin is awed by the magnificence of the house when it comes into view. He cannot see the end of it to the right or left. One must stand far back from the grand edifice to take it all in. Their driver pulls to a stop as they reach the front door, which is painted a brilliant white and framed by columns supporting a classical pediment with an urn at its apex.

A coachman, sitting next to the driver of the landau, jumps down to open Hanbury's door, then Franklin's. Franklin steps down and stands next to the carriage for a moment looking at the house, with his mouth agape.

Hanbury walks around to him. "Intimidating, eh?" he says. "That's why these nabobs build these piles… to make our knees bang together when 'in the presence'. Well, don't be afraid. The old boy drops his breeches to take a piss, just like you and me. Come." He leads Franklin to the entrance and bangs a brass knocker against the lacquered door. "I'm going to leave you to your devices. I will meet with you and His Lordship after you have had your talk with him."

A uniformed butler opens the door and invites Franklin and Hanbury into a cavernous entry hall. The foyer is filled with French furniture, including a bronze and marble center table supporting an elaborate floral arrangement. A massive crystal chandelier hangs above it.

Hanbury and Franklin part ways, as the butler shows Franklin through a pair of tall, gilded doors into a spacious drawing room, where Lord Granville sits slumped on a divan, reading a book. He is dressed in silks and satins, with monogramed pumps on his feet. His gray hair is worn pulled back and tied with a ribbon. He appears slender and fit, belying his sixty-seven years. He does not rise to greet Franklin as he enters the room.

The butler announces him. "Mr. Benjamin Franklin, Your Lordship." Granville looks up from his book.

Franklin nods, making a half-bow. "Your Lordship." He extends his hand.

Granville sits up, setting his book on a side table. He limply offers three fingers in return, while studying Franklin's plain brown suit. "You must have come directly from the country," he speculates.

"Yesterday, actually," Franklin replies.

"No time to change, eh? Well, welcome to Chiswick and to my home. D' ya care for some tea?"

"Not just now, thank you."

Granville dismisses the butler with a wave of his hand. "I hope you had a pleasant crossing. Smooth seas…"

Franklin stands awkwardly before his host. "Yes, very pleasant, thank you, sir."

"Good. We are impressed with reports we have received of your service to your province, as well as your success as a philosopher. Well done, sir. Please, do sit down."

Franklin sits on a settee opposite Granville. "Thank you, Your Lordship. I am flattered, indeed."

Granville suddenly becomes attentive. "Would you say that we are in a time of peace over there? With the natives and the bloody French, I mean?"

"For the moment, yes, but the security of the colony is of constant concern. It is the reason I have come here. We hope to obtain help from the Proprietors in paying for the defense of our borders. War is a costly business, as you know."

"We are sympathetic to your needs, but feel you are not yet clear regarding the role the Sovereign has to play in his colonies."

Franklin sits up straight. "Not clear?"

Granville leans back languidly. "You Americans have the wrong ideas of the nature of your constitution. You contend that the King's instructions to his Governors are not laws and think yourselves at liberty to regard or disregard them at you own discretion. But they are quite unlike the advice given to a minister going abroad, for regulating his conduct in some trifling ceremony."

Franklin sits on the edge of the settee. "But Your Lordship, a bill confirming your point of view was thrown out of the House of Commons twenty years ago."

"Perhaps, but that is of no import to us. Do you find it stifling in here?" Granville pulls at his cravat.

"No, I am quite comfortable."

"I deplore this summer heat." Granville rises. "Let's walk together. I should like you to see my garden. I may be prejudiced, but I think it the finest in Chiswick." He gestures for Franklin to rise. "Come now. Up we go."

Franklin rises and follows him through open French doors into the garden. The sweet fragrance and the beauty of the place escape Franklin, however. His mind reels, thinking of the distance between his point of view and Granville's. Franklin cannot foresee a meeting of the minds.

Granville has his back to Franklin as he walks. He stops to turn over a few leaves here and there, looking for insects or signs of fungus, Franklin surmises. The garden is a gridwork of graveled walkways, with parterres of lush flower beds in between. Franklin sees two gardeners at work with their pruning shears in the distance. It must take a dozen or more men, he thinks, to maintain the extravagant display surrounding him.

Granville stops, fondles a bloom and turns to Franklin. "Look here: rhododendron. New to this country. Some are evergreen… in flower all the year round. Have you ever seen such a delicate shade of pink?"

"No, I can't say as I have," Franklin admits.

"The King's wishes, you see, are first drawn up by learned judges, debated in Council, then signed by the King," Granville says, jumping subjects. "They are then the law of the land, for the King is the legislator of the colonies. Make no mistake about that."

"This is a new doctrine to me, Your Lordship," Franklin confides, hoping the conversation will stay with the business at hand.

Granville continues walking, pointing about the garden as he goes. "Camellias here, magnolias just there. Are they not lovely?"

"Yes, they are indeed lovely. But I have always understood from our charters that our laws were to be made by our Assemblies and presented to the King for his assent. Once that is given, the King could not appeal or alter them. Conversely, any law proposed by His Majesty must be approved by the Assembly."

I can assure you that you are mistaken." Granville stops and turns to face Franklin. "At issue here is your proposal to tax the Proprietaries, a scheme in which His Majesty has little interest. I do hope you haven't come all this way for nothing."

Franklin gathers his courage. "I should like to speak with the Penns directly if this can be arranged. Perhaps we could reach an understanding."

Granville stiffens. "The family is fully aware you have come to this country and what your mission is. If they wish to meet with you, you will hear from them, but, if you are a betting man, the odds of that happening are against you."

"Does all the Court share your sentiments?"

"Most definitely." Granville points to the other side of the garden. "In the wintertime, we plant white cyclamen mixed with blue iris over there."

Franklin cannot conceal his disappointment. "I am speechless."

"Yes, 'tis a breathtaking sight."

"At your revelation, I mean."

"Then, I am pleased to have set you on a right path with regards to the question of sovereignty," Granville says with an icy smile. "That done, I shall see to it you meet some interesting people whilst you are here, so your long voyage won't be for naught... if you like, that is."

"I need time to think."

"Of course, you do. I predict we're going to be great friends." Granville walks a few steps ahead of Franklin, caressing and sniffing roses along the way. "Your countryman, Hanbury, awaits us in the library. I'll wager he concurs with my point of view." Granville pauses. "You excel at so many things, Franklin. Is horticulture among them?"

Franklin catches up. "No, my wife is the gardener in our family."

"Pity. There's nothing like getting one's hands in the earth to focus the mind... it helps one to see things clearly. Of course, I don't muck about personally."

"Of course not." Franklin says, as he follows the tail of Granville's silk frockcoat into the house.

FRANKLIN'S BEDROOM, PHILADELPHIA   1790

Bobby spreads the quilt over Franklin's legs.

"His Lordship, that summer afternoon so long ago, had thrown down the gauntlet," Franklin tells him.

Bobby looks baffled. "Gauntlet?"

"I had been challenged to a fight... to match wits with a powerful and learned man. In the meantime, we settled into life at the Stevenson house. It is likely that Mrs. Stevenson and I knew each other in a previous incarnation. Such was the ease with which we lived together."

LONDON   SUMMER 1757

Margaret Stevenson, the proprietress of the boarding house on Craven Street, pulls the curtains closed against the afternoon sun streaming through the tall, paned windows of her dining room. The walls are papered above the wainscot and crowded with pictures, including portraits, landscapes and still-life paintings.

Benjamin Franklin is seated at the head of a long oak table. His eyes are on Mrs. Stevenson, who is still shapely and attractive in her fifties, as she stands on her tiptoes to reach the wand of the draperies. Polly, William and two gentlemen boarders in their late seventies, sit to his right and left. Miss Clark, a forty-five-year-old spinster with dun-colored hair and a forgettable face, is seated at the other end of the table.

William and Polly sit opposite one another. Peter and King are both dressed in the manner of English servants, carrying platters of food to the table, which are then passed along family-style.

Franklin calls to Miss Clark, "Did you enjoy a pleasant day, Miss Clark?"

"I did, Mr. Franklin," she replies, pleased with the attention. "I took a brisk walk down to the Thames and along the Embankment for a time, then returned to read a good book."

"I swam in that river as a lad, but would not dare do so these days." He turns to Mrs. Stevenson. "Margaret, who, may I ask, is in the portrait hanging behind Miss Clark?"

Margaret resumes her seat at the table next to Franklin. "That is my grandmother, Alma Robertson," she explains.

"Don't you find it fascinating how Englishmen made family names for themselves?" he comments, between bites of roast mutton. "'Son of Robert' becomes 'Robertson.' Yours is 'Steven's son'. Or, a man named himself after his trade."

"Like 'Mason' or 'Smith'?" Polly volunteers. "'Baker'? 'Potter'?"

"Precisely," Franklin continues. "Miss Clark's ancestor was a book-keeper, no doubt...a clerk, who became 'Clark.'"

Beneath the table, William has slipped off his shoe and rubs his foot on Polly's ankle. She keeps her eyes on her plate of food, struggling not to giggle. "Then there's 'Wainwright'," William suggests.

Franklin gives the table a slap. "Very good! A wagon maker. My forebears over here were farmers and smiths and dyers of silk, but somehow settled on 'Franklin'."

"'Johnson' comes to mind at the moment," Polly offers through a grin.

"My mother had a childhood friend," Franklin continues, "who married and moved up to Maine. Mother continued to write to Mrs. Carpenter until the lady died many years later, at which time Mother learned that her friend had actually married a Mr. Shoemaker."

The diners around the table laugh.

"Mother was terribly embarrassed, but there was nothing to be done about it."

One of the elderly boarders, Mr. Christie, turns to his dinner companion, Mr. Bennett. "I thought we had an intellectual come to live among us," he whispers.

Mr. Bennett nods. "The greatest thinker since Newton, they say."

"Is that so? Difficult to tell…" Mr. Christie says.

Polly's eyes widen as William moves his foot farther up her leg. She distracts herself by counting baubles hanging from the chandelier above her head.

A few days later, Margaret climbs the back stairs from the kitchen, carrying a small tea tray. She wears a pretty house dress with an apron over it, her hair is carefully arranged. She stops to part the curtains on a landing window with her free hand, and morning sun pours in. She continues on her way, reaching a landing another flight up, then a narrow hallway.

She arrives at Franklin's set of furnished rooms, and raps lightly on his door. "Mr. Franklin? I have your tea," she calls to him.

Behind the door, Franklin is in his under-drawers, shaving. He puts on his dressing gown, picks up his pocket watch from a side table, and looks at the time.

In the hallway outside, William Franklin, nattily dressed for the day in a gray suit with striped silk cravat, passes by. "Good morning, Mrs. Stevenson," he says in a cheery voice.

"Good morning, William. You are up bright and early."

"Yes, up at cockcrow. I have an early lecture at Lincoln's Inn Fields."

Margaret studies his attire. "Fancy dress for school today?"

William ignores her question. "Tell Father that King has run away, will you?"

"Run away?"

"His bed hasn't been slept in and his bag is gone. He didn't come to help me dress this morning. Father may wish to alert the authorities."

"I will tell him."

"Well, bye-bye. I won't be home for supper. I've been invited to White's Club in Mayfair."

"White's? Oh, very stylish. The members are known as 'the Gamesters of White's.' Did you know that?"

William doesn't answer and bounds down the stairs. Margaret calls after him. "Do be careful with your purse!" She watches him descend the stairs for a moment, then taps again on Franklin's door. "Mr. Franklin? You should be on your way soon!"

Franklin opens the door, pulling his dressing gown closed. Margaret enters the room and sets down the tray on a tea table. "Pray, why does the lady of the house herself deliver my tea?" he asks.

"Mrs. Jolliker demurred. She said you were sitting in a chair by the window naked as a babe when she came up yesterday."

"I was taking my air bath. A custom of mine. Most salubrious." Franklin pours himself a cup of tea.

"You mustn't frighten poor Mrs. Jolliker!" Margaret chides.

"Do you infer, madam, that my naked body is a fright?"

Margaret giggles and smooths the blanket on his bed. "No, of course not... how would I know?"

He sips his tea. "Speaking of frightful, I've been up half the night with a case of nerves. Never having attended a Royal Levee, I don't know what to expect."

"Follow Granville's lead. I suspect His Lordship hopes that if you are brought into the inner circle, you will come to see things his way."

"Never! What can you tell me about the King?"

Margaret walks around the bed, tucking in the sheets. "Mere gossip. He adored the late Queen, Caroline, but bedded the Countess of Suffolk. These days, the very Germanic Countess of Yarmouth is the Royal Mistress. The King calls her *'Yart-mouth'*."

"What else?"

"He loathes his son. The Prince of Wales has been banished from the palace."

"You can't mean it."

"Runs in the family. The present King's father despised him as well."

Franklin points to a suit hanging on a valet stand. "Peter thinks I should wear black this morning. What do you say?"

"A good choice. By the way, William says King has run away."

"Run away? More likely sleeping off last night's pints somewhere."

Margaret spreads marmalade on a piece of toast. "Get into your breeches and I'll help you with your cravat. It's a skill I learned from my late husband that I haven't forgotten."

Franklin opens a dresser drawer, lifts out a shirt, takes the pants from the valet stand and steps behind a screen in the corner. "Why have you never remarried?" he calls from behind the screen.

"The right man never came along."

"I don't believe it. A beautiful woman like you?"

"Flatterer. At least I won't have to wake up with some hoary old man next to me in my dotage. How is it that you travel so far afield without Mrs. Franklin?" she inquires, taking a bite of the toast.

"She is terrified of the sea. And, technically, she is not my wife. Deborah and I have a common law arrangement."

Margaret turns in the direction of his voice. "Is she not the mother of your children?"

"She is Sally's mother."

"Not William's?"

"Deborah was married to another man when William was born."

Margaret takes another bite and returns the piece of toast to the plate. "I see..."

"We had a son together, but he succumbed to the pox when he was only four."

"Oh. I am so sorry."

Franklin steps out from behind the screen, buttoning his shirt. "As am I... Eternally. What was your husband's trade?"

"Merchant. French silks, fancy trimmings for the Court dressmakers. He had a smart shop near St. James's."

"Did you help with the business?"

Margaret assists Franklin with his cravat. "Occasionally, when Giles was on the Continent buying yard goods. He was often away in France."

Franklin interrupts her work on his cravat and picks up the piece of toast. "Look here... a mouse has gotten into my toast! Whatever shall I say to the King?"

"A simple greeting, smile and bow to him. He speaks English reluctantly, his father, nary a word. The notorious Walpole was the old King's voice in Parliament, therefore, called Prime Minister. I am told the late Queen and Walpole were very close." Margaret finishes arranging Franklin's cravat.

"Told by whom?"

"A friend of mine who is a mistress of the Queen's wardrobe."

"Your friend has a keen ear."

"Well, she knows the back stairs of the palace." Margaret steps back to study her handiwork. "Look how handsome you are. You will be superb. I shall leave you to finish dressing," she says, and turns to leave the room.

"Thank you!" Franklin calls after her.

Margaret stops, takes a few envelopes from the pocket of her apron, and places them on the tea table. "I nearly forgot. The post has arrived," she says as she walks out the door.

Franklin House, Philadelphia   September 1757

Deborah Franklin is seated at the kitchen table, writing a letter, as she does every Friday night when a packet boat is scheduled to depart for Southampton on the coming Sunday. A wind howls outside, causing her candle to flicker in a draft from the door behind her, but she feels snug with an old wool shawl over her shoulders, a fire in the hearth, and a cup of hot tea at hand.

"Dear Ben, All is fit here, more or less," she writes, in her childish scrawl. *"Our Sally sprouts like a weed, and since you left has got so tall, she looks down on me like a bird to a worm. Mother is more feeble and disagreeable every day, but we must expect this in old age."*

Sally enters the kitchen, goes to the hearth, and pours herself a cup of tea. She fills her mother's cup and sits at the table across from her.

"Speak of the devil. I am writing to your Pa," Deborah says.

"Read it to me, Mama." Sally takes a biscuit from a small basket on the table.

Deborah reads aloud to Sally as she writes: *"'Your friend, Strahan, has already wrote how I should come over to London due to the temptations a famous and handsome man has with the ladies.'"*

"Who is 'Strahan', Mama?"

"Billy Strahan. A friend of your father's since the Creation. '*As I do not know of such a man, I will stay here and look after Sally and my old mother.*'"

"You're funny, Mama. Tell Papa I miss him."

"'*I hope Will is better with his studies over there than he was here. Sally misses you, and I miss your helping hand. We pray you come home soon. As ever, your loving Joan.*'"

"Why do you sign it 'Joan'?"

"A silly thing. Your father calls me 'Joan' for some silly reason."

"Do you think he will? Come home soon?"

Deborah looks up from her writing paper. "No."

CHAPTER SIXTEEN

The King

PALACE OF ST. JAMES'S, LONDON   OCTOBER 1757

A reception hall at the Palace is abuzz with the chatter of nearly one hundred men, awaiting the arrival of the King at his late morning promenade. They range in age from thirty to ninety, and several of the frail older men sit in straight-backed chairs lining the room, gossiping with their nearby neighbors. All are dressed in finery for the occasion, wearing bespoke suits, periwigs, and black leather shoes with stacked heels and silk bows on the vamp. The room has a high, ornately decorated ceiling, and voices bounce off its oak-paneled walls, adding to the din. Portraits and equestrian paintings of the royal family adorn the higher reaches of the walls. Tall leaded glass windows fill the room with light and cast patterns of tracery on the stone floor. A string trio seated on a balcony at one end of the hall plays the music of Haydn.

As they meander through the gathering of noblemen and grandees, Franklin and Lord Granville are offered refreshments from silver salvers carried by footmen in red jackets. Granville accepts a stemmed glass of wine, while Franklin declines the offer. Granville motions across the room. "That's Lord Montagu over there… the fair-haired gentleman. He is the master of Beaulieu Palace… built on the ruins of an old abbey in the New Forest."

Franklin strains to see Lord Montagu through the crowd.

"The land was given to his family by Henry the Eighth for their help in demolishing the Romish monasteries. That's how it works in this country. 'Grace and Favor', we call it."

"So, I understand."

"The struggle against Popery continues to this day, Franklin. The French are in the thick of it. Nothing more dangerous than religion, in my view."

"Or too much of it, in any case," Franklin muses.

"Quite. The old gentleman next to Montagu is the Earl of Bath… descended from a long line of notorious drunkards."

Franklin looks surprised at Granville's candor as he glances at the elderly Earl.

"When meeting His Majesty," Granville continues, "if I were you, I shouldn't speak of anything he may find taxing."

"But, may I brief him on my scheme for a proper colonial militia, which if…"

Granville wags a finger at Franklin. "A matter for the Council to consider and of no concern to His Majesty."

A pair of doors open at the back of the hall and a young page appears in the doorway. He pounds the Staff of State on the floor three times. The music and the din of conversation stop abruptly.

"His Majesty, The King!" the page shouts in his youthful, high-pitched voice.

An aide attempts to precede the King through the doorway, but is rudely pushed aside. "Out of my way, you fat blockhead!" the King commands in his thick, German accent. "Move! Move! Gott im Himmel!"

The retainer moves aside, cowering, as the King limps into view. At seventy-five, he is small in stature, pale and overweight. He, too, is dressed in business attire, and makes his way slowly through the gathering, nodding this way and that, unsmiling. His guests bow politely as the King greets them, occasionally by name. The music and murmur of conversation resume.

The King spots Lord Granville and Franklin. "Granville! There you are." He limps over to them. "You bring us company?"

Granville bows to the King. "Good morning, Your Majesty. You look exceedingly well today."

"I am old and fat, you liar," the King snarls.

"Sire, may I present Mr. Benjamin Franklin of Philadelphia?"

Franklin bows deeply, as he had rehearsed with Mrs. Stevenson. "Your Majesty."

The King's eyes are penetrating. "The famous Mr. Franklin. You are most welcome in my house." He turns to Lord Granville. "He looks civilized, Granville. Clean shirt, good shoes, not a wild man from the woods." He again turns his attention to Franklin. "Sprechen sie Deutsch?"

Franklin shakes his head. "Nary a word, sir."

"Too bad." The King gestures toward the orchestra. "You hear the beautiful music? German."

"Yes sir, very beautiful," Franklin concedes.

"You are a philosopher? A man of science?"

"In truth sir, I am but a printer, retired from the trade." Franklin's mouth is drying up. He wishes he had taken a glass of wine when offered.

"Me, I die in the job. You make new experiment with electricity?"

"I merely put forth a new way of describing the phenomenon, which I call *'conservation of charge'*."

"You will explain. Walk with me." The King continues his procession about the room, nodding to his guests as the three men walk, with Franklin on the Monarch's right. Men whisper to one another as they pass by, wondering who the stranger is who has His Majesty's ear.

"I determined, sir, that electricity is but a single fluid. When a thing is charged positively, an equal negative charge is generated. That is the law of *conservation of charge*."

"You take this electric fire from the sky, like a… like a…"

"Like a sorcerer?" Granville suggests.

"No magic involved, Your Lordship. I learned that the electric charge is naturally attracted to a pointed piece of metal. This electrical fluid is also a property of lightning and can be drawn into the ground by such a rod."

"What good is this?" the King asks.

"A tall structure, such as a church, can be saved from destruction with such a rod. Not to mention the bellringer in the belfry!"

The King manages his first smile of the morning "Very good, Franklin. Very good!"

A footman approaches, bows to the King, and offers the men refreshments from the tray he carries. The King and Lord Granville take a pastry. Franklin declines, again. They continue walking.

"One day we will learn to use the power in that lightning to our benefit. I haven't determined how, but someone will do it," Franklin explains.

The King stuffs his mouth with the sweet pastry. "I keep my eye less on the sky and more on my backside. So, Franklin, how goes the war with those French devils?"

"All is quiet for the moment, sir, but we are concerned that…"

Granville glares at Franklin, interrupting him. "I have advised Mr. Franklin, Sire, that he must discuss his concerns with your Privy Council beforehand."

The King stops in his place and wipes his fingers on the back of Lord Granville's coat. "Funny language, English. At Windsor, I make piss in privy in the woods. In town, I have Privy Council in the house. Has my Council invited Mr. Franklin for a talk?"

"Not as yet, Sire. We have many issues before us."

The King looks annoyed. "This man made long voyage to talk with us and we are too busy? Granville, go greet my guests. Talk with yourself a minute." He shoos Granville away with a wave of the back of his hand. The King watches Granville back out of his presence, then turns to Franklin. "There goes number one blockhead in my kingdom." He limps to an empty chair against the wall, sits down, and gestures to Franklin to join him. The King removes his slipper and rubs his foot. "Sit by me here," he says, patting the seat of the chair next to him.

As Franklin sits, a few gentlemen standing nearby stare in amazement. The King hands his shoe to Franklin. "This damn shoe hurts like der Teufel," he says. Franklin examines it and feels inside the toe. "A tack, you see?" He returns the shoe to the King. "You must get it fixed."

"Ahh. I hang the cobbler. You don't travel alone?"

"No. My son is here with me."

"So, I hear. Keep an eye on him."

Franklin looks puzzled but makes no comment.

The King produces a flask from his coat pocket, takes a sip and hands it to Franklin. "Scots' whiskey. Try some. Only good reason to live in this damn cold country."

Franklin takes a sip, gasps. "Blazes!" He coughs and splutters. "Delicious."

"So, you make crossing to talk things over?" Franklin coughs again. "My provincial Assembly has sent me to speak for them in Council… and to reason with the Penn family regarding sharing the expense of defending our frontier."

"You think this is important business?"

"I do, sir. Most urgent. Decisions made in Parliament are not always in our best interest. The people are increasingly unhappy about it."

The two men pass the flask back and forth between them.

"I have enemies in the middle of this?"

"A great empire is most easily diminished at the outside edges, rather like a cake."

The King smiles slyly. "Like we Germans nibbled at the Romans?" He pauses for a moment. "I do not ask much of a man, only that he be loyal."

"I understand, sir."

"My son is not loyal to me, but he will be King one day soon." He places a hand over his heart. "I am not good here. You will know him as King."

"I hope not for many years."

"What if the Penn plantations are a gift from the Crown and none of your business?"

"My reading of the Royal Charter would give us power, with your assent, to levy taxes. We ask only for help in paying for our defense."

"I am not opposed. You should have your meeting." The King points across the room with his shoe. "My friend arrives… the Countess."

Franklin looks at the entrance to the hall, where the Countess of Yarmouth is announced by a page. He sees a bird-like woman in her early fifties, very thin, with a Roman nose. She glides regally through the throng of men who gather to greet her, nodding to this one, shaking hands with that one. A diamond diadem glitters on the salt-and-pepper hair piled atop her head and a diamond and ruby choker sparkles around her frightfully thin neck.

"You think she is beautiful?" the King inquires of Franklin.

Franklin chooses his words carefully. "Very… stately. Like the music."

"Stately? Yes. She has a beak like parrot, but she fecks like rabbit, so I make her Countess of Yart-mouth." The King puts on his slipper and rises from his chair. Franklin follows suit. "She come to meet a bainter… a Mr. Gainsborough. He going to do her in oil. I hate bainting. How much this thief will cost me?" He sees Granville returning from his banishment.

"And here comes back the great Granville. I enjoy our little talk, Franklin."

Lord Granville approaches.

"Granville! You make a meeting for this man with the Penns. Let it be done," the King commands.

Granville bows. "Yes, Sire."

Franklin bows as the King takes his leave and limps over to his Countess.

When the King is out of earshot, Granville turns to Franklin. "You have made a mistake, Franklin, speaking to the King before speaking with the Proprietaries."

"I answered His Majesty's questions. What choice did I have?"

"And I thought we were going to be friends." Granville turns his back on Franklin and walks away.

That afternoon, Franklin lounges in Margaret's sitting room. He is slouched in an armchair with his shoes off, cravat undone, and shirt unbuttoned at the neck. A cup and saucer sit on the side table next to him. Margaret fills his cup with coffee.

Franklin looks up at her. "All said, I pronounce the morning a complete success."

"Do you?"

"And why not? A private audience with the King? Quite unexpected."

Margaret pours herself a cup of coffee and sits on the settee opposite Franklin. "Tell me… What did you think of him?"

"Smarter than he looks."

"The family wasn't favored with beauty, was it?"

'Not as you and I were!" Franklin quips and sips his coffee. "Well, at the very least, I shall have my meeting with the Penns."

"At considerable cost, I fear. You have made a powerful enemy."

"Oh, I think not... And, I intend to take you out to supper tonight to celebrate. Just the two of us!"

Margaret raises her cup. "To the two of us!"

Late that afternoon, Mrs. Jolliker climbs the stairs from a landing on the ground floor to a hallway on the floor above. She carries a stack of clean bed linen in her arms. As she enters the hallway, she sees William leave a bedroom and close the door behind him. A look of surprise crosses her face. "Are ya lost, lad?" she calls to him. "That's Polly's room."

"Yes, of course. I was... ah... returning a book I borrowed."

"They's lots of books in the library downstairs, lad," she reminds him.

"So, there are," he replies haughtily.

Mrs. Jolliker watches him suspiciously as he walks on down the hall.

Outskirts of London   January 1758

Franklin peers out the window of a fine carriage, a new acquisition, as it clatters down a cobbled street. His initials are woven into a gilded oval insignia painted on the doors. A coachman in uniform, sitting on the barouche box up front, guides the horses along the narrow lane. Ancient elm trees, their branches bare of leaves, reach overhead like the arches of a gothic cathedral. The coachman turns into a private drive and arrives at an impressive yellow-brick Georgian house, with a three-story center block and two-storied wings on its right and left. The entry door is lacquered black and framed on either side by topiary trees planted in terra cotta pots.

The coachman brings the carriage to a halt and jumps down from his seat to open Franklin's door. "Here we are, sir, Spring Garden."

Franklin steps down and surveys the manicured grounds surrounding him, now brown and dusted with a trace of snow. "I shan't be long," he says to his driver, and approaches the gleaming front door.

After a moment's hesitation, while he adjusts his wig, he pulls the bell cord beside the door.

A minute or two later, a butler opens the door, inviting Franklin inside. Franklin hands the butler his calling card. "Welcome to Spring Garden," the butler says pleasantly as he takes Franklin's coat. "My name is Woods. Mr. Penn is waiting for you in the library. Allow me to show you the way." He briskly crosses the marble-floored foyer with Franklin following close behind.

The butler opens a pair of tall, polished walnut doors leading to the library. Inside, Thomas Penn is seated behind a massive writing desk, sorting through a stack of papers. He is in his mid-fifties, dressed in daytime finery, with a curly powdered wig atop his head. The pallor of his pudgy face suggests it has been quite some time since he has seen the sun.

Woods announces his guest: "Mr. Franklin of Philadelphia, sir."

Penn looks up from his paperwork, but doesn't rise. "Ah, Franklin. Welcome to Spring Garden. Do sit down." He gestures to a chair opposite him.

"I am very pleased to be here," Franklin says as he takes a seat.

"I would stand to greet you, but I'm having trouble with this leg of mine… It wants to go out from under me."

Woods stands in the doorway, with Franklin's coat folded over his arm. "Shall I bring tea, sir?"

"Whiskey for me, Woodsie. Might stiffen the old leg, eh? You, Franklin? A brandy, perhaps?"

"Tea would be fine, thank you."

Woods leaves the room.

Penn looks Franklin over for a moment. "I say, your name is prominent in the booksellers' these days, is it not? Your *'Way to Wealth'* tome was on display at Whitney's."

Franklin is flattered by Penn's observation, but wishes to appear humble. "I *am* surprised at the success of it."

"What inspired the writing of such a… shall we say… *homely* book?"

"Merely the doodles of a long voyage. I pieced together a string of obscure English proverbs I had learned as a lad. Sharpened up the language, is all: '*Three can keep a secret if two are out of the room*' became '*if two are dead*', and so on."

"How very clever. Were your electrical experiments doodles as such?"

"One could say that. I knocked myself on my rear a few times in the process."

"On your arse?" Penn cackles. "I should have enjoyed seeing that!"

Woods re-enters the library with a tea service on a lacquered tray. He pours tea for Franklin and sets the cup on a drinks table next to his chair. He moves behind the desk and serves his master a dram of whiskey in a crystal glass. Franklin sips his tea.

Penn watches Woods leave the room again, closing the door behind him. His smile fades. "I don't wish to take up your time needlessly, so I shall get to the point. You might have found yourself on firmer footing with my brother and me if you had come to us before discussing your points with the King."

Franklin sets down his teacup and sits forward in his chair. "I could not stand mute before His Majesty while he questioned me."

Penn looks at Franklin suspiciously and drinks his whiskey, setting the heavy glass down with a *thud*. "Be that as it may, you must present your proposals, including your unprecedented taxation scheme, to our solicitor, Mr. Ferdinand Paris, in writing, for his consideration."

Franklin eyes narrow. "What does Mr. Paris know of Pennsylvania law?"

"You fail to see, Franklin, that we *are* the law in Pennsylvania." Penn picks up a large gold coin on his desk. "Lord Granville has already clarified this point for you."

Outside the library, Woods is eavesdropping with his ear pressed to the door. He hears Franklin's voice rising: "We are wide apart on that theory, sir. The right to make laws was given us by your father in his Charter of Privileges of seventeen hundred-and-one."

Penn tosses the gold coin from hand to hand. "You make an erroneous reading of that charter."

"I think not. The Charter plainly says, '*the Assembly shall have all the powers and privileges of an assembly according to the rights of freeborn subjects of England.*'"

"Those words were at odds with the Royal Charter, which allows no such thing. The King's word will forever trump some paper my dotty father may have written," Penn retorts.

Franklin rises and paces the plush Persian carpet behind his chair, "If your father had no right to grant the privileges he did, which were published all over Europe, those who settled in the province were deceived."

"Hardly… The Royal Charter was not kept secret. Anybody might have read it." Penn lays the shiny gold piece down on top of a copy of Franklin's book, '*The Way to Wealth*'.

"Those settlers were in no position to peruse the royal documents. They had trust in your father," Franklin reasons, with a note of passion in his voice.

"Misplaced, in my view." Penn resumes sorting through his papers. "I feel we have accomplished all we can here today, and I have other appointments. We will look forward to receiving your memorandum. And since you are already up…" He rings a bell on his desk. "Woods will fetch your coat for you." The butler quickly reappears. "Mr. Franklin is leaving, Woodsie."

Woods turns and goes to fetch Franklin's coat.

Penn rises from his chair. "How long do you intend to stay in this country?" he inquires.

"Long enough," Franklin replies tersely.

"We wouldn't want you to linger needlessly. You may experience an exceptionally cold winter," Penn warns, baring his over-crowded teeth.

Franklin braces himself with his hands on the back of a chair. "Your father, who was revered by all, would be appalled by what was said here today."

Penn straightens his waistcoat. "Fathers and sons are not always cut of the same cloth, are they?"

"It would appear not."

"I saw *your* son, William, the other night. He was supine on a sofa in a dark corner at Black's. You know, the club in Soho? Couldn't quite make out with whom…"

Woods appears with Franklin's coat.

"As you take your leave, I shall take mine." Penn drinks the last of his whiskey, and strides out of the room.

Franklin looks after him in disbelief. "He rises, like Lazarus."

Woods nods his head. "The whiskey done him a world of good."

"A miracle cure," Franklin concurs, as the butler helps him into his coat.

Woods pulls a banknote out of his pocket. "Truth evades the master sometimes. Would you kindly sign this for me, sir?" he asks, offering the note to Franklin.

"Sign it? Why?"

"To prove to the wife that I served the famous man today."

Franklin smiles warmly. "If you would like. Have you a pen?"

Woods places the banknote on the desk and smooths it with his hand. He hands him a pen and steps back as Franklin writes: *'To Mr. Woods, an Honest Man'*.

CHAPTER SEVENTEEN

The Heir

MAYFAIR, LONDON   FEBRUARY 1758

Outside an imposing whitewashed brick building, a brass tablet bolted to the wall next to the door reads: *"White's Club, Est. 1693"*. Inside, the décor is masculine, with ornate plastered ceilings, dark wood paneling above the chair rail, and heavy brocade fabrics on upholstered furniture and draperies. Landscape paintings of country houses and hunt scenes in gilded frames hang on the walls.

Twelve very well-dressed men, all in their twenties and thirties, are gathered around a table. They watch paper money and bank drafts change hands. William Franklin enters the club and looks about as his eyes adjust to the dim light. He sees the group of men, who are friends he has come to meet, and approaches the table.

One of the men looks up from the growing pile of securities. "Ah, Franklin! Glad you're here. Come and join us."

Sir Humphrey, seated across the table, counts bills and notes and records figures in a ledger book. He is slender, has honey blonde hair, and looks barely old enough to be out of short pants. "Hallo, Franklin!" he calls. "Are you getting what you need lately? Do tell us of your recent conquests!"

"At what are you blackguards playing?" William inquires.

"A new French game. Lots of fun. Come, join in," another young man enjoins.

A ginger-haired Irishman next to him explains the game. "We're making a '*Tontine*'. It's a shared annuity. We all put money in a pot, and whoever outlives the others wins the lot!"

William moves to stand behind Lord Hansen, who appears older than his compatriots. William surveys the impressive stacks of bills on the table. "You mean, one wins if all the other investors are dead?"

Hansen turns to look at William. "That's it! As we die off, the shares of the eventual winner compound in value. Pitch in one thousand pounds and be a player!"

William moves around the table and places his hands on Sir Humphrey's shoulders. "Certainly not. A rogue like Sir Humphrey here will poison the lot of you to win that pot of gold."

Sir Humphrey feigns a hurt expression. "Franklin! You call me a murderer! Just think how amusing your friends' funerals will be in the future! Come now…"

"Where would an honest law student come across one thousand pounds?"

"What about your father? He's a rich man," Hansen suggests.

"That he may be, but among his inventions he coined the word '*frugal*'."

"You infer that he's a stingy old bastard, then?" the Irishman teases.

"I do at that."

"May I say that your father is not doing you any favors, my friend?" A well-fed gentleman with a pinkish complexion and a pompadour wig askew on his head chimes in. "He stabs at the ruling class, which will ruin your chances in business… unless you are content to be a family solicitor all your life."

"What *do* you fancy getting into over here, Billy?" Sir Humphrey inquires.

"What about a dukedom?" William replies.

"That's the spirit! But our friend is quite right. You should distance yourself from the old man before the Penns take him down… which they *will* do eventually."

"I need a drink," William says forlornly.

Sir Humphrey taps the arm of a passing waiter. "My guest, here, requires a drink," he says, nodding toward William. Sir Humphrey pushes out an empty chair. "Sit down, Franklin, and think of something more pleasant. As my guest, I will lend you the thousand pounds to join in the *Tontine*. I know you're good for it."

William sits at the table. "You are very kind, but I'd rather not."

Undeterred, Sir Humphrey reaches into his coat pocket for his purse. "Live dangerously, old chap! We make of life itself a game of chance!"

Stevenson House   1759

Snow flurries drift down outside the music room window. An upright piano sits against one wall, with a violin and music stand next to it. Polly Stevenson is seated at a strange-looking instrument on the opposite wall, called an Armonica. It is the size of a harpsichord, with glass globes for a keyboard. Polly pumps foot pedals, spinning the globes, then slides her fingers up and down the globes to make music. The sound is akin to a combination of bellringing and playing a saw.

In a corner of the parlor nearby, boarders Mr. Christie and Mr. Bennett are playing checkers at a trick-track table. Although the music room doors are closed, they can clearly hear the eerie music emanating from the Armonica.

Mr. Christie stares at the board with his fingers in his ears. "Make your move," he says.

Mr. Bennett shakes his head. "How about Liverpool?"

Across the parlor, a Chinese vase filled with branches and autumn leaves decorates a sideboard. Franklin and Mrs. Stevenson are seated at the center table. He has a pen in hand, while she does needlework. They have teacups before them and are dressed for cool weather.

Franklin looks up from his writing. "The Armonica is a difficult instrument to master."

"Impossible, you might say," she concurs, pulling her shawl closed.

"Still, it is my proudest invention. Did you know that young Mozart has written music for it?"

"Has he? Listen… I can hear old Mrs. Hampton's hound singing along next door!"

"You have a wicked streak, Margaret. What are you knitting there?"

"A winter scarf for you, since you came with only one."

The music stops.

"For me? How very thoughtful!"

Polly enters the parlor. "Was I just awful? Tell me truthfully," she asks, in a pleading tone.

"Nay! You are doing remarkably well. Keep at it," Franklin says.

Margaret holds up her knitting. "Would you care to add a row or two?"

"I promised Mrs. Jolliker I'd help her with the shopping. We're going to the market at Covent Garden."

"Be careful, darling. Watch out for pickpockets and other unsavory characters."

"Yes, Mama," Polly says, and hurries off toward the kitchen.

Franklin sips his tea. "Have you considered, my dear, it is almost one year since I submitted my memoranda to the Penns' solicitor, as requested?"

"Is it? I thought just a month or two."

William walks into the parlor with a law book under his arm and joins Margaret and his father at the table. "Have you room for one more?" he smiles as he sits down.

"Bill Boy, have a look at this brief I've just completed on behalf of the Delaware Indians. The Penns have broken their treaties with the poor bastards and are annexing their lands." Franklin slides the document across the table to William. "I intend to file with the court in the morning. What do you think of my theory?"

William pours himself a cup of tea from the service on the table. "Why is it now that you choose to do battle on behalf of the Indians, when you wish the Penn family to favor your opinion on a more important subject? I am baffled."

"I intend to prod them along… Let them know I won't be ignored any longer."

William scans a few pages of the brief. "You've not been ignored. Thomas Penn asked you to speak with Mr. Paris on these issues."

"Ferdinand Paris is a haughty pig, and he loathes me, which is obvious whenever we meet. I predict my suit in favor of the Delawares will grease the wheels."

"It is your own personal declaration of war on a great family. People will talk…"

Franklin's face reddens. "Talk? About me?"

"Yes… and coldly. You attack the established order… hardly the means to making friends!" William opens his law book. "You asked my opinion. There it is."

Margaret sets her knitting in the basket next to her chair. "I'll just see if tonight's roast needs turning," she says as she gets up from the table.

"And your taxation proposal is outrageous," William adds, turning pages in his book.

Franklin watches Margaret walk away. "Is it? My theory is based upon historical documents I have studied in depth, which you, clearly, have not."

"The Penn plantations were granted to them by the Sovereign out of gratitude and, as such, enjoy special rights," William argues.

"If you don't agree that the Penns should share in the burden of our defense, why have you come here?"

William looks up at his father. "I think only of your good name, Father."

Franklin moves to sit next to William. "Do you? All your life you have enjoyed the rights granted by William Penn in his Charter of Privileges of 1701. His sons would neuter that charter!"

"I enjoy rights won for Englishmen in the Magna Carta of 1215."

Franklin raises his voice. "Remember, then, as an Englishman, that your expenses here, which are not paid from out of *my* purse, are paid by the Pennsylvania Assembly! You are, therefore, beholden to both of us!"

William closes his book and looks at his pocket watch. "I have an appointment," he says calmly.

"Consider too, that should I fail in my mission, we may very well witness the dissolution of the Empire!" Franklin shouts.

Messrs. Bennett and Christie, disturbed by the raised voices, quit their game of checkers. "Let's go to a tavern for a quiet tipple," Mr. Bennett whispers.

William rises, closing his book.

"This should be of some concern to you! Sit down! I haven't finished!"

"I never forget my loyalty to my King," William offers firmly.

"What of your loyalty to *me*?"

"I am late for my appointment."

"I am not finished with you!"

William ignores his father, picks up his book and marches out of the room.

Franklin yells after him, "I said I am not finished with you!"

A moment later, the door to the street closes with a *slam*.

The two elderly boarders pack up their checkers game. "If 'twere my son, that boy would have seen the back of my hand long ago," Mr. Christie says.

Mr. Bennett nods. "*I'd* sooner strike the old man."

Margaret returns with a small tea tray. "I come unarmed, bearing refreshments."

Franklin looks toward the front door. "Damned ingrate! Where he's acquired such ideas, I cannot imagine."

Margaret sets down the tray. "Out on the town. Fancy friends." She pours tea into their cups and uncovers a plate of biscuits.

"The King suggested I keep an eye on him."

"Perhaps you should."

"Do you think we are being watched?"

Margaret sits next to Franklin at the table. She offers him a biscuit, stirs her tea. "It wouldn't surprise me."

Covent Garden, London

Peter leads the charge into the jumble that is the farmers' market at Covent Garden.

"Watch where you step, Miss Polly, with them good shoes on," he says, as they navigate on cobbled walkways through horse-drawn carts, makeshift tables, and vendors' stalls. Baskets and sacks on the ground filled with vegetables and seasonal fruit define the various shops and specialties. Jugglers, mimes, magicians, prostitutes, and stray dogs vie for attention.

Mrs. Jolliker must raise her voice to be heard above the din of merchants hawking their wares, barkers announcing entertainments, and housewives jockeying for service. She, Polly and Peter are looking over vegetables displayed on a farm cart. They place their selections in baskets over their arms and stand for a moment examining an open sack of yellow onions on the cart.

Mrs. Jolliker points to a nearby cart brimming with fruit. "Peter, fetch me two dozen good green apples, will you? I'll make pies for tonight," she shouts. Peter nods and walks over to the fruit vendor.

Polly watches Mrs. Jolliker sort through onions, sniffing them before placing them in her basket. "Why do onions make me cry so terribly when I peel them?" Polly asks.

"Hang a slice of bread out of your mouth, child. It stops the tears."

"But then you can't see to chop the onion."

"'Tis an art to it." Mrs. Jolliker looks up from the display of onions. "Ooh! There's a sight to make you cry. Look! That's young Mr. Franklin with a cheap wench on his arm!" She grabs Polly's elbow and points across the courtyard toward the Theatre Royal.

Polly peers through the throng of shoppers and spies William with his arm around a young woman, whispering in her ear as they walk. The woman is not more than seventeen years old, curvaceous, and daringly dressed to reveal her attributes. Her bright yellow hair frames a heavily painted face.

Mrs. Jolliker takes Polly's hand and pulls her behind the cart. They peer over it, looking in William's direction. Mrs. Jolliker looks aghast. "Would you look at that now! He's kissing that rubbish!" William has the young woman backed against a brick wall and kisses her crudely.

Mrs. Jolliker whispers in Polly's ear. "As I've told you, missy, handsome is as handsome does. I know ye have a soft spot for the young man, *but*..."

"I have no such thing," Polly says defiantly.

Mrs. Jolliker gasps, grabs Polly's shoulders, and turns her to face the other direction. "Lord help us! Don't you dare look now, child. He's got his hands in places Mr. Jolliker never found in forty years of marriage!" She pushes Polly away. "Find Peter and help him with them apples! Go now!"

Mrs. Jolliker steps onto an empty crate for a better view as Polly reluctantly obeys and goes to join Peter at the apple cart.

STEVENSON HOUSE

A few evenings later, Polly is seated at the desk in her bedroom, studying a textbook. Her back is to the door, which is ajar. William pushes the door open, sneaks into the room, and stands behind her. He covers her eyes with his hands.

"Guess who?!"

Polly brushes his hands away. "Billy! I hate it when you sneak up on me like that!"

He smooths her hair with his hand. "What are you reading?"

"Your father has been tutoring me in Latin."

"*'Veni, vidi, vici'*. The busy man can always find time for you, can't he?"

She closes her book.

William places his hands on her shoulders. "I have time for you, Polly."

She brushes his hands away again. "You've been drinking."

"What if I have?" He sits on a chair next to her desk and leans close to her. "Something's amiss. You've been avoiding me."

"I have *not* been avoiding you."

He picks up another book from her desk. "What have we here? Geometry?"

"Your father's been helping me with that as well, but I'm hopeless at mathematics."

William flips through the pages of the book. "My father, my father, my father! I thought you and I were friends."

"Let's be friends, then."

He sets down the book and caresses her cheek with the back of his hand. "Friends sometimes do each other favors, don't they?"

Polly tilts her face away, repelled by his touch and the smell of his breath. "I shan't be doing anybody any favors." She attempts to push his hand away.

He slides his hand across her breasts. "Aw... we used to play such clever games. Don't you miss our amusing little games?" he asks, in a menacing tone.

"Kindly keep your hands away from me!" she orders, feeling her face flush.

William leans back in the chair. "One cannot help but notice that Father is ever so keen on your mother, isn't he? A union of our families would be brilliant, don't you think?"

Polly re-opens her Latin book. "Your mother might have something to say about that."

"Deborah? She's not my mother. She's my stepmother... the old cow."

Polly looks at her book. "I wish you would go now."

He reaches over and deliberately closes her book. "I'm going to make a name for myself, you'll see."

Polly sighs. "Well, carry on your father's good name. That should be enough."

"I intend to chart my own course. I've been getting to know the best people."

"Good. You do that." She pushes his hand off her book.

"You will never do any better, you know."

"I find this conversation tiresome, Billy."

William lifts her chin with his forefinger and moves his face close to hers.

Polly wraps her fingers around a heavy brass paperweight on the desk. "Please go now," she pleads.

William looks at the paperweight. "You wouldn't do that... you couldn't."

"I believe I could," she says, with her lip quivering. She tightens her grip on the paperweight.

William stands and goes to the door. He turns back to her, his face contorted. "You will never forget me... *Never.* I won't let you! He pushes a porcelain figurine off a tall chest next to the door. It falls to the floor and shatters. "How very clumsy of me!" he says innocently, looking at the mess.

"William! That was my grandmother's!"

DEAR BEN

"I'm such an oaf. I'll have it repaired." He bends down to pick up the pieces.

Polly stands. "No. Don't. Please... just go! Go!" she shouts.

"Well, accidents do happen," William offers and goes out the door, with a crooked smile on his face.

Polly's eyes fill with tears as she closes the door behind him. She picks up a few pieces of the broken figurine, then tosses them back onto the floor. She locks the door, noisily, firmly, standing with her back leaning against it. She closes her eyes, breathing heavily.

*****

LONDON   1790

William stands at the fireplace in his study on Savoy Hill with one hand resting on its carved oak mantel. As he stares into the fire, the flickering glow of dying embers is reflected in his face. He wears a smoking jacket and holds an empty crystal glass in his hand. He thinks back with a pang of sorrow. He pictures his beautiful first wife, Elizabeth, dead in her prime from pleurisy. He sighs, as he always does when he thinks of her.

He had been looking forward to a visit this evening with his old friend, Sir Humphrey, and his wife, Lady Wrey, but William's mood has darkened. He reflects on his long friendship with Sir Humphrey and the '*Tontine*', a shared annuity they formed many years ago with eleven other young men. Seven of those men are now gone. A sadness washes over him as he runs through their names in his head. Has he forgotten anyone?

Still, if he were to outlive the rest of them, he would win the *Tontine* and become a wealthy man... an alluring prospect, since his wife's money is running low, and he and Mary have grown accustomed to a certain style of living. William takes some comfort, however, in his father's impending demise. Surely, he will share a sizeable inheritance with his half-sister, Sally. His father is rumored to be one of the richest men in America, after all.

There is a tap at the door behind him and it opens a few inches. His second wife, Mary, leans in the doorway. She is brunette, slender, handsome and nearly twenty years William's junior. She is dressed in evening wear, with sparkling jewelry on her wrists, neck, and ears. "William?" she calls to him softly. She opens the door fully and enters the room. "Aren't you going to dress for dinner?"

He turns, glances at her, then turns back to the fire. "I will be along in a moment."

"You know Sir Humphrey and Lady Wrey always arrive on time, if not early," she gently scolds.

"'The Courtesy of Kings', my father would say," he says over his shoulder.

"Would he?" Mary crosses the room to the fireplace. She runs her hand tenderly across his back. "And what of Baronets?"

William does not answer her question.

"What do you see in the dying coals? An old flame?"

William speaks after a pause, still looking into the fire. "I see phantoms of a dark past, Mary. I think of my son, my father, my wife… What *could* have been."

"*I* am your wife now." She places her hand on his arm. "Come. Prepare for dinner darling."

William pushes her hand away, crudely, roughly. He pitches the glass in his hand against the brick back wall of the fireplace. It shatters in pieces. "Why will they not leave me in peace?" he shouts.

PART FOUR

The High Road

CHAPTER EIGHTEEN

When in Ecton

PHILADELPHIA   APRIL 1790

The wind has died down, but the rain comes in waves, roaring on the roof. Neighbors who have gathered on the walk below huddle together under the slender eaves of the house during the occasional downpour.

Bobby looks over at the old man, who sleeps with his eyes darting from side to side behind his eyelids, dreaming of tales not yet told. *'Whatever happened to that lawyer, Mr. Paris?'* Bobby wonders. He sings softly as he folds linens on a table near the fire. A housemaid attends daily to Franklin's room, but Bobby likes things 'just so…' - the folds in a pillowcase, the arrangement of books on a shelf, the placement of a letter opener on the desk.

It keeps him busy. Franklin's bedroom is a spacious suite, enlarged to its present size just a few years earlier. It is four windows long, with a sitting area at the far end of the room. Heavy linen curtains frame paned windows. Bookshelves lined with leather-bound books flank a fireplace, and a writing desk rests between two of the windows.

Bobby chuckles, recalling that on fair days, Franklin liked to lounge naked on an easy chair next to a window, taking his 'air bath,' with the window wide open and curtains flapping in the breeze.

Bobby looks again toward the carved oak headboard of Franklin's bed, where an oil lamp burns on a side table. He considers his master's offer of freedom. How would he fare on his own beyond the security of this big house? How far would he need to run before he felt safe?

Franklin stirs in his bed and struggles to sit up. He strains to speak in a raspy voice. "Bobby... Help me to stand for a few minutes, will you? It relieves the pain."

Bobby smooths the sheet he has just folded, goes to Franklin, and helps him out of the bed. "Put me in that chair again," Franklin says, pointing to the chair by the window.

Bobby walks him slowly to the chair and settles him in. "I been thinkin', Dr. Ben. Did you ever hear from that Mr. Paris?" he inquires, as he helps Franklin into his leather slippers.

"You remember Mr. Paris?" Franklin pauses for a moment. "Yes. I heard from him eventually. What have you decided, Bobby?"

Bobby takes a blanket from the bed and lays it over Franklin's legs. "I ain't decided nothin' yet. Tell me about that lawyer."

"Well, I was called to a meeting of the Privy Council at Whitehall. I had brought my own counsellor. Mr. Paris had come with counsel as well." Franklin wraps the blanket tightly around his legs. "Both men looked vicious, like a pair of hyenas, circling for a kill."

LONDON   1759

Hazy sunshine pours through the tall windows, bathing the room at Government House in light. Franklin, fifty-three, stands next to a conference table. His counsel, a man of about the same age, sits beside him, taking notes. Ten other men, advisors to the Monarch, are also seated around the table. All are dressed in fine suits and wear gray periwigs on their heads.

Lord Mansfield, the Chairman, a silver-haired gentleman with sagging jowls, is seated at the head of the table. A young clerk sits off to the side, recording the proceedings. Ferdinand Paris, the Penns' swarthy solicitor, and his colleague are also present. They whisper to one another as Franklin addresses the group.

"So, gentlemen," Franklin intones, "I believe we have made it clear that should our taxation scheme be made null and void, paper money currently in circulation in the colony and put to the King's use will be rendered worthless and bring ruin to many."

Paris rises from his seat abruptly, interrupting Franklin. "My Lords, you have listened with admirable patience to Mr. Franklin's specious argument," he sneers. "He has taken all morning to provide us with nothing of substance, nothing enlightening. I beg Your Lordship to end this charade and make a decision at once in favor of my clients, the Penn family."

Lord Mansfield stands, towering over the lawyer. "Thank you, Mr. Paris. You may sit down." Reluctantly, Paris resumes his seat.

"I do agree with Mr. Paris that we have heard a sufficiency from both sides," Mansfield continues, sounding as though he is gargling when he speaks. "I shall call a recess at this time. Mr. Franklin, please join me in my chambers. I wish to review one or two points of your testimony with you."

Paris and his cohort stare in disbelief as Mansfield leads Franklin out of the meeting room and into an adjacent clerk's office, a small room lined from floor to ceiling with shelves sagging with law books.

Lord Mansfield takes a seat at a writing table and gestures for Franklin to sit opposite him. He measures his words carefully. "Are you of the opinion, Mr. Franklin, that taxes could be levied fairly so as not to do harm to the Penn estates?" he asks, looking steadily into Franklin's eyes.

"I am most certainly of that opinion, Your Lordship," Franklin replies.

"Then you have no objection to entering into an agreement to assure that point?"

"None whatsoever," Franklin concurs.

Mansfield looks relieved. "Then I shall have such an agreement drawn up. It won't take long for my clerk to produce a draft. We will have Mr. Paris sign it, and you can go on your way."

Franklin cannot conceal his joy. "Thank you, Sir! Thank you, Your Lordship!"

Mansfield rises from his chair. "Well, then, let us inform Mr. Paris of my decision."

Moments later, Mansfield and Franklin return to the meeting room and resume their places at the conference table.

Paris is incredulous when Mansfield delivers the news. "What? That is preposterous!" He stands and gathers up his papers. "This unjust decision cannot, and will not, stand! The King himself will hear of it!" Paris says bitterly.

Mansfield speaks calmly. "You have just heard His Majesty's final word, Mr. Paris. My clerk is preparing a document confirming his decision. I suggest you sign it."

Franklin's Bedroom   1790

Franklin smiles, recalling the triumphant moment. He can still hear an indignant Ferdinand Paris huffing and puffing as he and his comrade flee the meeting room. "'Twas a great victory for me and for the Pennsylvania Assembly, Bobby. My reputation as an emissary was made."

Bobby resumes folding linens. "Time to come home, then?"

Franklin rests his eyes. "Not just yet. At Margaret's suggestion, I took William north on holiday that summer. Peter came along with us. Do you recall that King had run away?"

Bobby looks up from his chore. "He did?"

"Yes. I later heard that a widow in Suffolk took him in and made a good Christian of him. I'd wager he married her eventually." Bobby lingers on the thought.

Franklin opens his eyes. "I had been invited to an affair up in Scotland and hoped to pound some sense into my son's head along the way."

Northamptonshire, England   1759

A warm spring day under a glorious azure sky.

Franklin, William and Peter wander about an ancient cemetery in a churchyard. A stone plaque next to the entrance to the church reads: *'Church of Mary Magdalene. 1175.'* Dozens of gravestones lean at odd angles; some look on the verge of toppling over.

The men stop and brush away thick moss from two or three monuments with their hands.

The rector's wife, a white-haired woman of considerable girth, pretty in her day, hurries out of the church. She carries a pail and stiff brushes, wending her way through the gravestones to the three men.

"Here we are! Here we are!" she shouts in a voice suited to the opera house. "I have what you gentlemen need to scrub them stones so's you can make out the words."

"How very kind of you, ma'am," Franklin smiles.

She hands William and Peter a brush each, then places the pail on the ground. "Soap and a good stiff brush is what is called for," she says. "The moss grows so quick around here we can't keep up. Commit a body to the grave one day, and the poor soul's name has vanished the next."

She places her hands on her hips and looks around the cemetery grounds, now overgrown with tall grass, swaying in the breeze.

"Seems like the Sexton could do more about keepin' the grass down, but he's grown old and slothful. Then, ain't we all?" she sighs.

"There's some truth to that, my dear," Franklin replies. He turns to William and Peter. "Let's get to work now, men. I would like to find my grandfather's grave."

The rector's wife follows Franklin as he walks among the teetering stones. "My husband has been rector here for nearly thirty years, Mr. Franklin, and I have never seen him so excited over a visitor! Since you become so famous, he's had his nose in the parish books, writin' a history of the Franklins here in Ecton," she offers giddily.

"You don't mean it!"

"I do. He's waitin' on ye in his library, if ye can spare the time for a few words with him, that is."

"I would be delighted to meet the rector," Franklin says eagerly.

"Come along, then," she says, waving her chubby hand in the direction of the church.

"William! Peter! Keep at it!" Franklin calls over his shoulder.

Nearly one hour later, Franklin and the rector stand at a long table in the church library, a cozy room paneled in dark wood and lined with bookshelves. The shelving is interrupted on one wall by a painting of Jesus which hangs over an Elizabethan chest. The table is stacked with faded parish record books, abstracts of title, and parchment scrolls. The rector, a man in his late sixties, is tall and thin, with spectacles perched on his aquiline nose. He wears the collar of a man of the cloth, but his suitcoat is folded over the back of a chair.

The rector has the disconcerting habit of looking heavenward as he speaks, as though seeking divine approval for his words. "I hope you have learned today that your success in philosophy comes naturally to you. It was preordained," he says, with his chin tipped toward the ceiling.

"Do you really think so, Reverend?" Franklin asks, looking pleased as he scans a document.

"It is clear to me that the Franklins were an ingenious clan. Your great-grandfather, Henry, survived the seizure of his lands under James the First and made himself useful to the gentry by opening a smithy and a foundry. We believe the bells for this church were made in his workshop."

"You don't say! I've always enjoyed working with metals," Franklin volunteers. "In fact, I've been tinkering with an idea to improve those spectacles on your nose."

The rector opens another ancient book with a marker stuck between its pages. "Look here." He displays the open book to Franklin, moving his finger over the pages. "Henry's son, Thomas, was skilled in astronomy and chemistry and was a writer of wills and leases as well. You see, your writing skills are in your inherited blood."

Franklin studies the book. "My father spoke little of his early years here in Ecton."

"Four of Thomas's sons became dyers of silk in London. Your father, Josiah, was apprenticed to them," the rector explains.

"Apprenticed, was he? A family tradition from which I escaped."

The reverend looks at Franklin with a puzzled expression, then carries on with his history lesson. "Those were turbulent times. Charles the First was beheaded, then Oliver Cromwell ruled briefly, and Charles the Second was restored."

"And, of course, the most senior of Thomas's six sons would have inherited the foundry, is that not so?" Franklin adds as he walks around the table, touching various volumes which lie open.

"That is correct. Many freedoms were taken away during the Restoration, while bishops at the head of the Church of England were given more power. Your father was a Presbyterian and would have considered the rise of the high church akin to Popery. He determined it was time to go, so not a happy time."

"I suppose not," Franklin agrees.

"Did Josiah stay with his trade in America?" the Rector asks.

"No, Reverend. There wasn't much call for fancy silks in those days. My father became a candle-maker. It wasn't an easy life," Franklin says pensively.

The rector picks up paper and pen. "I shall make a note of that."

Franklin's tone brightens. "Well, I have enjoyed our visit immensely. Most edifying."

The rector points with his ivory hand to a pair of doors across the room. "Let us pay a visit to the chapel, Mr. Franklin, and say a prayer for your ancestors and for your descendants."

"I thank you, Reverend, but I have not set foot in a place of worship since my son died."

The rector is undeterred. "A quiet moment in the house of the Lord is a balm for the soul, Mr. Franklin. The church can re-acquaint us with the benevolent nature of our Maker."

Franklin goes to the painting of Jesus and examines the brush strokes. "I have crossed the Atlantic Ocean three times," he says. After a pause, he turns to the rector. "Out there, on clear nights, I gaze at the universe, an experience even the most magnificent cathedral cannot replicate. I do not disparage your chapel and I am profoundly grateful for your offer, but no. I have seen heaven itself." He turns back to the painting. "I hope I haven't interrupted the writing of your Sunday sermon."

The rector pats Franklin on his back. "Not at all. And I hope my wife did not offend in any way. She can be over-eager."

"On the contrary, she has been most helpful." Franklin returns to the table and closes the faded, frayed cover of a baptismal record book.

"She was our housekeeper when my dear wife died. I'm no good alone, so I married her. I was accustomed to her company, you see," the rector offers sheepishly.

"There is no need to explain a comfortable marriage to me, Reverend." Franklin extends his hand. "Well, thank you, and good day."

They shake hands. The rector, beaming, grips Franklin's forearm tightly.

Stevenson House, London　　　　　　　　　　1759

Two weeks later, a young woman in her twenties slouches on a divan in Margaret's sitting room, with a teacup balanced precariously on her knee. Her dress is trimmed with shopworn feathers, and she is abundantly adorned with cheap jewelry. Her dingy blonde hair is unkempt and topped with a gaudy little bonnet, which sprouts more molting feathers. She speaks with a Cockney accent.

Margaret sits opposite the young woman, also with a cup in hand. A tea service and vase of summer flowers rest on the tea table. Margaret studies her guest with a steady gaze, trying to ignore the sour odor of body and clothing in need of a wash, wafting over the table.

The young woman looks about, admiring her surroundings. "'Tis a fine place ye have here, Mrs. Franklin," she says.

"I am not Mrs. Franklin. I am Mrs. Stevenson. Please, call me Margaret."

"Oh? Beg pardon."

"The Franklins rent rooms from me."

"A kind of boardin' house, eh, Maggie?"

"It's 'Margaret', not 'Maggie'," she admonishes.

"Sorry, again. I got a room in a boardin' house down river. Nothin' to be ashamed of, mind ye, but not as nice as this. When do you say Willy will be home?"

"Not for a month or so. His father is to receive an honor in Scotland. William joined him on the journey," Margaret explains.

The young woman sips her tea. "Things will look different in a month or two. I was hopin' to see him today."

"What things?" Margaret asks.

"I come with good news. Willy and me is havin' a little 'un," she says with a sly smile, patting her tummy.

Margaret sets down her teacup. "You are with child?"

"You could put it that way, yes, ma'am."

"You are certain about the father?"

"Oh, yes. A girl knows about these things. Not my first time, ya' know."

"How did you meet William?" Margaret inquires cautiously.

The young woman takes a biscuit from a plate on the table, has a bite, and chews as she speaks. Wet crumbs fall in her lap. "I had business in Soho one night and Willy was goin' into Black's Club. He invites me in for a pint, don't he now. And, well, you know… it's like *pitch* in there."

Margaret looks at her with eyes wide. "I see. I shall tell him about your visit the minute he returns. What did you say your name was?"

"Name's Ada. 'Pearlie' to my friends. I appreciate you tellin' Willie I come to see him, Maggie." She removes a scrap of paper from her bodice and hands it to Margaret, who gingerly accepts it, as if unclean. "This here's my address… for now." She swallows the biscuit and brushes the crumbs onto the floor. She looks about the room again. "Truly is a lovely place you got here. I could move in with Willy, to be sure. After we is married, that is."

Margaret stands abruptly. "Allow me to show you out. I have a busy day ahead."

The young woman stands reluctantly, and Margaret leads her to the foyer at a pace.

"Everybody's in such a rush these days, ain't they?" the young woman notes as she adjusts her hat. "I do thank ye kindly for the tea, Maggie. I'm lookin' forward to the future!"

"Aren't we all?" Margaret mutters to herself as she leads the young woman to the entry hall and opens the door.

"Bye, dearie!" the young woman calls over her shoulder as she steps onto the street.

University of St. Andrews, Scotland   1759

Franklin is seated with five other men on a dais at the front of an assembly hall on the grounds of the ancient school. They wear caps and gowns and are dwarfed by the ornately carved, high-backed chairs in which they sit. Franklin fidgets nervously with a program he holds in his hand as he gazes about the gothic hall. Soft northern light spills from leaded glass windows high on the walls, while giant iron candelabra standing on the floor cast light on the heavily timbered ceiling.

A din grows as a few hundred scholars file into the hall through doors at the back, nearly all of whom are young men. Their leather boots *click* across the stone floor and they laugh and chatter as they take their seats on rows of benches below the dais. William, Peter, Billy Strahan and Peter Collinson have found seats near the front.

The Chancellor, a gentleman in his seventies, sits next to Franklin on the dais, conversing quietly with him. The Chancellor holds a rolled-up document in his hand. A mighty bell in a tower above the hall tolls three times. The Chancellor stands, moves to the lectern at the front of the dais and spreads the document on the lectern. He looks over the assembly.

The Chancellor clears his throat. The gathered students become quiet and come to attention. "I have a citation I should like to read to you," he says in a thick Scottish accent. He turns to Franklin. "Mr. Franklin, would you please stand next to me?"

Franklin rises and crosses the dais to stand next to the Chancellor. Another man gets up to join Franklin, standing near him at the lectern. He has a garment folded over his arm.

The Chancellor continues. "Ladies and Gentlemen, I am pleased to present Mr. Benjamin Franklin of Philadelphia," he announces, to light applause from the audience. "The ingenious and worthy Mr. Franklin has not only been recommended to us for his knowledge of the law, but the rectitude of his morals and sweetness of his life and conversation."

Franklin stands erect and motionless.

The Chancellor reads on. "He has also been recommended for his ingenious inventions and successful experiments, with which he hath enriched the science of natural philosophy and more especially of electricity, which heretofore was little known, and acquired so much praise throughout the world as to deserve the greatest honors in the Republic of Letters."

The Chancellor looks up to more applause from the assembly and turns to Franklin. "Therefore, the Regents of the University of St. Andrews do confer upon you the Doctorate of our College of Laws. Henceforth, you should be addressed by all as '*The Most Worthy Doctor*.'"

The assembly erupts in a roar of approval, stamping their feet and applauding wildly. Franklin's black gown is replaced with a red one and a white stole is lowered over his head. The Chancellor fixes a gold medallion around Franklin's neck.

Franklin acknowledges the applause with a bow to the audience. He places one hand over his heart, then admires the medallion with the other hand. He waits for the crowd to quieten down before he speaks. "I have often been accused of being a man of too many words, but at this moment I find myself quite speechless," he says humbly. "My deepest thanks and gratitude to The Regents. I am indeed honored."

Strahan and Collinson rise to join the assembly in a standing ovation. They shake hands with each other, then with William and Peter. Collinson leans close to Strahan so he can be heard. "I have arranged meetings for Ben with Adam Smith and David Hume in Edinburgh in the next few days," he shouts over the applause. "You know, the great economist and the equally famous historian. I hope you'll stay on here with us for a week or two!"

"I will!" Strahan shouts back. "Nothing of interest going on in London these days."

Stevenson House, London   1759

Margaret is engaged in conversation with Elizabeth Downes, who is perched demurely on the divan in Mrs. Stevenson's sitting room. Miss Downes is eighteen years old, very attractive, flaxen-haired, well-bred and well-dressed. Margaret is seated in a chair opposite her and appears to be enjoying herself. Flowers in a vase on the tea table speak of late summer, as does Margaret's thin cotton dress. Mrs. Jolliker serves the two ladies tea, then leaves the room, glancing over her shoulder on her way out the door for another look at the pretty young lady.

"It is *such* a pleasure to meet you, Mrs. Stevenson," Elizabeth says with a warm smile.

"The pleasure is all mine… A lovely surprise. Please do call me Margaret. Won't you have a pastry?" she asks, offering a plate of sweets from the table.

"I believe I will," Elizabeth says as she takes a small cake from the plate offered her.

"So, whence come your people, Elizabeth? What part of the country?" Margaret inquires.

"Most of Papa's estates are in Yorkshire, but he has land in Cornwall as well."

"A busy man, no doubt. And how did you and William meet, if you don't mind me asking?"

Elizabeth swallows her bite of cake before speaking, wipes her lips with a serviette. "I don't mind in the least. We met at dinner at Lady Cranleigh's. We enjoy many mutual friends."

Margaret takes a sugary biscuit from the plate. "How fortunate. Well, to answer your query of a moment ago, he and his father should be returning in a few days. They've been taking in the sights from here to Cambridge, then to Edinburgh and back… dilly-dallying in places, as it were. They've been away for several weeks." She has sip of tea.

"You will tell him that I called, won't you?" Elizabeth asks in a pleading voice.

"But of course, the minute he returns." Margaret takes a bite of her biscuit, wiping sugar from the corner of her mouth.

Elizabeth displays a gold ring on her finger. "I shouldn't be the one to tell you this, but William and I are betrothed," she says, beaming.

Margaret chokes on her biscuit, sets down her teacup, and pats her chest. "Forgive me, too many crumbs!" she coughs. Betrothed? Are you now? This is news, indeed," she says as she recovers. "Are you by any chance acquainted with a young woman named Pearl?"

"No. Why?"

"Nothing, really. A silly question."

"I miss William terribly," Elizabeth confides, taking a sip of her tea. "Father wants us to wait a year or two, but I want to get married now. I am *so* looking forward to the future!"

"Aren't we all?" Margaret says brightly. "I can hardly wait!"

CHAPTER NINETEEN

A Nightcap

Margaret's Bedroom   1759

Another fortnight later, Franklin stands outside Margaret's bedroom door. He wears his cap, gown, stole, and medallion from St. Andrews. He carries a lighted candle in one hand, a wrapped parcel in the other. On the other side of the door, Margaret lies in her bed, reading by the light of an oil lamp. Franklin raps lightly and whispers, "Margaret…"

She looks up from her book, hesitates before saying, "I am not receiving. Go away."

Franklin leans closer to the door, his lips nearly touching it. "Haven't you missed me?" he inquires sincerely.

Margaret sits up in bed. She wears a loose-fitting night gown and a flannel night cap. "If I succumb, I will have a devilish time getting rid of you," she says firmly.

"I have a gift for you," Franklin says enticingly.

Margaret sighs. "All right. You may come in… for one minute only."

Franklin enters the room and quietly closes the door behind him. He places the candle on a bureau opposite the bed. "May I sit?" he asks.

"You look a sight. Sit over there." Margaret points to a chair next to the bureau.

Franklin places the package on the end of the bed. "I brought you a present from Edinburgh."

"Did you? How sweet…" Margaret sets her book on the night table, reaches for the package, and picks it up. She holds it next to her ear, shakes it, then removes paper and string wrapping, revealing a small, framed painting. "A watercolor…It's lovely! Thank you," she says, admiring the picture.

"From a gallery on the Royal Mile," Franklin offers. "Shall we hang it now?"

"Don't be foolish. We mustn't bang on the walls at this hour of night."

"Why not? Other people do!" Franklin grins.

Margaret sets the picture next to her on the bed.

"I thought you might like me to recite the words of my investiture."

"Please, no, but I am *very* proud of you."

"Are you? I wish you had been there, Peggy."

"It's Margaret."

"'Twas a grand occasion… Truly memorable. May I come and sit next to you?"

"No. Go to bed."

A light knock at the door, and Polly peers in. "I was passing by and heard voices," she says, stepping into the room. She wears a robe over her nightgown, which is trimmed with satin ribbons. Her glossy, dark hair is worn down, spilling onto her shoulders.

Franklin greets her cheerfully. "Hello, Pigeon!"

"Welcome home, Papa. You were gone nearly forever!" She points to Franklin's scholars' cap. "Why the hat?"

"His head is swollen and he's unable to remove it," Margaret explains. "Ben was just leaving, darling."

Polly's face brightens. "Ah! You are '*Doctor Franklin*' now, aren't you, Papa? May I give you a kiss of congratulation?" Franklin offers his cheek. "I wish you would." Polly leans over and gives him a peck.

She sits on the edge of her mother's bed. "Mama, I've had an invite from Aunt Anne to visit her in Shropshire for a few weeks. I would so love to go," she pleads.

Margaret sits up straight in her bed. "A few weeks? I can't persuade you to visit Anne for even a few days at Christmas time!"

"It's hardly worth the journey for a few days," Polly says, wheedling. "The country air would do me good, don't you think?"

"Let's talk of it in the morning," Margaret says, sounding unconvinced.

DEAR BEN

They look toward the door as William raps loudly on the door frame. He is in evening wear and stands unsteadily on his feet. His cravat is untied. "Well, well! Isn't this a cozy little gathering?" he slurs, and staggers into the room.

Franklin studies his son's attire. "Bill boy, have you just now come in from the clubs?"

Margaret glowers at William. "Everybody is going to bed now."

Polly springs off the bed. "I think I'll go and read my book for a while."

William blocks Polly's passage through the doorway with his arm. "Must you leave so soon?" he asks, tousling a curl of her hair with his finger.

"'Scuse me, Billy. Good night, Mama. Good night, Papa Ben," Polly says as she ducks under William's arm and darts out of the room.

William's bloodshot eyes follow her for a moment, then he turns to his father. "*Papa Ben*? Now it's *'Papa Ben*'? My, my! I have another sister!" he exclaims, supporting himself with one hand on the door frame.

Franklin gets up from his chair. "I shall take my leave as well. William... Don't go near an open flame, or you will go up like a haystack," he cautions, shaking his head.

"Aw, I've wrecked your little party," William slurs with mock concern. "And I love a party. "Is there anything to eat in the kitchen?" he inquires, with glazed-over eyes.

"There's ham in the larder," Margaret replies, unsmiling.

"Wondrous!" William turns toward the hall. "'Night everybody," he calls over his shoulder as he staggers out of the room.

Franklin watches his son wander off. He hears William curse as he bumps into a wall. Franklin turns back to Margaret, his disappointment obvious. "I will leave you to sleep, then."

"Wait. Since you've seen fit to disturb my quiet, I wish to tell you something. A young woman paid a call on me whilst you were in the north. She was an unsavory sort of person."

Franklin tilts his head, as though baffled. "What does that have to do with me?"

"Close the door," Margaret replies, placing a finger to her lips.

Franklin goes to the door and closes it, as requested. He stands, arms folded, awaiting Margaret's news.

"Please sit," Margaret says, collecting her thoughts. Franklin resumes his seat. Margaret recounts the girl's visit, leaving no details out of her narrative.

Franklin's face loses color. "And you believed this 'Pearlie' creature?"

"I did. I do."

Franklin takes of his cap. "Have you anything to drink?"

"Brandy in the cabinet next to you."

Franklin sets his cap on the cabinet, opens the door, and produces a bottle. "Care to join me?" he asks.

"Perhaps I should."

He finds two glasses, pours the brandy, and offers a glass to her. "Did she ask for money?" Franklin inquires.

Margaret holds the glass with both hands. "Not yet… but she'll get around to it. She's a bold one."

"Damn him! We were together night and day for weeks and he told me nothing of this." Franklin sits in his chair again. He raises his glass to Margaret. *"Santé."*

Margaret lifts her glass. "To family," she snickers.

Franklin sips his brandy. "This will not be of help to me with matters of State. Damn him to hell!"

Margaret tucks a pillow behind her back. "Perhaps no one need know," she suggests.

"Yes! If I were to send him packing straight away, we may be finished with this."

Margaret twirls the brandy in her glass. "I was thinking of a settlement with the girl. You may meet with resistance to sending William home. He plans to marry."

"What? Marry the strumpet?"

"Nay. He would find purchase in higher society. I had another visitor whilst you were in Scotland… A charming girl named Elizabeth Downes. She and William are betrothed."

Franklin drains his glass, sets it on the bureau, and rests his head in his hands.

"Have I upset you?" Margaret asks after a moment.

Franklin raises his head. "I cannot say you have made my evening jolly. Have you any more good news?"

"You poor man. I am sorry." She pats the bed next to her. "Come, lie next to me. I'll smooth your brow. Snuff out that candle."

Franklin removes his stole, gown and medallion, and folds them on the chair. He blows out his candle and lies next to Margaret on her bed. She gently rubs his forehead.

"Deborah has always thought William to be evil," he whispers.

"Do you?"

"Not evil, but a man of dark secrets." Franklin looks into Margaret's eyes. "Shall I undress?" he asks boyishly.

"Turn out the light," she replies.

Franklin dims the lamp on the table next to the bed. "I should like to speak with the woman called 'Pearlie' who claims she is with child," he confides, as he removes his shirt and breeches.

"She left an address. Shall I fetch it for you?"

"Not now," Franklin says as he dims the light.

Polly has settled into the sanctuary of her bedroom. She latches the door behind her, pulls the curtains closed, removes her robe and hangs it on a hook near her bed. She kicks off her slippers, climbs into bed and pulls the quilt up around her. She sits up, plumps the pillows behind her and picks up a book from a side table. She finds her place, turns up the oil lamp next to her and begins to read, always a favorite pleasure.

William thought the narrow back staircase leading down to the kitchen to be fearsome in his condition. He decided to take the stairs at the front of the house, which are wider and more easily navigated when tipsy. In the hallway between staircases, he finds himself at Polly's bedroom door. He listens for a moment, then raps sharply on her door. He hears not a sound. He jiggles the handle, but the door is securely locked.

"Polly? It's me. Open up," he slurs.

Inside her room, Polly freezes in place, her eyes wide.

William whispers through the crack between the jam and the door. "I only wish to talk with you for one minute."

Polly sets down her book and turns down the lamp.

William taps on the door with his heavy signet ring. "Open the damn door!" he commands in a full voice.

"Go to bed, William!" Polly shouts from the darkness of her room.

"Pweeze? Just for a widdo minute?" he pleads in mock child speak.

"No! Go to bed!" she shouts again, not amused.

William pounds on the door with his closed fist. "You dirty little bitch!" he snarls before turning and weaving his way down the hall.

Polly listens to William's leather heels stomp away on the wooden hallway floor. She lies back on her bed and pulls the quilt over her head, sobbing, with his threat that she will never be free of him pounding in her ears.

A few nights after his visit with 'Pearlie' at her boarding house in East London, Franklin walks down a dark, narrow, winding street in Soho, London. As wretched as the young woman is, Franklin couldn't help but think he had known someone like her intimately in a previous life. The thought made him feel unclean. He arrives at the address he had set out to find: a shabby brick town house with a front door painted shiny black. A sign next to the door reads: *Black's Club. 8 Dean St.*.

Franklin looks at his pocket watch. It is eleven o'clock. His timing should be just about right, he surmises. He knocks on the door and a moment later, a rough-looking doorman opens it a crack. He looks Franklin up and down. The doorman is broad-shouldered, bearded, and a foot taller than Franklin.

The expression on the doorman's face is grim. "This be a private club, mister," he says in a gravelly voice.

"So I am told," Franklin says pleasantly. "I wish to see William Franklin. I trust he is inside this establishment?"

The doorman opens the door wider. "He may be at that. Who would be askin'?"

"I am his father."

"His father, you might like to know, is *Benjamin* Franklin," the doorman smirks.

"You are quite correct, young man. Step aside."

Franklin pushes past the dumbfounded doorman and strides into the inner sanctum of the club. It takes a few minutes for his eyes to adjust to the murky atmosphere of the crowded, candle-lit tavern as he wanders through it. He bumps into patrons standing at high tables in the smoky room, drinking, chatting and eating tavern fare. Most of them are young men, but there is a smattering of women among them. They glare at Franklin as ale splashes onto their boots and he awkwardly excuses himself. "Beg pardon, beg pardon," he says repeatedly as he negotiates his way through the gloom and across the littered floor, with sawdust and peanut shells crunching underfoot.

Franklin comes upon a narrow wooden stairway, looks up it, and climbs the creaky stairs. Reaching the top, he passes through a raucous gaming room, crowded with men at tables, playing cards and throwing dice. He moves on to a quieter lounge area at the back of the building. He spots William, slumped on a stained and tattered divan, conversing with four friends, all of whom look to be about his age. They are expensively dressed, but unkempt. Their jackets are thrown over chairs, their shirts open at the neck and cravats untied. The table before them is covered with drinks glasses, most of them are empty.

Franklin approaches the table. "William!" he announces in a loud voice. "I need to speak with you on an urgent matter!"

William looks up and is shocked to see his father. "Father? What are you doing here?"

"Let's step outside," Franklin orders.

William sits up and puts on his jacket, smoothing his hair. "That would not be convenient. You can see that I am with friends. You should be at home in your bed."

"Get up! We're going outside!" Franklin commands.

William picks up his drink from the table. "You are interrupting our conversation. I will speak with you later. Goodnight father." He resumes chatting with the gentleman sitting closest to him.

Crimson-faced, Franklin reaches over the table, grabs William by the lapels of his jacket and pulls him up, knocking over several glasses in the process. "I said, get up! NOW!"

A drunken young friend rises from his seat in William's defense. "Here, here, old man!" he slurs.

Franklin reaches across the table and pushes him back down into his chair. "Oh, sit down and shut up!" he scolds the teetering dandy, who falls onto his backside, wig askew. Franklin, his bulk half again that of his willowy son, leads William by his collar down the stairs and out of the club. Heads turn as they navigate through the noisy tavern, past the doorman and out to the street.

"How dare you embarrass me?" William gasps, as his father releases his grip on him in the dark lane.

"What do you intend to do about the child?" Franklin demands.

"What child?" William asks, sounding bewildered and innocent.

"The child you fathered with that strumpet. I've been to see her. She assumes you will marry her!"

William smooths his jacket collar. "'Pearlie?' You can't be serious! I certainly will not marry her. I have other plans."

"So, I've heard."

"Women like her know how to take care of these things," William says, rearranging his silk pocket kerchief.

"What if I had done that to you?"

William stares at his father, his mouth agape. After a pause: "I will have nothing to do with any child. That is a ridiculous notion."

"Then Margaret and I will arrange for the baby's care. You will pay."

William turns away, preparing to return to the club. "Fine. You do that," he says. "Have we finished now?"

Franklin grabs William by his shoulder and spins him around. "Yes, I am finished with you... And you will remove your belongings from Craven Street in the morning."

"Move out? Where will I live?"

Franklin gestures toward the decrepit club. "Why not here at Black's, the repository of black sheep pitched out of White's Club? It suits you!" He turns abruptly and walks down the winding street. "First thing in the morning!" he calls back.

William, humiliated, watches his father disappear into the darkness. He is astonished by the old man's fury... clearly a case of 'the pot calling the kettle black!' When did he 'get religion'? William wonders. Now, William would need money, and a goodly amount of it, for his accommodation and expenses in London. He has a few irons in the fire... perhaps a hasty visit to Chiswick is in order...

Near London   1759

A day or two later, William presents himself to Lord Granville at his mansion in Chiswick. A butler ushers him into Granville's study, where His Lordship is seated at an enormous marquetry and ormolu desk, in the French style. The walls of the room are lined with bookshelves rising to a great height, with family portraits in ornate gilt frames hanging in the gaps between bookcases. Granville bids William to sit in a chair opposite the desk, as the butler takes his leave. William is attired in a fine bespoke suit, silk cravat and powdered wig, as befitting an English gentleman. He long ago eschewed his father's simple, more homespun manner of dress.

Granville peers over his reading spectacles. "You understand that the post you have been offered is of utmost significance, given the times," he advises, as he pulls a silk cord hanging on the wall behind him.

"I do, sir," William concurs.

"You have the opportunity to be of special service to His Majesty," Granville continues. "The King desires peace and order to be restored in his colonies."

William can hardly contain his pleasure at having secured a position that is certain to annoy his father. "Your Lordship can be assured of my unswerving loyalty to the King."

"We appreciate all you have done for us thus far. Your appointment will convey a message to the Americans, most pointedly to your father," Granville says. "Take no offence, but I speak with candor."

"None taken," William says, thinking he shares those very sentiments.

Their conversation is interrupted when a maid appears through a hidden door in the paneling behind Granville's desk. She is an Irish girl, shapely, perhaps sixteen, her face dense with freckles and topped with a blaze of red hair. They both watch the girl serve them tea. His Lordship pats her behind as she turns, giggles, and retreats through the hidden door.

"An import from my estates in Ireland," Granville explains, waving a hand toward the hidden door. He rises from his seat at the desk.

"I find it puzzling that your father's friend, Strahan, has encouraged your appointment."

"Billy Strahan believes in the rule of law."

"There are those who say we risk an uprising unless we accede to your father's demand for representation in Parliament." Granville stops at a cabinet, opens a drawer, and takes out a hinged porcelain box. He opens it, takes a pinch of powder from the box, holds his fingers to his nostrils, and sniffs. He inhales deeply and returns the box to the drawer.

"You may rest assured that the Province of New Jersey will be kept subdued whilst I am its Governor, with or without such representation," William says.

"Your father and his associates cloak extortion of the Penn family as a scheme to assist us with military affairs… as if we needed their help!"

Granville resumes his seat at the desk. He takes a silver flask from his pocket and pours a splash of whiskey into his tea. "We have the most brilliant minds in His Majesty's service. Field Marshall Amherst has a clever idea to dispense with the Indian problem once and for all," he confides in a near whisper, offering the flask to William.

William shakes his head 'no'. "Has he now?" he inquires.

"Amherst proposes we distribute blankets which have been infected with the pox among the savages… Wipe them out completely! What do you say to that?" He sips his tea.

"It is certainly an *original* idea," William says, after a pause.

"You would not oppose such a measure then?"

"Why should I?"

Granville smiles. "The compensation provided will never make you rich. You are aware of that?"

"My fiancé is a woman of means. We shall want for nothing."

"Is she?" His Lordship raises his teacup. "You *are* a clever boy."

CHAPTER TWENTY

Into the Woods

STEVENSON HOUSE, LONDON   AUGUST 1762

An unusually hot, sunny morning in The Strand; there is no breeze blowing up the hill from the Thames. Windows are propped open in Franklin's bedroom and curtains hang limply from their rods. Leather-strapped travel trunks are stacked near the door. Peter perspires and wipes his brow with a kerchief as he packs items of Franklin's clothing into an open trunk.

Franklin stands with his back to Peter, organizing personal papers into a leather valise which sits open on the bed. "It is for the best, I swear to you it is. You will fare much better over here," Franklin calls over his shoulder.

Peter shakes his head. "As I see it, Dr. Ben, my place is on that boat with you. I don't like gettin' left behind one bit. We has been together an awful long time."

"You will stay here," Franklin replies firmly. "Margaret would be lost without your help."

"I should be goin' home… Be 'round some 'a my own people," Peter argues with a long face.

"This is your home. *These* are your people now." Franklin points to a small crate. "Take that box downstairs for me, will you, please? It's filled with glass and mustn't be jostled."

Peter lifts the box as requested and carries it to the doorway, where he meets Margaret as she enters, carrying a stack of folded shirts. "Mornin', ma'am," he says and stands aside to allow her to pass before he steps into the hallway.

Margaret nods a greeting and steps into the room. She places the shirts on top of a chest of drawers. "Mrs. Jolliker will be up shortly with the last of these. She has a few more to press," Margaret offers, with a brittle edge to her voice.

Franklin takes a few steps toward her. "I would like to say a few words to you."

"No need," she says, taking a silk fan from her apron pocket, and unfolding it. "Devilishly hot today, is it not?"

"It grieves me to leave you."

"Does it? Shall we pack your shirts? I'll help you. We should wrap them first."

"Please don't be angry." Franklin points to a stack of paper on his desk.

Margaret returns the fan to her pocket and wraps a shirt with the clean paper.

"I am *not* angry," she says. "I am befuddled. I do not understand why you cannot postpone your departure for two more weeks until after William's wedding."

"If I attend the ceremony," Franklin explains, "it will appear that I condone the affair, which I do not."

"Is William to be forever *persona non grata*?"

Franklin joins her in wrapping his shirts. "After a time, we may resume our exchanges. We *may*, I said."

"His investiture as Governor is but three weeks hence. I think it unwise of you to snub the Palace," Margaret warns.

"My departure will not be perceived as a slight to the Palace. Strahan has promised to see to it. He owes me the favor after politicking on William's behalf." Franklin places wrapped shirts on shelves in a standing trunk. Margaret sinks into an easy chair. "I admit I have dreaded this day."

"As have I. Five years have passed in a heartbeat. Anything I have accomplished here was due to your wise counsel, my dear."

"Hardly," she says modestly, brushing a damp curl of dark hair from her forehead.

Franklin stops what he is doing. "Will you be kind enough to look in on my grandson? Write with news? I may never see the boy again."

"You needn't worry," Margaret assures him. "Mrs. Noon will take good care of him."

The glass Armonica begins to play in the music room downstairs. Franklin cocks an ear and smiles. "Listen! Polly is playing!"

"She has sulked all morning," Margaret confides.

Franklin goes to her and takes her hands in his. "Come! Dance with me!"

"Dance?" Margaret pulls her hands away. "You are a silly old man."

Franklin coaxes Margaret out of the chair. She stands and they improvise a gavotte, dancing among scattered trunks and crates. "I shall close my eyes at night whilst I am at sea and dream of this moment," he says.

"You may tell Mrs. Franklin that nothing has transpired in this house of which we need be ashamed."

"I am ashamed of nothing," Franklin concurs.

"As I said…"

"I have been pondering something, Margaret: Was your Giles an agent of the French?"

"Impudent of you to ask. Let us leave Giles to rest," she replies.

Franklin stops their dance. He takes both her hands in his. "As you wish, but I shall return soon and learn the truth of it."

"Return to England?" Margaret shakes her head. "I hardly think so."

FRANKLIN HOUSE, PHILADELPHIA   APRIL 1790

Bobby is alone in the kitchen. He looks inside a cupboard, finds a bottle of wine, and secrets it inside his houseman's jacket. He looks up and down the hallway before crossing it. He hears conversation from the front of the house. Polly Hewson, Sally Bache and their guest, Thomas Jefferson, are in the parlor down the hall. The sound of their voices fades as he makes his way up the stairway to Franklin's bedroom on the third floor. Bobby stops on the landing, settles on a step, uncorks the wine bottle and takes a swig.

Upstairs, Franklin rests in the chair where Bobby had left him a short while earlier. Franklin dozes with his head lowered, his chin resting on his chest, one arm dangling outside the chair. He clings to an empty teacup with his other hand. His eyes are closed, darting from side to side. Franklin dreams of a candlelit salon, a room he had last seen ten years before.

The walls are of white damask, with crystal chandeliers hanging above a gleaming parquet floor. It is the ballroom in the Brillon mansion, his neighbors when he lived at Passy, outside Paris.

A trio of musicians in formal dress plays for Franklin and Madame Brillon as they dance. He is ten years younger and leads her skillfully in a gavotte, gliding and swirling through a white mist which floats above the floor. He wears gray satin breeches and waistcoat, with his beaver cap perched rakishly atop his head. She wears a dazzling emerald silk gown and sparkling jewels. Her raven hair is worn up. They are alone.

"John Adams thinks you are the most beautiful woman in France," Franklin tells her, looking into her eyes.

"Does he?"

"Yes, he has told me so more than once."

"And why have you not danced with me before, if I am so beautiful?"

"Because, my dear Hélène, you were dancing with your husband."

"Poor Henri. He is gone now."

"Yes, I know," Franklin says sorrowfully.

"Have you any regrets, Cher Papa?" she asks as she curtsies to him.

"I regret that I have felt anxious all my life."

Madame Brillon is surprised by his answer. "Anxious? Mais pourquoi? Why?"

"When a man stands at the pinnacle of success, he may easily slip and fall. It is a constant danger," he confides.

"No need to worry about such things at this late hour," she comforts him.

Franklin smiles, takes her hand, extends his arm, then releases her. With the grace of a ballerina, Madame Brillon performs a pirouette. When she turns back to him, her face is craggy and deeply wrinkled, her hair is thin and gray. Her opulent dress is shredded and falling to dust. The teacup falls from Franklin's hand, hitting the floor with a loud *thud*. He awakens from his dream with a start and jolts upright. Beads of perspiration dot his forehead. "Bobby!" he moans.

Bobby hears Franklin's call and hurries up the stairway. "Here I am! I ain't gone but a few minutes!" he says as he enters the bedroom. "You gonna wake the dead!" Bobby sets the wine bottle on a side table, picks up the teacup, and sets it on the dresser.

Franklin is agitated. "The lady came for me again!"

"Ain't no lady here, Dr. Ben, just you and me. You been dreamin'."

"I knew her well. I called her *'Hélène'*."

"I fix you some 'a your medicine... Might help your nerves."

Franklin raises a hand. "Enough opium. Let's walk a bit. It eases the pain."

Bobby helps Franklin to stand, bracing him with his hand under Franklin's arm. They pace the length of the room, then Bobby helps Franklin back into the chair and replaces the blanket over his legs. "You should be in bed," he chides.

A gust of wind rattles the windows. "Wind kick up again," Bobby notices. He goes to the window, closes it tightly, and stares out.

"What are you looking at?" Franklin inquires. "My Greek chorus down on the street?"

"Ain't no chorus. Jus' a few folks down there standin' around talkin.' I ain't lookin' at them."

"What, then?" Franklin asks.

"Ohio," Bobby replies.

"What do you see in Ohio?"

"My cousin, Jonas, he got himself a farm out there... His kids go to school now," Bobby says, still looking out the window.

"Perhaps you could go to them," Franklin suggests.

Bobby turns to Franklin. "That's what I been thinkin'."

Franklin's face brightens. "Good... excellent. I am very pleased. Let's drink to that," he suggests, looking around for his teacup. "I might like *'a spot of tea'*... Pour yourself a drink as well."

Bobby locates two teacups on the dresser, pours wine for Franklin and for himself.

"To your cousin Jonas and his good health," Franklin says, raising his cup.

"To *your* health," Bobby says, lifting his cup in return.

Franklin sips his wine. "The lady in my dream asked me if I had any regrets."

Bobby takes a drink of wine and sets his cup back on the dresser. "Do you?"

"Hundreds," Franklin admits. "But one in particular sticks in my mind. When I was a lad in London, I wrote an essay and published a booklet denying the existence of God."

Bobby goes to the bed and tidies the sheets and blankets. "Why you do somethin' like that?"

"I thought I knew everything. I have since come to be on better terms with Divine Providence... I hope."

Bobby fluffs the pillows on the bed. "My mama say it best if we forgive ourself 'cause they's so many sinners, Jesus maybe too busy to do the job."

"Your mother should be made a saint." Franklin pauses for a moment. "I dedicated my booklet to James Ralph."

"Ain't he the man who owe you fifty pounds?"

"I got my money's worth from James. He was the prettiest talker I ever met. He became a noted writer, a critic of the arts. David Garrick, the greatest actor of this century, wept at his funeral... As did I."

Bobby leans against the windowsill and folds his arms. "Mr. Ralph ever feel bad 'bout leavin' his wife and kids?"

"He never looked back. He had made his mark. When he died in 1762, the London papers called him *'The Celebrated Mr. Ralph'*."

"Seems to me that was the year you come home."

"You have a fine memory." Franklin gazes into his teacup. "James and I came home together after all." After a pause: "I landed ahead of William and Elizabeth, who took a rough winter crossing. I had softened toward my son when I learned the Penns had done all they could to block his appointment as Governor. He and his new bride came to Market Street and spent a few days with us, recovering from their arduous voyage. To my delight, Elizabeth was a perfectly decent woman and we grew fond of her."

Mid-Atlantic   January 1763

A schooner under sail is tossed about like a toy, on mighty swell after mighty swell. For weeks on end, the sea has been black, the skies a dismal gray. A freezing drizzle washes over the ship's deck, rendering it

DEAR BEN

impossibly slippery. Blustery winds howl endlessly through the rigging and sails. In her cabin at the stern, gray light from a porthole falls across Elizabeth Downes Franklin's face as she lies in her berth. The appalling weather has made her seriously ill. She is weak, her hair is matted and her skin is ghostly pale.

William Franklin sits on the edge of her bed, attempting to comfort her. He mops her brow with a damp towel. "It has been three days since you have taken any nourishment," he says with a concerned look on his face.

Elizabeth answers him in a thin voice, "I couldn't possibly…"

"You *must* try to eat something," he pleads.

Elizabeth attempts a wan smile. "No… please."

"Why don't you come up for tea? The fresh air may help you," he cajoles.

"The fresh air may *kill* me. Just let me be for now. Please, William," she moans.

He pats her hand and rises to leave. He bends down to kiss her forehead, then lays the towel next to a basin on a chest of drawers. He backs out of the cabin, bracing himself with his hands on the door frame against the motion of the ship.

I will come back to see you in an hour or so," he says, closing the door behind him.

A few weeks before the Franklins embarked on their Atlantic crossing, Thomas Penn sat at the desk in his splendid library at Spring Green, writing a letter by the light of an oil lamp. A glass of brandy rests on the desk next to the lamp. Penn addresses the envelope to his nephew, John Penn, whom he and his brother have appointed Governor of Pennsylvania, the colony in which the family's vast plantations are located.

"My Dear Nephew," Penn writes, "*Franklin the Younger will soon arrive on American shores with his new bride, to assume his post as Royal Governor of New Jersey. Some good may come of it. He is obligated to follow orders from London, and his father dare not oppose them.*"

Penn picks up the brandy glass, sniffs it, then takes a drink of the auburn liquid. He swirls the glass a few times and considers that his nephew is instrumental in his scheme to neuter the nettlesome

Benjamin Franklin. Penn fully intends to end that wretched man's life in England. "Somehow I will do it!" he says aloud.

Several weeks later, Governor John Penn is seated in a wing chair in the library of his home in Philadelphia, reading his uncle's letter. The Governor is in his thirties, of fair height and good figure, but prone to his family's trait of a feminine softness in his features. His house is comfortable, but humble when compared to his uncle's place at Spring Green. Penn drinks tea and continues reading. *"Do us a great favor and befriend William Franklin."* his uncle writes. *"Take him under your wing and show him the ropes, as it were. You know how to do it."* Penn puts down the letter and smiles. Skilled and crafty in business, he knows precisely how to do it.

FRANKLIN HOUSE, PHILADELPHIA   MARCH 1763

The kitchen door flies open and Sally darts out, her black spaniel bounding ahead of her. "They're here!" she shouts over her shoulder, pulling her shawl closed about her as she crosses the yard in the chill spring air. Sally has made a special effort with her hair today, wears a pretty frock, powder on her face, and a spot of rouge on her cheeks.

As she hears a carriage clatter into the mews, Jake emerges from the barn to help the driver calm the skittish horses and to bring the coach to a stop. The coachman jumps down and opens William's door, which bears a golden oval insignia, with the letters 'BF' intertwined therein, glistening in the afternoon sun.

A bedraggled-looking William steps out, offering his hand to Elizabeth. She steps down, wearing a rumpled travelling cloak and looking weary from her journey.

Sally, now twenty years old, runs to her brother and throws her arms around his waist. "Billy! Billy!" she cries. "You've been away so long!"

William drops the valise he carries and places his hands on Sally's shoulders, holding her at arm's length. "Look at you! Grown into a woman whilst my back was turned!" He turns toward his wife. "Elizabeth, meet my sister, Sally."

Elizabeth extends her hand. "How do you do?"

"Very well, thank you," Sally replies tentatively, like a shy schoolgirl.

Franklin negotiates his way between puddles as he crosses the drive to greet his son and his English wife. "I am the father of these two," he calls to Elizabeth, pointing to Sally and William. "Welcome to Philadelphia, my dear."

"Dr. Franklin…" Elizabeth, who has not yet found her land legs, attempts a wobbly curtsy in return. Father and son look at each other in silence for a moment, then shake hands and embrace warmly. Franklin's eyes brim over as he offers his arm to Elizabeth. "Come inside. You just have time for a wash before dinner," he says, leading her toward the house, with the spaniel barking and circling about them. "How was the voyage?" Franklin inquires.

"I will not be making the return trip, I can assure you of that!" she replies sweetly, but firmly.

"Mrs. Franklin is of the same mind. Tomorrow I will give you a tour of the place," he says, gesturing toward the vacant property adjacent to his. "I am about to commence a building project on that land… We will make this old house large enough for grandchildren, which are sure to come along." He shouts back to William, who walks a few paces behind. "There will be grandchildren, will there not, Son?"

William seems not to have heard the query. "It looks like there's rain coming," he comments, looking up at the sky.

"You're too skinny, girl," Deborah remarks and shakes her head, as she watches Elizabeth take her seat at the dining table that evening. "Aggie, give Miss Elizabeth some 'a those potatoes, will ya?"

Elizabeth is refreshed and transformed: she wears a pretty dress and good jewelry, with her hair worn up stylishly. William is freshly scrubbed, his is hair washed and combed. He wears a velvet frockcoat and silk cravat.

His father stands at the head of the table. He is in his shirtsleeves, carving a roast chicken on a platter. Aggie serves side dishes as Jake pours the wine. "Aggie, you've roasted the bird perfectly, as usual," Franklin tells her. Aggie smiles proudly as he resumes his seat at the table and passes the platter to Elizabeth, who is seated on his right.

The dining room is a pleasant chamber with a beamed ceiling, walls painted deep red, a brass chandelier overhead, and a pegged oak floor. Tall windows extend from floor to ceiling and are flanked by printed linen curtains, tied back with woven ropes and tassels, revealing the twilight outside.

The table is set with Irish linen and Deborah's finest English china. The glow of candlelight is reflected in the diners' faces. William looks about the room and thinks that his father's house has taken on a polish unknown before his years in London with Margaret.

"I hope you come with an appetite," Deborah says to Elizabeth. "The chickens is from our own coop. Do you like rutabaga? Root vegetables is all we got this time of year, greens being so scarce."

Sally, wearing her Sunday best and seated next to Elizabeth, whispers, "You don't have to eat it. I *hate* rutabaga."

"It is all wonderful to me," Elizabeth says cheerily. "I didn't eat much aboard the ship."

"It shows," Deborah says. "Have some of Aggie's stuffing."

Aggie offers the bowl of cornbread stuffing to Elizabeth.

"Well, we *are* grateful you come across safe," Deborah continues. "Two ships went down already this winter. Near two hundred souls lost, if you was to count the crew," she says as she passes the chicken platter on to William.

"Oh, dear! That is truly horrible!" Elizabeth laments.

Sally looks at Elizabeth earnestly. "I think you're a very lucky lady. When I get married, I want to marry somebody just like my brother."

"An admirable ambition," Elizabeth concedes.

"I am flattered, indeed, little sister!" William says.

"I was thinking, Bill Boy, I might accompany you to Perth Amboy," Franklin volunteers between bites. "Help you get settled into your new home…"

"Oh, you needn't bother. We'll be fine," William responds.

Deborah's expression sours. "Your father is only happy when he's off somewhere!"

"I think it's a lovely idea," Elizabeth says brightly. "It would be a fine chance to get to know one another!"

"That's it! We can have a chat about Billy's new position. You have a great challenge ahead of you, son."

"Oh? How is that?" William raises his empty wine glass and looks at Jake.

"You must serve two masters: The King *and* the people."

Jake fills William's wine glass. "I am beholden only to His Majesty and come prepared with instructions from his government. It is really quite simple."

"Is it? Perhaps not." Franklin rests his knife and fork on his plate. "There is change in the wind, Billy… Imperceptible, but coming nonetheless."

William sips his wine. "The rabble up in Boston are forever kicking up a rumpus if that's what you refer to. It is not a worry."

"We love our King, but you must never forget your obligation to the people. You want to come out on the winning side, do you not?" Franklin cautions.

"The Americans have neither the resolve nor the resources to enter into a confrontation with the King." William says confidently. "I shan't lose any sleep over it."

Franklin sighs and resumes eating his meal.

Rain begins to patter on the windows, as William had predicted.

CHAPTER TWENTY-ONE

Two Governors

A few days later, the Franklin carriage drives along a narrow, deeply rutted road. The trees on either side of the lane have sprouted tender green buds, hinting of springtime, but the day is brisk and the driver and coachman wear heavy coats and leather gloves. The passengers inside are bundled in warm clothing and have woolen blankets spread over their legs. The coach rocks from side to side as it navigates the furrows of the roadway. The men are dozing, with Benjamin Franklin leaning against one door and William against the other. Elizabeth sits primly on the seat opposite, looking a shade nauseous.

When they are not napping, Elizabeth fills the distance between the two men with chatter. "I must admit, there is *nothing* to recommend the roads in New Jersey," she says as she is jostled about in her seat.

William places a hand on Elizabeth's knee. "There's a project for you, my dear. Organize work gangs to smooth out the bumps. I shall propose it to the legislature."

Franklin looks out the window. "Thank goodness we're nearly there. My bladder can't take much more of this." He looks over at William. "Ask the driver to stop again, will you, please?" Franklin pushes his blanket onto the floor.

"You can't wait?" William replies churlishly.

"As somebody once said to me, '*the piss fairy calls*'," Franklin confirms.

William's face reddens. "Good Lord, Father! Who would make such a vulgar remark?"

Franklin conceals a smile. "A woman you once knew, briefly."

William looks bemused.

One hour later, the carriage rolls into the cobbled drive of the Governor's mansion at Perth Amboy. Elizabeth looks out the window and puts her hand to her cheek. "My goodness," she says with wide eyes. "There is quite a crowd of people out there."

"Smile, my dear, but not excessively," Franklin suggests. "Or they will think you're a mad woman."

Dozens of local citizens have come out to get a look at their new Governor and his English bride. They surround the carriage as it stops in front of the house, a handsome three-story red brick building in the Georgian style, with window trim, Ionic columns, and front door painted a crisp white.

A young African-American stable boy runs up to open William's door, who steps out of the coach to light applause. There is a murmur of approval from the ladies in the gathering as Elizabeth alights from the carriage. They remark on her beauty and on her finely tailored travel costume: a dove gray, fur-trimmed greatcoat with matching hat and kid gloves.

William shakes the hand of a rosy-cheeked, middle-aged man named Mr. Earl, who has come to represent the Provincial Legislature, a body William considers a mere formality, and before long, a nuisance.

As William introduces his wife to Mr. Earl, a man's voice booms out from the crowd. "Ay, Mr. Governor!" he shouts. "When ye are at St. James's, who sleeps in the middle? You or the Duchess?" Several people gasp, while others titter at the shocking outburst. A militia guard parts the crowd and lunges at the heckler, but the man runs into an adjacent field and escapes into the woods. William pretends to have not heard the nasty gibe, but Elizabeth looks ashen and wears a pained expression. *'What am I in for?'* she wonders.

The unexpected appearance of Franklin, who chooses that moment to step down from the carriage, brings a cheer from the crowd, many of whom push in close to touch him or shake his hand.

With Mr. Earl leading the way, William takes Elizabeth's hand and climbs the steps to the front door of the mansion. They stop at the portal, look back, and see Franklin shaking dozens of outstretched hands.

"Your father appears to be on the winning side," Elizabeth whispers.

"I wish he hadn't come," William says bitterly.

Franklin House, Philadelphia — February 1764

Franklin doesn't take his eyes off the newspaper he is reading, as he sips his tea. He has a plate of freshly baked bread and a crock of butter before him on the scarred old kitchen table where he is seated. Sally's spaniel is curled at his feet, whimpering occasionally, begging for another bite of crust. Franklin looks up when the kitchen door opens and Deborah, followed by Aggie, enters from the backyard. They stamp snow from their boots on a rag rug at the door. They wear woolen capes and bonnets and carry market baskets filled with dry goods, produce, and a few paper bundles from the butcher.

"Good morning, ladies," Franklin says, returning to his newspaper.

"Ben, there's somethin' crazy goin' on," Deborah says breathlessly, as she hangs her cloak and bonnet on a hook by the door. "Shops are closing up early and pulling their shutters tight."

"We had to hurry along," Aggie adds, as she hangs up her cloak and bonnet.

Deborah arranges their purchases on a sideboard. "There was frightening talk about a gang of settlers camped outside town."

Franklin lowers his newspaper. "I was just reading about the tragic events out Germantown way… Shocking!"

"Farmers out there have been slaughtering peaceful Indians, taking the ax to men, women, children… Christians, no less!" Deborah empties her pockets on the table. "I picked up the post while I was in town."

Franklin puts down the newspaper. "'Tis revenge for Chief Pontiac's raids on their farms… Bloody and brutal, at that."

Aggie sets packages on shelves in the pantry. "Now they comin' to kill all the Indians here in town! I hope they ain't comin' after us black folk too!" she says anxiously.

"Even the Quakers are takin' up arms. We are gonna have us a war before this is over." Deborah hands an envelope to Franklin. "This letter come for you from Mrs. Stevenson."

"Read it to me." Franklin says, stirring his tea.

Deborah takes her spectacles from her pocket, sits at the table, and opens the envelope with a butter knife. She scans the first page of the letter. "Well, here's some news straight off," she says, reading slowly: *"I had a visit with the little one yesterday. He thrives and is three years old now. Plump and pink and bright as can be. There is quite a family resemblance."* Deborah looks up at Franklin. "I thought Margaret was past the age."

"Of course, she is," Franklin says nonchalantly. Deborah gasps. "You didn't, did you?!"

"Heavens, no! It's William's little boy."

"What? With Elizabeth?"

"No. With another woman."

"*There's* a family resemblance, all right," Deborah says smugly. "Why did you not tell me about this child?"

Franklin picks up his newspaper. "We've kept it quiet. Margaret's daughter, Polly, knows nothing about it, either."

Aggie takes her cloak and bonnet from a peg near the door. "I best go attend to my own business," she grins, and hurries out the kitchen door.

Deborah looks baffled. "How could William leave this boy in England?"

"The child is in the care of a good woman in the country," Franklin answers calmly.

"Dear Jesus! A sorry state of affairs if I ever heard one!" Deborah says as she pours herself a cup of tea.

A tap at the kitchen door and Jake peers in.

"'Scuse me, Dr. Ben, a gentleman come to see you."

"Who is it, Jake?" Deborah asks.

"The Governor, Ma'am," Jake replies.

"Governor Penn? Is he alone?" Franklin folds his newspaper.

"Yes, sir." Jake steps aside to reveal the Governor standing behind him. He wears leather riding breeches, a greatcoat and wide-brimmed hat.

Franklin jumps up and tosses the newspaper onto the chair next to him. "Your Excellency," he cries. "Come in, come in! This is an unexpected pleasure! Please allow me to introduce Mrs. Franklin."

The Governor offers a polite bow to Deborah and she attempts a curtsey in return.

"Mother, make a cup of tea for the Governor, would you?" Franklin invites Penn to join him at the table. Deborah goes to the fire and prepares tea.

Penn removes his hat and sits at the table across from Franklin. "I wish I were here on more pleasant business, but I have come to ask for your help in diffusing a crisis."

"Is this about the tragic business at Germantown?" Franklin inquires. "I have read something about it."

"Paxton Village, to be precise." Penn clarifies. "Before I continue, I must say I *am* sorry Uncle was not more kind to you at Spring Green."

"Think nothing of it," Franklin says.

"I have been getting on well with your son, by the way."

Deborah raises an eyebrow as she prepares tea.

Franklin looks surprised. "Have you?"

"Charming fellow… Good company. He's doing wonders with the roads in the province."

"That is good news," Franklin says with a half-smile. "How can I help you?"

Penn's tone darkens. "A gang of farmers is camped in the woods, not more than a few miles away. They threaten to invade the city and carry on with their massacre of the Natives. They call themselves God-fearing men! I fear a blood bath if we don't stop them."

Deborah serves tea and cake to Franklin and the Governor. "What do you propose?" Franklin inquires.

"Help me organize a defense of the city. Take command of the militia for the duration of the crisis," Penn replies.

"Forgive me, Governor, but would it not be more appropriate for me to carry a musket under your command?"

Penn adds milk to his tea. "Better you lead the way. You have the respect of the militia. They would rather take orders from you," he confides.

Deborah stands next to the hearth, with her arms folded across her chest.

"Have you a plan?" he asks the Governor.

"Yes. You will take a delegation of armed men out to the settlers' camp. Reason with the farmers and talk them out of coming into the city."

Deborah places her hands on her hips. "Have a party out in the woods with a gang of Germans that's got rifles and pickaxes? I won't have that!"

Franklin raises his hand. "Hush, woman."

Deborah bristles. "Don't you shush me! You ain't trained for such a battle. You will all lose your heads!"

Franklin ignores Deborah. "Have you any volunteers?" he asks the Governor.

Penn raises a forkful of cake. "I've spoken to ten men who are willing, and two young Indian guides."

"This is madness!" Deborah shrieks. She tears off her apron, tosses it onto a chair and storms out of the kitchen. Penn looks out the window, where snow is falling, quickly covering brown patches of grass. "My wife is also a woman of strong opinions," he offers.

They hear a door down the hall slam shut, quivering on its hinges.

"Aren't they all?" Franklin smiles weakly and sips his tea. "When do you propose we head out?"

"Tonight… after ten… to keep them off-guard," Penn replies. "They will be on the move before daybreak, if we wait."

OUTSIDE PHILADELPHIA

It nears midnight as Franklin and ten volunteer militia men walk in single file along a trail through dense woodland. They carry rifles and are led by two Indian guides, who have their knives bared. The troop moves along quietly, not speaking. Snowfall has stopped and a full moon lights their way. The woolen coats, fur hats and leather boots the militia men wear hardly warm them on this crisp, cold night, but their guides appear comfortable in deerskin clothing, moccasins on their feet, with their heads bare.

Franklin was surprised when meeting the guides at the trailhead to discover that one of them is a young woman with jet-black hair and skin the color of honey.

After a long trek through fresh-fallen snow, the guides signal they are near the German camp. A wisp of smoke from a campfire rises above the trees ahead. Franklin signals the column to stop. "Remember, when I give the word," he whispers, "cock your rifles sharply, rustle the leaves under your feet, make noise. Until then, not a sound."

One of his men looks ashen. "Couldn't this wait until morning?" he whispers.

Franklin raises his finger to his lips. "No. We'd be too late. Hush now."

Their Indian guides lead the volunteers to the edge of a clearing in the woods, where the German farmers have set up camp. Most of them are asleep in makeshift tents. A few are curled up near a campfire.

Two older men are posted as sentries. They are wrapped in blankets, warming themselves by the fire. They pass a bottle of spirits back and forth.

Franklin hears them speaking in German: *"I say we send a party at first light to burn the Quaker church. That is where they will hide the women and children,"* one of the sentries says.

"Good idea," the other man concurs.

Franklin gives a hand signal to his men, who surround the camp. A minute later, the Indian guides sneak into the camp and snatch rifles leaning against the primitive tents. They retreat back into the darkness.

Franklin takes a deep breath, gathers his courage, and strides boldly into the camp. "Good evening, gentlemen," he says cheerily, in full voice.

The two sentries are startled and freeze, their jaws drop, mouths open.

"Do you speak English?" Franklin calmly inquires.

One of the sentries nods his head.

Franklin forces a smile. "Good. I have come to have a visit with you. I *am* sorry to invade unannounced like this. Just the same, you might offer me a drink." One of the men hands the bottle to Franklin, who takes a swig and winces. "Ouch! Did you make that?" he gasps.

The sentry nods his head in agreement. "Da," he says.

"Very good. Very good. I am Benjamin Franklin."

"I know who you are. I seen you in town," the other man says. "I am Kraus."

A settler sleeping near the fire wakes up, rubbing his eyes.

"Fine, Herr Kraus," Franklin says, offering his hand. They shake hands. "I have come with a few friends of mine." He points to surrounding forest. "They are all around you, amongst the trees." He shouts into the woods. "Now, my friends!"

The militia men cock their rifles and stir the ground, shouting commands to one another. The sound in the camp is of a hundred men hidden in the trees.

Kraus is stunned. "Mein Gott!" he says to the other sentry.

A settler lying on a blanket nearby reaches for his rifle. Franklin sees the movement. "I wouldn't do that!" he shouts. "Tell your men, Herr Kraus, if one shot is fired in this camp, my men will open fire and you will all be killed, instantly!"

Kraus yells to his men, in German, to hold their fire. A few farmers sit up, groggily curious about the midnight visitor.

"Now, Herr Kraus," Franklin goes on. "Can we talk for a minute? Then we will be on our way and let you get back to sleep."

Kraus looks dazed, but offers Franklin a seat.

Franklin lowers himself onto a log by the fire. "I have a proposition for you. You lay down your weapons and go back home at first light, and I will arrange a meeting with Governor Penn and a delegation of your men to settle your grievances."

A young farmer lying outside the ring of firelight raises himself onto his elbows, picks up his rifle, and aims it at Franklin. An Indian guide, the woman, sees him from her hiding place behind a stout tree. She slides her knife from its scabbard and throws it at him. The blade whirs through the air and strikes the German in the shoulder with a *thwack!*

"Scheisse! Scheisse!" he cries and drops his rifle. He pulls the bloody knife from his shoulder, tossing it onto the ground. Blood gushes between his fingers as he covers the wound with his hand. "Verdammt!" he cries in pain.

The Indian retrieves her knife and retreats back to her hiding place.

Franklin continues his conversation with Kraus. "You will have an opportunity to air your grievances with the Governor. If you carry your arms into town, you will be annihilated."

He draws a finger across his throat. "Finished! Killed!"

"What about Pontiac?" Kraus demands to know.

"The Governor will enlist the help of British troops to punish Chief Pontiac and to protect you from raids on your farms in the future," Franklin assures him.

"You believe this Governor?" Kraus asks.

"Yes, Herr Kraus. I do. Do we have a deal?"

Kraus thinks hard for a minute. "Ya, we have a deal."

Franklin rises and offers his hand again. The two men shake hands over the dwindling fire. "Give me a few days to make arrangements. I will be in touch," he says. Thank you for the drink… Delicious."

Franklin shouts to his men, still hidden in the trees. "Let's go home, boys!" He doffs his fur cap to Kraus and walks calmly out of the camp, fighting the urge to break into a run. He disappears into the darkness.

CHAPTER TWENTY-TWO

Double-cross

FRANKLIN'S BEDROOM   APRIL 1790

Bobby rises from his seat on the edge of Franklin's bed. "I throw another log on the fire," he says, going to the fireplace.

"That homemade whiskey saved me, Bobby. The drink kept me from fainting dead away."

"That a true story, or you makin' it up?" Bobby calls from the end of the room.

"'Tis true... as I remember it now," Franklin replies thoughtfully.

Bobby settles an oak log onto the coals. "What about that Indian lady? The guide?"

"It turns out she was a princess of the Chippewa Tribe, from the northern Territory of Michigami. Winona was her name. A lovely creature. I believe she came to be the wife of a wealthy white man," Franklin says, hiding a grin.

Bobby stokes the fire, sending sparks swirling up the chimney. "You makin' that up, too."

"Has Mr. Bache come back home yet?" Franklin inquires.

"No, sir." Bobby leans the iron poker against the hearth.

"My grandsons?"

"Not that I know." Bobby brushes dirt from the log off his hands.

"Damn." Franklin goes on, "So, a week or two later, the settlers had their meeting with the Governor, as I had promised."

Philadelphia 1764

Kraus, the sentry from the camp in the woods, chose three other English-speaking farmers to join him in a delegation to meet with the Governor. They have ridden into town wearing the stiff attire they might wear to Sunday services at the Lutheran church in Paxton Village. Now they sit opposite John Penn at the large mahogany desk in his office, with their well-worn hats resting on their laps. They listen intently to what Penn has to say.

"You are, therefore," the Governor concludes, "exonerated of the charges which have been brought against you. I will sign papers to that effect, and have my secretary make a copy for you."

One of the farmers leans forward in his chair. "What means 'exonerated'?" he asks in a thick German accent.

"It means," Penn explains, "your alleged crimes have been forgiven, and you are free to go."

The foursome smile and nod to one another.

"You must keep your quarrels out of the city in the future, gentlemen," the Governor clarifies. "You angered the 'do-goods' around here. That caused me no end of trouble. Agreed?"

Kraus speaks up. "We agree. What about my idea for bounty?"

"I like it," Penn replies enthusiastically. "If word gets around that we are paying a five pound bounty for Indian scalps, the savages might stay well away from our plantations!"

"You pay same thing for man or woman?" Kraus asks.

"Makes no difference to me, Penn replies. "But make certain you bury the dead properly, or we'll have the Quakers up in arms again! He rises from his chair.

"Well, that should do it," he says with a broad smile.

The farmers rise from their seats and shake hands with the Governor. They put on their hats and coats and file out of his office in high spirits, jabbering in German, as they head for the tavern across the road.

FRANKLIN'S BEDROOM   1790

"As a means of thanking me for risking my life, the wretched man went on to veto every bill that came to him from the Assembly." Franklin looks into his teacup. "I'm empty, Bobby. Can you hear me?"

The new log has ignited and burns brightly, casting a warm glow on Bobby's face. "I can hear you." He fetches the wine bottle and refills Franklin's cup.

"I've been curious," Franklin says, raising the cup to his lips. "You said you hit something with your rifle the night you and Deborah were confronted by the mob. What was it?"

Bobby points out the window. "I shot the head off that cockerel across the street."

"What?" Franklin looks incredulous. Bobby looks outside. "Maybe too dark to see now, with the rain and all."

Franklin rises from the bed, shuffles to the window, and peers out. A streetlamp illuminates the roof of the carriage house across the street, where a weathervane topped by a headless rooster turns in the wind. "So you did! Well done, my boy!" Franklin exclaims.

Bobby chuckles. "Let's get you back to bed now 'fore Miss Sally come up here and make trouble." He escorts Franklin back to his bed.

"How to rid ourselves of the Penns once and for all became the question," Franklin continues. Bobby helps him into his bed and pulls the quilt over him as he lies back. "The Assembly chose to circulate a petition among the voters, asking for their assent in a plea to the Crown to assume control of the Colony. Why don't you pour yourself a cup, Bobby?"

"I wouldn't mind," Bobby replies.

"The Governor put up a fight."

OUTSIDE PHILADELPHIA   1764

John Penn is at the reins of a horse-drawn cabriolet as it rolls along a country lane on a warm, sunny afternoon in late summer. Trees lining both sides of the road are thick with leaves, casting cool shadows over him and his open carriage. Beyond the trees, golden fields of grain and corn wave in the wind. He turns into the drive of a modest, white-washed farmhouse.

He sees a woman sitting on a bench on the front porch with a dog curled at her feet. She is fiftyish, plain looking, and wears a house dress and apron. Her faded blonde hair is pulled back into a bun with strands falling here and there. She plucks a chicken and is surrounded by white feathers fluttering about her in the breeze. Her black and white hound jumps off the porch to greet Penn's arrival.

Penn pulls his carriage to a stop, steps down, and walks to the porch. The hound follows, barking and wagging its tail, sniffing at Penn's heels.

"Fritzie!" the woman calls from the porch. The hound obediently returns to her side, settling into the pile of feathers.

"Afternoon, Ma'am. Are you Mrs. Kraus?" Penn inquires, tipping his hat to her.

She looks at him with a blank look and continues plucking the chicken.

"Frau Kraus?" Penn asks again.

"Ja?" she replies.

"Is your husband at home?"

She does not respond.

"Herr Kraus?"

The woman motions toward a weathered barn across the yard and makes a gesture indicating 'around the back'.

"Thank you," the Governor nods. "Danke." He strides through tall grass on an uphill trek to the barn and wends his way around the board-and-batten barn. Rounding the corner, he comes upon farmer Kraus holding a squawking chicken under one arm, its neck resting on a tall tree stump. Kraus brings down an axe on the chicken's neck. Blood flies in all directions, splattering over Penn's face and over his good suit.

"Shit!" Penn exclaims.

"I am sorry, Governor!" Kraus looks appalled and takes a rag from his pocket, wiping blood off Penn's face. "I harvest some birds… Scheisse! Please forgive me!"

"No matter," Penn says, attempting to sound unperturbed. "I have come to ask for your help." He takes a kerchief from his pocket and wipes blood from his clothing.

"What can I do for you?" Kraus asks eagerly. He rinses his hands in a pail of water and wipes them on his trousers.

Penn dabs at his frock coat with his kerchief. "Convince your friends out here in the country to come into town and vote in the forthcoming election."

Kraus looks puzzled. "Vote for what?"

Penn speaks in confidence. "It is very important to my family. I will explain…"

Philadelphia　　　　　　　　　　November 1764

Late afternoon sun washes over a meeting room in the Assembly Hall. Moses Brooks, the Chairman of the Pennsylvania Assembly, listens patiently as Franklin paces the room and pontificates, his voice quivering with anger. "He should have hanged the bastards! Instead, he gave them a banquet!" Franklin fumes. "The bloody farmers, of course, owed Penn a favor. That cunning son-of-a-bitch… Our petition fell like a rotted tree!"

"Calm yourself, Ben," Brooks pleads. "Sit down and reason with me." He reaches for a carafe of wine on a sideboard behind him and pours two glasses.

Franklin joins Brooks at the table. "Do you not think it criminal, Moses, that such an act should go unpunished? I am ashamed to have been roped into the scheme."

"How could you have known? I see only one right move ahead for us, Ben. We must make an appeal to the King himself."

Franklin picks up a glass of wine. "The people fear a crown colony will bring the Church of England with it."

"That may not be so. Penn rigged the election. Let us write a draft of a Royal Petition and I will take it to the committee leaders for ratification in the morning."

Franklin sips his wine. "Who do you propose makes the journey to London to present this petition?" he inquires.

The Chairman looks squarely at Franklin but says nothing. After a moment, Brooks rises from the table and takes pen and paper from a drawer of the sideboard. "You dictate, I will write," he says. "You can redeem yourself."

Franklin's Bedroom   1790

Franklin pushes the quilt away and sits up in bed. "I felt it my duty to go to London, as you may well imagine."

Bobby looks into his cup of wine. "Mm-hm."

"I was most curious to see my grandson."

"Mm-hmm. 'Course you was. You best lay back down now and get some rest, or the 'lady' might come get you!" Bobby teases.

"You might have guessed that Deborah had something to say on the matter."

"I ain't surprised if she did."

Deborah's Bedroom   1764

Franklin walks along an upstairs hallway, balancing a silver salver set with a China tea service. He arrives at Deborah's bedroom door and hesitates there a moment. He raps lightly, then pushes the door open to find Deborah seated at her desk in a corner of the room, intent on her ledger books. Morning sun pours in from a window next to her desk. Her hair is pulled into a single braid at the back of her head, and she wears a light cotton robe over her night clothes. Embers of an early morning fire glow in the hearth nearby.

Deborah's bedroom is pleasant, if sparsely furnished. The walls are painted sage green, with creamy linen curtains on the windows. A four-poster bed occupies one wall, a settee sits opposite. The petite upholstered chair in which she nursed Franky sits in a corner of the room, like a relic. A small oil painting of Franky and one of Sally in her Christening gown hangs over the settee. A still life hanging on the wall next to her bed and two porcelain figurines on the fireplace mantel are the only other artworks adorning the room.

Deborah sits with her back to the door. "Set the tray on the bed, Aggie," she calls out, pouring over a column of figures.

"Yes, Ma'am," Franklin teases, in a falsetto voice.

Deborah turns with a start. "Ben! Where's Aggie?"

"I told her I would bring you your tea this morning. I'd like to have a visit with you."

Deborah waves a sheaf of invoices at him. "And I want to talk to *you* about your building project. Expenses have got out of hand."

Franklin sets the tray on a tea table in front of the settee. "You should take over, Mother. You are a much better manager than I."

"The good news," Deborah adds, "is our stationery shop had a very good month... Near twice the business we had last year. 'Course the warmer weather had somethin' to do with it."

Franklin sits on the edge of the bed. "I met with Moses Brooks over at the State House yesterday."

"How is the old bandit?" Deborah asks.

"He asked me to return to England on a mission for the Assembly."

Deborah closes the ledger book and turns in her chair. "Don't even think about it," she says firmly.

"'Tis but a brief assignment. A month or two at most."

"Don't lie to me! A month or two? Pshaw! I'll never see you again!"

"I will have one or two meetings with the Privy Council to present a petition to the King, then I'll turn around and sail home."

Deborah stands, tying her robe closed. "Why can't they send a younger man more fit for such a journey?"

"We haven't time for a new man to find his way. I wish you would come with me."

She walks to the settee and sits down. "You know I won't do that," she says.

Franklin rises from his seat on the bed and pours tea for her.

"I want you to do me a favor before you go," Deborah says calmly, squeezing lemon in her tea.

"Anything. What is it?"

"Marry me, Ben." Franklin joins her on the settee and caresses her cheek. "We *are* married."

"Not proper. Not by a preacher, not in a church," she pouts.

"And make a bastard of Sally?"

"It would give me peace. I don't want to lie all alone in the cold ground out in that cemetery until Jesus come for me. They bury married people together… as a regular matter."

"Our little Franky is there," he reminds her.

"You think I've forgotten?" she replies sharply.

"I assure you, my dear, that I will spend eternity at your side. I shall most likely precede you. A wedding ceremony is quite unnecessary." Franklin pats her knee, rises, and walks toward the door. "Drink your tea while it's hot."

"I know what the attraction is over there! I'm not a fool!" Deborah shouts.

Franklin stops and looks at her with a pained expression.

"I will be dead before you get back!" she predicts.

"Nonsense. I shan't be away long. You'll see." Franklin smiles weakly, turns and leaves the room, pulling the door closed behind him.

"I will *not* be here!" Deborah screams after him. She picks up the porcelain tea pot and hurls it at the door. It hits with a loud *bang* and smashes to bits, with tea flying in all directions. "I will not be here!" she screams again.

Franklin pauses in the hallway outside her door, wincing at the noise. "'Til death do us part, Mrs. Franklin!" he yells through the door. He shakes his head and walks on down the hall.

PART FIVE

The Cockpit

CHAPTER TWENTY-THREE

Mr. Temple

STEVENSON HOUSE, LONDON	DECEMBER 1764

The parlor at the front of the house is bathed in twilight as Benjamin Franklin settles into a comfortable wing chair near the entry hall, book in hand. He is in his shirtsleeves, his jacket is draped over the back of the chair. He removes his shoes, adjusts his wire-rimmed spectacles, and opens the book. Heavy velvet curtains on the windows are tied back with braided ropes, allowing a view of Craven Street outside, where a light snow falls on the cobbled street. Franklin's eyelids soon grow heavy. He dozes off and drops the book on the floor. It lands next to his shoes on the Turkish carpet beneath his feet. The room grows dark.

Peter enters the room. He lights an oil lamp on a bureau and candles on the side tables. He is a tall Negro man, nearing forty years of age, as far as is known. He bends down to look at his former master, smiles, picks up the book from the floor, and sets it on the table next to the chair. Peter goes to the fireplace at the far end of the room and stokes the coals. He pulls the curtains closed on the three tall windows facing the street, then leaves the room.

A few moments later, Margaret Stevenson opens the front door and enters the foyer. She wears a hooded opera cape and gloves, stops to brush snowflakes off her shoulders, and closes the door behind her. She removes her gloves, sets them on the entry table, and hangs her cape on a rack behind the door. She adjusts her hair in the looking glass above the table. Margaret is pleased with the reflection she sees. She finds it quite agreeable for a woman of fifty-six years. She steps into the parlor and places a folded program from the Opera House on the roundtable in the center of the room. She does not see Franklin in the chair behind her.

He is awakened by the sound of the door closing. "Hello," he says in a near-whisper.

"Ben!" Margaret shrieks as she turns to see him sitting in the wing chair. "How long have you been here? You are days early!"

"I was anxious to see you. I took a bellows to the sails! I've been here a few hours. You've been to the opera?" he inquires, bending to look for his shoes.

"Yes. Covent Garden. Handel. *Julius Caesar*", she says, resting her hands on the table behind her.

Franklin rises from the chair. "Glad I missed it," he comments. "Dull as a sober vicar."

"It was lovely. We had supper afterwards."

He stands with his hands in his pockets. "Out with a gentleman friend?"

"An old friend… Arbogast," she replies.

"Persistent, that Arbogast!" Franklin teases.

Margaret clasps her hands together in front of her, not moving from her place by the table. "Have you settled in? Did Peter carry up your bags?"

Franklin closes the buttons on his shirt and straightens his shirt collar. "He did, bless him, and he helped me to unpack."

"He must have been delighted to see you."

Franklin moves closer to her. "My rooms are just as I left them," he says with a note of surprise.

Margaret looks at her hands. "I haven't rented them."

"Why not?" he presses on.

Margaret ignores his question. She goes to the fireplace and warms her hands over the glowing coals. "You must be hungry," she suggests over her shoulder.

"Dear old Mrs. Jolliker fixed me something. Is Polly in? Mrs. Jolliker wasn't certain."

"Up in her room, sleeping, I hope."

"Shall I go up and wake her?"

"No!" Margaret turns to face Franklin. "Certainly not. Wait 'til morning. She will want to tell you all about her new beau."

Franklin moves still closer to her. He smells a hint of orange blossom in her perfume, a scent he remembers fondly. "I am happier to see you than I can say," he says, his eyes glistening.

"And I am happy to see you," Margaret says evenly. "How long will you be staying with us? Billy Strahan wasn't certain."

"Three, perhaps four, months," Franklin replies.

Margaret returns to the center table and toys with an arrangement of branches and dried leaves resting on it in a tall porcelain vase. "Oh, very good," she says.

"Have you seen little William Temple?" Franklin inquires anxiously.

"Not more than a week ago. He is very well." Margaret snaps a dried flower off its stem and offers it to Franklin. "It is time to dispose of these and get out the Christmas baubles, don't you think?"

Franklin sighs. "I was thinking that it might be nice to bring Temple to stay with us here for a while."

"He is quite content where he is. I think I'm going to keep Christmas simple this year," she says, changing the subject. "Perhaps just a small tree, in the German style." She walks around the table, picturing her holiday decor. "If Queen Charlotte can have a tree, so can I."

Franklin follows her. "He would bring some cheer to this old house," he offers brightly.

Margaret looks at him with a stern expression. "It would upset the boy to take him from Mrs. Noon for a few months, then return him to her. And I am not keen to return to the business of child-rearing. You should go for a visit tomorrow."

"Why don't you think about it?" Franklin persists.

"My answer is 'no'. Are you staying up? I am going to bed."

"I'm going to read a while longer."

Margaret walks toward the stairway. "Goodnight, then."

Franklin calls after her. "Not even a handshake?"

Margaret turns, walks back to him and extends her hand. "Welcome back, dear Ben."

He takes her hand in his and kisses it gently.

"Goodnight," she says, and goes to the stairway. She stops. "Look, Ben, I am not going to delude myself with an illusion of a blissful family life here, only to have you leave after a few months. It hurts too much."

Franklin nods his head. He watches her climb the stairs, then he returns to the wing chair and his book, which he does not bother to open.

Two weeks later, Margaret's parlor is decorated for Christmas. Branches of holly and evergreen adorn the fireplace mantel, garlands festooned with red ribbons and pinecones frame the archways. A small fir tree decorated with handmade paper ornaments and tinsel rests on the center table, which is draped with a green velvet cloth to the floor. Gaily wrapped packages surround the tree, and a gilded tin star atop the tree sparkles in the waning December sun.

Margaret's two elderly boarders, Mr. Bennett and Mr. Christie, are seated in easy chairs in the corner of the room, reading newspapers. A table between them is strewn with books and teacups. Both gentlemen wear waistcoats and stiff high-collared shirts. Mr. Christie holds a small, unlighted pipe in his mouth.

Polly enters the room. Now twenty-four, she has blossomed into a lovely young woman. Her auburn hair is combed off her forehead and is tied at the nape of her neck with a frilly ribbon. She carries a few gift packages and arranges them under the tree. She kicks something under the cloth. She lifts it, peers underneath, and finds Franklin hunched under the table.

"What are you doing down there?" she inquires incredulously.

Franklin is folded in two, his chin resting on his knees. "I've lost my spectacles," he replies.

Polly lowers the tablecloth as William Franklin's illegitimate son, Temple, runs across the room. He wears short breeches, a flannel shirt and leather tie shoes. "I find you, Papa Ben!" he screeches and runs out the doorway to the library.

"You are hiding, aren't you?" Polly says to the draped table.

Margaret enters the room. She wears an apron over her housedress, and has a scarf tied around her head to keep her hair in place.

She holds a dusting cloth in her hand. Margaret looks askance at Polly. "Why are you speaking to the table?" she inquires.

Polly points under the table. "Papa's down there."

Margaret lifts the cloth, and bends down to see Franklin. "Ben! Come out of there! You look ridiculous. It's teatime!"

Franklin crawls out from beneath the table, polishing his glasses with a kerchief as he struggles to stand. "Found 'em! How the wretched things got down there, I'll never know!"

"I have two five-year-olds on my hands now," Margaret says in mock disgust.

Mrs. Jolliker enters the parlor carrying a tea service and a plate of cakes on a silver salver. She wears a long white apron and a bonnet on her head. She sets the tray on a table in front of the settee near the fire. "I left the post on the hall table, Dr. Franklin. 'Tis a letter from Mrs. Franklin with it… all the way from America!" she says.

Franklin sorts through packages under the tree. "Wait… I have a little gift for you, Mrs. Jolliker. It's here somewhere." He finds the item he was looking for and hands it to her.

"Thank you kindly, Dr. Franklin." Mrs. Jolliker accepts the parcel, gives a little curtsey and scurries out of the room.

"What did you get for Mrs. Jolliker?" Margaret asks.

Franklin smiles. "A framed portrait of myself. I thought it might cheer up her dingy room in the basement."

In the corner of the parlor, Mr. Bennett lowers his newspaper, and leans close to Mr. Christie. "That's what he gave me two years ago," he confides.

Mr. Christie lowers his paper. "He gave me his book, 'The Way to Wealth'. I never read it," he admits.

"I'll trade you," Mr. Bennett offers.

Franklin and Margaret go to the settee and sit next to one another. Polly pours the tea, serving her mother first, then Franklin. "You know, Papa," she declares, "I don't recall ever meeting Temple's father, your friend… what was his name?"

"Newcomb. Edmund Newcomb. Perhaps you didn't." Franklin adds milk to his tea. "He lives in the Caribbean. Treacherous country for a child, that. Vipers. Mrs. Newcomb succumbed to a snake bite."

"Snakes? I hate snakes!" Polly says wide-eyed, pouring herself a cup of tea.

Margaret shouts into the next room. "Temple! Come! Teatime! We have cakes!"

"Mr. Newcomb will come for Temple eventually, won't he?" Polly asks.

"Perhaps sooner than you may think," Margaret volunteers, stirring her tea.

Temple squeals as he runs into the room and clambers onto Franklin's lap. He reaches for a cake from the plate on the table.

"Careful, lad! Don't spill the tea!" Franklin cautions.

"Shall I fetch Deborah's letter for you?" Margaret inquires.

"Yes, please do," Franklin replies.

Margaret rises from her seat and walks toward the entry hall. Franklin follows her admiringly with his eyes, which does not go unnoticed by Polly.

FRANKLIN HOUSE, PHILADELPHIA   OCTOBER 1764

Several weeks earlier, Deborah is seated at the kitchen table, writing a letter by candlelight. It is pitch dark in the yard outside, save for a sliver of light falling across the yard from a streetlamp on Market Street. Bobby stands behind her, tea towel in hand, drying dishes on the draining board of the wooden sink. The last of the evening's fire burns in the hearth and both wear warm clothing. Deborah has a black crocheted shawl draped around her shoulders.

"Dear Ben," she writes. *"All goes here as usual. I partake of none of the diversions, as work prevents it."*

"Pardon, Ma'am. You writin' a letter to Dr. Franklin?" Bobby inquires, not looking away from his chore.

"Yes. Would you like me to read it to you?"

"Yes, Ma'am, if you don't mind."

Deborah begins to read aloud as she slowly writes: *"The building work goes on apace, when the men show up, that is. Some days, Bobby and Jake must go down to the tavern on Bush Street and round up the boys."*

"Ain't that the truth!" Bobby says, chuckling.

"Now Christmas and cold weather is around the corner, all will go slow for a time."

Deborah lifts the paper, blows on the wet ink, and dips her pen in the inkwell. "What else should I tell him, Bobby?"

STEVENSON HOUSE, LONDON   DECEMBER 1764

Franklin stands by the fire, reading aloud from Deborah's letter. Temple has moved to sit in Margaret's lap. She and Polly listen to Deborah's news. Franklin adjusts his spectacles. "*'There is a great odds between a man's being at home and abroad, and a body is afraid she shall do wrong, so some things get left undone.'*"

He hears the bell ring at the front door.

"Shall I go on?" Franklin asks.

Margaret sips her tea. "Poor Deborah is afraid of making a mistake. I can't say as I blame her."

"What building works, Papa?" Polly inquires.

"We're putting up a large addition to our house on Market Street. I doubt I will see it finished." He folds the letter, sticks it in his pocket, and sits next to Margaret again. "I heard the bell," he says, looking toward the foyer.

"You've left Mrs. Franklin to look after all this?" Polly asks.

"Do not concern yourself, child. Deborah has a gift for telling men what to do."

Peter enters the parlor. "Mr. Strahan is here, Dr. Ben," he announces.

Franklin looks pleased. "Show him in, Peter."

Polly rises from her chair. "I'll fetch another teacup," she says, walking toward the stairway down to the kitchen. Temple jumps down from Margaret's lap and runs after Polly.

A moment later, Billy Strahan strides into the room. He is fuller of face than two years earlier, but he is still robust and smartly dressed. He juggles gift packages under his arms and pulls a wooden toy horse on wheels behind him.

"I come with glad tidings!" he announces cheerily.

"Is it something about a virgin birth in the East?" Margaret teases.

"Do you know of it?" Strahan replies. Franklin stands and places his arm around Strahan's shoulder. "We've already heard the good news. What have you in the packages? And the Trojan horse?"

"The pony is for the wee lad," Strahan explains. He offers a wrapped box to Margaret and a bottle tied with ribbon to Franklin. "Chocolates from Brussels for this lady, and French brandy for the gentleman. I do not intend to depart the premises until both have been consumed."

Margaret unwraps the candy box. "You are a dear man. I adore chocolate and Temple will be mad for the horse."

Strahan pulls a cigar from his pocket and displays it for Franklin. "And a rare cigar from Cuba, which I plan to share with you, sir."

"I've not tried one before," Franklin admits.

"Because they were unheard of here until we took Cuba from the Spanish in '62. So, some good came of our brief occupation!"

"Then, let us retire to the 'smoking room'," Franklin suggests. "Margaret, will you join us?"

Margaret unwraps the box of chocolates. "No, no. I am content here with my tea and my chocolate."

"We'll need our coats," Franklin advises Strahan.

As the two men leave the room, Margaret pushes the toy horse under the draped table. Franklin carries the brandy, and takes two glasses from a tray on a sideboard as they go to the entry hall to put on their coats. He leads Strahan through the house and out the back door to the yard.

The late afternoon sky is gray and dismal as the two men seat themselves on the back steps, pulling their coats closed about them. "Margaret won't have smoking in the house,"

Franklin says meekly. "I don't care for the smell of it, myself."

"She's a good girl, that Margaret… Runs a tight ship. Well, you must try this." Strahan takes the cigar out of his pocket. "'Tis fine tobacco, wrapped in tobacco leaves," he explains as he lights the cigar and passes it to Franklin.

Franklin studies it. "It resembles a dog's turd," he says. He takes a timid puff and coughs.

"Tell me, has your 'Pennsylvania as Crown Colony Petition' come before the Privy Council as yet?" Strahan inquires.

Franklin coughs a deep cough, and hands the cigar back to Strahan. "It slowly percolates up through the bureaucracy, but something else has got my attention at present."

"Oh?"

"The Prime Minister has proposed a bill forcing the Colonists to buy a government stamp for every piece of paper passing though their hands."

Strahan looks curious. "What kind of paper?" he asks, taking another puff of the cigar.

"Every kind! Deeds, leases, wills, newspapers, almanacs, even playing cards." Franklin opens the brandy bottle and pours them each a drink. "Deborah will be forced to collect the damned tax in her stationery shop."

"Has Grenville lost his mind?"

"His stamp tax will enrage the Americans. There is already a separatist fervor erupting around Boston, flowing south like molten lava."

Strahan takes a sip of brandy. "What will you do?"

"I am going to reason with Grenville before the bill passes the House. There are better means of raising the revenue which he claims to need so badly."

Strahan raises his glass in a toast. "Here's to the speedy demise of Grenville's Stamp Tax."

Franklin raises his glass. "Or of George Grenville!"

CHAPTER TWENTY-FOUR

A Dinner Party

London   February 1765

It is a sunny winter's day, but the air is chilling. Franklin and George Grenville, the Prime Minister, are walking at a leisurely pace through an avenue of stone statuary in a park. Grenville wears a woolen coat and silk scarf over his velvet jacket. Fancy ruffles on the cuffs of his shirt protrude from the sleeves of his coat. The curls of the silver wig on his head nearly reach his shoulders, framing the refined features of his face. Franklin wears a warm coat and has a scarf Margaret knitted for him wrapped around his neck. They tread carefully in their low-heeled pumps through patches of snow and ice.

Grenville sounds exasperated. "You see, Franklin, you really *must* leave these matters to the experts who know something about it."

"I beg to differ, sir. I do know something about the Americans. Your Stamp Tax will stir up a hornet's nest."

"I have made it a priority as Prime Minister, to right the Imperial finances. Your Indian wars have been a drain on the Treasury. It is time the Colonies pay a fair share for their defense." Grenville points to a park bench. "Let's sit here."

"We have put forward millions of pounds and thousands of men in arms to that end," Franklin argues, joining Grenville on the bench.

Grenville takes a cigar from his pocket and lights it. "I foresee a steady stream of income for the government with the stamps. Perfectly painless, in my view." He puffs on the cigar. Franklin fans away smoke drifting his way. "There is a better means of raising revenue," he suggests. "Let the government issue paper currency, paying six percent interest. Those who buy it will have the use of the principal, and the money supply will be increased for all. The rich will pay the tax, with no harm done to the poor," he offers brightly.

"Such paper must have something of intrinsic value behind it," Grenville retorts.

"His Majesty's *word* is of value, is it not?"

"Yes, yes," Grenville concedes. "But the Stamp Tax is much simpler. We need only hire a few agents to sell them, whereas your idea requires an entire new government department. However, I shall give it some thought." He pulls a second cigar from his pocket and offers it to Franklin. "Care to try one? The very finest tobacco from Cuba…"

Franklin shakes his head. "No, thank you, sir."

Grenville drops his lighted cigar on the ground and replaces the other cigar in his pocket. "You mustn't worry yourself, Franklin. We have been at this business a very long time. I *do* know what I am doing. Shall we be on our way?" He rises from the bench.

Franklin forces a smile, rises, and follows the Prime Minister along the gravel path.

STEVENSON HOUSE   APRIL 1765

Franklin and Margaret have dressed for a night out, a special occasion. He wears his black velvet suit and a crisp white shirt. She wears a shimmering long dress of gray satin trimmed with seed pearls, and a stylish feathered concoction in her hair. They stand together before a looking glass in the parlor, attending to details of their attire.

Franklin helps Margaret into her fur-trimmed evening cape. "Your costume, my dear, must include garments from your late husband's fashionable emporium. You look heavenly."

"So it does," she concurs.

"Did I mention that Sir John and Lady Pringle are joining us tonight?" he inquires.

"Good! They are delightful company."

"What time is Lady Shelburne expecting us? I don't recall…"

Margaret looks in the mirror, adjusting her hair and her diamond earrings. "Seven-thirty. Now, do remember to address her as 'Lady

Anne.' As the daughter of an Earl, she is 'Lady' by birth. Hannah Pringle is 'Lady' by marriage."

Franklin stands close to her, fussing with the gray wig on his head he had chosen for the occasion. "What's the difference?" he asks.

"The daughter of an Earl always goes through a door before the wife of a physician," she explains with a knowing smile.

"What was your father?"

"A fishmonger."

"Fishmonger? Then, henceforth, you shall be known as 'Lady Mackerel!'"

Margaret laughs and slaps him on his arm.

SHELBURNE HOUSE, LONDON   APRIL 1765

A passerby might not glance twice at the ordinary-looking façade of Shelburne House, cleverly configured to conceal what is behind it. Two older townhouses were combined into one, and a house at the rear of the property had been demolished to make way for a greenhouse and mews. When Franklin and Margaret arrive, the Shelburne's butler opens the door to an opulent interior: an entry hall with a gleaming marble floor, Chinese scenic paper on the walls, a massive crystal chandelier overhead, and a view through French doors to an orangery beyond.

Franklin and Margaret are shown to a relatively cozy damask-lined reception room, where they are greeted by the Shelburnes and aperitifs are served. Sir John Pringle and his wife, Hannah, arrive shortly thereafter, and animated conversation ensues.

Lord Shelburne, who is in his mid-thirties, has attained high status in the court of King George III; surprising, since Shelburne had been a confidant of Frederick, the late Prince of Wales, who was loathed by *his* father, King George II. Lady Anne, who is a few years younger than her husband, was born into a lofty position in society, and wears her beauty and title with the ease of a kid glove. Franklin looks into the fire burning in the black-and-white marble fireplace. *'What is the son of a candlemaker doing in such grand company?'* he wonders to himself.

After a time, dinner is served in a baronial dining room. His Lordship sits at the head of a long ebony table. Sir John is on Shelburne's right and Lady Pringle on his left. Franklin and Margaret sit opposite one another, with Lady Anne seated next to Franklin.

The diners are dwarfed by the high ceiling, where candles burn in crystal chandeliers. Tall windows are draped in voluminous yellow silk and topped with carved, silver gilt pelmets.

French chairs are covered in silk brocade, and the table is set with Dresden china and Irish crystal. Silver epergnes lift arrangements of petite roses above their faces, which glow with the light of candelabras in the center of the table.

Franklin looks at Lady Anne, seated on his left. She wears a billowing silk gown, with a sparkling diamond tiara on her head, and an emerald necklace about her neck. The necklace, Franklin notes, mirrors her lively green eyes.

Lady Anne sets down her fork and pats her mouth with her serviette. "Sir John, tell me," she says, while keeping an eye on the footmen serving the table, "have you attended to Queen Charlotte of late?"

Sir John sets down his fork. "I visited her just the other day. She is in excellent health. Sturdy German stock, you know."

"That is good news," Lady Anne says.

Pringle turns to Margaret. "I mentioned to Her Majesty that I would be dining here and with whom, and she told me, surprisingly, that you are an acquaintance of hers."

Margaret takes a sip of wine. "Yes, but only in passing. The wife of a dressmaker will always be a dressmaker."

"Whatever do you mean, my dear?" Lady Anne inquires.

Margaret sits back in her chair as a footman removes her dinner plate.

"My late husband was in the silk trade. From time to time, I take tea with an old friend from those days who assists the Mistress of the Robes. On rare occasions, the Queen herself joins us. We share a bit of gossip. You know…" Lady Anne smiles engagingly. "After dinner, you must tell me all!"

Hannah Pringle joins in. "Yes, Margaret… And don't spare the details!"

"If you ladies reveal any state secrets, I shall be very cross," Lord Shelburne teases. He turns to Franklin. "It would appear, Dr. Franklin, the Prime Minister is going to have his Stamp Tax after all."

"I might as well have stopped the sun from setting as talk him out of it," Franklin concurs.

"As long as it is to be, why not think of a few good men to help us collect the tax?" Shelburne suggests.

"I do owe you that favor, My Lord. You have been more than generous with lands granted to me," Franklin offers.

"Before long, you will be expected to pay taxes on thirty thousand acres of Nova Scotia," Shelburne reminds him.

"I happily assume the challenge," Franklin says. "That is why my partners and I have formed the Grand Ohio Company. We propose to create an entire new colony for His Majesty in the West."

Sir John looks up from his food. "Is your son, William, a partner in the venture?"

"Yes. As I wish you were, John."

Lord Shelburne's brow is furrowed. "As I am Colonial Secretary for the South only, you must get your scheme past Lord Hillsborough. He is not as fond of things American as am I."

Lady Anne looks at the other ladies. "Would you care to see the conservatory after dinner? Let us leave the men to talk of their land swindles!"

"I would be delighted," Margaret says.

Later that evening, Franklin, Sir John and Lord Shelburne retire to His Lordship's oak-paneled library. Pringle holds a pipe in his hand, while Lord Shelburne takes a cigar from a leather box on his desk and lights it.

Pringle draws on his pipe. "Are you not concerned, Ben, that lobbying for tracts of land as vast as Ohio and Illinois will be perceived as feathering your own nest?"

"To what shall I return, Sir John, if not these new territories? I retired from my business to come here at the behest of the Assembly."

Shelburne sets his cigar on a plate on the table next to his chair. "He is quite right, Pringle. Such are the spoils of diplomatic service. Our people have taken plantations all over the world, whether or not the natives like it." Shelburne rises, goes to a drinks cabinet, and pours three glasses of brandy. "Ancient stuff… From the Armagnac region," he says as he serves Franklin and Pringle each a glass.

Pringle twirls the amber liquid in his glass. "Your son is Royal Governor, after all. What are his constituents to think?"

Franklin sniffs his brandy. "William may need to come in out of the rain one day," he confides.

Shelburne looks at Franklin. "Do you sense a storm brewing?"

"I am afraid I do. And it will be fierce."

Shelburne raises his glass. "If such a disturbance is to come, may it pass with little damage done." Franklin and Pringle join in the toast. "Here, here!" they cry in unison.

STEVENSON HOUSE   APRIL 1765

Margaret sits up in her bed with feather pillows propped behind her. An oil lamp burns on the night table next to the bed. Franklin sits on the edge of the bed with a glass of brandy in hand. "The nerve of that woman! 'Land swindles', indeed!" he barks.

"Oh, come now. Lady Anne was teasing you."

Franklin offers his glass to Margaret. She takes a sip of brandy and smiles devilishly. "What would you call your scheme, if not a land swindle?"

"Pringle *is* concerned about the appearance of our enterprise."

"Because he is a true friend and cares about you."

"By the way, he and I have decided to travel in Germany together next summer… to ogle the frauleins," Franklin says smugly.

"Good! Stay over there!" Margaret jests.

Franklin removes his wig and sets it on the dresser. He begins to unbutton his linen shirt. "I thought I might stay here with you for a moment."

"For a moment only. Dim the light."

Franklin turns down the light.

"I warned His Lordship that unrest in the Colonies may soon boil over," Franklin says, laying his shirt on the back of a chair. "He was not overly concerned."

"Nor was Pharaoh." Franklin turns off the light.

Hughes Residence, Philadelphia   August 1765

John Hughes is seated at the desk in his study writing a letter by candlelight. He wears a nightshirt and looks as though his sleep has been disturbed. He dips his quill pen into the inkwell. *"Dear Ben,"* he writes. *"This may be the last letter you will receive from your old friend, as the spirit of rebellion has reached a high pitch among the Americans."* A rock flies through the window behind him, shattering it. Startled, Hughes drops to the floor. A moment later, a hammer is thrown through another window, shattering it and knocking an oil lamp off a table. Burning oil spreads over the wooden plank floor. Hughes grabs a blanket folded on a wing chair and damps the fire with it. He hears the angry shouts of a mob surrounding his house. Windows break in the parlor as more rocks are thrown. He cowers under his desk, doubting he will live through the night.

Stevenson House, London   September 1765

Several weeks later, Franklin stands in the parlor reading John Hughes's letter.

Margaret sits in a chair nearby, knitting. "You look troubled. Does Mr. Hughes send bad news?"

Franklin looks over at her. "I stupidly put forward his name as Stamp Tax Commissioner for Pennsylvania, which has caused the poor man no end of trouble. It was John, by the way, who moved in the Assembly that I be dispatched over here to do battle with the Penns."

"Bless John Hughes," she says. "What news has he?"

Franklin adjusts his spectacles and returns to the letter. *"A sort of frenzy or madness has got such a hold of the people,"* he reads aloud. *"I fancy some lives will be lost before the fire is put out. I am threatened that my house shall be pulled down and the stamps burnt. I will defend my house at the risk of my life!"* Franklin looks pale. "My God, what have I done?"

Margaret rises from the chair and goes to Franklin. She places her hand on his arm.

"Let us pray that Mrs. Franklin is not in danger," she says.

FRANKLIN HOUSE, PHILADELPHIA   SEPTEMBER 1765

Daylight fades as Deborah crouches under a window in the sitting room. She peers out, watching as several men outside gather around the house. She hears them crunching through fallen leaves and murmuring to one another. The men appear menacing: some wear masks, some are disguised with Indian war paint, a few of them carry lighted torches.

"Christ! What new hell is this?" she wonders aloud.

Deborah gets up and moves quickly from room to room, blowing out candles, trying not to be seen. She runs to the kitchen, out the back door, and across the yard to the servants' quarters. She pounds on the door with her fist. "Jake!" she yells. "It's me! Open up! We got us a bad situation!"

LONDON   SEPTEMBER 1765

Franklin and Margaret walk arm-in-arm along a gravel path in a park, disturbing fallen leaves as they go. The afternoon sun is weak, but there is little wind and the air is too warm for winter coats. Margaret has a shawl draped over her shoulders, he wears a waistcoat over a linen shirt.

"You *will* accept his invitation, won't you?" Margaret asks.

"Yes, but I do find it odd that the King's equerry has invited me to tea at Carlton House."

Margaret tightens her grip on Franklin's arm. "Perhaps Major Price seeks your advice on something or other."

"Why me? Why Carlton House?"

"Lord Shelburne may have put your name forward… or Dr. Pringle might have. You should be flattered."

"That I am… but still baffled." Franklin places his hand on Margaret's hand and they walk on, not speaking for a time, relishing the last hours of summer.

CARLTON HOUSE, LONDON

A few days later, a footman in royal livery shows Franklin into a sunny drawing room on a front corner of the massive, white stucco house. The footman advises Franklin to wait a few moments and leaves the room, pulling the double doors closed behind him.

Franklin surveys the generous room, where velvet curtains hang from swags and tassels. Ivory damask covers the walls above painted wainscoting, and ornate gilded mirrors hang over commodes sitting between the tall windows. He looks in one of the mirrors, straightens his wig, and brushes dust from the shoulders of his frock coat. He adjusts his spectacles and studies a landscape tapestry hanging on one wall and portraits hanging on another. Franklin looks at his pocket watch, wondering how long Major Price, the equerry, will keep him waiting. He sits in a French-style chair, crossing and uncrossing his legs. He flicks a speck of dirt off a black leather pump.

Suddenly, the door opens. A page stands at the threshold and announces, "His Majesty, the King!" Franklin is astonished to see King George III stride into the room. The king is attired in scarlet for riding, with tall black leather boots on his feet and a tricorn hat in his hand. Franklin had forgotten how young the man is: he is just twenty-eight. Franklin had seen him, but infrequently, since attending his coronation in 1760. Franklin jumps to his feet and bows.

"Your Majesty." Franklin's legs feel weak under him.

"The famous Dr. Franklin," the King smiles. "I hope I haven't kept you waiting."

"Not at all, sir," Franklin stammers.

"Major Price thought it best if we meet privately. Do sit down." Franklin resumes his seat.

The King throws his hat on a table and sits in a gilded chair opposite Franklin. "I thought it might amuse you to see this rambling old house. My father, Frederick, was fond of it. As Prince of Wales, he kept his family at Leicester House and his affairs here… A neat arrangement. The gardens out the back are quite pretty. You must see them afterwards."

Franklin lays one hand on top the other to keep them from trembling. "I would enjoy that very much," he says.

"My mother thinks to renovate this house. I would rather tear it down. Are you comfortable on Craven Street?" the King inquires.

Franklin is surprised by the question. "Yes, sir, very," he replies.

"Good. You haven't travelled much this summer, I am told."

"Dr. Pringle and I hope to tour Germany next year," Franklin offers.

The King leans back in his chair. "Good man, that Pringle. A Scotsman, you know. He looks after my uncle, the Duke of Cumberland, and my wife, the Queen. Stupid *English* doctors killed my grandmother. You are aware my people are from Germany?" he asks.

"Yes, sir."

"My grandfather wished to be buried over there, but protocol would not allow it." The King reaches for a silk cord on the wall behind him and pulls it. "Quite frankly, my father would have preferred it."

A uniformed butler opens the door. "Sir?" he asks.

"Bring us some tea," the king commands.

The butler bows and shuffles out of the room, backwards. "Now, down to business. You may not know, Franklin, that my old friend, the Earl of Bute, put the Prime Minister up to instigating the now notorious Stamp Tax."

"I had no idea," Franklin admits.

"Well, the Earl has changed his mind. He suggested I get your thoughts on the matter."

"I see…" Franklin imagines pieces of a puzzle coming together.

"The Americans have gone quite wild over those little stamps, have they not?" the King says.

"The people wish to have a say with regard to internal taxation. That is at the heart of the disturbance," Franklin explains.

"*'Render unto Caesar, sayeth the Lord,*'" the King says.

"Yes, but the colonies strain under massive debts left from the French and Indian Wars," Franklin responds. "There is a better way."

"Is there?" The King takes a newspaper clipping from his pocket and opens it. "I have here a letter published recently in the papers, written by a person calling himself 'Homespun'."

The butler enters with a silver tea service and sets it on a tea table between the two men.

"Leave it," the king orders brusquely.

The butler backs out of the room again.

"The letter is addressed to 'Master John Bull'."

Franklin looks at the herringbone pattern of the wooden floor as the King reads:

"*'You have mixed with your virtues a haughtiness and contempt to all but yourself, that will, if not abated, procure you a handsome drubbing one day.'*"

The King tosses the paper aside. "You may lay down your pen. We have instructed Lord Rockingham to form a new government. Grenville is out. We wish an end to the rebellion."

"That is good news indeed, sir," Franklin looks relieved.

"I want you to address the Commons… Explain the situation in my Colonies."

"I am no orator, but I would be pleased to speak, if it is your wish."

"Good." The King points to the tea table. "You may pour," he says.

Franklin pours tea for the King, then for himself, his hand shaking slightly.

"Here's some help for you," the King offers. "Rockingham will provide the questions to be put to you in advance. You will have time to prepare your responses. If you make a good job of it, your insolence may be forgiven." The King takes a sip of tea. "There is talk of an appointment for you as Colonial Undersecretary. We shall see. My Council will soon take up another matter of interest to you, 'though I am not inclined, as you are, to pitch the Penn family into a dustbin."

"I shall look forward to the Council's deliberations," Franklin says.

The King sets down his teacup and rises from his chair. Franklin rises and sets down his cup.

"If you will excuse me, I must change my clothing for the evening. Since much substance has been taken from us, we must rely more on appearances," the King says. "Finish your tea. A page will show you out."

Franklin bows as the King leaves the room and closes the door behind him. Franklin takes a sip of his tea while waiting for the page to come for him. He feels euphoric.

In the hallway outside, Thomas Penn leans against the wall near the door. He stands to attention when the King emerges from the room. "Did you hear all that, Thomas?" the King asks him.

"I did, sir. Very smoothly done, sir," he replies.

"We shall see how well he plays his part. Come. Let us have a drink," the King says, leading Penn down the corridor at a pace.

CHAPTER TWENTY-FIVE

The Swimming Lesson

WILTSHIRE, ENGLAND

It is an exceedingly pleasant day for early October. A hawk flies lazily, circling over a grand manor house which is surrounded by manicured lawns and gardens. The mansion is in the Tudor style, with slate roofs sprawling in several directions. Pruned yew trees line a long cobbled drive from a country road leading to the estate. A half-dozen carriages are stopped under the porte-cochere to one side of the house. The hawk looks down on the stables nearby, where grooms attend to the horses, brushing their coats and covering them with blankets bearing the heraldry of their owners.

The hawk flies on over a pond beyond a knoll, well-removed from the house. The color of the pond is the azure of the sky above it. Three or four acres in size, it is surrounded by tall reeds, save for a few yards of sandy beach at the foot of the grassy knoll.

Margaret sits on a blanket spread over the grass, preparing a picnic lunch. She takes bread, slices of ham, a wedge of cheese, and a jar of pickled tomatoes from a hamper. She wraps cutlery in cotton serviettes.

She wears a light summer dress, its short sleeves and scooped neckline revealing a bit of her upper arms and shoulder blades. She had left the manor house earlier, decorously wrapped in a colorful India shawl. Her skin is very white, including on her legs and bare feet.

Franklin kneels in the sand at the edge of the pond. A stiff breeze ripples the surface of the water. He rolls up a cuff of his shirt and tests the water with his hand. "Water's perfect for a swim!" he calls to Margaret with boyish enthusiasm.

"Then you must take one!" she calls back to him.

Franklin looks about the countryside. The leaves on the trees have gone to color. Some fall, drifting in zigzags to the ground like feathers. The warm breeze caresses him. "Back home, we call this an 'Indian Summer'," he shouts to Margaret.

Margaret laughs. "Here, we call it a rare day!"

Franklin picks up a cane he has hidden in the grass. "Look, Margaret! I have found a magic cane! I wager I can calm the waters of the lake with it!" He reaches out and waves the cane over the water in a sweeping motion, smoothing the ripples to a glassy surface.

"I know that trick!" Margaret shouts. "You have oil hidden in that cane. Now come and eat something!"

Franklin joins her on the blanket. He stretches his legs and wiggles his bare toes. He leans over and kisses her neck. "So, I've shown you that one before, have I?" he asks.

"'Tis endlessly fascinating," Margaret teases. She smiles and touches her hand to the spot on her neck where he kissed her. She butters a slice of bread for him. "Open the wine, will you, Ben?"

Franklin takes a bottle of wine from the wicker basket. "Aren't you blessed to know people with a lovely place such as this?"

"I've been coming to the De Guignes' since I was first married. Maurice was Giles's cousin."

"Another French connection," Franklin says, pulling the cork from the bottle. He studies Margaret's placid expression, then changes the subject. "I lay awake last night fretting about my forthcoming appearance before the Commons. A command performance!" He locates two wine glasses in the hamper.

"We'll rehearse again when we get home. You have plenty of time…"

Franklin sniffs the cork, then pours two glasses of wine. "I always say, '*If one fails to prepare, one prepares to fail*'."

Margaret groans and looks heavenward. After a pause: "Will you book passage to Philadelphia for Sally's wedding?" she inquires.

"Why? Do you wish me to go? I would be a least a half year on the return."

"No… I was just curious." She raises her wine glass. "Santé," she says.

Franklin clinks glasses with her. "I had William look into the finances of this Mr. Bache of whom Sally is enamored, and they are a scandal. I wrote to Deborah suggesting they wait until he can support a family."

"A woman in love cares little for a man's finances."

"I won't be going to any wedding. I have too much to do here." Franklin takes a bite of bread and ham.

Margaret sits close to Franklin with a plate on her lap, her legs stretched out, her foot touching his. "I predict that young Dr. Hewson will propose to Polly before long," she says.

"The brute! He had better not! She's just a child!" Franklin chuckles.

"She will ask for your blessing."

"Well, I shan't give it. I would prefer she marry me." Franklin sets his plate and wine glass aside. "Let's go for a swim! We'll eat afterwards."

"I'm sure the water is too cold for me," Margaret demurs. Franklin pulls Margaret up from the blanket. "Come! The water is perfect!" He strips off his breeches, runs to the pond wearing only his linen shirt, and dives in. He swims submerged for a few strokes, then springs up, shaking water from his thinning hair. "Come!" he shouts to her.

Margaret strips down to her cotton shift. She runs to the pond, laughing and screaming, "You are a crazy man!" They stand in shallow water and circle one another, splashing each other with their hands. Franklin falls onto his back and does a perfect backstroke for several yards. Margaret is unable to keep up using her dog-paddle stroke and watches him swim away from her.

Franklin stops, standing in waist-deep water, his wet shirt clinging to him. "Why do I think the King is keeping an eye on me?" he shouts to her.

"This is no time to think of that!" she shouts back, crossing her arms over her breasts, now visible through her wet shift.

"Is that the only stroke you know?" he asks, wading over to her.

Margaret nods, brushing wet hair off her forehead.

"Did I tell you I once swam the Thames from Chelsea to London Bridge, on a dare?"

"And you lived to tell of it?"

"Allow me to demonstrate," Franklin offers. "You do not breathe on every stroke, and then on one side only… Watch me." He swims a crawl stroke. "You try it. I will help you." He places his arm around Margaret's waist and urges her to lie prone in the water. "Try the stroke I just showed you. Kick your legs," he commands.

Margaret attempts the crawl stroke, reaching her arms in an arc into the water. Franklin holds her tightly and walks with her. "Do my arms look all right?" she asks, kicking furiously.

"No," he replies. "But your bum is perfection."

"Put me down!" she cries.

Franklin releases her and stands next to her in the shallow water. He brushes water from her brow with his forefinger, lifts her chin and looks into her eyes. He gently kisses her lips. They embrace, his hand following the contour of her back through her wet clothing.

"I find myself in a place I promised myself I would not go," she whispers.

"I am happy to be in that place with you," Franklin says.

Westminster, London — February 1766

As usual, a wet and dreary winter follows the Christmas season in London. Franklin's appearance before the Commons is to take place on a particularly gray and gloomy day. As he walked to his carriage early that morning, Franklin's eyes burned and he struggled to breathe air laden with the smoke of countless coal fires.

Inside the House of Commons, faint light streams through the Gothic windows of the lofty chamber, adding luster to the dark paneled walls.

Franklin is called to testify before the Commons late in the morning. He stands on one side of a long oak table facing the Marquess of Rockingham, who stands at a lectern opposite him. Lord Rockingham, recently made Prime Minister at only thirty-five years of age, is slender in figure and in face. His nose is sharp and prominent, his eyes dark and penetrating. His chestnut-colored hair is combed off his forehead and into a ponytail tied with ribbon at the nape of his neck. Franklin's simple frockcoat contrasts with Lord Rockingham's rich green velvet coat, trimmed with gold applique and braid, under which he wears a shirt trimmed with lace and ruffles.

Members of the House, including George Grenville, are seated in the gallery behind Rockingham. One of the members concludes his questioning of Franklin: "And you would say the people have not the same respect today?"

"No, it is greatly lessened," Franklin replies.

Another member stands and shouts a question: "You, sir, would have us believe the colonies are unable to pay the Stamp Duty?"

"There is not enough gold or silver in the colonies to pay the Stamp Duty for one year," Franklin replies.

A third member stands. "Do you think military force could be employed to compel the colonists to pay the tax?"

"I do not see how a military force could be applied to that purpose," Franklin argues.

"And why not?"

"Suppose such a force is sent to America. They will find nobody in arms. What are they to do then? They will not find a rebellion, but they may indeed make one!"

Murmuring arises from the members.

George Grenville jumps up, waving his hand in the air.

"I recognize the former Prime Minister," Rockingham calls.

Grenville locks eyes with Franklin. "You make a distinction between 'internal' and 'external' taxes, which is ridiculous. If the Stamp Tax is 'internal', are we to expect 'external' taxes to be paid willingly?"

"'Internal' taxes must be levied in the constitutional way, by vote of the colonial assemblies. 'External' taxes, such as a duty on manufactured goods imported into the country, are another matter," Franklin clarifies.

"You are splitting hairs!" Grenville retorts. "The colonies must pay, one way or another, for the defense provided for them by Royal Forces!"

"During the last war we raised near 25,000 men and spent many millions," Franklin replies calmly. "We must come together now to restore harmony within the Empire. The Stamp Act is onerous in that regard."

A din of voices sweeps over the gallery. Lord Rockingham pounds his gavel on the table.

"Let us not, my lord Prime Minister, belabor the distinction between 'internal' and 'external' taxes," Franklin continues. "The Americans, who have heretofore seen a difference, may come to see merit in an argument to the contrary!"

Shouts of "Here, here!" arise from the gallery. Grenville resumes his seat, a sour look on his pretty face.

Outside London   1766

Thomas Penn is seated at the desk in his study at Spring Green, composing a letter by candlelight. He sips brandy from a glass on the desk, then dips his quill into the inkwell and writes: *'My Dear Nephew. Dr. Franklin revels these days in his victory in the House of Commons. The Stamp Act has gone down to defeat by a wide margin. Poor Grenville. Our friends are down, but clearly not out.'*

Philadelphia   1766

Some weeks later, after its voyage across the Atlantic, Penn's nephew, John, reads the letter from Spring Green. He is seated in a comfortable chair in his library, with a coffee cup in his hand. *'There is better news,'* his uncle writes. *'The Privy Council has deferred action on Franklin's petition to wrest our plantations from us. The issue is, therefore, forever dead. You shall enjoy your governorship into the foreseeable future. Do keep close to William Franklin in New Jersey, however, as we may yet need him.'* John smiles, sets the letter on the table next to him, and drinks his coffee, pondering his uncle's words.

CHAPTER TWENTY-SIX

Holy Matrimony

Stevenson House, London   Spring 1766

Messrs. Bennett and Christie are seated opposite one another at a trick-track table in the library, playing a game of checkers. They strain to see the game board in the fading evening light, but have not yet bothered to light a candle. Mr. Bennett rests his chin in his hands, with his elbows on the table, determining his next move.

Distracted, Mr. Christie looks through the archway to the parlor, where an arrangement of garden flowers adorns the center table. He sees Margaret enter the room. She is dressed in evening wear, her hair worn up and jewels sparkling on her ears and neck. She adjusts her long white gloves as she walks toward the entry hall to retrieve her cloak.

A shoeless Franklin hurries into the parlor, waving a letter he holds in his hand. "Margaret! Wonderful news here from John Hughes!" he cries.

Margaret stops in the foyer and looks in the mirror as she dons her velvet cape.

"Listen to this!" Franklin reads excitedly from the letter: "*Dear Ben, There are bonfires and rejoicings in the streets at the news of Lord Rockingham's ascension to power. I remain armed, but hopeful my house is spared.*" Franklin speaks to Margaret in the mirror. "Just think of the joy to come when people hear the Stamp Act has been repealed!" He looks her up and down, noticing her attire. "And where would you be going, my dear?" Franklin inquires.

"To the opera," she replies off-handedly.

"What opera?"

"Monteverdi. *L'Orfeo*."

"Heavens! That old war horse? You didn't tell me you were thinking of going to the opera," Franklin says, sounding miffed.

"It didn't occur to me. You hate ancient music."

"And so I do," he allows. "With whom are you going? Wait! Don't tell me… Arbogast?"

"Yes," she confirms, adjusting her cloak.

"Is he picking you up here? Good! I shall get to meet the old bastard… at last!" Franklin says gleefully.

"No, no. I am walking to the Opera House."

"Then, give me a minute to find my shoes. I shall walk with you."

"No need. Don't worry, it's just a few streets away. There are many people out and about, I'll be fine. Enjoy your solitude. Read a book. Better yet, write one!" Margaret gives him a peck on his cheek. "I shan't be late," she says and hurries out the door.

Franklin looks after her with a bewildered look on his face. After a moment, he finds his shoes on the stairway, puts them on, takes a jacket from a hook in the front hall, and scurries outside.

In the library, Mr. Bennett has made his move on the checkers board. "Franklin can't shake that Arbogast, can he?" he comments.

Mr. Christie nods in agreement. "No, he's like the rash on my testicles."

It is nearly dark in the West End when Franklin finds Margaret standing on a corner of the Strand. Throngs of theatregoers pass by her as she waits… *'Waits for what?'* he wonders. He hides behind a building and peers around it. Moments later, an elegant coach-and-four, with the royal insignia embossed on its side, clatters up to the corner and stops. Franklin has a clear view of the grand rig from his vantage point.

A coachman in royal livery jumps down and opens a door for Margaret. Franklin sees a bejeweled young woman seated inside. Her tiara sparkles in the light of the streetlamp. She smiles as Margaret steps up and into the carriage. The coachman closes the door and resumes his position at the back of the coach and the carriage lurches on down the street. "Arbogast, be damned!" Franklin mutters to himself.

DEAR BEN

Franklin House, Philadelphia   October 1767

Sally stands at the kitchen table, kneading bread dough. Her mother stands opposite her. Deborah has floured a board on the table and works a ball of dough into the form of a loaf of bread. Both women wear aprons streaked with flour. Baskets at the far end of the table are piled high with pumpkins and squashes and other bounty of the autumn harvest.

Aggie takes freshly baked loaves from the oven and places them on a cooling rack. Sally's spaniel is curled up on the floor near the oven and Aggie is careful to step over him.

Deborah speaks across the table to Sally, "I wrote to your Pa and told him, as I am obliged to be both mother and father to you, the least he could do is attend your wedding. Well, we'll see."

"I *will* be heart-broken if Papa doesn't come," Sally admits. "He wouldn't do that to me, would he?"

"There will be a wedding with or without him. I ain't gonna make an old maid out of you on his account," Deborah says, punching the ball of dough into shape.

"What's keeping him over there? He got rid of that stupid Stamp Act. He should come home now!" Sally places the dough in a bowl, covers it with a tea towel, and sets the bowl on a sideboard to rise.

"There's only one thing I know of that will keep a man from his family," Deborah says with bitterness in her voice.

"Mm-hm. Listen to your Mama, now," Aggie says.

Sally covers her ears with floured hands. "I don't want to hear about it!"

"You will soon enough," Deborah warns and cuts a slit in the top of the loaf with a long, sharp knife.

The wedding proceeds, as Sally's fiancé, Richard Bache wishes, before the first snowfall blankets Philadelphia. Mr. Bache is not about to let the daughter of a wealthy man slip away, plain looking though she may be. It is Bache's supposition, what is more, that Franklin cares not at all for church weddings, since he couldn't be bothered with a ceremony before a preacher for himself and his own spouse.

MICHAEL KOSKI

Stevenson House, London   Spring 1770

It is nearing noon as Peter assists Franklin with the finishing touches to his formal attire. Franklin wears a gray coat with tails, flared in the back, and matching waistcoat over a crisp white linen shirt. Franklin stands still, with his chin raised, as Peter ties his white silk cravat. Peter unties it, and ties it a second time.

"Hurry up, Peter," Franklin urges. "How are the ladies coming along?"

"I ain't allowed to see the bride, but she be along in due time." Peter steps back and studies his handiwork. "You look real nice, Dr. Ben."

"Thank you." Franklin studies his own reflection in a cheval mirror.

A light tap at the door. "Come," Franklin calls out.

Mrs. Jolliker opens the door a crack and peers in. She wears a frilly pastel frock with a bonnet to match. The crags in her face seem to have smoothed out somehow. "I'll be along with the maid soon as the church service is over and tidy up your rooms for ye," she says apologetically.

"Not to worry, Mrs. Jolliker," Franklin assures her. "Let's have a look at you!"

Mrs. Jolliker blushes and steps into the room. Her skirt flares as she does a turn. "Do I look a fright?" she asks shyly.

"You are as pretty as a picture, my dear."

"How you carry on!" she giggles and dashes out the door.

Franklin turns to Peter. "Have we finished here? Let's go downstairs and have a drink."

Peter follows Franklin as he hurries down the stairs to the parlor. Peter takes a key from his pocket and unlocks the doors of a tall mahogany cabinet. He takes out a bottle of whiskey and pours a shot for Franklin. Franklin gulps the drink down. Peter pours him another.

"Leave the bottle," Franklin says. "My nerves are wound like a cuckoo clock."

Peter pockets the key to the cabinet and goes on his way. Franklin paces the room and looks at his pocket watch.

Mr. Shearer, a newcomer to Craven Street, saunters into the room. He is portly and gray-haired, with a widow's peak that has not receded with the rest of his hairline. His olive-green wool jacket is buttoned closed over his midriff with considerable effort. He carries a newspaper folded under his arm and has a teacup in his hand. He settles into a comfortable chair.

Mr. Shearer opens his newspaper and watches Franklin pace back and forth. "You getting married, Franklin?" he asks after a moment's hesitation.

Franklin looks in Shearer's direction. "No, no. I am giving the bride away."

"Oh? And who would that be?" Shearer inquires, lowering his newspaper.

"Polly. Margaret's daughter," Franklin replies.

"Margaret's little girl? To whom is she betrothed?"

"A Dr. Hewson… Fine young fellow."

"Let us hope Dr. Hewson shows up at the church. My Alice was jilted. She fell into a deep depression afterward," Shearer says.

"That's terrible!" Franklin consoles. "Care to join me in a tipple? I have a fine Scots' whiskey opened here."

Shearer raises his cup. "I wouldn't mind a jot in my tea."

"What became of your Alice?" Franklin asks, pouring whiskey into Shearer's teacup.

"She met a lady in her church choir. They raise sheep on The Isle of Man."

"To a good Christian vocation," Franklins says, raising his glass. "With a name like Shearer, it was pre-ordained, you might say."

Mr. Shearer lifts his teacup. "'To each his own', I always say."

"I couldn't agree more. 'À chacun son goût!'"

Franklin sees Margaret descending the stairway. He points to the whiskey bottle. "Help yourself," he tells Shearer and goes to meet Margaret at the bottom of the stairs.

She wears a light beige floor-length gown, snug in the waistline. The bodice is of pleated silk, but the dress is otherwise without ornamentation. Her jewelry is simple as well, with an ivory brooch at her neck and golden earrings on her ears. The hat she carries in her hand is another matter. It has a broad turned-up brim at the front, fastened with a pin of pearls. Silk flowers and feathers sprout from the hatband.

"This cannot be the mother of the bride!" Franklin says effusively. "She is far too young and beautiful!"

"I smell alcohol," Margaret says stiffly.

"I had a drop to calm my nerves," Franklin concedes. "Would you like to join me?"

Margaret softens her tone. "I don't mind if I do." She displays her hat to Franklin. "What do you think of my *chapeau*? Is it too much?"

Franklin takes her hand. "You, my dear, could wear the entire chicken coop on your head and look marvelous."

One hour later, invited guests fill the pews of the Royal Chapel on Savoy Hill. Built during the reign of Henry VII, the ancient chapel is of modest size, but airy and charming. A glorious rainbow of light pours in though outsized stained-glass windows. Intricate fretwork on the ceiling, ornate altar carvings, and marble statuary combine to entertain the eye.

An organ fanfare announces the procession of the bride. The wedding guests stand and look to the back of the church, where a blissful Franklin proceeds slowly up the aisle with Polly on his arm. Polly is lovely in a white satin gown, with her dark hair worn up and crowned by a floral tiara, which holds her veil in place.

A snowy-haired vicar awaits the bride and her surrogate father at the altar steps, as does Dr. Edward Hewson, the bridegroom. Hewson, thirty-four years of age, is a tall, slender man. He is considered handsome, with fair wavy hair and pale blue eyes. Hewson's best man and Polly's maid of honor stand on the other side of the vicar, smiling broadly as they watch her process up the aisle.

Franklin and Polly reach the dais of the altar. Beaming, Franklin raises Polly's veil, kisses her on her cheek, and 'gives away' his adoptive daughter to her betrothed.

FRANKLIN HOUSE, PHILADELPHIA   SUMMER 1770

It is late in the afternoon as Deborah and Jake rattle into the drive between the stables and the barn in a wooden horse-drawn wagon. They were up early for a journey to the port, where they collected four wooden crates which had arrived on a packet boat from London the previous day. Deborah steps down when Jake brings the wagon to a halt. "Get a man to help you smooth out this driveway, Jake. It's like a damned washboard. I am tired of bein' jostled."

"Yes, ma'am," Jake says, as he jumps down from the wagon.

Deborah carries a leather portfolio under her arm. "Come and get me when you have those crates open. We'll see what foolishness Ben has wasted his money on now."

Jake unhitches the horse from the wagon. "Yes, ma'am."

Deborah treads through tall grass peppered with wildflowers as she heads for the house. The scent of lilac bushes planted along the fence on her left brings a smile to her face.

Aggie doesn't look up as Deborah enters the kitchen. Aggie prepares a chicken for the oven, humming a tune as she works.

Deborah drops the leather folio on the kitchen table. "I brought the post from London," she announces.

"That's fine... it's been a while," Aggie says, interrupting her song.

Deborah empties the mail onto the table and sorts through the envelopes. "Stuff some celery in that bird along with the onion," she suggests.

"Yes, ma'am. I already done that."

Deborah holds up an envelope. "Look here: a letter from Ben's old friend, Billy Strahan. He's such a gossip. Should I read it to you?"

"Ain't no such thing as bad gossip."

Deborah opens the envelope, unfolds the letter, and reads haltingly. "*I had a letter from your son, William.*" She looks at Aggie. "Why would William write to Mr. Strahan?"

Aggie wipes her hands on her apron. "Can't say as I know, ma'am."

Deborah continues reading. "*He pleads with me to in-ter-cede with his father, who has asked him to resign his post as Governor of New Jersey.*"

"Ain't that somethin'!" Aggie says, with a note of surprise.

"*I trust this is a means of ret-rib-u-tion for the Privy Council's denial of the Pennsylvania motion. I advised William to stand firm and be his own man.*" Deborah looks up from the letter. "Hmph! William will never quit that job. He's a hog in manure up there in that grand Governor's mansion."

Aggie wipes her hands with a cloth. "You right about that."

"He has big pictures of the King and Queen in his dining room... makes Ben plain crazy. Anyway..." Deborah returns to the letter.

"*'Dear old Ben looked mighty dapper Saturday last as he escorted Polly Stevenson up the aisle at the Royal Chapel.'*" She looks at Aggie again. "You listening?"

Aggie nods. "Mm-hm. I think I make you some tea." She uses the towel to lift a dented old kettle from a grate over the fire and prepares a cup of tea for Deborah.

Deborah's face darkens as she reads. "*The bride looked ra-di-ant as she wed Dr. Edward Hewson. Dr. Franklin hosted a dinner afterwards for near two hundred guests at the Vintners' Hall.*" She smacks her hand on the table and stands, staring out the window. "That son-of-a-bitch! He told me *"Don't make a big feasting wedding"* for Sally two years ago. Polly's a different story, ain't she?"

Aggie sets the teacup before Deborah. "Ain't her mother a widow? Maybe he trying to help the poor woman out," she offers.

"Poor woman? I'll tell ya who the widow is! ME!" Deborah screeches. "He's made a goddamn widow outta ME!" She crumples the letter and pitches it into the hearth. It ignites and flares up in the coals of the cooking fire.

Aggie shakes her head as Deborah thunders out of the room. She hears Deborah cursing as she climbs the stairs to her bedroom.

Stevenson House, London   December 1772

Franklin and Dr. Hewson are intent on a game of checkers in the library. Both are dressed comfortably, with the sleeves of their shirts rolled up. Franklin is shoe-less. Half-filled drinks glasses and a decanter of port rest on the table. Books, newspapers and plates littered with scraps of food are scattered about the room.

Franklin watches impatiently as Dr. Hewson ponders his next move. "I wish you would take up chess instead of this mindless game. I could beat the pants off you," he says.

"I prefer to keep my breeches," Hewson replies. He makes his move.

Franklin follows the move quickly, jumping a few of Hewson's men. "King me," he gloats.

Hewson tops Franklin's aggressor with a game piece of his own. "Ben, I hope you don't mind if Polly and I stay on with you a while longer. I have yet to find the right house for us and I hate to move her in her condition…"

"We are delighted to have you here. Besides, Margaret and I are moving out shortly," Franklin confides. "Margaret has bought a small house for the two of us a few doors away. You can stay here as long as you like."

Hewson looks surprised. "Did she? I didn't know that."

Polly walks into the library, leaning back on her heels, with a hand on her swollen belly. She holds a sheet of paper in the other hand and waves it at her husband. "Edward! Papa has written scandalously about us in his 'Craven Street Gazette.'" She reads from the paper: *"All revelers were truant at church services, having lain abed, recovering from the festivities of the previous night, during which three bottles of Queen Margaret's finest Tokay wines were drunk."* You must find and destroy all copies before Mama gets home from Aunt Anne's!"

"Heads will roll!" Hewson concurs.

Polly bends down to pick up a newspaper. "What a mess you gentlemen have made!"

Hewson jumps up from his chair. "Don't exert yourself, darling. We'll do it… Ben, let's tidy up." He gathers up cups and plates and stacks them on a side table.

"Have you seen Temple?" Polly inquires. "It's nearly suppertime."

"He's gone off somewhere with his friends," Franklin replies, stooped under the table, looking for his shoes.

"Come to supper now!" Polly commands and toddles out of the room.

Franklin finds his shoes and sits to put them on. "Edward, I need your professional opinion," he says. "With regard to a letter I have received from Mrs. Franklin."

"Oh?" Hewson picks up a book from the floor and replaces it in a secretary.

Franklin takes the letter from his pants pocket and hands it to Hewson, who reads aloud from it: "*'Dear Ben, I could bear no more loneliness, so I fell down and could not get up again. The doctor says these are bad signs that auger danger.'*" Hewson gives the letter back to Franklin. "She's had a stroke, Ben. You might want to go to her."

Franklin returns the letter to his pocket. "I couldn't possibly, but I *am* concerned…"

"She has written that letter, which means that she is recovered, but it is impossible to know to what extent," Hewson explains.

Franklin gathers up newspapers from the floor. "There is mischief I must attend to here. I put out one fire and Parliament lights another. Boston is a tinderbox. I dare not leave now."

Hewson folds the game board into a wooden box. "You have broad shoulders, Ben, to take on the government by yourself."

"I believe I have found the heart of the disturbance." He opens a drawer in the secretary and takes out a stack of letters. "I want to show you something… See what you think."

Franklin drops into an easy chair by the hearth and Hewson takes a seat opposite. Franklin scans through the letters and hands one to Hewson. "These were written by Governor Hutchinson of Massachusetts to ministers over here," Franklin explains. "Hutchinson calls for stern measures to subdue the Colonies, as well as the curtailment of English liberties for our people."

Hewson looks over the letter. "Troubling to an American, I should think."

"It's plain treasonous! If I were to forward these letters to the right people, they will learn it is Hutchinson who conspires to subjugate the Colonies. The culprit will be ousted, and the people will come to love their King again."

"How did these missives come into your hands?" he asks.

"A reliable source," Franklin replies coyly.

Hewson returns the letter to Franklin. "They were pilfered from royal ministries. If it comes to be known that you touched them, you may well find yourself in the Tower."

"Oh, I hardly think so," Franklin says.

Hewson rises from his chair and shakes his head. "Although tempting, I would be *very* careful what I did with those letters."

Franklin finds his wine glass on the table and drains it. "I shall consider your learned opinion with care," he sighs.

CHAPTER TWENTY-SEVEN

A Snake Pit

FRANKLIN'S BEDROOM, PHILADELPHIA   APRIL 1790

Franklin stands, braced against a window frame, peering out at the street. Five neighbors are huddled under a streetlamp on the walk below. A light rain falls, sparkling like diamond dust in the light of the lamp. The men pull down the brims of their hats against the rain, two ladies raise their umbrellas.

Bobby removes a bedpan from beneath Franklin's bed and places it in the hall outside. "What you lookin' at out that window?" he calls to Franklin.

"I see a few neighborhood spirits down there. What is the hour, Bobby?"

"Goin' on nine o'clock."

"Is Jefferson still in the house?"

"Don't rightly know. I ain't heard him leave. How you feelin'?"

"Woeful. Any Madeira left in that bottle, or have we drunk the house dry?"

Bobby finds the bottle on the dresser and pours wine into Franklin's teacup.

Franklin holds the cup with both hands. "Of course, I ignored Dr. Hewson's advice. Those letters did not have the calming effect over here I had hoped for."

Franklin continues as Bobby helps him back to his bed: "Parliament handed the East India Company a monopoly over the tea trade, adding fuel to the fire up in Boston. Later, I was called to a hearing before the Privy Council to consider the Massachusetts petition to remove Hutchinson as Governor." Franklin lies back on the bed and snuggles his head into the pillows. "Alexander Wedderburn, the Solicitor General, attended. Now, there's a bitter piece of old fruit," Franklin says, closing his eyes.

Stevenson House, London   December 1773

Snow whirls in the wind outside the music room windows as day turns to dusk.

Margaret sits on the piano stool, her back to the keyboard, with a coffee cup in her hand. "So, what was the point of the hearing?" she inquires.

Franklin tinkers with the glass armonica, making a haunting sound. "The hearing was a sham. Wedderburn wanted to know from whom I had obtained the Hutchinson letters. It had nothing to do with the Massachusetts Petition."

"Did you tell him?"

"Certainly not."

Margaret sets down her coffee cup, turns to the piano and plunks a few keys. "Perhaps you were mistaken to publicly confess your role in the affair."

"Two men fought a duel in Hyde Park, accusing one another of the deed. One of them was seriously injured… not killed, thank God. I had to reveal the truth."

"What next?"

"Another hearing."

Margaret rises and goes to a cabinet across the room. She takes a decanter off a shelf and pours sherry into two crystal glasses. She hands one to Franklin "Who is behind this… hearing?" she asks.

"A consortium of my enemies: Lord Granville, Lord Hillsborough, the Earl of Sandwich. They will all be there."

"Where is *there*?" she asks.

"The Cockpit."

"The… *what*?"

"The Cockpit. A large room in Whitehall where cockfights were held during King Henry's time. I anticipate a new rendition of the same. I have three weeks in which to prepare. I shall engage a lawyer to represent me. I pray Boston stays quiet in the meantime."

Margaret raises her glass. "Yes, let us pray," she concurs solemnly.

Boston   December 1773

Moonlight shimmers on the water, illuminating the rigging of sailing vessels anchored in Boston Harbor and moored at the wharfs. Gilt lettering on the stern of one of the ships reads: *'Dartmouth, Liverpool.'* On the deck of the *Dartmouth,* several men heft wooden crates from the hold of the ship onto the deck. The crates are labelled, *'TEA. East India Company.'* A second group of men aboard the ship pries open the crates with crowbars. A third gang dumps the contents of the crates overboard, the tea splashing into the sea. All are disguised as Native Americans, their faces slathered with war paint. They wear loincloths over their breeches, moccasins on their feet, and have feathers stuck in bands wrapped around their heads. They work steadily and stealthily in the moonlight.

One of the crew opening crates whispers to the man working next to him: "I've got a big urge to let out a 'whoop' or two, just to make it authentic!"

"Well, don't," his comrade whispers. "You'll have the troops on us. Shut your mouth and keep working!"

Whitehall, London   January 1774

The meeting hall set amidst the houses of government known as 'The Cockpit' buzzes with the din of hundreds of spectators taking their seats on the main floor and in the galleries above, as Franklin's 'hearing' before the Privy Council is about to commence. A crimson canopy and royal coat of arms hanging over the dais at the front of the hall indicate the occasional presence of the King himself. Chairs and benches are filling up quickly with the beau monde, many of them courtiers. Women wear fashionable hats and are layered in silk and satin, and adorned with diamonds and furs. The crowd chatters and waves greetings to one another as though arriving at a family gathering.

Ionic columns frame soot-coated windows high on the walls of the lofty room, which provide gloomy light. Billy Strahan and Sir John Pringle are seated in stiff chairs under the mezzanine. Strahan's jaw drops when Sir John jabs his shoulder and points out the arrival of the Archbishop of Canterbury, who is dressed in ecclesiastical garb and is shown by a page to a seat near the front of the room. Ten men of the Privy Council are seated at a long table below the dais. They wear gray periwigs on their heads and robes of state draped over their shoulders. Their robes are abundantly decorated with sashes, medals and ribbons. The Chairman of the hearing, a silver-haired man in his sixties, is seated in a gilded chair on the dais. He surveys the crowd with a stern expression on his face, waiting for the rustling of hooped skirts and the chattering of voices to calm down.

Alexander Wedderburn, the Solicitor General, is seated at a table on the floor facing the Chairman. Franklin and his lawyer, John Dunning, are seated at a table next to Wedderburn's. Franklin hears the murmur of gossip behind his back as he and Dunning confer quietly. Dunning is a short, lean man of sixty-eight years and frail-looking. Both his hair and skin are pale shades of gray. He is, however, a barrister of some reputation.

The hall goes quiet as the Chairman stands. "Order! Order!" he bellows, pounding his gavel on the lectern. He nods to Franklin. "The gentleman before me will please identify himself to the assembled Lords."

Strahan and Sir John look at each other, aghast at the absurdity of the request.

Franklin rises and stands before the Chairman. He wears a simple blue velvet suit and black leather shoes, his head is bare. He strikes a pose in a shaft of light falling from a window above him, with one hand in his waistcoat. He hears ladies' silk fans swooshing the stuffy air. "I am Dr. Benjamin Franklin," he announces in a clear voice. "Agent to His Majesty's Government for the Colonies of Pennsylvania and Massachusetts."

"Lord Hillsborough informs us that you are *not* the agent for Massachusetts, as your credentials were refused," the Chairman replies curtly. "An important point, as we are here to consider that Colony's petition to remove Governor Hutchinson from his post." Chatter arises among the visitors. Franklin keeps his composure. "Lord Dartmouth, who replaced Lord Hillsborough as Secretary for Colonial Affairs, approved the appointment. I have that paper in my pocket."

After a pause: "You make keep it in your pocket," the Chairman says tartly. "Have you counsel with you?"

"I do. Mr. John Dunning will represent me and the Massachusetts Assembly." Franklin looks at Dunning, seated at the table next to him.

Dunning rises to address the Chairman, standing unsteadily. His back is stooped, and his voice is scratchy and weak. "Your Excellency, I should like to reiterate Dr. Franklin's point of three weeks ago…"

The Chairman interrupts him. "Please speak up, Mr. Dunning! I cannot hear you!" he barks.

Dunning attempts to raise his voice. "With respect, Your Lordship, as Dr. Franklin pointed out previously, we were summoned here on a political matter, not one that requires a legal proceeding such as we have today."

The Chairman interrupts him again. "Speak louder, Sir!" he shouts impatiently.

Dunning's face reddens. He coughs and clears his throat. "I do apologize for my sore throat." He raises the volume of his speech a little. "I say that this is a *political* matter, not one suited to a trial."

"Today's proceeding is *not* a trial," the Chairman argues.

"Well, it looks like one to me," Dunning retorts. He turns to acknowledge laughter from the crowd behind him, smiling weakly. The Chairman pounds his gavel, calling for order.

Across the room, Strahan and Sir John smile at one another, looking hopeful.

Alexander Wedderburn jumps up from his seat. "Mr. Chairman! May we please get on with the business at hand?" he demands.

The Chairman waves a hand at Dunning. "You may sit down, Mr. Dunning. I recognize the Solicitor General, Mr. Wedderburn." Dunning, clearly annoyed, resumes his seat.

Wedderburn takes his place on the floor between Franklin and the Chairman. He is tall and robed in a black serge gown which drags the floor. His wig is full and flowing, spilling onto his shoulders. His eyes are dark and darting, his skin white as marble.

He addresses the Chairman: "We have the matter of certain letters to review before we consider the Massachusetts Petition," he says smugly. "These are letters obtained by Mr. Hutchinson's accuser by fraudulent and corrupt means!"

He turns dramatically to face Franklin.

Franklin stands poised with hands behind his back and a serene expression on his face.

Wedderburn goes on: "Letters he employed so successfully to inflame the populace of the Province against the Governor, who is a defender of freedom, not the betrayer of liberties as he is so painted to be by Dr. Franklin!"

Murmuring arises again in the galleries.

Wedderburn wags an arthritic finger at Franklin. "I hope, my Lords, you will mark and brand this man, for the honor of this country! Private correspondence hitherto has been sacred. No longer! Gentlemen, *lock your secretaries*!" he howls to the rafters.

Cheering erupts from the galleries.

Wedderburn carries on, shouting and pounding his fist on the table. "He has forgone the respect of societies and of men! He makes the ridiculous claim that letters between public officials are public property, lest they have something to hide! Yet, he kept his part in the theft and publication of these particular missives secret for one year! What, my Lords, did *he* have to hide?"

Visitors stamp their boots on the floor, jeering in Franklin's direction. Strahan and Sir John look at each other, alarmed at the hostile mood of the crowd. They look up to the gallery, where men lean over the edge with their elbows on the railing, hissing and catcalling to their friends. Franklin doesn't move. *'Why am I vilified so? How has it come to this?'* he wonders, as Wedderburn continues his tirade.

After nearly one hour of scathing invective, Wedderburn pauses and announces calmly, "I am ready to examine the witness."

Blindsided, Dunning rises from his chair. He stammers in a scratchy voice, "Your Lordship, Dr. Franklin does not choose to be examined, as we are not in a court of law."

The Chairman looks at Dunning with contempt. "Very well. If I heard you correctly, Mr. Dunning, I shall adjourn this proceeding and beg the Privy Council make their deliberations regarding the Massachusetts Petition privately."

The crowd groans with disappointment. The Chairman turns and makes a hasty exit to chambers with his fellow members of the Privy Council. Spectators stare at Franklin, tittering and whispering to one another as they file out of the hall. Franklin keeps his position, statue-like, until Dunning takes his arm and leads him back to his seat. As they confer, Strahan and Sir John come to rescue Franklin and escort him from the hall. The trio smiles politely at straggling spectators as they walk out to the street and a drizzly gray sky. Sir John places his hand on Franklin's shoulder as they approach his waiting carriage. "I am shocked that not *once* did a member of the Council step forward to check Wedderburn's indecent behavior. *Shocking*, I say!"

"Unbelievable," Strahan concurs.

"I heard gunfire as I was standing there," Franklin shares with his friends.

"I didn't hear anything, other than Wedderburn droning on," Strahan says.

"The first shots of the American Revolution rang in my ears," Franklin confides.

Strahan and Sir John do not require clarification.

The London newspapers report a few days later that Dr. Franklin is relieved of his position as Colonial Postmaster, robbing him of considerable income. The papers further state that the Massachusetts Petition was rejected as 'groundless and scandalous' by the Privy Council.

Perth Amboy, New Jersey   1774

William Franklin is seated at the desk in his book-lined library in the Governor's mansion, writing a letter. He looks well beyond his forty-five years, thanks to his silver hair and sallow complexion. A varnished portrait of the King looks down on him from the wall behind his desk chair. William sips tea as he writes, a cozy fire crackles in the fireplace. A tall window to his right sheds afternoon light on his embossed writing paper. The letter is dated, *'December 19, 1774.'* He dips his quill in the inkwell. *'Dear Father,'* he writes. *'I rode to Philadelphia Thursday last to attend the funeral of my poor old Mother, who died on Monday. She was grown feeble in the past year and succumbed to a stroke.'* He sips his tea and looks over what he has written thus far, pondering what he might write that will arouse his father's sense of guilt.

Stevenson Townhouse, London   1774

A light burns in an upstairs window of Margaret Stevenson's new townhouse in the Strand. It is considerably smaller than the Craven Street house, but not far away, so she can easily look in on her boarding house business down the street. The new house is large enough to accommodate her favorite things, as well as Franklin's scientific paraphernalia and printing press. There are pleasant rooms in the attic with generous dormer windows for Peter, and for Margaret's maid. Mrs. Jolliker's quarters are adjacent to the basement kitchen.

Margaret's bedroom suite includes a sitting area with a settee, an easy chair and hassock, and a writing desk in the French style. She sits up in bed with a book at her side. A candle burns on the table next to the bed. Her reading has been interrupted by Franklin, who is seated on a bench at the foot of her bed. His cravat is untied, his shoes lie on the floor next to the chair. He holds a letter in his hand.

Franklin looks up from the letter. His face is strained. "William says there was a fine turnout for her funeral. That's terribly nice, isn't it, in the dead of winter?"

"It shows how people loved and respected her. I am so sorry, Ben. Truly, I am."

"William says my presence might have given her the strength to go on."

"You could have done nothing to save her. It was her time."

"I hope you are right." He looks down at the letter again. "William says I should flee England… that I am looked upon with an 'evil eye' in this country."

Margaret speaks in a consoling tone. "You have many friends here. This storm will soon pass. Come to bed."

"I don't know, Maggie. There is talk of sedition. I hear rumors of Newgate Prison for me."

Margaret sits upright in her bed. "They wouldn't dare! Your arrest would bring Armageddon to the Colonies."

Franklin sets William's letter aside and begins to undress. "You would anticipate such a reaction? Honestly?"

"Nothing less. Think of the furor the King's blockade of Boston Harbor has unleashed," Margaret reasons. She pats the quilt next to her.

CHAPTER TWENTY-EIGHT

The Spy

PERTH AMBOY, NEW JERSEY   FEBRUARY 1775

Amos Beaumont, William Franklin's secretary, peers in the window of a tea shop on the town square, searching for something, or someone. A sign over the door reads: *'Pine St. Tea Salon. J. Baggott, Prop.'* Amos is a wispy, bookish-looking man in his early twenties. It is a blustery, wintry day, and he is wrapped in a warm woolen coat with a thick scarf tied around his neck. Amos spots a well-dressed gentleman in his late fifties, sitting alone in the back of the shop. He enters the tea salon and approaches the gentleman, who greets him cordially and invites him to join him at his table.

Amos takes a packet of letters from his coat pocket and passes it across the table to the gentleman. The letters are bundled together with a string, which the gentleman cuts through with a pocketknife. He sets the letters in his lap and sorts through them. Amos takes off his scarf and coat and drapes them over the back of his chair.

"Care for tea?" the gentleman inquires.

"Tea would be nice," Amos replies.

The gentleman signals a waitress with a raised hand.

"I thought those might be of particular interest to you. The Governor marked them *'Personal and Confidential'*. I am instructed to post them to England by the fastest ship."

The waitress approaches the table and the gentleman orders tea for Amos. When she leaves, the gentleman displays one of the letters to Amos. "Indeed they are of interest. This one is addressed to Lord

Dartmouth, himself. We will copy them, re-seal them and send them on their way. The Governor won't be any the wiser."

Amos squirms in his chair. "I don't feel entirely comfortable doing this. He trusts me completely."

The gentleman leans across the table. "Governor Franklin is a dangerous man," he whispers. "He considers himself immune to prosecution for espionage, due to his illustrious father. But his day will come. In the meantime, you do us a great service."

Amos smiles.

"Are you the Governor's only secretary?" the gentleman inquires.

"There's another fellow, but he doesn't know…" Amos replies.

"Let us keep it that way," the gentleman advises. He reaches into his pocket. "What do we owe you for your trouble, young man?"

Amos shrugs his shoulders.

Palace of St. James's, London   February 1775

King George III and Thomas Penn are seated at a round oak table in an intimate dining room in the King's private apartments. Although it is early afternoon, the winter light coming through the windows is weak and candles have been lit in a silver candelabrum resting on the table. A footman in royal livery clears their luncheon plates, while a second footman serves a pudding. The King waves away a third footman offering coffee to him and to his guest. It is unsettling to His Majesty that Penn, who was virile and hearty-looking when last seen by the King, appears wan and gaunt. The King raises his wine goblet to his lips. "I tell you, Penn, the die is now cast. The colonies must either submit to my wishes, or they must triumph," he says.

Penn looks alarmed. "You think it has come to that, Sire?"

"Without question. The New England governments are in a state of rebellion. Blows must decide whether they are to be subject to my rule, or completely independent of it."

"I cannot help but worry about my own family's interests," Penn says, cutting a piece of lemon cake.

"In the case of independence, your family is doomed. You will be wiped out," the King says gloomily and sips his wine.

Penn coughs and has trouble swallowing his bite of cake.

"It is ironic, is it not, that my most reliable man over there is William Franklin, who continues to feed us valuable intelligence about the rebels?"

Penn clears his throat. "The son of the great instigator of unrest?"

"None other." After a pause, the King's face brightens. "Come, Thomas, you look pale. Let's take a steam. It might do you some good," he offers.

"A steam?"

"I have had a new Turkish bath installed, sent to me by the Sultan, replete with Eunuchs," the King explains cheerily. "Great fun!"

"But I haven't brought my bathing gown," Penn pleads.

"I have plenty." The King drains his goblet and stands. "I shouldn't worry too much about this American business. No gang of ruffians is going to run over my glorious army. I have half the Royal Navy and thirty thousand ground troops in New York alone. The Howe Brothers know what they are doing. Come."

The King strides out of the room.

Penn's frock coat hangs loosely on his frame when he stands. A footman pulls out his chair and Penn follows the King out of the dining room, with a fretful look on his very thin face.

STEVENSON TOWNHOUSE   MARCH 1775

Franklin and Peter carefully pack books and scientific instruments in crates strewn about Franklin's first floor study. Margaret taps sharply on the door, tying her dressing gown closed about her as she enters.

Peter looks up from his chore. "Good morning, ma'am," he says.

"Good morning, Peter," Margaret replies curtly. "Ben, I wish to remind you that we have a long journey ahead of us today." She pauses and looks around the room. "You are not thinking of taking all this down to Cornwall with us, are you?" she asks.

"I am not going to Cornwall," Franklin replies.

"Not going? Don't be silly. You have always wanted to see Clovelly."

"I have started my packing. My enemies are closing in on me."

"Nonsense! You will *adore* Clovelly! Charming little cottages cascading down to the sea, the scent of roses and honeysuckle everywhere…" She draws a picture in the air with her hand. "There is a lovely manor house atop the hill with a comfy inn at the bottom. I don't know which we will stay in, but the Portmans have a good cook in both places, so it really doesn't matter. Johnny's family has owned Clovelly forever."

Franklin sets aside a glass beaker. "I *am* sorry, but Wedderburn's dogs are nipping at my heels. I've had a visit from Pringle… and a warning."

Margaret turns to Peter. "Leave us, please," she says.

Peter stops what he is doing and leaves the room. Margaret closes the door after him.

"To the devil with Pringle!" She wends her way through a maze of boxes. "Clovelly will be perfect for us," she argues. "We can stay there for a month or two… until the dust settles."

Franklin shakes his head. "I sail on the 20th from Portsmouth." He resumes wrapping glass instruments. Margaret moves closer to him.

"With most tender respect, one cannot help but think we are free to marry now! We could live in France! Giles had many friends there. The Charrons would take us in!" she offers enthusiastically.

Franklin places his hands on Margaret's shoulders and looks into her eyes. "If I am indicted, they will find me. If I am hanged, I will have made you twice a widow."

Margaret's eyes fill with tears. "And what will you make of me if you *leave* me?"

"You are in grave danger if I stay."

"Then take me with you!" Margaret pleads.

"Nay. The war I have struggled so long to prevent is nigh. The King himself encourages a decisive conflict." Margaret stares out the window. "Then I must live with vain hope that when hostilities are concluded, you will return to visit your grandson."

"I am taking Temple with me," Franklin says quietly.

Margaret turns from the window and looks at Franklin wide-eyed. "You cannot be thinking of taking Temple with you!"

"He is my grandson."

"And mine!" Margaret fires back. "I have raised him since he was a little child!"

"It is time for him to meet his father," Franklin reasons.

"His father is a rake and a villain!" Margaret declares. "Have you already booked passage for Temple?"

"Yes."

"Then you are a scoundrel!" she cries.

"I will send the money I owe you. It is a considerable amount," Franklin says, hoping to calm her.

Margaret glares daggers at him. "Some say you are a gifted philosopher. I say your genius is in the leaving! There is never a look back, is there? Never a glance over your shoulder to view the carnage strewn behind! You may keep your money, sir! I spit on your money!" Margaret shrieks and runs out of the room.

Franklin looks after her for a moment, but makes no attempt to follow. He resumes packing his books.

A few days later, Franklin, Billy Strahan and Dr. Pringle are seated in the library on the ground floor of the townhouse. The mood is somber. Strahan and Sir John hold empty drinks glasses in their hands. Franklin sits with his head in his hands, his elbows resting on his knees.

Sir John picks up a bottle of brandy and refills his glass. "I think in the end, you know, Margaret may be proven right. The present storm will blow out to sea and be quickly forgotten."

Franklin raises his head and lowers his hands. His eyes are red-rimmed. He looks out the window, where he sees two boys playing with sticks and a ball in the street below.

Strahan sets his glass on the table. He rises from his chair and pats Franklin on his shoulder. "Well, old man," he says. "I must be going. I will see you on the other shore."

Franklin turns to look at him. "The other shore of what?" he inquires. "The River Styx?"

"I was thinking of the Atlantic," Strahan replies. He smiles at his friend, turns and leaves the room.

Franklin looks again at the boys in the street. He watches them laugh and jostle one another in the early spring sunshine.

Peter follows Strahan into the foyer. He finds Strahan's coat and helps him on with it. "Now you take care, Mr. Strahan," he says. "I

DEAR BEN

hope you come visit Miss Margaret sometime." Peter opens the front door for him.

Strahan arranges his scarf around his neck. "Thank you, Peter," he says.

Strahan looks back toward the library.

After a moment, he pulls up the collar of his coat and steps outside into the crisp air.

Franklin's bedroom, Philadelphia   April 1790

A candle burning on a side table flutters in the draft from an open window. Franklin sits up in bed with pillows propped behind his back.

"I wish you get some sleep now," Bobby says.

"I am afraid to sleep. I might dream of the lady again."

"Ain't no dream ever hurt nobody. Bobby crosses his arms. "So… you finally come home that time."

"Temple and I sailed on the first day of spring of 1775. The war I dreaded began in earnest whilst we were at sea." Bobby smooths the quilt over Franklin's legs. "British troops set out from Boston to seize weapons the rebels had stashed outside the city. The Redcoats faced fierce resistance from a rebel militia up near Concord. After a bloody skirmish, a detachment of Redcoats took a route through the forest back to Boston, intending to regroup, I would suppose."

Near Concord, Massachusetts   April 1775

A company of British Redcoats marches along a rutted road through a dense wood. They are young, most of them not yet twenty years old. Several had been wounded earlier in the day and are bandaged in battlefield triage. They march in formation behind their Captain and two fife and drum majors. A few of the wounded are carried, strapped to makeshift litters. A number of members of the local militia are hidden in the trees along the road. They have been following the British troops for a mile or two. The British are unaware they are being stalked, until a hunting dog breaks free from the lead of a militia man.

"Homer! Homer! Feck! Get back here!" the militia man calls in a whisper after the dog.

The dog runs onto the road and nips at the heels of a Redcoat holding up the rear of the company. The Redcoat stops and takes aim. The dog's master sees the move and shoots the Redcoat, who falls to the ground. The British Captain orders the company to halt its march. The Redcoats look around for the source of the gunfire, shouting to one another in confusion.

The militia men take cover behind trees and open fire on the surprised Redcoats. Several of them fall where they stand. The repeat of gunfire is deafening, smoke and the acrid smell of gunpowder fill the air.

"Retreat, men! Take cover!" the Captain yells over the roar of musket fire.

"Retreat? Bloody hell! Where to?" a panicked Redcoat shouts to a comrade.

The Redcoats break into a run, struggling with the burden of wounded men on stretchers. A drum major throws his drum on the road as he flees. A dozen Redcoats stand their ground, drop on one knee and return fire into the woods. They bravely stand and re-load as the rebels pick them off with musket fire. Several militia men are hit by the British and fall, dead or injured, into the weeds.

The muddy road is strewn with dead and dying Redcoats, including every man who stayed behind to fight. The shouts and curses of those who fled the ambush diminish as they disappear down the road. The militia men emerge from their hiding places in the woods. They look for signs of life among the bodies lying in blood-streaked puddles. Homer, the hunting dog, circles about, sniffing at the fallen men, his tail wagging.

One of the militia men is sickened by the carnage. "Good Christ! This is a slaughter!" he cries. "We were going to take them prisoner! How many men have we lost?" he yells to nobody in particular in the woods.

"Maybe eight or ten of our men," a man shouts from the trees.

A militia man steps over bodies lying on the road and picks up the drum left behind by the drum major. "Look here!" he shouts, holding up the instrument. "A souvenir for my boy!"

A man who appears to be an officer of the militia steps out of the trees and surveys the grim scene. "Let's get our wounded loaded onto the wagons and make for home!" he shouts. "The British will be back before long with half the King's army to gather up the fallen."

MID-ATLANTIC   MARCH 1775

A bright, clear, sunny day. Puffy white clouds line the horizon. Franklin stands mid-ship, with his shirt sleeves rolled up, leaning on the railing, looking out at the indigo sea. His wispy hair whirls about his head and the collar of his shirt flutters in the stiff breeze. Despite the brilliant day, his face is a picture of despair, of regret over having left behind in London the life he loved and over having failed at his mission.

He turns to his left and sees Temple, fifteen years old, on deck ten yards down the way. He and a young sailor, a Mr. Cainey from Birmingham, sit on the deck, cross-legged, facing one another. Both are shirtless, bare-footed, wearing only cotton breeches. Temple watches intently as Mr. Cainey demonstrates tying a complex sailors' knot.

Temple has grown into a strapping lad, broad-chested, with well-muscled arms. His hair is sun-bleached, his face and back are tanned to a deep bronze from sun and sea. Franklin recalls that Temple's mother could have been a handsome wench, if only she had known how to dress herself.

Temple and Mr. Cainey chat and laugh as the knot-tying lesson proceeds.

Franklin walks toward the young men. Temple's face breaks into a grin when he sees his grandfather approach. "'Afternoon, Grandpapa!" he says. "Mr. Cainey is going to make a sailor of me yet."

Cainey stands and lowers his head, out of respect for the famous older man.

"Sit, my boy, sit," Franklin commands. "Don't let me interrupt your class. Rope-tying is important business aboard a vessel such as this."

Cainey lowers himself to his cross-legged position on the smooth planks of the deck.

"I don't suppose, Mr. Cainey, you are able show my grandson how to tie a hang-man's noose? Now there's a knot with which a man could earn his living," Franklin teases, eliciting laughter from the young men. "Well, carry on, boys. Keep up the good work."

Franklin pats Temple on his shoulder and proceeds on down the deck.

Franklin stops when he reaches the prow of the ship.

He leans into the wind, tasting the salt air, rummaging through his thoughts. In Temple, he sees the means to his salvation. He sees what his own son, Franky, might have been.

Still, he is consumed with shame and guilt at having taken the boy from Margaret to use as a pawn against his father.

William has made no mention of Franklin's brutal treatment at the hands of the Privy Council. He has cast his lot solidly with the British, while Franklin has chosen the opposite path.

"Temple is my trump card!" Franklin shouts to the wind, ready for the contest ahead.

He turns, descends the stairway behind the wheelhouse and disappears from view.

PART SIX

O' Canada

CHAPTER TWENTY-NINE

The House that Deborah Built

MAY 1775

May 5th, 1775, is a day of celebration. Word had spread about town that a packet boat from Portsmouth, England, had docked at the Port of Philadelphia just before daybreak. The local citizenry began gathering at the port shortly thereafter to greet the ship's most illustrious passenger, a renowned native son. Not since the untimely death of the young poet and town clerk, Aquila Rose, in 1723, has the community so taken a man to its collective heart.

In the belfry of the Lutheran Church of St. Mark, Mr. Jackson, the sexton, grins as his son, Peter, a slight lad of thirteen years, pulls on the heavy rope which rings the French-made iron bell above. The weight of the contraption raises Peter three feet off the floor with each pull of the rope, and Peter's younger brother, Hiram, grabs Peter's legs and pulls him back down to the floor, swinging and ringing the bell in the opposite direction.

The Jackson boys' bell ringing joins the peal of bells from churches all over the city. Rifles and muskets fired into the air at regular intervals in surrounding farm country add to the cacophony. At the port, the crowd has grown to several hundred well-wishers of all ages. Some are dressed in their city finery, while others wear simple calico frocks or coveralls better suited to the farm.

They chatter excitedly as they watch passengers struggle off the vessel, most of whom carry hand baggage and look weary from many weeks spent in the confines of the ship. The three-masted, square-rigged vessel appears enormous to an onlooker standing on the dock, but she is diminutive to those aboard who struggle in confined quarters with a sparse, salt-laden diet, seasickness, boils, dysentery, scurvy, heat, dampness, lice, and other miseries of life at sea. Deckhands hoist trunks and cargo on winches from the ship's hold, lowering them to stevedores waiting on the dock below with dozens of push carts and wagons.

A cheer erupts from the crowd as Benjamin Franklin appears on deck and steps onto the gangway. Fathers lift young children onto their shoulders and nudge their wives forward for a better view of the famous man. Franklin, and the young gentleman who walks closely behind him, look refreshed and no worse for the wear, as is noted by some of the ladies in attendance. Franklin, seventy years of age, and his grandson, Temple, who has recently attained fifteen years, are followed by three burly longshoremen with an assortment of trunks and crates piled on handbarrows. Franklin stops and smiles broadly, waving to the crowd below, who cheer and wave in return. Temple, wary of the attention, smiles nervously.

Franklin cocks an ear and listens for a moment to the chorus of church bells ringing throughout the city. He taps Temple on the shoulder and points heavenward. "The bells ring for ye, lad!" he says cheerily.

Several people in the crowd shout, "Welcome home, Ben!"

A man standing near the gangway yells, "We are grateful to ye, Ben, for all ye done for us!"

Franklin acknowledges the man's remark with a slight bow. "'Tis good to be home!" he calls in the man's direction.

"Will ye be missin' Merrie Olde England, after all these years, Dr. Franklin?" A woman shouts.

"Only my landlady's puddings, ma'am!" Franklin responds, to laughter from the crowd.

He shakes outstretched hands as he descends the gangway and makes his way across the wharf. Temple looks mistrustful of the crowd as it closes in on them.

A young man grabs Franklin's arm. "Dr. Franklin! I write for the *Mercury*. My readers would like to know what your plans for the future might be!" he inquires in a demanding tone.

Franklin jerks his arm free of the newspaper man's grip. He speaks in full voice, so all can hear. "I return to this country an old man, but I still hope to be of service," he replies, not looking at the rude young reporter. "Think of the merchant who says of the rag end of a bolt of cloth, '*Go ahead, take it. Make of it what ye can.*' I am that rag end, sir!"

The crowd roars with laughter. "We need you in the Congress, Ben!" another man in the crowd shouts. The man standing next to him pipes up. "Are we goin' too fast, Ben, rushin' as we are to prepare for war?"

Franklin looks in the man's direction. "*You* may delay, my friend, but *time* will not!"

Many in the crowd cheer and applaud Franklin's response.

A middle-aged man and woman standing at the back of the assembly do not join in the applause. "Look-a-there. Caesar re-enters Rome with a ton of booty, I would wager," she sneers to her companion. The man holds his hand to his mouth, so he won't be heard by the man standing next to him. "A quick about-face, eh?" he says to the woman. "He sups with King George one day and dances with the rebels the next. Wouldn't surprise me if he's come to spy on us." The woman confides, "His son all but sleeps with the King, I hear."

Jake, Franklin's manservant, weaves his way through the crowd. He is powerfully built and a head taller than any other man in sight. He gently pushes people out of his way as he approaches Franklin, who sees him and offers a warm smile and a wave in his direction. They meet and shake hands vigorously. "Jake!" Franklin cries. "Dear old Jake has come to rescue us from this melee!" Franklin turns to Temple and urges him forward. "Meet my godson, Mr. Temple."

Jake and Temple shake hands. Temple, who has had little experience with people of color, is taken with the countenance of this ruggedly handsome, towering black man. He feels his fear of this new world melting away.

The crowd parts as Jake relieves Franklin and Temple of their hand baggage and leads them along the wharf to a waiting coach-and-four, with a horse-drawn drayage wagon standing behind. "I help the men with your trunks and such. You go on ahead. Miss Sally waitin' on ya at home. She real anxious to see ya!"

A coachman in livery, an African-American slave, opens the door and helps Franklin up and into the carriage. Temple follows. The driver sits on the box up front with reins in his hand. Franklin leans out the window, waving to the crowd as the driver cracks his whip and the carriage jerks into motion.

Minutes later, the coach rocks gently from side to side as it rolls down a dry, dusty road toward the city. For a time, Franklin and Temple are quiet, content to watch the passing scenery. The countryside is bursting with the fresh green of springtime and is as familiar to Franklin as the back of his hand, but strange and foreign to Temple. Franklin clears his throat. "Are you happy you have come, lad?"

"Oh yes, Grandpapa," Temple replies without hesitation.

Both are silent for another few minutes, until Temple inquires, "Will my father be at the house, Grandpapa?"

"No," Franklin replies. "We will go to him."

"When?"

"Soon enough." Franklin raises an index finger. "Listen…" he says. A military band plays in the distance. The sound of it grows louder as the carriage approaches the city.

Curious, Franklin leans out the window and shouts up to the driver. "Driver! Is that band I hear playing for us, perchance?"

The driver shouts down to Franklin. "No, sir. The bells was for you. The music is for General Washington. He come to town same day as you. They's a thousand militia men with him!"

"A thousand?! My God, that's an army!"

"Yes, sir," the driver agrees. "I think they's war comin' 'fore long."

"I think you are right. That is what armies are for!" Franklin settles back into his seat in the carriage. Absorbed in thought, he and Temple do not speak again until they reach Market Street in town and the carriage pulls up to an impressive three-story mansion. The house is built of stout timbers, clapboard and brick, and set back from the street on a quiet, shady courtyard.

"There it is, lad," Franklin says, nodding toward the imposing edifice. "The house that Deborah built."

Aggie, Jake's wife and the Franklin housekeeper, stands on the front step waiting to greet Franklin. She wears a house dress with a long white apron over it and a cotton bonnet on her head. She clasps her hands together when she sees Franklin peer out from the carriage.

The coachman jumps down and opens the door. Franklin steps out. He sets his valise on the walk, goes to Aggie, opens his arms, and wraps them around her in a hug. He takes a step back. "Dear, dear Aggie! My, don't you look well!"

Aggie beams. "Old as I am, I thank you, sir! I turned fifty-two while you was gone!

It been such a long time!"

The front door opens and Sally Franklin Bache steps out. She wears a pretty frock and has done her best to look attractive. Her hair is arranged pleasingly, her cheeks are rouged. Tears streaming down her face leave a trail in her face powder. "Hello, Papa," she says quietly.

Franklin opens his arms and the two embrace. "My dearest, sweet, Sally. Always in my heart!" he says. He takes a kerchief from his pocket and wipes away her tears. "You look lovely, child!"

"Eleven years, Papa. Eleven long years," Sally says, choking on her words.

"I have been with you in spirit every minute of those eleven years, child. Every moment," he consoles her.

A little boy in short breeches peeks out from behind Sally's skirts.

"And who have we here?" Franklin asks.

"Your namesake, Father." Sally urges the little boy forward. "Meet Benjamin Bache."

"Benjamin?" Franklin's face lights up. "I can see that you are going to be my favorite."

"My name is Benny. I am six years old!" the little boy says in a strong voice.

Franklin bends down to Benny's eye level. "Are you, now? Then, 'Benny' it shall be."

Franklin straightens and turns to Sally. "Meet my godson, Mr. Temple. Temple, this is my daughter, Sally."

Temple extends his hand to Sally, and they shake hands politely. "A pleasure I have looked forward to, ma'am," he says. Franklin looks around. "And where is Mr. Bache?"

"He'll be along," Sally replies. "Come inside now. You have time for a wash before lunch."

Franklin pats Sally's hand. "You go ahead... show Temple to his room. I'm going for a little walk to find my land legs." He removes a wrapped package from his valise, sticks the package under his arm, and passes the valise to Aggie. He walks away down the street at a determined pace. The others look after him for a moment.

"I know where he's going," Sally says, as she shepherds Temple into the house.

A rusted iron gate creaks as it swings open, and Franklin enters the cemetery in the shadow of the Anglican Church. The balmy spring morning is agreeable for a meander through the graveyard. Juggling the package under his arm, he puts on his spectacles to better read the names and dates carved into the headstones. Many inscriptions are obscured by lichen or faded by the elements, or both.

Franklin wanders through the stone tablets, some of which totter precariously. He sees that while he has been abroad, several men and women he once knew have been laid to rest next to their spouses. Like his Franky, more than a few children have succumbed to the pox or other scourges of the day. Their lives cut short, they lie for eternity in fenced-in family plots. He finds what he came to see in a newer section of the graveyard. It is a modest stone, of white marble with a Christian cross affixed to the top of it. He stops before it, sets down his package, and with his hands folded in front of him, studies the inscription: *Deborah Read Franklin. B.1708 - D.1774. 'Tarry with me here whilst I wait for Him.'*

Franklin ponders the words for a minute, takes a kerchief from his pocket and wipes a tear from his cheek. He polishes the face of the stone with the cotton cloth. "Deborah, I find this marker ye had made for yourself to be entirely unsatisfactory," he says aloud. "It is unclear whether '*Him*' refers to me or to the Lord Jesus." He pauses for a moment. "I have brought you something." Franklin picks up the package, unwraps a toby jug in the shape of a jolly, plump matron, and places it before the stone. "It reminded me of you."

He continues speaking to the monument. "In due time, I shall order a less puzzling marker with both our names on it, of ample size, but with no additional decoration… perhaps just a simple frame around our names. That is what I shall do." Franklin hesitates another moment, then turns away and takes a few steps. Overcome with grief, he stumbles and reaches out to a stone monument for support, sobbing into the arm of his coat.

Franklin's return to the house on Market Street goes unnoticed. He hears voices and laughter from the kitchen, which fade as he climbs the stairs to the second floor. He hesitates on the landing outside Deborah's suite, then tries the door. It opens to a darkened room, gloomy with all the curtains pulled closed. He draws back the curtains on the street-side windows and sunlight pours in. It appears untouched since Deborah's passing, though it has been kept clean and dusted. Nothing has changed since Franklin last saw the room twelve years previously.

He sits on Deborah's four-poster bed, smoothing the counterpane. The coverlet had been sewn for Deborah by her mother, the poor soul, who perished in a hideous kitchen fire in 1760, an event seldom mentioned, but not forgotten.

He goes to Deborah's desk and flips through a neat stack of letters written by him and posted from England. He removes a familiar-looking creamy envelope from the bottom of the pile. The return address is Stevenson, Craven Street, London. He opens the envelope and reads Margaret's florid hand: *'Dear Mrs. Franklin, how we wish you were here with us, as Benjamin returned from travels on the Continent with a summer cold. He suffers like a child with his sniffles and sneezes. A wife's skills alone can nurse him properly.'*

How clever of Margaret to have written thus, Franklin reflects. He returns the letters to their place on the desk and goes to Deborah's wardrobe cabinet, opens it, and touches a few hanging garments. It is time to give these things to the poor, he concludes. He will speak with Sally about it.

He closes the wardrobe, pulls the window curtains closed, and leaves the room which he will not see again for another ten years.

A few mornings later, Franklin sits at the kitchen table, attempting to read a newspaper, with Benny bouncing on his lap. Benny gleefully eats spoonbread.

Sally enters the kitchen from the backyard with a bouquet of cut flowers in her hands. She places the arrangement in a crock on the pine table. "From Mama's garden," she explains.

Franklin looks up from his newspaper. "I shall have Dr. Pringle send you some tulip bulbs from Holland in the fall. Your mother would have loved them," he smiles. "If you like, that is…"

Sally hangs her knit shawl on a hook by the door. "I see you found Aggie's spoonbread," she says. She makes herself a cup of tea and joins him and Benny at the table. She reaches for a pitcher and adds some milk to her tea. "You should have been here, Papa," she says.

"When?" Franklin asks.

"When Mama was low."

"It was not possible."

Sally stares into her teacup. "She might have recovered from her stroke had you been here. She gave up hope."

Franklin sighs. "If I could have come, my dear, I would have."

"Will you see my brother, William?" Sally inquires.

"Of course, I will. And very soon."

They both look up as Temple rushes into the kitchen, putting on a jacket.

"Jake wants to show me how to drive the phaeton! May I, Papa Ben?" he asks, short of breath. "He's waiting for me in the stables."

"You may, but over here, we call it a buggy, and Jake awaits you in the barn. A lesson in American nomenclature for you, lad."

Temple dashes out the door and crosses the yard at a brisk pace. Franklin calls after him, "Temple! Ask Jake to harness up a sweet nag for you!"

Benny squirms his way off Franklin's lap. "Me, too!" he pleads.

"All right," Sally concedes. "But put your coat on. It's chilly outside."

Benny finds his jacket hanging behind the door, snatches it, and chases after Temple. Franklin and Sally sit quietly for a few minutes. They feel the distance of lost years between them.

She takes a bite of spoonbread from her father's plate. "Papa, I swear I see a family resemblance in Mr. Temple. Was his father a cousin of yours?"

"Something like that," Franklin replies. "Where is Mr. Bache this morning?" he inquires, changing the subject. "Not around much, is he?"

"No, Papa," she concedes. "Richard's import business went to hell with the boycott of British goods, and he has taken more to the drink, the poor man."

Franklin folds his newspaper and sets it on the table. "He has a fine roof over his head, and I pay you well to look after my affairs since your Mama died. He is not suffering."

Sally stares out the window. "We're not starving, Papa, but I am… hungry."

Franklin considers the remark. "That is entirely your affair, my dear." He reaches for the teapot. "And I shan't say 'I told you so'."

"I still love him, Papa."

Franklin looks into Sally's eyes. "I see. Well, there you are."

Temple is at the reins of an open carriage pulled by a gentle old mare as it rolls lazily along an unpaved country lane. Benny sits close to him, pleased to be included on the journey. Jake rides on horseback alongside the carriage. The spring air is cool on the tree-lined roadway, but they are warmed pleasantly when they ride through patches of bright sunshine.

"Missus Franklin was real fond of that little carriage, Mr. Temple," Jake says. "She take it out all the time. She go wherever she like, all by herself."

"Did she?" Temple says.

"Missus Franklin ride all the way to New Jersey a few time. She take Aggie with her. They visit Governor Franklin and Miss Elizabeth."

"Wasn't that dangerous?" Temple asks, keeping his eyes on the road. "Two women alone, I mean?"

"Oh, no. Aggie got a loaded pistol under her apron, and they got a musket under the seat with the picnic basket. Missus Franklin ain't afraid of nothin', except it maybe gonna rain. But it don't rain."

"Is New Jersey far away, Jake?" Benny inquires.

"Not too far, Master Benny. Missus Franklin real fond of Miss Elizabeth, but she never take kindly to the Governor, even when he was a boy like you."

Temple looks up at Jake. "The Governor is my father."

Jake's eyes widen. "He is? I didn't mean nothin' by what I said, Mr. Temple."

Temple smiles. "I know you didn't, Jake. I thought you would find out sooner or later."

Jake rides along quietly for a time, deep in thought.

Perth Amboy, New Jersey — 1775

That same morning, sunlight floods the kitchens of the Governor's mansion. William Franklin is seated at the breakfast table in a bow window, drinking coffee from a demitasse cup. He wears a silk robe over his dressing gown and monogramed slippers on his feet. He has settled into his role as Governor and is pleased that he has attained a station higher than that of his father. He has, further, added a patina of aristocratic bearing to his persona, creating a cool distance between him and his associates.

The citizenry have taken warmly to his wife, on the other hand. Her beauty and genteel manners combine to win people over. Elizabeth misses her family in England, but she is content in her marriage. Occasional loneliness is a price she is willing to pay for happiness.

William holds a newspaper at arm's length before him, scanning up and down the columns of type. He stops at a news item, gasps, and shouts to the next room, "He's come! Do you hear me? He's come!"

Elizabeth drifts in unhurriedly from the hallway. She wears a satin dressing gown and a floppy flannel bonnet on her head. Her feet are bare. "Who has come?" she asks. She pours herself a demitasse of coffee, adding a splash of milk.

"My father! He kept his return a secret from me!" William quotes from the newspaper: "*Benjamin Franklin has landed on our shores after a six-week voyage from Portsmouth. Bells rang out in Philadelphia to celebrate his arrival.*' I have to learn about it in the newspaper! That son of a bitch!"

Elizabeth snatches a piece of bread from William's plate. "Six weeks? That is rather swift, is it not?"

William continues reading from the newspaper. "*Dr. Franklin is pleased to find us armed and preparing for the worst events. He thinks nothing else can save us from the most abject slavery.*" He tosses the newspaper onto the chair next to him.

Elizabeth sets down her coffee cup, picks up the paper, and scans the article. "We mustn't shout, William. The servants will hear us."

William lowers his volume a notch. "*Slavery*, no less! The old man has become a warmonger! 'Tis just the sort of wrong thinking that has led my Legislature to run amok!"

She points to the newspaper. "Did you see this? It says here that Papa has brought his godson with him, a Mr. William Temple, aged sixteen years."

William looks surprised. "Temple is with him?"

"So, it says." Elizabeth looks at William with a curious expression. "I wonder why he would bring his godson along. How strange…"

William takes a deep breath. "Sit down, Elizabeth," he says.

She sits in the chair next to him, looking puzzled.

Philadelphia   1775

A few days later, Temple runs his finger along the tooled leather lining the edges of the shelves as his grandfather gives him a tour of his new library.

"Mrs. Franklin had this room built to my specifications, God bless her," he says. Franklin appears pleased, although the room already strains under his growing collections. The furnishings include cozy damask wing chairs flanking the fireplace and an ancient refectory table anchoring the center of the room. Book stands, library ladders and a large globe of the earth complete the décor.

Temple stops to peruse the title of a book on a shelf. "It is splendid, Grandfather."

Franklin points to a row of books. "Look here, lad. These are my Almanacs, '*Poor Richard*', '*The Way to Wealth*', all my scribblings are assembled here. Deborah had them beautifully bound."

Temple's crisp English accent has faded under the influence of new friends in Philadelphia. "I never expected to see such a library in America," he says.

Franklin takes one volume of a six-volume set off the shelf. He opens the cover and shows the frontispiece to Temple. "Here's a treasure. David Hume's '*History of England,*' signed to me in 1759 by Hume himself." He points to the autograph. "Look at that! Do you know who David Hume is?"

Temple looks at Franklin sheepishly. "No, sir."

"Well, you should," Franklin scolds. "He is a great philosopher of the Enlightenment." He replaces the book on the shelf. Franklin leads Temple across the room to another collection of books. He runs his hand along their spines gently. "Here are all the plays of William Shakespeare. You have heard of *him*, haven't you?"

"Of course, sir," Temple says.

"This is a very early folio and worth a king's ransom. Don't you forget that, lad."

"I shan't forget," Temple promises.

"Good. Come sit with me," Franklin says, pointing to the wing chairs. "We are going to visit your father on Friday next. I wish to speak with you about it."

Temple looks as though he has let a cat out of a bag. "I told Jake about…"

"I am aware that you did, son. And I told Sally, so that is that. They had to know eventually."

Temple reaches for his grandfather's hand. "So that is that," he says. They smile knowingly and shake hands.

CHAPTER THIRTY

His Excellency

Temple's face is pressed to the window of Franklin's gleaming new coach as it rolls northeast on the Post Road. He is interested to see countryside he has never seen before. His frock coat lays on the seat next to him. Within a few miles, his grandfather is fast asleep on the bench opposite, his head tilted back, his mouth open and snoring loudly.

Heavy rains of the night before left the unpaved road muddy and pitted with puddles. The coach rocks from side to side as it navigates through the watery craters, jostling the riders inside.

After a while, Franklin awakens. He looks out the window to get his bearings. "Where are we? Have I been asleep long?" he asks.

"For an hour or so," Temple replies.

Franklin reaches into the pocket of his coat and produces a silver flask. He takes a swig, then hands it to Temple. "Here. This should settle your innards," he says.

Temple accepts the flask and takes a sip. "I can't say much for the roads hereabouts."

"You are not the first person to say that," Franklin grins.

Temple returns the flask to his grandfather.

"May I remind you again that you will stay with your father only for the summer, then you will return to Philadelphia to resume your studies."

"Yes, Grandpapa." Temple looks out the window again at the passing scenery.

"Look at me," Franklin orders. "I don't want your head filled with your father's Loyalist drivel. If he comes to his senses, you may return next summer."

Temple looks at Franklin. "I should like that, Grandpapa."

"Let us hope we encounter no surprises," Franklin says and takes another drink from the flask. He and Temple ride along quietly for a time.

Suddenly, three armed highwaymen on horseback spring out of the woods and block the passage of the carriage on the narrow road. Their faces are covered with bandanas, their hats are pulled low over their eyes. The horses pulling the carriage are startled. They rear up, snorting and neighing.

"Halt!" one of the highwaymen yells in a gravelly voice. He trains his rifle on the driver and coachman up front.

The driver brings the carriage to a stop. Franklin and Temple look out the windows.

"What in hell?!" Franklin says. "We're being robbed!"

"What goods do ye carry, man?" the bandit shouts up to the driver, pointing his rifle at a trunk strapped to the back of the coach.

"Only Mr. Temple's baggage," the driver yells in reply.

"No gold? No jewels? 'Tis a rich man's rig ye be drivin'!"

"Our cargo be the boy's personals is all, sir," the driver replies.

Inside the carriage, Temple and Franklin look at each other, alarmed, but keep quiet.

"They's got jingle in their pockets, I'll bet ya," the highwayman sneers. He dismounts and walks around the carriage, while his comrades keep their rifles trained on the driver.

Franklin touches Temple's knee. "Remain calm, son. Our men are armed, but let us pray it doesn't come to that."

The bandit jerks Temple's door open. "Stand down!" he orders. Temple leans out of the carriage. "Would ye be aware that it is Dr. Benjamin Franklin, on state business, who ye detain, sir?" he asks in a quivering voice.

The bandit peers into the coach. Franklin raises his hand and offers a weak smile.

The bandit courteously removes his hat. "My God, so it is…" he whispers to himself.

"Are ye a Republican or a Royalist, sir?" Temple further inquires of the bandit.

"A rebel, to be sure!" the bandit replies emphatically.

"We go to meet with the Governor of New Jersey to convert him to your cause," Temple clarifies.

"That so?" The bandit thinks for a minute. "Then ye best be on yer way! Beg pardon, Dr. Franklin," he says as he doffs his hat." The bandit slams Temple's door shut and remounts his horse. "Let's be off, boys!" he calls to his comrades. "They is Patriots on important business!"

Franklin and Temple watch the trio of highwaymen disappear into the dense forest from whence they came. Franklin's driver whips the horses and the coach lurches forward.

Color returns to Franklin's face and he takes a deep breath. "I thought I told you to keep quiet, lad," he laughs.

"Where's that flask?" Temple asks, reaching out with a trembling hand.

That evening, Franklin's carriage clatters into the cobblestone drive of the Governor's mansion at Perth Amboy. A stable boy, an African American slave, runs up to help with the horses as Franklin's driver brings the coach to a stop.

William and Elizabeth step out the front door of the mansion, awaiting their guests. Elizabeth smiles warmly, clasping her hands before her anxiously, while William appears nervous, even from a distance.

Howard, the Franklins' butler, an African American gentleman with salt-and-pepper hair, comes to open the door of the carriage. Franklin and Temple step down. Their legs are stiff after the long day's ride on bumpy roads.

William approaches Temple and gazes at his face for a moment. "I never thought I would see this day," he says.

"Hello, Father," Temple says as they embrace.

William steps back, overcome with emotion.

Elizabeth and Franklin meet and shake hands "Hello, Papa," she says, sounding chipper. "Did you have a pleasant journey?"

"Yes, uneventful," Franklin lies. He turns to his grandson. "Elizabeth, my dear, I would like you to meet Mr. William Temple."

Elizabeth and Temple shake hands. "A pleasure, ma'am," he says.

Franklin looks at his son. "Aren't you going to say something, Bill Boy? It has been more than ten years!"

"Hello, Father. Welcome." William offers his hand, and they shake hands.

"I believe a cool drink is in order for all," Elizabeth says as she places her hand on Temple's back and leads him into the house. Franklin and William follow, while Howard and the coachman attend to Franklin's bags.

The family retires to the parlor of the mansion, an elegant salon with long windows hung with heavy red velvet drapes. Settees and chairs upholstered in golden damask are arranged in groupings for ease of conversation. Tables and cabinets are of polished mahogany, in the Chippendale style. Large gilt-framed portraits of King George III and Queen Charlotte hang over the fireplace. Windows are open, and sheer curtains hanging behind the velvet draperies waft lazily in the breeze.

Elizabeth directs Franklin and Temple to a settee to one side of the fireplace, while she and William take seats on the settee opposite. Howard enters the room carrying a silver salver and serves glasses of wine.

Elizabeth nods toward Temple. "He's not too young for a touch of sherry, is he Papa?" she asks.

"Heavens, no." Franklin replies. "The boy was *raised* on Madeira."

"You are a blessing to us, Temple, in many ways" Elizabeth continues cheerily. "I have been unable to bear a child. Now I have one. We are a family at last!"

Franklin is relieved to learn that Elizabeth has been apprised of Temple's parentage.

William raises his glass. "A toast! To our family!"

The others raise their glasses and share in the toast. Howard sets the bottle of sherry on a sideboard and leaves the room.

"It is beautiful country around here, Temple. You won't think of London for one minute," William offers.

"I do miss Aunt Margaret," Temple concedes. "And Polly. She is like a sister to me."

"Polly Stevenson? Did she ever speak of me?" William inquires.

"Not that I recall. She's Polly Hewson now. I lived with her and her husband in the big house when Grandpapa and Aunt Margaret moved down the street to their townhouse. Dr. Hewson kept skeletons in our basement!"

William looks at his father with a surprised look. "You moved with Margaret to another house?"

"Yes. Margaret couldn't abide the skeletons. Hewson is a medical man, you see."

"I should have moved as well!" Elizabeth volunteers.

Howard re-enters the parlor. "Dinner will be served shortly, Mrs. Franklin," he advises politely.

"'Tis very kind of you, Elizabeth, to wait your evening meal for us," Franklin says.

"It is our pleasure," Elizabeth assures him. "You have time for a quick wash, then let us meet in the dining room."

Darkness falls outside the dining room windows, the candles on the table have been lit and a chandelier shines overhead. A framed oil portrait of the King looks down somberly on the Franklins as they take their seats around the oval table, which is polished to a high shine. The men wear dressy jackets over their waistcoats, with cravats tied at the neck. Elizabeth's smooth, rosy complexion belies her forty-seven years. She is lovely in pale blue silk with strands of flawless pearls around her neck. Franklin grimaces at the King's portrait as he settles into his Queen Anne-style chair. Howard and a second, younger manservant attend to the table with quiet efficiency.

The younger servant offers vegetables to Elizabeth from a porcelain bowl. "I think we should take a picnic lunch to the seashore on Sunday," she announces, placing carrots on her plate with a silver spoon. "Would you like that, Temple?"

"Very much!" Temple says. "Grandpapa taught me to swim."

Elizabeth looks pleased. "Will you join us at the shore, Papa? Perhaps give me a swimming lesson?"

"Thank you, but no," Franklin replies, as Howard fills his wine glass. "I must return home on the morrow. The Continental Congress is in session and resumes deliberations on Monday."

"A Congress which is pointless and illegal," William says, through a mouthful of roast meat.

"I happily serve in that Congress, Bill Boy, having been appointed the day after we landed. I advocate separation from the mother country, as do many other delegates."

"Independence can only be won by revolution, which would be suicidal," William argues.

"As the Crown wishes nothing less than the subjugation of the colonies, there is no other path open to us!" Franklin retorts, raising his voice.

"Don't be shy, my dear," Elizabeth says to Temple, as a platter of roast venison is offered to him. "Please eat your fill."

"You must consider, Father, I swore fealty to my King!"

"A King who is half-mad and entirely dissolute," Franklin says impatiently.

"I believe, sir, you would be wise to remain neutral in the conflict. You are an easy target for His Majesty's retribution."

Franklin waves his fork at the King's portrait. "He is no threat to me here, nor will he protect you. He is too far away and hasn't the resolve - or money enough - to prevail."

"May I suggest, gentlemen, that you continue your discussion in Billy's study after dinner?" Elizabeth says lightly. "Let's talk now of something more pleasant," She turns to Temple. "Do you plan to continue your schooling in America?" she inquires.

"Yes, ma'am," he replies eagerly. "I plan to attend college in the fall."

"Good! We will send you to King's College in New York. It enjoys a fine reputation," William chimes in.

Franklin slams his hand on the table. "You will not!" he snaps. "He will attend the college I established in Pennsylvania. New York is awash with Loyalists!"

Elizabeth remains calm. "What do you plan to read whilst at university?"

"I have a keen interest in history, Ma'am."

Elizabeth places her hand on Temple's arm. "Do please call me 'Mother'," she says.

"I would be honored to do so, Mother."

The warm glow of their smiles is unable to thaw the icy atmosphere in the room. Franklin and William continue eating their dinners in silence.

Later that evening, Temple stands in the central hall of the mansion with his ear pressed to the pair of doors which lead to William's study. He hears his grandfather's and his father's raised voices on the other side.

Behind the doors, Franklin and William are seated in easy chairs on either side of the fireplace in the candlelit room. Howard serves the two men glasses of whiskey from a silver salver. He returns the tray to a sideboard and lays kindling wood from a bin next to the fireplace on a grate in the hearth.

Franklin twirls the amber liquid in his glass, watching it drip down the sides of the crystal. "Do not cling, William, to a corrupt institution!" he advises. "You would be wise to resign your post and make peace with your Legislature."

William slumps in his chair. "I believe His Majesty's troops already amassed in this country to be invincible, and another fifteen thousand Hessian fighters have landed at New York."

"Men who defend their own property and a way of life will not be defeated by mercenaries!" Franklin argues.

"Father, you speak of a ragtag band of farmers armed with shovels and pitchforks versus the British Army? It's laughable!" William smirks.

Howard ignites the fire, then quietly leaves the room, opening and closing the double doors behind him. Temple retreats around a corner as Howard leaves.

"Do not be naïve, Bill Boy. A large army of patriots has organized under General Washington, who is a brilliant tactician. Cunning and bravery will win the day... I promise you that!" retorts Franklin.

William sips his whiskey "You ask me to commit treason."

"What treason? You are not a British subject, per se. You are an American," Franklin reasons.

William shakes his head. "That's ridiculous."

"Why is it you have made no mention of the bludgeoning I suffered at the hands of the Privy Council?" Franklin continues. "Cause enough for a son to come over to his father's side."

"Wedderburn was excessive, I admit, but you *had* stolen those letters."

The fire glows and crackles in the fireplace.

"I most certainly had not stolen them! They were *given* to me!" Franklin snaps. "You must realize we cannot coexist on opposing sides of this great issue."

"I stand by my King and my work here," William says resolutely.

"Are we to be Caesar and Pompey? Vanquished in victory?"

William sits up and takes a sip of his drink. "Caesar and Pompey were allies and friends, not father and son. A poor analogy."

"Friends… as I thought we once were."

"May I suggest, Father, if you are determined to set the colonies aflame, you run by the light of it!"

Franklin holds William's eyes. "Very well. You have made your position clear." He tosses back his drink, slams the glass down on the table, and rises from his chair. "Run I shall. I am going to bed."

William takes a long pull of his drink and stares vacantly into the crackling flames as his father leaves the room.

Temple hears Franklin's footsteps pound across the wooden floor of the study. He retreats around the corner again as Franklin opens the doors.

"Good night!" Franklin shouts to William. He slams the heavy doors closed behind him.

Franklin hears Temple breathing around the corner. He pauses for a moment. "Temple? Do not forget that I will come for you at the end of August!" Franklin says, before thundering on down the hall to his room.

WATERFRONT, PHILADELPHIA   APRIL 1790

Raindrops dance on the river across the road from a seedy tavern. Small boats tied to the wharf bob up and down, tugging at their ropes. A sign over the entrance swings back and forth in the wind. It reads: *'Two Mariners. Tavern and Publik House.'* Piano music and the sound of laughter drift out the door and over the water.

Inside the noisy, smoke-filled establishment, a few scantily clad women wander through ale-soaked sawdust on the floor, serving drinks and flirting with customers. The heavily powdered and rouged servers are well along in years and from appearances, may well have been professional entertainers in their prime. Although candles burn on the tables, the tavern seems dark and murky. Patrons sit at tables in the shadows, drinking and chatting. A pianist in the next room plunks out an Irish folk tune.

Temple and Benny lounge on tattered upholstered chairs in a quiet nook, with their feet propped on a hassock shared between them. A near-empty whiskey bottle rests on a table next to them. They both have drinks in hand.

Temple recalls his visit with his grandfather to Perth Amboy several years earlier. "A chasm opened between the two of them that night, like a fresh dug grave," he recalls, slurring his words. "I fell into it and never climbed out."

Benny shakes his head. "It's a shame you were stuck in the middle all these years. A damn shame. But it ain't ever gonna change." He takes a sip of his drink. "Way too late now."

"You're right," Temple agrees. "They're both stubborn bastards."

"Stubborn bastards," Benny concurs. He chuckles and points to one of the 'hostesses'. "Temple, look there, at that damsel. She might very well be your mother!"

Temple points out an ancient 'hostess'. "And that old dear is likely my grandmother!"

Benny laughs. "'Tis lovely to drink with family, ain't it?"

"'Tis at that. Are you going upstairs?" Temple asks, sounding tempting.

"No, you swine, and neither are you." Benny empties his glass. "It's getting late. Drink up. Time to go home. Let's go see Grandpa."

Temple lifts his glass. "To our family!" he says as he drinks the last of his whiskey.

They both stand, weaving unsteadily through tables and chairs toward the door to the street. A distant clock strikes nine.

Franklin House   April 1790

Jefferson's carriage waits in the mews behind the mansion. His two coachmen lean against the carriage, bored, their arms folded across their chests. They chat and share jokes. One of them takes a small pipe from his pocket and lights it. A clock in a church tower a few blocks away chimes nine. The other coachman looks at his pocket watch to confirm the time. He shows his watch to his fellow coachman, who looks at it and shrugs his shoulders. On the walk out front of the house, three neighbors, two women and a man, stand under a streetlamp, quietly conversing. They hear the clock in the belfry of the Romish church on Maple Street strike the hour.

As the man checks his pocket watch, a second man approaches him. "Jefferson still in there?" he inquires.

"Seems so," the first man replies. "We ain't seen him leave."

"Where'd Emeline go to?"

"She went home… worried about her old man," one of the women explains.

The second man looks toward the big house. "I'd like to get a look at him," he says.

"Emeline's old man?" the other lady asks.

The second man glares at her. "No! Jefferson!" he growls.

Aggie descends the stairs at the center of the mansion carrying a basket of laundry destined for the wash house out back. She hears a distant clock strike the hour, passes a grandfather clock on the landing and stops. With her free hand, she opens the door of the clock and moves the big hand to nine. The clock begins to chime the hour. She smiles and closes the door of the clock. She is startled to see a hazy reflection in the glass of a raven-haired woman standing behind her. Aggie shrieks and drops her basket on the floor. She slowly turns to see a broom leaning against the wall with a dust rag draped over its bristles.

Aggie takes a deep breath and holds her hand to her heart. "I swear," she says aloud, "someday this big ol' house gonna scare me to death!" She gathers up her laundry basket and continues down the stairs.

DEAR BEN

Franklin's bedroom   April 1790

Franklin reclines on his bed, with his head propped up by pillows, and his eyes closed.

Bobby sits in a chair near the bed, darning stockings. He looks up when he hears the grandfather clock on the landing below strike the hour.

Franklin opens one eye. "You're still here," he whispers.

"Mm-hm… so are you. That lady ain't come for you yet."

"So, she hasn't. Did your mama teach you to do that? Darning?"

"Mm-hm."

Franklin turns onto his elbow, with both eyes open. "You should go, Bobby, before Sally gets wind of our scheme," he says earnestly. "She may be of another mind."

"I go when the time come, Dr. Ben. You ain't finished your story yet."

"Story?" Franklin strains to sit up. "Oh. Let me think. Well, we had a full Congress that summer. Sixty-two delegates, half of them my enemies."

CHAPTER THIRTY-ONE

An Act of Congress

Philadelphia   1775

Light from the tall, paned windows topped with fanlights floods a large hall in the State House. Thirty men stand about in small groups, conferring with one another. Another ten men meander from group to group, stopping to introduce themselves and to join in with the informal debate. All wear stiff business attire, most wear wigs on their heads. Franklin sits off to one side in the lofty room. He is alone, with his cane in hand, his head bare, observing his fellow delegates. Chairs are lined up in rows facing a head table draped with blue cloth. The Continental Congress is about to get underway.

John Adams walks up to Franklin, his stocky frame casting a shadow over him. "Well, Franklin," he inquires, "have you decided if you are an Englishman or an American?"

Franklin looks up. "Ah, Adams! I have a foot in both countries, but my heart is firmly planted here."

Adams pulls over a chair and sits next to Franklin. "I am happy to hear it. What are your thoughts, then, on the 'Olive Branch Petition' as proposed by Dickinson?"

"It seems several colonies are bent on this one last chance for reconciliation with the Crown. What say you?"

"I think it's demeaning and a waste of time." Adams leans close to Franklin. "We beg the King for clemency, while being pummeled by his troops, and then we wait. For what, I do not know."

"It will be a long wait," Franklin predicts. "The King will ignore the petition, but I feel I have no choice but to sign it."

"As do I, out of solidarity with the other delegates, but I hold out little hope for its success." Adams points to Franklin's walking stick. "Gout bothering you again?" he asks.

"Yes, and other complaints of old age. If we live long enough, John, and drink life to the bottom of the bottle, we must come to the dregs."

"That all depends, Franklin, on how one lives it," Adams sniggers. He stands, turns his back to Franklin, and walks away.

Two southern delegates sitting nearby have been observing Franklin's exchange with Adams. One of them nods in Franklin's direction. "We would be wise to keep a sharp eye on that crafty old buzzard," he says in his southern drawl.

"Yes, too many years spent in England, to my liking," the other delegate concurs.

"My guess is that every word said here will find its way to His Majesty's Privy Council."

"One way or another, to be sure," the other man agrees.

Franklin's bedroom   April 1790

Bobby sets his darning in a basket on the floor next to his chair, rises, and fluffs the pillows behind Franklin's back.

"Thank you," Franklin says and goes on with his story. "Before long, I was appointed to a commission bound for Canada. With me were delegates Sam Chase, Charles Carroll, a French-speaking gentleman, and his brother, John, a Romish priest. Have we any more of that tea left Bobby?"

Bobby finds the wine bottle and pours some in a teacup. He hands it to Franklin.

"The Congress had appointed an army under General Shuyler to seize Canada the previous year, hoping to fend off a British invasion from the north. This was no easy task."

Bobby picks up his darning basket and resumes his chore.

"Shuyler managed to take Montreal, but Quebec withheld his assault," Franklin continues. "General Arnold laid siege to the impenetrable fortress throughout the cruel winter. My party set out in early spring. We witnessed the last of that endless winter."

Franklin wheezes and coughs, then takes a drink of his Madeira. "We were sent to report on affairs there and to advise the Congress if reinforcements should be sent to Quebec. I surmised that my enemies had encouraged my appointment, hoping I would succumb to the elements… Not an unlikely prospect since I was seventy years of age."

Northern New York   March 1776

Franklin recalls a bitter cold, gray day. He and his companions trudge on foot across a frozen lake. The ice is covered with a layer of pristine, crisp snow, which crunches under foot. The men are bundled in fur coats and wear warm hats pulled down over their ears. They lead four horses laden with supplies and bedrolls.

Two hundred feet ahead of Franklin, a party of eight men crosses the frozen lake. Six of those men lead heavily laden horses. A seventh man rides in a horse-drawn carriage, piled with gear. The eighth man drives a Conestoga wagon filled with material and supplies. Franklin sees patches of bitterly cold, open water fifty feet off to the left of their path across the ice.

Franklin slips on the ice and falls. Samuel Chase and Charles Carroll see him fall, stop, and help him up. The team of eight men ahead of them treks on.

As Franklin brushes the snow off his breeches, he and his comrades hear a loud 'cracking' noise, followed by another loud 'crack'.

"What was that? Rifle fire?" Carroll asks anxiously.

Chase holds up his hand. "No, not gunfire."

The priest stops walking and listens. They hear another loud 'crack'.

Suddenly, the carriage, horse, and driver ahead fall through the ice. A man screams, men shout in confusion. Another loud 'crack' is heard and the Conestoga wagon, along with its horse and driver, plunges through the ice into the water. Franklin's party is stunned for a moment, not moving. They hear more screaming and mad shouting from the men ahead.

"Mother of God!" the priest yells. "They've fallen in!"

Chase and Carroll regain their senses. "Retreat, men! Run! Run for your lives!" they both yell at once. Franklin's party turns and runs back toward shore, the ice cracking behind them as they go.

Later that afternoon, Franklin and his company plod along a path through snow-laden trees on horseback. They ride in single file; their progress is slow. The sun is low on the horizon, occasionally peeking through the trees. The men have not spoken for a long while, as they replay in their heads the tragic scene they had witnessed earlier in the day.

The priest, riding at the rear of the group, is the first to speak. "We will never be forgiven for not going to the aid of those men!" he shouts to his companions.

"Nonsense, Father!" Chase calls back to the priest. "We would have surely drowned, had we tried to help them!"

Franklin rides just ahead of the priest. "When we camp for the night, Father, you will hear our confessions and grant us dispensation. Is that not what you do?" he teases.

"'Twas a nightmarish thing to see! Horrid! I am still in shock!" Carroll admits.

The four men ride on in silence.

As darkness falls, they come to a clearing in the woods. They see an abandoned farmhouse at the far side of the clearing. The house is derelict, with many roof shingles missing and several windows broken, but still a welcome sight.

"There's a piece of luck, lads!" Chase shouts as he points to the old weather-beaten house. "Shelter for the night! With a proper outhouse!"

They pick up their pace and head for the farmhouse.

"Come Father John," Franklin calls to the pouting priest, "Let's find some kindling." He and the priest dismount and scour the edge of the forest, collecting sticks of wood.

Inside the farmhouse, the four men wander through barren rooms stripped of furnishings. They do what they can to make themselves comfortable, huddling around a fire they build in the old parlor fireplace. They sit on blankets spread on the worn plank floor, with their coats over them, fending off the chill coming in from a broken window. A few stubs of candles are lighted and fixed to floorboards with spilled wax. The candles flicker and cast yellowish light and deep shadows on the foursome. The men share a meal of jerky, hardtack and cheese, as they have for many nights.

Charles Carroll chuckles to himself. "I don't know about you gentlemen, but I could use a change of menu," he offers.

"And a change of *venue*," the priest concurs.

Franklin leans down to write in a notebook by the light of a candle stuck to the floor.

"What do you write, there, Franklin?" Samuel Chase inquires. "A journal about our sad lodgings?"

"Nay, 'tis a farewell letter to a friend," Franklin replies. "I am beginning to doubt I will live to see Montreal."

"Was it ever this cold in England, Ben?" Carroll asks, while chewing on a piece of jerky.

"Much worse… a damp cold. 'Tis why Englishmen roam the world."

Carroll takes a sip from a flask and passes it to his brother. "There were plenty of Englishmen in Paris when I studied there as a boy."

Franklin perks up and sets down his notebook. "Did you perchance meet the Frenchman on the Pont Neuf who loved to nettle the English?"

"No. What of him?"

Franklin takes a sip from his flask. "He kept a brazier of hot coals with a glowing red poker in it. When an Englishman would walk by, he would stop him and say, *'Pardonnez-moi, Anglais, would you kindly bend over so I can stick this hot poker up your arse?'* The Englishman would respond, *'Are you mad?! No, I will not bend over! Get that thing away from me!'*"

Chase looks up from his meagre meal. "Is this a true story?"

"Of course, it is," Franklin replies. "Then the Frenchman would say, *'In that case, may I at least have fifty pence for the cost of heating it?'*"

The others roar with laughter; despite himself, the priest laughs too.

"Shall I tell you another?" Franklin grins and takes a long pull from his flask.

"No! Go to sleep Franklin," the priest snaps, and lies back on his blankets.

Franklin is undaunted. "When my grandson and I were crossing from Portsmouth last spring, we watched two sailors…"

The priest interrupts Franklin, speaking to shadows on the water-stained ceiling. "Your grandson? The bastard son of a bastard son, no?"

Franklin hesitates for a moment. "So he is. Does that bother you, Father?"

"Shh!" Carroll 'shushes' the two men. "Écoutez! Listen!" he says, with his finger to his lips. A rain shower begins to patter on the leaky roof of the old house. "It's raining!" he says excitedly.

"Yes! Rain!" Chase concurs, looking very pleased. "It's getting warmer, thanks be to God!"

PERTH AMBOY   MARCH 1776

William Franklin is seated at the desk in his study, intent on a letter he is writing: '*I hope this finds Your Lordship in good health. It is of keen interest that Dr. Franklin and three others passed through here en route to Canada. With him were a delegate to the Congress, a French-speaker, and a Romish priest.*'

William reaches for and rings a bell on the table behind him. He stirs his tea and takes a sip. He dips his pen in the ink well again and continues writing: '*My father's mission is to persuade the Canadians to join their confederacy and to send delegates to Congress. Montreal has already fallen, and Quebec is under siege. He will assure the Quebecois their estates will remain intact and their Catholic faith sacrosanct.*'

A tap at the door and Amos Beaumont, William's secretary, enters the study.

"Sir?"

"When I finish here, I want you to post this letter to Lord Germain in London by speediest means. It is most urgent. Use my seal."

"Yes, sir. I will wait outside," Amos says, and retreats to his office.

William resumes writing the letter. '*Should they succeed, Canada will be lost.*'

The window of an apothecary across town from the Governor's mansion displays colorful beakers, canisters and other wares of the pharmacists' trade. A bell atop the door rings as Amos enters the shop.

He has the letter William had given him to post earlier hidden inside his jacket. He waits nervously at the shop's sales counter. After a minute or two, the gentleman Amos had met with previously, at the Baggott Tea Shop, parts a curtain and approaches the counter from the back room of the apothecary.

Amos looks about. "Are we alone, sir?" he asks.

"Yes, son."

"I have here an urgent letter from the Governor to Lord Germain," he says, patting the side of his frock coat. The man holds the curtain open. "Come with me," he says as he leads Amos into the interior of the shop, which is lighted by a window high on the back wall. Amos takes the letter from his pocket and hands it to the man, who opens it. He spreads it out on a worktable and smooths the paper.

"Unbelievable," the gentleman says, as he looks over the letter. "He sells his father to the King, as Judas sold Jesus to Pontius Pilate."

"I'd best be on my way," Amos says anxiously.

"My wife will transcribe the letter and I will have it for you in an hour or two, ready to post. Come back then," the man instructs.

"Yes, sir."

The gentleman takes silver coins from his pocket and lays them on the table. "Thank you, Amos," he says. "You are a true patriot."

Amos looks at the coins and shakes his head, leaving them on the counter. He turns, parts the curtain, and scurries out of the shop.

MONTREAL   MAY 1776

Twelve men, including Franklin's party of four, are seated at a long table in a dining hall, in the midst of a meal. Several of the men wear uniforms of the American Continental Army. Conversation is lively and loud. General Benedict Arnold, aged thirty-five, sits at the head of the table, hosting the dinner. His younger aide sits at his right. Candles burn on the table, which is covered with a white linen cloth. The table is laden with epergnes of fruit and sweets. The diners have an array of fine china plates, stemmed crystal glasses and silver flatware before them.

Four pretty French Canadian girls, not one of them more than seventeen years old, attend to the table. They wear revealing attire, especially considering the chilly weather outside. The girls speak French as they clear the plates and pour wine for the General's guests. A fifth young woman plays a harp in a corner of the room.

Samuel Chase, seated mid-table, turns to General Arnold. "We are surprised by the bountiful table you set with a paucity of means," he shouts above the chatter of the other diners.

"To the victor belong the spoils!" the General calls back to him.

Franklin is seated opposite Chase. His eyes are fixed on the bosom of one of the girls, who is filling his wine glass at that moment, "The logic of your mission, General Arnold, is unclear to me," Franklin says in full voice. "We invade, then ask the Canadians to join our confederacy?"

Franklin's eyes follow the girl as she moves around the table. "Conquer and make new friends? Was that the idea?"

General Arnold pats the backside of another girl who pours wine into his glass from a decanter. "Along those lines, yes," he replies.

Charles Carroll raises his voice from the far end of the table. "Who conceived of this plan?" he asks.

Chase answers the question. "It was General Shuyler who convinced Congress of the viability of the scheme, Charles."

"You are quite right," General Arnold confirms. "Then Shuyler fell ill, and General Montgomery took over, but was killed at Quebec. I sustained injuries there as well."

"After an arduous journey north, I have heard," Franklin adds. "We can attest to the difficulties you encountered."

"I lost nearly half my men to the brutal weather or to desertion."

"How many men would that be?" Carroll asks.

"Hundreds," the General replies.

The priest, who has kept his head down while dining, looks up. "Lord have mercy," he whispers.

Arnold's adjutant turns to Franklin. "We hoped, Dr. Franklin, that your delegation had come with at least 20,000 pounds to restore our credit in the region."

Chase sips his wine. "My dear boy," he says. "I doubt that kind of money can be had from the Congress anytime soon!"

The priest looks stricken as one of the girls hovers over him, tempting him with her offerings. She pours sweet wine into his crystal glass.

Carroll sits back in his chair and looks toward the General, as one of the girls serves him a pudding. "The Bishop of Montreal told my brother and me that he is quite satisfied with British assurances of religious freedom. He has no interest in joining our cause."

Franklin looks concerned. "Is there any hope, General, you will succeed in taking Quebec?" he asks.

"Without fresh troops and money to pay our debts, none whatsoever," Arnold replies.

Chase waves away a girl offering him a pudding. "A quagmire, I would say. Ill-conceived and ill-fated," he grumbles.

General Arnold looks up and down the table. "If you do not succeed, gentlemen, in sending what we require, we will be contemptible in the eyes of the people. The Quebecois will turn their backs on your federation. They will not be alone."

His dinner guests look at one another, without comment.

After a moment, Arnold's tone lightens. He pushes his back chair from the table and stands. "Come! Let us retire to the ballroom. The girls have arranged an entertainment for us. They will sing and dance! Bring your wine glasses!"

The diners rise from the table and follow the General out of the dining hall.

Franklin catches Carroll's eye. He bids him to stay behind. "I am going to gather my things and head for home on the morrow. There is nothing more I can do here," Franklin confides.

"Take my brother with you," Carroll suggests. "His work here is finished as well. Chase and I are of a mind to stay another week or two and try to kick life into this dead horse."

Franklin gestures toward two girls clearing china and glassware from the table. "And take in the local scenery, perchance?"

"You rogue. What will you advise Congress?"

"I shall recommend that we withdraw our troops at once. The Canadians have no quarrel with the English King."

"Chase and I will likely agree with you, Ben, but kindly wait until our return to make your report."

"Agreed. *Je suis d'accord.*"

Franklin's bedroom   1790

"The General's words, Bobby, proved prescient. He soon turned coat and went over to the British side. I spent the next weeks making the long trek home with the priest. We said little. He was an opinionated, irritating man."

Northern New York   May 1776

A fair spring day. Franklin and the priest ride along a sodden trail through the woods. Trees are in bud, and a bright sun shines through the tender green leaves, dappling the muddy path with sunlight. Their horses are laden with supplies and bedding, their rifles secured in scabbards. The two men ride in their shirtsleeves, with their heavy winter coats strapped to the top of their bedrolls. Franklin's horse plods along a few yards behind Father John. The men haven't spoken to one another during the past hour or so.

Franklin decides to strike up a conversation. "So, Father John, you live in Harrisburg?" he shouts ahead to the priest.

"Yes," Father John replies over his shoulder. "In the church rectory."

"Do you live alone?"

"Yes, but I have a woman who comes in to cook and clean for me."

"Is she the only woman in your life?" Franklin grins.

The priest slows his horse's pace to hear better. "I am celibate," he responds.

Franklin's horse catches up with the priest's. "No other woman?" he taunts. "Only the Virgin."

"Do you believe in the virgin birth?" Franklin asks, as he pulls alongside the priest.

"Of course."

"And that Mary is the Mother of God?" Franklin persists.

"As Jesus in the Holy Trinity is the Son of God, it follows naturally," the priest answers peevishly.

"Naturally? I find it incredible."

"You are not a man of faith? You are an agnostic?"

"I am a man of science. I believe in that which is rational."

"You are also a rich man. Beware the 'eye of the needle'," the priest warns ominously.

Franklin's expression sours. He whips his horse and pulls ahead of the priest and his mount.

CHAPTER THIRTY-TWO

A Long, Hot Summer

PHILADELPHIA   MAY 1776

Shortly after his return from Montreal, Franklin recovers from his arduous journey in his library at home. He is content, reclining in an easy chair, savoring a book he had put off reading before he embarked on his trip north. The window behind him is open a few inches, the curtains flutter in the warm breeze. He is comfortably dressed in well-worn cotton breeches and a frayed linen shirt, but one of his feet is bandaged and elevated on a hassock. A teacup rests on a small table next to him.

There is a tap at the door, and he hears Sally's voice in the hall outside. "Papa?"

"What is it, Sal?" he calls to her.

She opens the door a sliver and peeks in. "You have a visitor."

"Who is it?"

"General Washington."

"Jesus! Show him in!"

General Washington pushes past Sally, opens the door wide, and strides into the room. At forty-four, he is tall and commanding in his military uniform. "You are thinking of another gentleman! My name is Washington!" he says in a jovial tone, a wide smile on his face.

Franklin attempts to stand.

"Don't get up, Ben. Don't get up," Washington commands.

The two men shake hands with Franklin still seated. "I *am* a little lame these days," Franklin offers.

"You've been through one hell of an ordeal!" Washington concedes.

"I wish I had brought you better news. I saw little hope of success. Please, General, sit down. My neck won't bend far enough to get a good look at you."

Washington laughs and turns a desk chair to face Franklin.

"May we offer you tea?" Franklin asks.

"I can't stay long. You witnessed a classic military blunder first-hand, Ben. We over-reached our ability to succeed."

"I say, take food off your neighbor's plate and you may get your hand slapped."

"Or your arm broken. British ships arrived in time to turn our retreat into a rout."

"So, I heard." Franklin's face brightens. "I am so *very* pleased to see you. Are you sure you won't stay for tea?"

"No, no. I have come to thank you for bringing the Congress to its senses."

"I have been unable to attend any sessions due to my poor health. Boils and gout have got the better of me. I do believe I'm finished with public service."

Washington smiles. "Well, we are not finished with you. Rest and get your strength back. You're needed at the State House." He rises and pats Franklin on the shoulder. "I wanted to have a look at you. You will survive this."

"Your visit has been restorative," Franklin says, looking up at the man towering over him.

Washington takes a few steps toward the door and turns back. "Congress is drafting a paper of separation from the Mother Country," he says. "Adams and Jefferson are on the committee writing it. They will need your advice. I'll see my own way out."

Washington strides out of the room as briskly as he entered it.

One evening, a week or two later, the candle on Aggie's tea tray lights the hallway outside Franklin's library. She taps lightly on the door, opens it, and enters the room. Aggie finds Franklin and Thomas Jefferson seated on either side of Franklin's leather-topped partner's desk. They are looking over papers by light of an oil lamp. The two men don't look up as Aggie sets her candleholder on a commode, then serves them tea and biscuits.

"Thank you, Aggie," Franklin murmurs.

Aggie smiles and curtsies to Jefferson. She retrieves her candle and leaves the room, closing the door quietly behind her.

Jefferson sips his tea. "Otherwise, do you find the document sound? Is it reasonable?" He looks at Franklin anxiously.

"Damned near flawless," Franklin replies.

"Adams stepped aside. He said a Virginian should do the honors."

"Well, you have done a magnificent job," Franklin rises from his chair and limps around the room. "There are a few minor points I would mention, however. *'Truths we hold to be sacred'* sounds to be from a religious tract. How about making that *'Truths we hold to be self-evident'* instead? Sounds more rational to me."

"I shall make a note of it," Jefferson says, picking up a pen from the desk. "I suppose the Congress will tear my draft apart."

"Congress will have its way with it. 'Tis why I avoid writing papers for review by committee."

"I must try to control my temper," Jefferson says.

"Yes, you must." Franklin rests on a wooden stepstool next to a bookshelf. "Think of Dr. Jones, a medical man, who settled in a small town and specialized in piles and perversion and hung out his sign saying so. The town fathers were horrified and asked that he change the sign to something more dignified."

Jefferson looks askance. "You're making this up."

"Nay, 'tis a true story."

"So, he hung a second sign which read, *"Dr. Jones. Queers and Rears."*

Jefferson spills his tea, laughing.

"Now the town council was truly offended and demanded something more subtle. The solution was a sign reading, *"Dr. Jones. Odds and Ends."*

Jefferson laughs a belly laugh.

"It is predictable that the Congress will make some edits to your Declaration, but there is so much good in it, Tommy, it will survive the assault. Enough blasted tea! Let's open a bottle of wine." Franklin rises from the wooden stool and limps to a cabinet opposite the desk. He removes a bottle of French wine and two glasses. He pulls the cork and pours them both a drink. "Let us toast your brilliant success!" Franklin says, raising his glass.

Jefferson, beaming, raises his glass.

Perth Amboy   June 1776

William Franklin's desk in his office is, as usual, piled with stacks of paperwork. He studies a tract which has come to him recently from the legislature. He hears a knock at the door. "Come!" he calls impatiently through the closed door.

His secretary opens the door and enters the room. "There are two gentlemen here to see you," he says.

William looks up from his papers. "And they are…?" he inquires.

"They say they have come from the Provincial Assembly," Amos replies.

"Show them in, then." William says and returns to his papers.

A moment later, Amos directs two young men into the office. They wear military uniforms and carry muskets. They have grave expressions on their faces.

Surprised by the men-at-arms, William gets up from his chair. "Hello… I don't recognize you gentlemen from the Assembly," he says. He walks around the desk and extends a hand to the visitors. "William Franklin here. Who are you, my I inquire?"

The taller of the two men reaches out and shakes William's hand. "How d'ya do," he says, in an attempt at courtesy. "We is officers of the Militia. You is under arrest by orders from the New Jersey Assembly."

"I beg your pardon?" William cocks his head, as though he hasn't heard the soldier correctly.

The other officer moves toward William. "He said, you are under arrest."

William retreats behind his desk. "You can't arrest me! What are the charges?!"

The taller soldier takes a step forward. "The new Congress is removin' all Royal Governors. That be you."

William is indignant. "Have you a warrant for my arrest?" he demands to know.

The other officer takes a folded paper from his vest pocket and lays it on William's desk. "Says here you are *an enemy of the liberties of this country.*"

William's eyes are wild as he scans the paper. "Does my father know of this?"

"He will," the taller soldier says. "So's the Assembly asked us to treat you with respect... Sir." He waves his musket toward the door. "Let's go," he orders sharply.

"Where are you taking me?" William asks meekly.

"We take you to stand for trial," the soldier explains. With that, he ushers William out of his office, with the barrel of his musket pressed to William's back.

Amos is seated at a writing table in the outer office as they pass by.

"Amos! Call for my guards!" William shouts to him as he stumbles forward.

"They went home, sir. You might want your coat, sir!" Amos jumps up and fetches William's jacket from a hook by the door in the inner office. He stuffs it into William's hands, which have gone limp.

Blinking his eyes in the bright sunlight, William is pushed out the front door of the mansion by the two militia men. "You will pay for this!" he yells, his voice raspy and cracking with anger. The officers do not appear concerned by the threat.

Franklin's bedroom   1790

Bobby is seated in a chair near Franklin's bed, with his darning basket in his lap. Franklin has been silent for the past several minutes and Bobby's mind wanders.

Franklin breaks the quiet. He grunts and raises himself up onto his elbows. "The hour grows late, Bobby. Where *are* my boys?" he asks, sounding annoyed.

"Oh, they be along," Bobby replies. "This time 'a night, I know where I could go find 'em, but I ain't welcome there."

Franklin sits up straighter. After a pause, he says, "I understand."

Bobby looks up from his darning chore. "Where those soldiers take William that time, anyway?" he asks.

Franklin gazes at the streetlamp outside his window. "The Assembly had incriminating letters of his, which painted him a traitor. How they got hold of them, I don't know. I didn't dare attend the trial. My son and I had parted ways."

Franklin pushes his blanket aside and struggles to rise from the bed. "Nothing like a misplaced letter to get a man into trouble," he says.

"Ain't that the truth," Bobby concurs.

"Where are Jefferson's maps?" Franklin inquires. "I should attend to them."

"You sit back, Dr. Ben. I bring 'em to you." Bobby sets down his darning basket, goes to Franklin's desk and sorts through papers.

Franklin sits back on his bed. "William was convicted. He was taken to Connecticut and placed in the custody of Governor Trumbull, a confirmed patriot."

Connecticut   June 1776

William, flanked by two sentries in uniform, is led to a modest frame cottage on the grounds of the estate of the Governor of Connecticut. It is the guest house of a Greek Revival-style mansion, which rises on a knoll fifty yards away. The sentries prod William over the threshold with their bayonets. William wears an ill-fitting uniform of plain indigo cotton. Governor Trumbull, a tall man in his mid-fifties, with wavy gray hair and a round, pleasant face, follows the trio into the cottage.

William is quietly seething but has gathered his wits and is sure his release will come in a matter of a few days. He enters a front room, sparsely furnished with a few straight-backed chairs and a writing table pushed against the walls. A small window above the table and another next to the door provide weak light. He peers into the next room, a tiny bedroom with a single window, a double bed, a washstand with basin and a battered chest of drawers.

The Governor ducks his head under the low doorway and enters the bedroom. "It may not be what you're used to, but you are much better off here than the prison in Litchfield," he says.

William smiles icily and moves to the bed. He pushes his hand into the thin mattress. "Would you mind, Governor, if I send to my house for proper linens?"

The Governor raises an eyebrow. "As you wish, but you would be wise to keep your head down. Your Assembly has branded you a 'virulent enemy' of the Revolution. They would rather have seen you at Litchfield."

"Will my wife be allowed to visit? She is in poor health, and I am worried about her."

"Not just yet," Trumbull replies. "She *may* write to you and you to her. Let us hope the hostilities between our two countries will be brief." He walks toward the door. "Make yourself comfortable, Franklin. Your meals will be brought to you here. If you behave yourself, perhaps I will invite you to dine with me up on the hill."

William looks about the room and says nothing.

The Governor turns back to him. "I don't suppose you play whist?" he inquires.

William shakes his head, 'no'.

"Well, then." Trumbull steps out the front door. "If you need anything, one of these gentlemen will be outside your door," he calls, pointing to the sentries. And then he is gone.

FRANKLIN HOUSE, PHILADELPHIA   JUNE 1776

A few nights later, Aggie's sleep is disturbed by the noise of a horse-drawn carriage clattering into the mews. She jabs Jake in his shoulder with her finger. "Somebody has rode into the driveway out there!" she whispers. She gets out of bed, takes her robe from a chair next to the bed and wraps it over her nightgown. She goes to the window for a look outside. "Jake! Wake up! Miss Elizabeth come from New Jersey!" Aggie finds her slippers and steps outside to meet the late-night visitor.

Aggie circles around the coach to greet Elizabeth. "Miss Elizabeth! What you doin' here this time 'a night?" she inquires.

Elizabeth looks tired and frail. Her head is bare, her hair tousled. "I have come to see Dr. Franklin on the most urgent business," she replies. "Everybody in bed by now," Aggie advises. "Where is your coat? You gonna freeze in this night air."

Elizabeth points to the coach.

Aggie reaches into the coach, retrieves Elizabeth's greatcoat and drapes it over her shoulders. "We go inside and I make you some tea."

Jake emerges from his quarters, yawning and tucking his nightshirt into his breeches as he walks toward the Governor's coach. "Throw them reins down and we get these animals watered," he calls up to the driver. Jake smooths the sweaty neck of one of the horses with his strong hands "Look to me like they been rode hard."

The driver, another African American man, jumps down from the front of the coach. "Yes, sir. They sure been rode hard," he agrees.

Inside the kitchen, Aggie hangs Elizabeth's cloak on a hook by the door. She lights an oil lamp, stokes embers still glowing in the hearth and places a kettle on the grate. She takes a log from a basket and settles it on the fire. She points to a chair at the kitchen table. "You sit here Miss."

Elizabeth takes a seat at the table. Aggie pours a glass of water and places it before her. "I get you somethin' stronger, if you like."

"This is fine, thank you."

"I have your tea ready in a minute." Aggie leaves the room, adjusting her bonnet as she goes, to bring the news of Elizabeth's visit to Dr. Franklin.

A moment later, Temple, groggy with sleep, wanders into the kitchen. He ties a long robe about his waist and smooths his blonde hair. "Mother! What brings you here?" he asks in a gravelly voice. "I heard your carriage. Where is Father?"

Elizabeth rises from her chair and they kiss each other on the cheek.

"Dear Temple!" she cries. "Your father has been imprisoned!"

"Imprisoned? Why?"

"His Assembly tried him for treason and sent him off to jail," she cries.

Temple looks incredulous. "I don't believe it! That's impossible."

"'Tis the Assembly that should be tried for sedition! They are a passel of traitors!" Elizabeth sobs, resuming her seat at the table.

Temple hears the kettle simmering in the hearth and fetches two teacups from the china cabinet. "What did they have as evidence?" he asks.

Elizabeth takes a kerchief from her pocket and wipes away tears. "Letters written to his superiors in London, as was his duty!" she replies, "The letters were stolen by a thief in the Provincial Government... How, I cannot imagine."

Temple makes a pot of tea and sits next to his stepmother. "What was in the letters?"

"Private matters! Your father was spirited away like a common criminal!"

Temple pours tea. "Surely Grandpapa can do something about this," he offers.

"I pray that he can," she sniffles into her kerchief.

Franklin enters from the hall, with Aggie a few steps behind. He is bright-eyed for the late hour, with a silk robe worn over his shirt and breeches. His slippers shuffle across the wooden planks of the kitchen floor. "My, goodness, Elizabeth! It is awfully late to be out for a buggy ride!" he says as he bends to give her a peck on her cheek.

Franklin nods toward the teapot. "Aggie, I will have a cup as well." He joins Temple and Elizabeth at the table.

"Oh, Papa, I have come with the most dreadful news about your son," Elizabeth says, unleashing another flood of tears.

"I know why you have come. Where have they taken him?"

"To Governor Trumbull in Connecticut," she replies, blowing her nose in her kerchief.

Aggie serves Franklin a cup of tea.

"It could be worse," Franklin offers. "Trumbull is a fair man. I am not surprised at this turn of events... Nor should you be, my dear."

"Can you not arrange a parole for him? I worry for his life in some dark prison!"

"He is not in prison," Franklin assures her. "More likely a sort of house arrest."

"Then, think of me, honorable sir!" Elizabeth pleads. "I am too weak to survive this ordeal... my asthma, you know. I worry the mansion will be sacked in Billy's absence. A woman alone..."

Franklin looks at Elizabeth as he stirs his tea. "Temple, you will go with Betsy and stay with her for a few days. Make certain she is safe in her home. I will send enough money with you so she will not be in need."

"If that is the best we can do…" Elizabeth whimpers.

Temple places a consoling hand on his stepmother's shoulder.

"Now, my dear," Franklin says over the rim of his teacup, "Aggie will get you settled in the guest room so you can get a night's rest. Let me do some thinking. Things will look brighter in the morning I can assure you." Franklin gives Elizabeth a gentle pat on the back of her hand. "Go along now."

Aggie takes Elizabeth's elbow and helps her up, then out of the kitchen.

A minute or two later, Temple turns to his grandfather. "Is there nothing more you can do for my father?"

Franklin sets down his teacup. "A sniveling woman in the middle of the night is of no help whatsoever. How can a man think?" Franklin huffs as he rises and leaves the room.

Temple calls after Franklin, "Shall I go to see him?"

"Do only as I tell you. Nothing more!" Franklin retorts.

After all the commotion, he fully intends to get back to the book he dropped on the floor next to his chair in the library earlier in the evening. Perhaps a spot of brandy…

CHAPTER THIRTY-THREE

The Gift

CONNECTICUT JUNE 1776

A few days later, a sentry, with his musket in hand, steps out of the guard's hut near William's cottage as Amos Beaumont approaches.

Amos carries a paper-wrapped package under his arm and a small basket in his hand. "I am told I can find Governor Franklin here," he says courteously.

"Aye, that be so," the sentry says. "And who would you be?"

"Amos Beaumont. I am the Governor's secretary."

"Secretary? Ye might like to find another line of work." The sentry points to a small table next to his hut. "Put 'em down here," he orders, indicating the parcel and basket.

"I have the Governor's bed sheets and some baked goods," Amos explains.

The sentry probes the paper-wrapped package with his bayonet and rummages through the basket. "All right, you can go on in," he says. "Bed sheets!" he mutters to himself as he raises the wooden bar securing the front door of the cottage. Amos doffs his cap, gathers up his package and basket, and steps inside.

"Governor Franklin?" It takes a moment for Amos's eyes to adjust to the dim light. He sets his parcels down on the writing table. "It's me, Amos!" he calls.

William wakes from a nap and jumps off the bed. He straightens the wrinkles in his cotton suit and smooths his hair as he goes to the front room. "How very good of you to come!" William says, offering his hand to Amos. Amos is surprised to see how much weight the Governor has lost since he last saw him, and how pale he is. "I have brought your bed linens, sir."

"Wonderful! I shall have a good sleep tonight!" William takes the parcel from the table and tosses it through the doorway and onto the bed. "How is my dear Elizabeth?" he inquires.

"Her spirits are very low, I am sorry to say, and her breathing trouble is bad."

"My poor darling wife. I pray my father rectifies this injustice soon."

"Mrs. Franklin was in Philadelphia when I went to the mansion to gather your things. Howard showed me in."

"Good! She has gone to talk some sense into the old man!"

Amos opens the basket. "I brought you a cake and strawberry jam from my mother, who is a fine baker."

"I am very touched," William says. "Please sit down." Amos sits in a spindle-backed chair. "Would you care for a cup of tea? It's the one luxury I am allowed…" William gestures to the little fireplace at the other end of the room, where coals glow under an iron grate and tea kettle.

"No, thank you," Amos replies. "My heart is heavy at your present circumstances. I wish I could have done more."

"Your loyal friendship cheers me," William says, his voice cracking. "But what could you have done? Trumped up charges and a farcical trial! I was defiant, Amos. You would have been pleased." William pauses a moment. "There *is* one small favor I would ask of you."

"Of course…"

William takes an envelope from a drawer in the writing table and hands it to Amos. "Post this to London for me. Keep it close to your breast as you leave, so the guard can't see it."

Amos studies the envelope.

William picks up a letter he has just finished writing. "Hold this letter to my wife where the guard can readily see it. It will distract him."

Amos secrets the first envelope inside his waistcoat. "I understand, sir. I will send your letter on its way."

William places his hand on Amos's shoulder. "You are a dear boy," he smiles.

Amos rises from his chair. "I must be going…"

"Won't you stay for a cup of tea? We could have a taste of your mother's cake! I have so little company…" William pleads.

Amos shakes his head. "I have a long journey ahead of me. Shall we make up your bed before I leave?"

"No. I will do it… An entertainment for me."

"Well, then," Amos says, extending his hand to William.

William shakes the hand offered. "Godspeed," he whispers, his voice choking with emotion.

Amos taps on the front door, the sentry opens it, and Amos steps out into the late afternoon sun.

PHILADELPHIA   JULY 1776

Jared Potter, the Chairman of the Congressional Committee for Secret Correspondence, listens patiently as Benjamin Franklin speaks and paces the floor of a meeting room in the Carpenter's Hall. At the same time, Potter watches a patch of the late afternoon sun retreat from the oak conference table at which he is seated.

After a pause, Franklin clears his throat. "Elizabeth's pleas, I tell you, were heart-wrenching, but I have done nothing to help my son."

Potter, a tall and wiry man who suffers with palsy on his right side, lights a candle on the table with some difficulty. "Why should you help him? He's never come to your aid, and the man is a bloody traitor! You are wise to distance yourself from him. Now, come sit down. I have another matter to discuss with you."

"Still, it is a painful business…" Franklin looks at his pocket watch as he takes a seat at the table. "Where are the other committee members?"

"Not coming. I invited only you."

Franklin looks surprised. "But why, Jared?"

"Our committee's covert pleas to foreign powers for aid in our conflict with the British have yielded little more than good wishes - and outrageous proposals from nefarious arms dealers. It is time to be less circumspect, to take the fight to the Europeans."

"How do you propose to do that?"

"The Congress wishes you to take another voyage," Potter advises.

Franklin sits up in his chair. "A voyage? Where?"

"To France. To plead with the French King for his help in our war with the English. We are in desperate need and running out of time!"

Franklin waves his hand in the air. "Oh, no, no, no. I am much too old for such a journey."

Potter pushes a decanter of wine on the table toward Franklin. "You are the only man who can do it, Ben. You have met Louis XVI."

"Briefly, once. He was only a child," Franklin argues.

"You speak French fluently, and your fame will smooth the way for you."

Franklin pours wine into his glass. "What you ask is an impossible task. We have been making war on the French and their Iroquois allies here for decades. Do you remember the battle of Louisbourg, up in Nova Scotia in '45? We captured the French fort there. They won't have forgotten it." Franklin rises again and goes to the window, looking out at the gathering twilight.

"Blame it on the British," the Chairman retorts. "Louis will be pleased to have us as an ally against those English devils. The Congress has asked John Adams to travel to The Hague on a similar mission."

Franklin turns back from the window. "Has he agreed?"

"Yes, I think so," Potter replies.

"What would you have me ask of the French King?"

"A loan of at least ten million… Twenty would be better. We require arms, ships, you know… the stuff of war."

"A tall order, my friend."

"Yes. We are aware of that." Franklin turns to the window again. "Let me think about it."

NEW JERSEY   JULY 1776

Temple stands in the doorway of Elizabeth's bedroom in the Governor's mansion. He wears sleeping attire and a long silk robe tied at his waist. His stepmother lies in her white-painted, four-poster bed. Her face, seen through the sheer draperies hanging at the corners of her bed, is still beautiful, but alarmingly pale. "Are you certain you are going to be all right?" Temple asks in a concerned voice.

"Yes, yes. I will be fine," Elizabeth replies softly. "Go to bed, son."

"I will see you then, early in the morning. You know tomorrow is my last day here."

"Yes, I am very sad," she says.

"Good night," Temple closes the double doors behind him with a 'click' as they latch.

A candle burns on the night table next to Elizabeth. Her head is propped on feather pillows and a book lies open on the bed next to her. She stares at the ceiling. Her mouth begins to quiver, her eyes fill with tears. She coughs, then coughs again, deeply, uncontrollably. She reaches for a water glass on the bedside table but knocks it onto the floor. The glass shatters, spilling water over the Persian carpet next to her bed.

FRANKLIN HOUSE, PHILADELPHIA   OCTOBER 1776

A drayage wagon piled with travel trunks and crates filled with Franklin's scientific paraphernalia had left for the seaport earlier on this crisp autumn morning. Now, Jake and Bobby strap the last of Franklin's bags onto the back of his shiny black carriage. Four fine quarter horses rear up and whinny in their harnesses, restless and ready for the journey to the port. Two coachmen, wearing Franklin livery, take their places atop the carriage drivers' box, awaiting their passengers.

Franklin, looking fit and eager, walks briskly into the mews. Temple languidly follows. Both wear comfortable travelling clothes, and Temple carries a wide-brimmed felt hat. They throw their leather satchels onto the seats of the coach.

"Did you get both boxes of books from my library?" Franklin calls to Bobby.

"Yes, sir," Bobby replies.

Franklin turns to Temple. "Did you remember to bring the games box?"

"Yes, Grandpapa. It's already in the carriage."

Franklin is concerned by Temple's long face. "Why so glum? Aren't you excited, lad?"

Temple thinks for a moment. "Yes, of course I am, but I'm sad to leave Mother here alone."

Franklin places his hands on Temple's shoulders. "Elizabeth is a very nice woman, son, but she is *not* your mother. Don't you worry. Women are very resilient."

The kitchen door flies open with a 'bang' and Benny Bache runs across the yard toward the mews, stirring up fallen leaves as he goes. His mother follows, with three-year-old William Bache clinging to her full skirt. Richard walks a few steps behind. Benny holds a rag doll tightly under his arm and carries a small valise. He runs down the drive to his grandfather, drops his bag, and hugs Franklin around his legs.

Franklin's eyes brighten. "Good morning, lad!" he says, prying the boy off his legs. "It appears 'Mister Rags' is ready for a voyage!"

"We are ready, Grandpa!" Benny says, squirming with excitement.

Sally approaches her father. Her eyes are red-rimmed. She picks up Benny's valise and sets it inside the open door of the carriage. "Papa? Are you sure this is a good idea? I was awake all night."

"I am very sure!" Franklin replies reassuringly. "Benny is off on an adventure other boys can only imagine." He pats little William on his white-blonde head. "Billy, you look after your mother whilst we are away."

William puts two fingers in his mouth and giggles.

Richard approaches his father-in-law. "You *will* be certain to give Benny his lessons, won't you? I don't want him to get behind in his studies."

"I will do that," Franklin assures Richard, lifting the lapel of his stained waistcoat with his forefinger. "And you try not to be sauced every night of the week!"

Aggie hurries across the yard carrying a basket covered with a tea towel. "Yoo-hoo!" she calls to Franklin as she approaches. "I determined, Dr. Ben, you gonna have *one* good meal on that boat! I roast you a chicken."

Franklin accepts the basket from Aggie. "You are a treasure," he smiles, patting Aggie on her shoulder. He sets the basket on the floor of the coach.

Sally begins to sniffle. "Benny is only seven years old, Papa!" she cries, holding a kerchief to her mouth.

Franklin turns to Sally and caresses her cheek. "Dearest daughter, I shall ingratiate myself with the King of France, snatch his purse, and run for it. We will be home before you know it. You need not worry. Come, boys," Franklin calls. He turns his back to Sally, walks to the carriage, and climbs in.

Benny scurries to the coach and Jake lifts him up and onto the seat inside. Temple follows him. Sally folds her arms across her bosom and sighs heavily as she watches Jake close the door.

Jake yells a command, and the coachman cracks his whip. The carriage lurches forward. Franklin and the boys lean out the windows, waving and calling 'goodbye'. The horses' hooves clip over the cobbles as the carriage turns onto the street and vanishes around the corner.

CONNECTICUT   OCTOBER 1776

Viewed from the road leading to it, Litchfield Prison appears to be an abandoned wreck of a building. Inside, its brick walls are decaying, the corridors are dank and dreary. William, with his arms handcuffed behind him, surveys his surroundings as he is led along a narrow passageway of the prison by two uniformed sentries. They come to the rusted iron door of a cell. One of the sentries unlocks it with a huge key on a ring he carries and throws open the door.

William is dazed and confused. "What is this place you have taken me to?" he inquires timidly.

"'Tis where we takes prisoners waitin' for the hangman," one of the sentries replies.

"But I have done nothing wrong!"

"You been a naughty boy," the sentry disagrees. He unlocks the cuffs on William's wrists and pushes him through the door.

William stumbles into the cell. "Where is Governor Trumbull?" he demands to know.

"Busy," the younger of the two sentries replies tartly.

William looks about the tiny, dark chamber. "Does my father know about this?"

"Your papa has gone to France, I heared," the other sentry replies.

William takes inventory of his new home. There is a single small window high on a crumbling brick wall, providing a sliver of light. The cell is bare but for straw mats covering parts of the slate floor. His eyes brim with tears. "I cannot live in a miserable hole such as this! I will die!" he says, his voice choking with emotion.

"You got the idea," the younger sentry smirks. He and his comrade step into the corridor, close the door with a loud 'clang', and lock it firmly behind them.

William sinks to the floor in a corner of the cell and drops his head into his hands.

MID-ATLANTIC   NOVEMBER 1776

Gilded letters painted on the stern of a warship under sail can be seen clearly in the bright moonlight. They read: *'Reprisal. Baltimore.'* Overhead, the night sky is as black as printers' ink and ablaze with stars from horizon to horizon.

Franklin leans against a railing of the ship, his thin hair rustling in the wind like the sails above him. Temple and Benny sit on a bench nearby, wrapped in warm cloaks against the brisk wind and spray of the sea. They scan the brilliant night sky, shouting to one another over the wind.

"Remind us, Temple, how one finds the North Star," Franklin shouts to him.

"You follow the handle of 'The Seven Stars'," Temple replies.

"Very good. In Africa, 'The Seven Stars' are called 'The Drinking Gourd', aren't they?" Franklin clarifies.

"'The Drinking Gourd' was over the carriage house on the Fourth of July, Grandpa!" Benny adds cheerfully.

"So, it was!" Franklin concurs. "It is by knowing the location of the North Star, Benny, that sea captains navigate this vast ocean."

"I'm hungry, Grandpapa," Temple says.

"We all are," Franklin agrees. "Let's go have our supper and see if there's anybody interesting at table tonight."

He and the boys rise and walk toward the dining saloon. "Lord Granville once told me there are only three hundred people worth knowing in the entire world," Franklin shouts as they walk into the wind.

"Are some of them in France?" Temple asks, looking puzzled.

Franklin laughs. "Oh, let us hope so!"

DEAR BEN

FRANKLIN'S BEDROOM   1790

Franklin lies back on his pillows with his eyes closed, recalling the journey. "I took the boys along, Bobby, so as to have a child with me to close my eyes and dispose of my remains, should I die over there."

Bobby doesn't respond.

"Well, I didn't die over there. On the contrary, we had quite a big time. Bobby?"

Franklin raises himself up on one elbow and sees Bobby in the chair next to him, with his eyes closed and mouth open, fast asleep, quietly snoring.

PART SEVEN

The Man Who Kissed Voltaire

CHAPTER THIRTY-FOUR

Maison Valentois

Philadelphia   1790

April in Philadelphia is more a time of hope than promise. It is spring by the calendar, but not yet warm and often blowing a gale. Melba Perkins, a Franklin neighbor, treads carefully in a light rain along a slippery path toward Market Street. She pulls a woolen cape closed around her as she walks. Her bonnet is tied tightly under her chin to keep the blustery wind from snatching it off her head.

She sees two ladies standing under a streetlamp, huddled under an umbrella, on the walkway in front of the Franklin mansion. The lady holding the umbrella looks up as Melba approaches. "Hello, Melba," she says. "You get Ephraim his supper?"

"I warmed up a pasty," Melba replies. "Any change here?" she asks, pointing to a light in a third-story window.

"Not so far as we can see," the other lady offers.

The three women hear the 'click' of a man's leather heels coming toward them on the glistening street. They turn to see Horace Powers, a tall, gray-haired, balding gentleman in his sixties, approaching them. He wears a heavy cotton cloak over his shoulders, shielding him from the rain shower.

"I seen you ladies out my window," Horace says. It's gettin' late, ya know. Goin' on ten o'clock." He takes a silver flask from his pocket and hands it to Melba. "I bring somethin' to take the chill off ya's."

"Mighty thoughtful of you, Horace," Melba says. She takes a sip and passes the flask to the lady holding the umbrella.

"Oh, no, thank you," the umbrella lady says. "Me and Edward are not partakers." She passes the flask to the woman standing next to her, but quickly snatches it back. "However, I will make an exception tonight." She takes a long pull from the flask and passes it on again.

"Any word?" Horace asks, nodding toward the Franklin house.

Melba points to the window three flights up. "Well, his light's still on… Means he is still with us."

"I'd like to know what's goin' on up there," Horace confides.

"We saw Franklin's man, Bob, look out that window maybe a half hour ago," the umbrella lady offers. "Where's that flask?" she asks.

Franklin's Bedroom

Bobby dozes in the chair next to Franklin's bed, snoring. Franklin opens one eye and looks at Bobby. He reaches out and pokes Bobby's knee with an extended finger. Bobby awakens with a start, his eyes darting around the room. "What's goin' on?" he asks in a raspy voice.

"He lives!" Franklin chuckles. "For a moment, I thought the lady came for me and took you in error."

Bobby reaches for a glass of water on the table next to his chair. "I nod off. So sorry."

"My story put you to sleep," Franklin teases.

"No, I was listenin'. I was just restin' my eyes a minute. You was on a ship to France with your boys."

"Yes, with Temple and Benny. My fellow Commissioners, Silas Deane and Arthur Lee, had arrived in Paris ahead of me."

Bobby rises from his chair, goes to a dresser against the wall, and replaces a candle that has burned down. "Go on," he says.

"Edward Bancroft, who was to be our mission's secretary, arrived with Deane and Lee. I did not look forward to seeing Mr. Lee again, who was mistrustful of me when I served in England." Franklin settles back into his pillows.

Paris   December 1776

Franklin's carriage rolls along toward the center of town under a cloudless blue sky. The sun is bright, but the air is cold and sharp.

Throngs of citizens of Paris of all ages line both sides of the street. They are bundled in warm woolen coats against the winter cold, but they are in a holiday mood.

A roar of voices arises as Franklin's coach comes into view along the narrow, winding lane. The crowd waves and shout greetings as it passes by: *"Vive Franklin! Bienvenue à Paris! Vive Franklin!"* they shout.

Temple and Benny ride with their faces pressed to the windows. Temple is astonished by the boisterous, friendly crowds lining the way. Benny holds Mr. Rags to the window for a better view.

"Grandpapa! These people know you!" Temple says in amazement.

"They seem to, don't they?" Franklin concurs. He pushes open his window and leans out, shouting to the coachman up top. "Driver! Slow down!" he commands in French. "Let them get a look at us!"

The coachman complies and the carriage slows its pace.

"How do they know you, Grandpapa?" Temple asks.

"The French are a congenial nation. Let us hope the Foreign Ministry is as cordial as are these dear people!" Franklin smiles and waves to the crowd in return as the carriage moves along.

Temple opens his window and ventures a wave to the onlookers.

"When we have some free time, I am going to take you boys to see the sights of Paris," Franklin announces. "Would you like that?"

"Oh, yes, very much," Temple replies enthusiastically as he continues waving to the cheering crowd.

VERSAILLES   DECEMBER 1776

Even in winter, the vast courtyard in front of the Palace swarms with activity all day long. The clatter of grand horse-drawn carriages coming and going over stone pavers through its massive gilded iron gates competes with the din of a legion of merchants peddling their wares from booths lining the perimeter of the courtyard. Vendors sell hots drinks suited to the cold day and sausages roasted over the coals of braziers glowing next to their stalls. Rosy-cheeked children, many of them dressed in rags, wander about peddling apples and oranges from baskets they carry strapped to their bellies. *"Des pommes! Des oranges!"* they shout.

Some merchants offer ceremonial swords, periwigs, medallions, and other paraphernalia touted as required for a visit to the Royal Court. An artist, wrapped in a warm coat and wearing gloves, paints a view of the palace on a board resting on an easel before him, while another artist draws a charcoal portrait of a voluptuous woman who poses for him. She sits, chipped teeth chattering, cleavage exposed, with a feathered hat tipped rakishly on her head.

The cacophony of this marketplace will go on until twilight, when guards shoo the vendors out to the street and lock the gates for the night. The merchants will queue up the next morning at first light, waiting for the gates to swing open again.

The common folk who populate the courtyard of the Palace during the day have never seen the glorious gardens and fountains on the west side of the palace. They are a pleasure reserved for the noblemen and diplomats who call on the King. Emissaries to the Court of Louis XVI will meet with his advisors in the golden Council Chamber, located in the garden façade of the Palace. The Chamber enjoys a view of the park outside, which seems to stretch to infinity.

The lofty Chamber is ornately decorated, with intricately carved and gilded panels on the walls and brilliant crystal chandeliers suspended on silk sleeves from a frescoed ceiling. Glazed French doors open toward the endless lawn, which is now brown and dusted with snow.

King Louis XVI sits at the head of a conference table in the Council Chamber. He is twenty-two years of age, slender, and simply dressed for the day's business. He wears his dark curly hair loose, spilling onto his shoulders. His cabinet of twelve men, all of whom are older than he, sits along the sides of the table. All wear daytime attire, but a few of them wear tall powdered wigs piled on top their heads, likely because their pates are shaved to ward off lice.

The Comte de Vergennes stands at the far end of the table, addressing the group. He is of medium height, stout, gray-haired, fifty-nine years of age. There is a commanding presence about him.

"A delegation has arrived in Paris from the English Colonies," Vergennes says in French, with urgency in his voice. "They request an audience with Your Majesty. Among them is the famous Dr. Franklin."

"Good! I should like to meet him," the King smiles. "My father spoke highly of Monsieur Franklin. What do you anticipate they want of us?"

"They will ask for your help in their war with the English. Money, arms, ships…" Vergennes replies.

The King's smile vanishes. "Well, we haven't any money to give them, what with the amount you are spending to refit our navy. And I am not a proponent of such rebellions against authority."

A door to the hall outside is opened, and two footmen enter the room. They move around the table, unobtrusively serving demitasse and pastries.

Vergennes declines the refreshments offered to him.

The King stirs his coffee with a tiny silver spoon and looks down the table at Jacques Turgot. "So, what does my Comptroller think of all this? What do you have to say, Monsieur Turgot, at the Foreign Minister's news?"

"I am in complete agreement with Your Majesty. Monsieur Vergenne's ship-building program has all but drained the treasury," Turgot says, with a stern look on his face. "And we must not appear to encourage such an uprising!"

Vergennes places his hands on the table. "Need I remind you, Monsieur Turgot, that England is our fiercest enemy, and her unswerving goal is to humble and destroy France? It may be in our interest to align ourselves with the Americans and secure our possessions in the West. We should listen to what Dr. Franklin has to say."

Turgot crosses his arms in a petulant gesture.

"It cannot hurt to meet with the Americans," the King says. "But you will not do so here at Versailles. Let us sound them out before they are seen loitering around the Palace." He wags his fork in Vergennes's direction. "Do you understand?"

Vergennes nods his head. "I do, Sire."

"I do not wish to raise the ire of the British just now, before we are ready. But do bring Dr. Franklin to me." The King sips his coffee. "In due course…"

Turgot stares out the window at the wintry garden, fretful about the Royal finances.

"What else have we on our agenda?" the King inquires, looking up and down the table.

PARIS   DECEMBER 1776

Though elegant in its day, the suite at the Hotel Russe which presently serves as the American Embassy, is shop-worn and shabby. The curtains are frayed, and the carpets and upholstery are threadbare and stained. Wooden legs of chairs and tables are scraped and scarred. The parlor of the suite is piled high with portfolios, legal tracts, books and newspapers. Franklin works at the dining table, looking over papers, with his spectacles perched on the tip of his nose. His leather valise sits on the floor next to him.

Temple and Edward Bancroft, the mission's secretary, work at a writing table fitted into a corner of the room. Small desks have also been squeezed in for Silas Deane and Arthur Lee, who, like Bancroft, are gentlemen in their thirties. Franklin and Temple share a bedroom off the dining area, while Bancroft's room is through a door next to the fireplace on the other side of the parlor. Deane and Lee share a bedroom across the hall. The accommodation may be cramped and dowdy, but it is in keeping with the meagre budget allocated by Congress.

The bell rings, Temple rises from his chair and goes to the door.

Franklin turns to his colleagues. "If you will allow me, gentlemen, I will do the talking. My French is better than yours. Mr. Bancroft, perhaps it would be best if you wait in your room."

Surprised, Lee and Deane look at each other. Lee raises an eyebrow. Bancroft huffs, but does as requested and retires reluctantly to his bedroom. Temple opens the door and invites the Comte de Vergennes into the suite. Franklin rises to greet him. Lee and Deane stand next to their chairs.

"Monsieur le Compte." Franklin says as he bows to Vergennes.

"Dr. Franklin." Vergennes puts out a hand and the two men shake hands.

"Votre Excellence, je voudrais vous presenter Messieurs Lee et Deane, mes associes."

Vergennes walks toward Lee and Deane, looking about and sniffing the air as he goes. Lee and Deane give a slight bow, and Vergennes offers his hand to them. They note that Vergennes is dressed as befits his station. He wears a crushed velvet coat, velvet knee breeches and silk stockings, with low-heeled black pumps on his feet. The coat, across which he wears a deep blue sash, is topped with a black velvet stand-up collar. A large silver medallion denoting his rank is pinned near the lapel of his jacket. His close-cropped gray wig is so finely made, it looks as though it may well be his own hair.

Franklin carries on in French. *"Nous avons venir en France, Votre Excellence, pour…"*

Vergennes raises a hand. "Please, let us speak English, Franklin."

Lee and Deane smile a mocking smile at one another.

"I know why you have come," Vergennes volunteers.

"Do you?" Franklin looks surprised. "Shall we sit down?" Franklin directs Vergennes to an armchair upholstered in tattered brocade.

Vergennes sweeps the seat of the chair with his hand before he sits. "His Majesty prefers we discuss matters here, in private, whilst we get to know one another. Tongues would wag if we were seen together, would they not?"

"I suppose that is so," Franklin accedes.

Franklin glances toward the next room, where Bancroft stands with his ear pressed to the door. He sees a pair of shoes interrupting the light coming under the door.

"For your government to have sent such a distinguished delegation to us, indicates a mission of some importance," Vergennes suggests generously.

Temple takes wine glasses from a silver tray on a sideboard and serves Vergennes, then the other men, a glass of wine.

"You have requested an audience with His Majesty," Vergennes says. Deane interrupts. "We wish to propose an alliance between our country and your government," he blurts out.

"And what country would that be?" Vergennes inquires.

"The United States of America," Lee offers earnestly. "We believe such an alliance would be of great use to your King. The interests of our two countries are aligned. We have both suffered repeated injury at the hands of King George."

"Beyond a mutual loathing of the English King, I am not sure what you have to offer us," Vergennes argues.

Franklin raises a hand to hush Lee and Deane. "With your help, Your Excellency, we can ensure our independence and humiliate the English. We will terminate the commerce that has made Britain rich, and France and Spain may divide her Caribbean possessions between them."

Vergennes sniffs the rim of his glass as he considers Franklin's words. "You must first present your proposals to me. I will decide if they are of interest to His Majesty. I warn you, however, that my Sovereign is in the business of *being* a ruler, not deposing one."

Franklin sips his wine. "We do not topple a monarch. King George sits on a throne thousands of miles away from us. We merely ask him to leave us in peace."

"You have not demonstrated an ability to prevail against your enemy thus far, so we do not share your optimism," Vergennes says frankly.

"The tide is turning, as you will soon see." Franklin lifts his glass. "To His Majesty, the King of France!"

They all raise their glasses and join in the toast, "To the King!" Vergennes sets his glass on the table. "Put your ideas in writing, Dr. Franklin, in a memorandum. Get it to me as soon as possible. I will study it and perhaps bring it to His Majesty. In the meantime, pray for victory on the battlefield."

"We are grateful to you, *Votre Excellence,* for journeying from Versailles to meet with us," Franklin says.

Vergennes takes a last sip of wine and rises from his chair. He glances around the suite again. "This is not a fit embassy for you, Franklin. We must do something about it."

Franklin rises from his chair. Lee and Deane follow.

Temple escorts the Foreign Secretary to the door.

Vergennes stops in the foyer and turns back. "And better sooner than later," he calls to Franklin. "Enjoy your time in Paris. *Au revoir.*" Temple accompanies Vergennes down the stairs and out to the street.

Lee and Deane take seats at the dining table.

"Now what?" Lee asks peevishly as he drinks his wine.

"I shall write a memorandum," Franklin replies.

"Then what?" Deane wonders.

Franklin joins them at the table. "We wait," he says. "And we enjoy Paris."

ÎLE DE LA CITÉ, PARIS   JANUARY 1777

As recommended by the Foreign Minister, Franklin wrote his memorandum and delivered it to him within a few days of their meeting at the hotel. Meanwhile, Franklin and his grandsons fill the time by taking in the sights of Paris. They will have three months free for sightseeing before any word comes from the Palace, but the time passes quickly. Franklin has decided it is time for the boys to view the splendors of the Royal Chapel of Sainte-Chapelle, situated on an island in the Seine.

They stand outside the building, craning their necks to see the top of the Fleur-de-Lys tower which rests at the mid-point of the roof. "This church was built by Louis IX as a Royal Chapel in about 1238," Franklin explains. "There you see the stone columns, called buttresses, which support the structure from the outside so the walls inside can be made mostly of glass. Come, boys," he says, and leads them through the heavily carved wooden doors and into the church, where they are surrounded by more than one thousand windows, all ablaze in a dazzling display of multi-colored light.

They walk up the aisle of the cathedral, gazing upward, dwarfed by the lofty vaults of the ceiling. Benny keeps his rag doll stuffed securely under his arm.

"Say 'great' five times before 'grandfather' and you have that king's connection to the present king." Franklin turns to Benny. "What do you think, Benny?"

"I think the windows are very pretty," he replies.

"They are among the most splendid in all of Europe. There is iron hidden in the buttresses and in the eaves outside which makes this transparent interior possible." Franklin points to a row of wooden chairs with woven rush seats. "Let's sit here and collect our thoughts, which have settled in our feet after our long day."

Benny settles with Mr. Rags in his lap. "Great, great, great, great, great grandfather!" he exclaims. "Well done!" Franklin reaches over and pats Benny on his back. "And you, Temple, what do you think?"

"I don't know what to think. I am overwhelmed." he replies, his mouth agape.

"'Tis precisely what the architects intended: for you to sense the Glory of God, the grandeur of the Romish Church, and of the Monarchy… To diminish one's sense of self and to keep one from enlightened thought."

"It is a temple for people of faith, Grandpapa."

"Yes, *faith* is the word. The windows around us tell stories from the Old and New Testaments." Franklin points to the enormous rose window over the altar. "There you see the End of Days as told in the Book of Revelation. Originally, these were tales told around campfires in tents in the desert."

An old woman seated near them shushes Franklin, with her finger to her lips.

Franklin lowers his voice. "Louis IX built this church as a repository for a treasured relic: the Crown of Thorns worn by Jesus at his Crucifixion. Louis paid a princely sum for it to the Emperor in Constantinople, who had mortgaged it to the Venetians." Franklin points beyond the nave where they are seated. "It is ahead of us, there, in a priceless jeweled reliquary in the apse of the church."

The old lady shakes her head and gets up from her chair, growling as she shuffles away from the Franklin party.

"Do you believe, Temple, the Crown of Thorns worn by The Christ is *truly* in that jeweled box?" Franklin asks.

"Men of faith believe it." Temple replies.

"Think of the men of faith who fell to their deaths while constructing this edifice. Still, it is an achievement of the greatest magnitude. You boys will decide for yourselves what is true and what is not."

Benny perks up. "I learned in school that the true church is in Rome."

Franklin reels and turns to Benny. "Rome? We shall see about that! I will not have your head filled with Papist rubbish in that school you are attending here. You were baptized a Presbyterian and you will remain one whilst I am still alive." He huffs and rises from his seat. "Come! Let us find a tea salon. I will treat you boys to a refreshment… perhaps a profiterole."

Paris 1777

Weeks later, Franklin stands before a low dresser in his bedroom at the Hotel Russe, shaving with a long blade. He rinses soap from the blade in a porcelain basin filled with water. A tap at the door and Temple peers in.

"Yes, lad?" Franklin says, with his face covered in frothy soap, the razor poised.

"There is a gentleman here to see you, Grandpapa," Temple advises. "A Monsieur de Chaumont."

Franklin lowers the razor. "So early in the morning? Who is he?"

"He says he is a friend of Count Vergennes." Franklin rinses the soap from his face. "I will be with him in a moment." He wipes his face with a towel.

Temple directs the visitor to a seat on a well-worn settee in the parlor. He is in his fifties, with salt-and-pepper hair, slightly overweight, but smartly dressed.

Franklin enters the room, wiping his hands with the towel. "Bonjour, Monsieur," he says, extending a hand to the gentleman, who rises and introduces himself.

"I am Jacques de Chaumont. The Comte de Vergennes suggested I come."

"Did he? Please sit, Monsieur de Chaumont."

Franklin sits opposite him on an armchair, his face composed, concealing his curiosity.

"I know you are a busy man, Dr. Franklin, so I will get to the point," de Chaumont says. "I have a fine house on my estate, known as the Maison Valentois, which I am not using. It sits, sadly empty. I invite you to take up residence there."

Franklin's eyes widen with surprise. "My goodness!" Franklin calls to Temple. "Temple, can you arrange a cup of coffee for Monsieur de Chaumont?"

Temple nods and leaves the room.

"Where is this 'Maison Valentois'?" Franklin inquires.

"It is located at Passy," de Chaumont clarifies enthusiastically. "A lovely village midway between here and Versailles. Very convenient, and a suitable place to conduct business. Vergennes found this hotel to be, shall we say… '*insufficient*'."

Franklin leans forward in his chair. "Your offer is most kind, but my Congress has set a strict budget for board for our mission here, which does not allow for such a fine house."

Temple returns, carrying a tray bearing a demitasse service. He serves coffee to his grandfather and his guest.

"I offer you Maison Valentois free of charge. How can your Congress object?" de Chaumont asks.

Franklin considers the offer for a moment. "If I were to accept, I must pay you *something*."

De Chaumont smiles. "I am a businessman, Dr. Franklin. Rest assured we will think of some way you can help me in return," he says, with a twinkle in his eye.

"An intriguing prospect. And what of my associates?" Franklin inquires.

"I think just you and your boys." De Chaumont sets down his cup. "Shall we have a look at the house? My driver is waiting downstairs."

Franklin studies de Chaumont for a few seconds. "Why not? Temple, get your coat!" He sets down his cup. "Allow me to fetch my cloak." Franklin scurries through the door into his bedroom. "And find Benny!" Franklin calls to Temple.

After a pleasant journey out of the city and into the fresh air of the countryside in de Chaumont's elegant carriage, Franklin and his grandsons ride along the Seine to the pretty village of Passy and to the stone walls of the Maison Valentois. The coach passes through massive wooden gates and into a stone courtyard, covered with patches of snow. "Take care," de Chaumont warns the trio as they step out of the coach and follow him to the house. He unlocks an imposing front door with a rusty iron key. The door swings open with a mournful groan. Inside, light streams from a pair of French doors on the wall opposite the entrance, revealing a splendid foyer. Franklin and the boys stand on a gleaming parquet floor, surrounded by walls hung with landscape tapestries and varnished equestrian paintings. They look up to cherubs painted on the ceiling, flying circles around a glistening crystal chandelier. Gilded mirrors are mounted over intricately carved console tables sitting against the walls.

"Will this please you, Dr. Franklin?" de Chaumont asks.

Franklin is dumbfounded. He and the boys peer into the adjoining rooms.

"I should say so," Franklin says at last. "Magnificent!"

Franklin catches his breath and leads Temple and Benny into a spacious salon, which looks onto the street. It is furnished with sumptuous furniture resting on fine Aubusson carpets. Family portraits in gilded frames hang on the walls. Turquoise silk curtains puddle on the floor alongside tall windows, which rise to an eighteen-foot-high ceiling. Chinese porcelains and marble sculptures cover every surface.

"Could you be happy here, boys?" Franklin asks, taking an inventory of the trappings surrounding them.

"Oh, yes, Grandpapa," Benny sighs.

Temple runs his hand over the silk brocade upholstery of a settee. "How could we not?" he says, sounding a bit sullen.

"You hesitate," Franklin scolds.

"I think of my father and how miserable his circumstances may be," Temple admits.

"Your father lies in a bed of his own making." Franklin places a consoling hand on Temple's shoulder. "Let us go and pack our things!" he suggests cheerfully, and leads his grandsons back to the foyer and Monsieur de Chaumont, who awaits their decision.

CHAPTER THIRTY-FIVE

A Day at Camp

McConkey's Ferry, Pennsylvania   December 1776

A fierce wind whips fallen snow through avenues of canvas tents and make-shift huts in a military encampment. As darkness settles on the camp, hundreds of soldiers, many in their 'teens and twenties, huddle together around meager campfires. They are bundled in threadbare blankets and wear tattered uniforms of the Continental Army. Some are shoeless, their feet wrapped in rags.

The soldiers' rifles lean against 'sawhorses' made of tree branches. Their horses graze on scarce strands of grass in a snow-covered field beyond the camp.

Dr. Blaire Mercer, a trained physician and surgeon, strides purposefully down the gentle slope leading to the camp. He is a sturdily built man in middle age. He carries a leather satchel and wears tall boots and a heavy greatcoat, firmly pulled closed around him. A fur cap on his head is dusted with snow. He approaches two soldiers who are cooking over a campfire using a metal skillet. "What's for supper, lads?" he inquires.

"Fire cake, sir," the younger of the two soldiers answers.

"Fire cake? What the hell is that?" Dr. Mercer asks.

"We mix flour and water and fry it, like you see," the soldier replies, holding up the pan.

Dr. Mercer looks incredulous. "Is that all you have to eat?"

The soldier pulls his blanket closed tighter. "That would be it. 'Tis *the specialty of the house.*"

"For Chrissake." The doctor shakes his head. "Where is General Washington's headquarters?" he inquires, sounding cross.

The soldier points to a rise in the distance. "On yonder hill."

Dr. Mercer gives the two young men a nod of thanks and heads for the knoll a few hundred feet away. When he reaches Washington's tent, he removes his cap and taps with his knuckle on the wooden frame of the tent's doorway. "General? You in there?" he calls.

"Enter!" comes the reply from inside.

Dr. Mercer parts the canvas flap and enters the tent. He sees sparse furnishings: a single cot, a few folding stools, and scattered trunks. General George Washington is seated at a camp table writing a letter by the light of an oil lamp. He has a blanket draped over the shoulders of his uniform and pulled closed around him. His boots are caked with dried mud, and his close-cropped gray periwig could use a scrubbing.

Washington doesn't look up. "Who are you?" he asks in a surly tone.

"Dr. Blaire Mercer. The Congress engaged me to come and look at conditions here."

Washington sets down his pen and stands. Dr. Mercer is awed by the forty-four-year-old man's height and powerful physique. He puts out a hand to the General.

Washington shakes the hand extended to him cautiously. "Oh, they did, did they?" he growls.

"I am told there is no surgeon attached to this battalion," Mercer replies meekly.

"You are correct. We have no surgeon in the camp," Washington confirms.

"Do any of your men need my attention?"

"Most of them. Do you have the time?"

Dr. Mercer considers the question.

Washington persists. "What will you report to the Congress?"

"I would say things look very grim. Have the boys nothing to eat here but flour and water?"

Washington folds his arms across his chest. "My men are hungry and naked. I provision them by taking from the local farmers, paying them with worthless promissory notes. You can tell the Congress this army is either going to starve or dissolve soon unless the funds I need are forthcoming."

"I would like to stay on for a few days, if a bed can be found for me," Dr. Mercer offers.

"We'll find you a bed. You will bunk here with me. Have a seat."

Washington pulls a folding stool up to his writing table. He moves a pile of maps out of the way and retrieves a bottle and two tin cups from a trunk. "Join me in a spot of port. We'll write your letter to Congress."

Dr. Mercer sits on the stool and sets his hat and satchel on the ground next to him.

"The British, under General Howe, pushed me from New York to this side of the Delaware. We are penned in here by an army of Hessian mercenaries camped on the other side of the river at Trenton." Washington pours two cups of wine.

The doctor takes a notebook and pen from his satchel and begins to write. "How many Hessians, would you say?"

"More than a thousand," Washington informs him.

"Good Lord," Dr. Mercer says, his eyes wide.

Washington sips his wine. "General Howe has retreated up to New York to winter in comfort. Come spring, the prize will be Philadelphia."

"And you plan to keep the Hessians from crossing the river in the meantime?"

"Precisely. I have sent two runners over to spy on them… see if the bastards are preparing to move anytime soon. Thus far, the Hessians have favored us with their bad behavior."

Dr. Mercer sets down his pen and takes a drink of his wine. "How is that?"

"They are a horde of drunken thieves, which has brought us volunteers and donations of supplies from their neighbors." General Washington looks the doctor squarely in the eye. "I do not intend to sit here and wait."

PARIS   1777

A slate gray morning sky outside the windows of the Americans' suite at the Hotel Russe threatens rain. Edward Bancroft scurries about the parlor with his hair disheveled, and his shirt open at the neck and untucked. Franklin and Silas Deane wear robes, cinched at the waist, over their nightshirts. They wear slippers on their feet. Coffee cups and soiled breakfast plates cover the dining table. The three men work at packing Franklin's books and papers into open boxes scattered about the floor.

Deane points to a desktop. "What about these journals?" he inquires. "Leave them," Franklin instructs. They belong to Arthur. We're only taking my things."

They hear the front door open and close and Temple enters from the foyer. "I've brought the post," he says, setting a stack of envelopes on the sideboard.

"Have you finished your packing?" Franklin asks him.

"Yes, sir. There's a letter here from home, from Aunt Sally."

"Open it, son. What news has she?"

Temple sits at his desk next to the window and opens the letter.

Arthur Lee opens the front door, crosses the foyer, and enters the room. He looks with curiosity over the disarray he finds. "Somebody going somewhere?" he asks of no-one in particular.

Franklin raises his hand. "I am. I'm moving to Passy to a large house where we can better conduct our business."

Temple lowers the letter. "It's not good news about my stepmother. Elizabeth has been very ill with her breathing trouble," he calls to Franklin.

"I am sorry to hear that, son," Franklin responds.

A sour expression crosses Lee's face. "And how do you propose to pay for a fine house at Passy?"

"The house is rent-free," Franklin advises.

"There is no such thing," Lee argues.

"'Tis a generous gift from a gentleman who supports our cause," Franklin explains.

Temple continues reading the letter.

Lee inches closer to Franklin. "My brother Richard, who serves in the Congress, writes of his concern that public monies are being sacrificed to private purpose over here."

Dean looks up from his packing chore. "As our mission's accountant, I can assure you that is not so. And you may tell your brother I resent his inference!"

Temples watches a few drops of rain hit the window. "Aunt Sally and Uncle Richard are doing what they can for her."

"God Bless the Baches," Franklin says.

"I suppose you plan to keep me and Silas out of your deliberations with Vergennes henceforth," Lee whines. "Well, I won't have it!" he snarls.

Franklin looks up from a stack of books he is sorting through. "For Lord's sake, Arthur! Now is not the time!"

"I should have stayed with Elizabeth, Grandpapa. She has no family," Temple offers sadly.

"There is nothing you can do to help poor Elizabeth, and you are needed here. We have a war to prosecute," Franklin responds impatiently.

"This is not the time to squander resources when our need for funds is desperate!" Lee fumes. "It is time to present Louis with an ultimatum. Either he comes to our aid *now* or we make an accommodation with the English. We've dallied here for months!"

Franklin pushes aside his stack of books. "Sit down, Arthur, calm yourself." Franklin invites Lee to sit next to him at the dining table, then speaks with care. "If we were to present such an ultimatum to the King at this time, Arthur, all would be lost. We would frighten him away. You must be patient and wait for good news from General Washington." Bancroft joins the two men at the table. "There is little hope of that, Ben," he says. "Arthur has a point. A quiet talk with the British Ambassador may well be in order."

Franklin slams his fist on the table. "Never!" he shouts.

NEW JERSEY   1776

Two soldiers of the Continental Army lie on their stomachs on a snow-covered hillock near Trenton. Their muskets lie on the ground next to them. They look through spyglasses at the enemy camp below, where dozens of tents lined neatly in rows give the appearance of a small town. A mess hall, a bakehouse and an ordnance shack anchor the center of the 'village'. Many of the tents are strung with evergreen garlands and pinecones in a nod to the Christmas season.

The American spies see, and can hear, groups of Hessians wandering about, laughing, drinking, and cursing loudly in German. They wear warm woolen greatcoats and the leather boots on their feet show little sign of wear. The spies hear a metallic *'clank, clank'* as eight Hessians play a game with horseshoes at the base of the hill. A fiddler begins to play.

The Americans look at each other, fold their field glasses, pick up their muskets, and back away on all fours from their observation post. They run to their horses, mount up, and ride as fast as their steeds will carry them to the ferry crossing the Delaware River. The journey from Trenton to Washington's camp will cover some nine miles.

The soldiers reach the rebel post before nightfall. The General invites them to join him and his guest, Dr. Mercer, for a drink. The four men stand outside Washington's tent, warming their hands over a meagre campfire. They hold tin cups filled with port wine in their hands. The spies eagerly share intelligence with Washington and his visitor.

"They got women over there, too," one of them confides.

"Have they?" Washington asks, looking surprised.

"They was dancin' by the time we sneaked away," the other soldier adds. "Somebody was playin' a fine fiddle."

"I'll be damned," Washington says. "General Howe must have sent some 'working girls' down from New York. Could you identify the Commander's quarters?"

One of the soldiers clears aside some slush with his boot, picks up a stick, and draws in the mud. "Right here, in the middle-front," he demonstrates.

"We will hit them at first light. They'll be sleeping like dogs after dinner. We'll cross the river in darkness," Washington says, with a steely glint in his eyes.

Dr. Mercer drinks from his mug. "Mind if I come along?"

"You any good with a musket, doctor? A bayonet?" Washington inquires.

"I know how to wield a knife, General."

Washington tosses the last of his drink on the ground. "I will tell the men at parade tonight they are about to embark on a secret mission." He turns to the two young spies. "Go to the supply sergeant and tell him to get every man a fresh flint. Then go to the cook shack and ask the officer to provision the company for two days' march. It won't be much, I know. Mercer, you had better get some sleep. We leave in four hours."

Passy 1777

The front door of Maison Valentois is wide open. Franklin directs porters carrying trunks and boxes into the house from a horse-drawn drayage wagon standing in the courtyard. Temple and Benny carry personal items into the entry hall. A bitterly cold rain falls and splashes onto the stone pavers and over their shoes. A degree or two colder, and it would freeze.

Monsieur de Chaumont passes through the open gates from the street and walks into the courtyard. He carries an umbrella and holds his cloak closed snugly about him. "May I enter?" de Chaumont calls to Franklin.

Franklin sets the box he carries on the wet stones and greets his landlord. "Jacques! Yes, please do!"

De Chaumont lowers his *parapluie* and they shake hands vigorously.

"I am pleased to see that today is moving day," de Chaumont says. "You must get settled quickly because I want you to meet some of the neighbors."

"I would be delighted to." Franklin wipes rain drops from his spectacles.

"The Brillons, who live nearby, are having '*une soirée musicale*' on Thursday. You must come! Madame Brillon has the voice of an angel and the face of a goddess. Six o'clock. Bring your boys. *D'accord?*"

"Nothing would please us more! *Je suis d'accord.*"

DEAR BEN

NEW JERSEY   1776

Bone-chilling rain has turned to freezing rain, then sleet, blowing sideways in a gale.

General Washington has defied the brutal weather and loaded his troops onto longboats for a crossing of the Delaware River and an assault on the Hessian garrison near Trenton. His troops count more than two thousand men, who march eight abreast from the rebel camp to the ferry boat landing. Horses and artillery, loaded onto barges, accompany the soldiers on their treacherous journey across the ice-clogged river. Cavalry and infantrymen stand upright for the trip across a narrow bend of the river, praying the canon lashed to rafts behind them will make the crossing successfully. Mercifully, only a few men plunge into the icy waters.

Upon reaching the New Jersey side of the river, the cavalry mount their horses and infantrymen begin the march toward Trenton and the Hessian camp. The soldiers move silently in the dark, in miserable wet and cold, for nearly four hours. They will rely on the element of surprise at their destination. Washington leads the advance. Dr. Mercer slept soundly through the General's departure from camp.

As daylight breaks, Washington's forces reach the Hessian post and regroup at the edge of the field. All is quiet; it is Christmas Eve and there is no sign of a watchman. With a hand signal from Washington, two infantrymen dash across the field and into the Hessian camp. They run to the Commander's hut and barge in. A shot is fired. The foot soldiers charge across the field and spread out through the camp, with muskets and bayonets poised, bursting into the quarters of the sleeping Hessians.

A carrot-topped American soldier aims his musket at two burly mercenaries he finds sleeping on their cots. One of the Hessians has his arms wrapped around a naked woman.

"Wake up! Get out!" the young American yells, his hands and musket shaking.

The woman wakes up and screams as she attempts to cover herself with a blanket. The Hessian opens his eyes, grabs his rifle from beneath the cot, and takes aim at the American boy, who fires his musket. The Hessian drops his weapon and falls back onto his cot, dead. The naked woman pushes the dead man out of her way, wraps the blanket around her, squeezes her swollen feet into her shoes, and runs out of the tent, screaming hysterically.

The Hessian lying on the other cot stirs and crawls out of his bed, with his hands raised over his head. The American prods the Hessian out of the tent with his bayonet.

The scene is repeated hundreds of times as Hessians emerge from their tents in various states of dress, with their hands high above their heads, herded along by American infantrymen. Gunfire is heard throughout the post as nearly one thousand cursing mercenaries are lined up in rows as prisoners.

Several half-naked women emerge from tents, confused by the chaos in the camp. They scream and wrap cloaks and blankets around themselves as they run across the icy parade ground. The young red-headed American soldier wonders how far those women must run, the weather being what it is.

CHAPTER THIRTY-SIX

Nightingale

Passy												1777

Three pairs of French doors, separated by faux marble columns, look out to the gardens of the Brillon mansion. The music room is an exquisite salon, with Savonnerie carpets scattered on a polished parquet floor and crystal chandeliers igniting a frescoed ceiling overhead. Buttery silk curtains frame the French doors, puddling onto the floor. A piano sits against one wall, a harpsichord against another, and two golden harps stand in a corner of the room.

Twenty-four guests are seated for a performance on gilded side chairs arranged in rows facing the piano. Franklin and Monsieur de Chaumont are among them. The audience is dressed in finery for the Thursday evening musicale. The ladies wear hoop-skirted satin gowns and are adorned with brilliant jewels. The men wear frockcoats over brocade waistcoats, cravats tied at their necks, and powdered wigs atop their heads.

Temple stands stiffly at the rear of the assembly, looking somber and quiet. He struggles to acquire French and avoids conversation when possible. Benny sits in the front row next to Juliette Brillon, a raven-haired nine-year old girl, stifling the giggles. He and Juliette communicate perfectly well through sign language and her pidgin English.

Henri Brillon is seated next to his daughter. Monsieur Brillon is a ruggedly handsome fifty-four-year-old, with a decidedly Roman nose. He surveys the room with pleasure tonight, as his wife, Anne-Louise, stands on a dais next to the piano, entertaining his aristocratic guests.

Madame Brillon faces her audience wearing a low-cut white silk gown, which compliments the white streak in a forelock of her ebony hair. Diamonds glitter on her fingers, neck, and in a diadem atop her head. She sings an aria from *'Lucio Silla'* by Mozart, the *wunderkind* young composer. Madame Brillon's lyric soprano voice is well-trained and silky. Sophie Brillon, her pretty sixteen-year-old daughter, accompanies her mother skillfully on the piano.

Franklin listens to the performance with rapt attention. He is enchanted.

After the concert, the two dozen guests from the 'musicale' cross a hallway to the dining room, where they take their seats at a long table. The gardens outside are lit in their wintry repose by oil lamps in glass shades, a charming effect one can see through a row of French doors facing the terrace. The room is soon abuzz with conversation and laughter. Candles burn in golden candelabra lining the table, which is set with Sevres china, Belgian linens and Italian crystal. Six footmen, wearing the livery of the house, attend to the diners, serving them plates of food and filling their glasses with wine.

Franklin is seated next to Madame Brillon. He is unable to take his eyes off her bodice for any length of time.

"We are honored, Dr. Franklin," she says brightly, demurely covering her *décolletage* with her left hand while eating with her right, "that you have come to live in our midst."

"*Au contraire,* Madame Brillon, I cannot believe my good fortune to have you as a neighbor," he replies, taking a bite of his *veau en croute.*

"Let us be friends, as well as neighbors," she says, raising her glass. "Please, call me 'Anne-Louise'."

Franklin wipes his mouth with his serviette. "I look at you and cannot help but think of Helen of Troy and her legendary beauty. I shall henceforth call you '*Hélène*'."

Madame Brillon's face reddens. "You make me blush, Dr. Franklin. Then I shall be '*Hélène*' for you. Have you met my husband, Henri?"

"I have not yet had the pleasure," Franklin replies. "Your daughter had begun playing when we arrived."

Madame Brillon gestures to the head of the table. "Monsieur Brillon sits there, with the blonde lady at his right."

Franklin turns and sees Henri Brillon engrossed in conversation with the heavy-set blonde woman who is seated next to him. Though elegantly coiffed and gowned, her features are quite plain. Monsieur Brillon leans close to her and whispers in her ear. "They appear to be close friends," Franklin observes.

"Too close," Madam Brillon confides. "Mademoiselle d'Armond is my children's governess."

"She is, therefore, often under this roof, is she not?" Franklin deduces.

Madame Brillon sips her wine. "Perhaps more often than one might like."

Franklin laughs. "'*What is good for the gander is also good for the goose*', it is said."

Madame Brillon places her bejeweled hand on Franklin's. "Tonight 'the goose' could be tempted to stray from the coop," she teases, her green eyes shimmering.

They keep each other's gaze for a moment.

"Welcome to the neighborhood, Dr. Franklin," Madame Brillon says, lifting her hand from his and diverting her attention to the potatoes *dauphinoise* on her plate.

Passy   1777

Two weeks later, Franklin stands next to a map of North America displayed on a wall in the library of Maison Valentois. The map is dated '*1755*'. Franklin moves a wooden stick across the map, pointing out various features of the Continent to Silas Deane and Edward Bancroft, who are seated at a library table, looking in Franklin's direction.

"When the time comes," he says, circling his stick around the Great Lakes region, "I am of the opinion we should demand this area to the north and east of Lake Huron be included in our territory."

Silas Deane rests an elbow on the table and his chin in his hand. "The British will say that area is part of Canada and not open to negotiation."

Franklin lowers the stick. "It is adjacent to the Great Lakes and naturally belongs to the United States."

"There is little need to debate the point now," Bancroft interjects, "as the British appear to be winning the war. Before long, General Howe will have chased Washington into the Gulf of Mexico."

Franklin glares at Bancroft. "Mark my words, Edward. We will demand all of Canada as reparation and settle for a northern boundary delineated by Lake Superior extending eastward to the sea."

Bancroft crosses his arms, scowling. He turns toward the foyer when he hears the front door slam shut. Boots hurry across the stone floor of the entry hall and toward the library. Temple rushes into the room, removing his coat as he walks. He carries a packet of letters in one hand.

"Gentlemen!" he says, breathlessly. "A courier from Nantes has brought us good news!"

Deane sits up in his chair. "What is it, boy?"

"General Washington won a great victory at Trenton!" Temple takes a letter from the packet and spreads it on the table. "He took nine hundred Hessian troops prisoner!" he says, pointing to the document. "The news has been weeks in crossing to us. Look for yourself!"

Deane moves around the table to the open letter. "But... *how?*" he wonders.

"In a bold stroke on Christmas Eve, he attacked in darkness, killed their Commander, and the Germans laid down their arms and surrendered. Very few American lives were lost, it says here."

Franklin looks at the letter and claps his hands together. "What did I *just* say? The tide turns!" He spins on one foot, does a lively little jig, and dances his way out of the room.

"What did I say?!" he calls back from the entry hall.

Bancroft looks after Franklin, surprised and bewildered.

Paris

That night, Bancroft walks in the Tuileries Gardens near the Louvre Palace. His fur cap is pulled low over his forehead. He approaches a stout tree beside the walk, looks around, senses he is alone, and takes a bottle from his coat pocket. He removes the cork and stuffs a paper into the bottle. He ties the neck of the bottle with twine, re-corks the bottle, and lowers it into a hole in the back of the tree. He looks around again to make certain no one is watching, and inserts a peg in the ground. He attaches the twine to the peg. Bancroft glances at his pocket watch, looks around, then scurries away.

Moments later, a gray-haired man steps cautiously out of the darkness of the woods and retrieves the bottle.

LONDON   APRIL 1777

King George III and two companions are out for a morning ride in Hyde Park. The King, forty years old, appears robust and in good spirits, at least for the moment. General John Burgoyne, fifty-two, and a head taller than his monarch, pulls his horse alongside the King. John Penn, the forty-eight-year-old Governor of Pennsylvania, catches up a minute later.

"A perfect day for a ride, isn't it?" Penn says, looking up at the azure sky.

The King laughs. "My father often said, '*Ah, jetzt im Frühling in Deutschland in zu sein.*"

Penn and Burgoyne look at each other with a puzzled look.

"'*Oh, to be in Germany in springtime*', or something like that." The King chuckles and whips his horse to trot on. Burgoyne and Penn follow.

The King's mood darkens. He shouts over his shoulder to Burgoyne. "I fail to understand, General, why the American war drags on so. We commit more men and endless money to the contest and we are still at a draw!"

"One does lose patience, Your Majesty," Burgoyne replies.

The King looks at John Penn. "If your late uncle, *may he rest in one piece*, had been more kind to Benjamin Franklin, I wouldn't be in this mess!"

"I did apologize to Dr. Franklin for Uncle's transgression, Your Majesty," Penn offers.

"On your *knees*?" the King persists.

Penn casts his eyes down sheepishly.

"General Howe has loaded twelve thousand troops onto ships and taken to the sea, going where, we know not. What say you, Burgoyne? The Carolinas, do you suppose?"

The General catches up again with the King. "I suspect not, Sir. I think he takes aim at the capital."

They come upon a watering trough. The King dismounts and walks his horse to water. The other two join him.

"Philadelphia? Why not march there overland from New York?"

"General Washington stands in his way. General Howe will surprise him and attack from the rear," Burgoyne surmises.

The King's face brightens. "How clever of him. I *love* surprises!" He pulls a silver flask from his pocket, takes a sip, and passes it to Governor Penn.

"I can win this war for you, Sire," Burgoyne offers.

"And how would you go about doing that, General?"

"Give me ten thousand troops. I will cross to Quebec, join forces with the Native Indians, and march south to New York," Burgoyne explains earnestly. "The northern colonies will be cut off, and we will buy General Howe time to take the South."

Penn passes the flask to the General. "You could destroy the Congress, which they so richly deserve!" he says, looking gleeful.

Burgoyne drinks from the flask. "I foresee a speedy surrender."

The King claps his hands together. "Burgoyne, you shall have your troops!" he concludes.

He looks into the dense wood a few yards away. "If you gentlemen will excuse me for a moment..." The King turns and walks briskly toward the trees, unbuttoning his breeches as he goes.

Passy

Franklin and Madame Brillon ride side by side on a trail following a bend in the River Seine. They trot along as though they are in no great hurry to get anywhere. She rides side-saddle, with her long skirt splayed out over her legs. Her dark hair is worn down and falling over her shoulders in billowing curls. Franklin sports a beaver cap covering his wispy hair. It is a flawless spring day, with a warm sun on their backs and trees overhead bursting with spring green.

They have not spoken for a while, until Franklin says, "It concerns me that Benny has been indoctrinated with Papist beliefs at his boarding school here."

Madame Brillon is startled by Franklin's comment. "You must not demean the one true faith, Papa," she retorts. "It is the only right path to heaven!"

"Then, perhaps it would be sensible of me to entrust you with the charge of my eternal soul," he says mischievously.

They both bring their horses to a stop.

"A wise decision!" she replies, her eyes sparkling. "I shall be your spirit guide here, and in the hereafter!"

Franklin feigns a troubled look. "How can she who provokes me to sin, also be my confessor?" he inquires.

Madame Brillon giggles. "I know my penitent's weakness, and I shall tolerate it."

"Even though I am prone to breaking that Commandment which forbids coveting thy neighbor's wife? I am helpless in that regard," he tells her.

Madame Brillon smiles. "As long as you love God, America, and *me* above all, I absolve you of all your sins… present, past, and future!"

Franklin's face brightens. "My future looks very rosy, indeed!"

Franklin reaches out and touches Madame Brillon's hand. She withdraws it, whips her horse and gallops ahead.

He whips his horse and chases after her, shouting, "Hélène! Wait! I am condemned to hell if you leave me!"

FRANKLIN HOUSE, PHILADELPHIA   1777

Two stable boys load crates and boxes into a drayage wagon stopped in front of the house. The sun is hot for September and both boys are perspiring; they have stripped to the waist. Inside the house, the sitting room is cluttered with trunks and packing crates. Sally, Aggie, Jake and Bobby rush about, packing valuables. Little William Bache, five years old, tries to help his mother.

"Billy, don't break anything," Sally warns him. "We don't have much time, so just pack our best things," she calls to Aggie.

"I take this full box out to the wagon," Jake announces, lifting a crate with Bobby's help and backing toward the open front door.

"Did you pack the tea set Mrs. Stevenson sent from England for my wedding?" Sally asks Aggie. "I don't want to lose that."

"Yes, ma'am. Them dishes is in the wagon already. I got the silver from the dining room, too." Aggie wraps a blue and white Chinese vase in paper.

Richard Bache enters from the street, looks around the room, and blinks his bloodshot eyes as he takes off his coat. "What in hell is goin' on, Sal?" he inquires, weaving slightly.

"It's about time you showed up!" she glowers. "We are packing up to leave town!"

"Leave? Why?" he asks, sounding befuddled.

Sally places her hands on her hips. "There's near a hundred British warships loaded with troops out in the Bay, all primed to invade any minute! You ain't heard about that down at the tavern?" she fumes.

Bache braces himself against the back of a chair. "Yes, but there is no cause for alarm!"

"Don't be stupid, Richard. My father is their sworn enemy. General Howe will march our family off in chains to a prison ship, then burn down this house. Get busy!" she snaps, impatiently.

"I'll fetch the strong box," he volunteers.

"And pack up Papa's Shakespeare books!"

Bache staggers out of the room.

"Thank God Benny is out of harm's way," Sally says with a sigh, wrapping a piece of crystal in paper.

"Praise Jesus!" Aggie looks heavenward, while nestling a parcel into a crate.

CONNECTICUT 1777

William lies on the cot in his tiny cell in Litchfield Prison. He is wrapped in a blanket, reading a book by the light of a candle resting on a small wooden table next to him. The chamber is barren but for these two pieces of furniture, both delivered to him out of the kindness of Governor Trumbull. Woven straw mats covering parts of the cold slate floor are the only other furnishings to be seen. William is grateful for a steady supply of books, also sent to him by the Governor.

William looks up as a key turns in the lock of his iron door. A shaft of light pours in as the door creaks open. A guard in militia uniform enters and winces at the odor of the place.

The guard waves his hand in front of his face. "Jesus! What's that smell?"

"Me. You smell me," William replies in a weak voice.

The guard waves the barrel of his musket toward the door. "Your turn at the latrine." William sets down his book and stands with considerable effort. He appears frail and gaunt, his hair thin and matted. His eyes are encircled as though with charcoal, and he is missing a front tooth. "What is the hour?" he inquires.

"It's dinner time, Mr. Franklin. I'll bring your meal after you use the latrine," the guard advises.

William looks at the young man with watery eyes. "You seem like a kind fellow. Would you get a message to Governor Trumbull for me?"

"I ain't been invited to tea with the Governor lately, but ya never know. What's the message?" the guard inquires, placing his musket in one hand and taking hold of William's elbow with his other. He guides William out the door, along the corridor, and down the stairs to the prison yard.

William is blinded by the bright sunlight when they step outside. He pulls his blanket close around him and walks with difficulty through the slushy snow. He stumbles and leans on the guard's arm. "Please tell the Governor I can bear my dark cell no longer. I am alone all day and night. I speak to no-one, get no exercise…"

"Aw, but we're goin' for a walk right now!" the guard says sarcastically, as he leads William along a rutted, muddy path.

"Ask the Governor, please, if he would take me out to the parade ground and have me shot," William whimpers, looking pleadingly into the guard's eyes. "Tell him I would be grateful to him if I were shot dead!"

"That is a very poor attitude, Mr. Franklin, very poor indeed. But I will see what I can do for ye." The guard says no more as he leads William to a row of outhouses ahead.

NEW JERSEY   1777

Elizabeth Franklin reclines on a settee in the parlor of the Governor's mansion. Her eyes are closed, and one arm is raised over her head. She appears to be napping. Her blonde hair is worn down and arrayed over the pillow behind her head. She has reached thirty-five years and is still lovely, her skin milky and pale. She looks serene. A thin blanket of pale blue wool covers her legs, and a book lies open on her lap. A candle has been lit on the table next to the settee and a fire glows in the fireplace across the room.

A female servant, an African American girl of about sixteen years, enters the room. She carries a small silver tea tray and approaches Elizabeth. She sets the tray on the table next to the settee. The maid doesn't wish to disturb Mrs. Franklin, but she feels she must make her presence known.

"I bring your tea, Ma'am," the girl announces in a near-whisper. "Sorry I a little late, but the tea cakes just come outta the oven."

Elizabeth doesn't stir.

The girl studies her for a moment. "Mrs. Franklin?"

Elizabeth does not answer.

The maid reaches out and gently taps Elizabeth's shoulder. There is still no reply.

She touches Elizabeth's hand, which is icy cold. The girl shrieks, backs away, her eyes wide, with her hand to her mouth. She turns and runs from the room, screaming.

CHAPTER THIRTY-SEVEN

Nine Sisters

NORTHERN NEW YORK   OCTOBER 1777

Daylight breaks over the recently plowed fields of a farm near Saratoga, casting deep shadows between rows of furrows. A light burns in the kitchen window of a white-washed farmhouse situated at the edge of the fields. A horse, tethered to a fence near the house, waits for its rider. A man's pair of boots sits on the covered porch next to the kitchen door. A rifle leans against the porch rail.

Inside the house, Albert Wick, who farms this land, and his neighbor, Bernard 'Buzzy' Brooks, who is in his stockinged feet, are seated at the kitchen table studying a map of the area. Cups of coffee sit on the table before them.

Wick sips his coffee as Brooks points to the map. "I figure we can catch up with 'em 'bout here, on the Old Emerson Road. I seen 'em a mile or so from there," Brooks tells him.

Wick looks at Brooks over his coffee cup. "How many militia men was there, you suppose?"

"Maybe a hundred, maybe more. I didn't talk to nobody."

Evie, Albert's wife, appears in the kitchen doorway. She is in her late thirties, strawberry blonde, and pretty even without make-up. She wears a flannel nightgown and carries a lighted candle. "I thought I might's well join in the conversation, since I can't sleep through it," she says curtly and blows out the candle.

"'Mornin', Evie," both men offer politely. Evie takes bread and butter from a box on a sideboard and places them on the table. She nods toward her husband's rifle leaning next to the door. "Looks to me like you two ain't goin' fishing today."

Albert sets his cup on the table. "We was talkin' about the British army that's marching this way from Lake Champlain. Some of our neighbors has gone to help the militia surprise them British in the woods."

Evie places a jar of jam on the table. "You're not thinking about joining the neighbors, are you?"

Albert shrugs and looks at Brooks.

Brooks helps himself to a slice of bread. "We were thinking about it, yes, ma'am," he admits.

Evie pours herself a cup of coffee from the pot in the hearth. "Buzzy Brooks, every time you come by here, you and Albert take off on some crazy crusade. A handful of farmers are no match for the King's army."

"We'd like to lend a hand," Albert says, buttering a slice of bread.

Evie joins the men at the table. "What about lending *me* a hand? There's plenty to do around here. Buzzy, you best go on your way now."

"We'll be home before dark," her husband offers.

Evie shakes her head. "You won't come home, Al. I can feel it in my bones." She slams her coffee cup down on the table and rises from her chair. She takes a shawl from a hook by the door, wraps it around her, and slips into a pair of clogs. "I'm goin' to milk the cows, since you ain't goin' to!" she says crossly, and steps outside, slamming the door behind her. Albert takes a sip of his coffee, rises from the table, and picks up his rifle. "Let's go, Buzzy. Get your boots on. She'll be all right."

There isn't much to see on the Old Emerson Road, save for hearty blue spruce trees and a few dilapidated, abandoned homesteads. After an hour's ride north, Wick and Brooks dismount, tether their horses to a tree next to a clear creek, and shoulder their rifles.

They march through the forest on foot and, as Brooks predicted, they come upon a company of the Colonial Militia hiding in the dense woods, who plan to ambush the British troops and their Indian cohorts heading their way. Most of the Militia are known to Wick and Brooks from the Community Church in town or from barn-raisings around the county. It is the Indian warriors recruited by the British who most incense the locals. The Indians have been paid generously and were a menace before they were stirred up by the British.

Wick approaches a man whose face is familiar to him. "Buzzy and I thought we'd give you a hand," he says.

"Fine, fine," the Militia man says in a whisper. "The English should be along here anytime now. Make yourselves at home, but keep quiet."

General John Burgoyne rides along a narrow trail through the forest. He is dressed as a field marshal, with a gold-braided stand-up collar on his coat and matching bicorn hat perched atop his short-cropped gray wig. Four British officers ride on horseback behind him. They are followed by a battalion of foot soldiers, aged from sixteen to forty. Most have been conscripted for Burgoyne's campaign in North America. A company of Indian fighters brings up the rear.

As Burgoyne mounted his horse at first light, he thought again that only the British Empire could move so many men, so grand an army, over so many miles, and so efficiently.

Thus far, he has met with little resistance as they marched from Montreal to New York, but for a token skirmish here and there. *'The prize is within reach!'* Burgoyne thinks as he looks back over the legions trudging behind him. He is certain to earn the gratitude of his Sovereign.

It is a glorious autumn day. The trees are changing color and are a riot of bright yellow and red-orange leaves. Other than an occasional aside or quip, the soldiers speak little as they trek along. Burgoyne has not spoken a word to the officers near him for the past mile or so. The woods are quiet… perhaps too quiet, he thinks, as he approaches a crossing with another unnamed trail.

Burgoyne and his officers enter the intersection where the Militia Men are waiting for them. A rifle is fired. One of Burgoyne's four officers moans and falls from his horse. An ear-splitting volley of musket and rifle fire ensues, coming from all directions. Dozens of British foot soldiers are shot and fall where they stand. Burgoyne orders a retreat, but his men can find nowhere to run. Another of his officers is shot, screams in pain, and falls from his horse. Burgoyne is confused by the noise and smoke. He cannot see the enemy as more of his soldiers fall and pile up, dead, on top of others. Many of the British soldiers raise their muskets and take aim into the trees, firing at the invisible enemy. They are an easy target for the Militia Men and most are promptly dispatched. Another of Burgoyne's officers groans and falls from his horse.

Some British soldiers manage to hit their mark. Brooks takes a shot in his shoulder, screams in pain, and drops to his knees. Wick is hit by musket fire square between his eyes. He falls backward, his blood spilling over a bed of crimson maple leaves.

With their leaders dead or in disarray, hundreds of British soldiers farther back along the road turn tail and run. The Indians quickly vanish into the woods. Fleeing British troops are chased by the Americans, who organize the British soldiers into gangs of prisoners which, at the end of the day, will number in the thousands.

Burgoyne is frozen in place, paralyzed by the fury of ceaseless gunfire and the screams of the injured and dying soldiers. His horse is spooked by the chaos of the battle, rears, and throws the General. Burgoyne regains his footing, stands, and surveys the carnage around him. *"The prize is lost!"* he moans. He feels sick and staggers into the underbrush and retches.

PASSY   DECEMBER 1777

Franklin stands on the front steps of Maison Valentois, speaking in French with three young men who face him in the stone forecourt. Franklin looks at them sympathetically. "We appreciate your interest, gentlemen, but I have no commissions in the American Army to hand out, and all officers' positions are filled," he tells them. "Please share with your friends what I have said here today."

The disappointment the young men feel is plain on their faces. *"Merci, Dr. Franklin, merci"*, they say courteously, as they back out of Franklin's presence and turn to leave.

As the trio walks to the entry gates, a man on horseback rides into the courtyard. The three young men press themselves against a brick wall to make way for the rider. He is a messenger and appears agitated. He quickly dismounts, removes his cap, and approaches Franklin, who is made curious by the visitor and has stepped down into the courtyard.

"Dr. Franklin! I bring you a message from Nantes!" the courier says excitedly in French.

"Has Philadelphia fallen to General Howe?" Franklin inquires.

"Yes, sir," the courier replies in English, handing a packet to Franklin.

Franklin's expression is grim. He looks at the packet without opening it. *"Merci beaucoup,"* he says, turning to walk back to the house.

"There is better news, Dr. Franklin!" the courier calls after him.

Franklin pauses at the steps. "What is it?"

"General Burgoyne has surrendered at Saratoga! More than a thousand of his army killed or wounded! Six thousand men taken as prisoners!"

Franklin opens the packet, removes a document and studies it briefly. He looks up with a joyous smile. He goes to the courier, places his hands on either side of the young man's head, pulls him closer and kisses the boy on his forehead. "Thank you, my son!" he exclaims. He fishes in his pockets for some coins and gives them to the courier.

Franklin turns and walks back into the house with a bounce in his step.

Passy   February 1778

Arthur Lee and Silas Deane approach Maison Valentois on foot. They pause when they near the entrance gates of the mansion to avoid a string of fine carriages exiting the front courtyard and onto the cobbled street outside. A function seems to be coming to a close. Arriving at the front door, Lee and Deane stand aside as four ladies leave the house. The women are dressed in daytime finery, including fur coats, fashionable hats and plenty of jewelry. They hold the hands of three children, an eight-year-old boy and two girls of about ten years, and chatter happily with one another in rapid-fire French. The butler holds the door open for the departing guests and bids them *'au revoir'*.

Arthur Lee addresses the butler. "We are here to see Dr. Franklin."

"*Oui, Monsieur Lee,*" the butler replies. "*Monsieur Le Comte de Vergennes* has already arrived."

"Who were all those people leaving just now?" Lee inquires snootily.

Dr. Franklin's '*rassemblement*' has just ended," the butler explains.

"'*Rassemblement?*'" Deane poses a question.

"*Oui*. On Tuesday and Friday mornings, people come to be near him… to receive his blessing. You know, for the children."

Lee looks at Deane with an eyebrow raised.

"His *blessing?*" Lee asks. "Just when was Franklin declared a saint, and by whom?"

Deane chuckles. "Well, he is a holy relic, Arthur."

The butler invites Lee and Deane to enter the house. He leads them into the library, where he announces them. Vergennes is seated at a large ormolu desk, with a sheaf of papers before him. Turgot stands to one side of the Foreign Secretary and Franklin on the other. Temple and Bancroft are seated across from one another at a writing table across the room. They have journals open before them and are taking notes of the proceedings. Franklin directs Lee and Deane to stand next to him on Vergennes' right.

Vergennes raises his pen dramatically. "At this moment," he says, "your United States becomes a sovereign nation, recognized as such by His Majesty, King Louis XVI." He signs a paper in front of him with a flourish and passes the pen to Turgot. Turgot adds his signature to the document. Franklin, Lee and Deane take their turns at signing the paper.

A footman enters the library. He carries glasses of wine on a silver salver and places a glass before each of the men.

Deane lifts his glass. "I trust, Your Excellency, that an accommodation for commerce and a schedule for financial aid are included in the treaty we have just signed. 'Tis the accountant in me that inquires, you understand," he says apologetically.

"It is all there, Monsieur Deane. You may sleep tonight," Turgot assures him.

Vergennes looks at the Americans. "His Majesty extends an invitation to you gentlemen to affirm our alliance in his presence at Versailles. Do you accept?" he inquires.

Temple looks up from his journal. "I do!" he calls across the room.

The Frenchmen and the American diplomats all laugh.

Vergennes raises his glass. "To the great work done here today!"

DEAR BEN

Paris   April 1778

Franklin and his grandsons ride in a horse-drawn carriage through crowded city streets. Benny tugs at the collar of his shirt and at the knees of his breeches, trying to make himself feel more comfortable. "Why do we have to wear these fancy suits, Grandpapa?"

Franklin sinks back into the tufted leather seat of the coach. "Because Voltaire, the great poet, is being inducted into my Masonic Lodge tonight and Monsieur de Chaumont arranged for you boys to attend. You both look very dashing."

"Sophie Brillon was going to give me a piano lesson," Temple sulks.

"Piano lesson indeed!" Franklin retorts.

"Will Monsieur Vergennes be there?" Benny inquires.

"Alas, no," Franklin replies. "The King would disapprove. Voltaire was exiled long ago for his republican views. He has only recently been allowed to return to Paris."

"Why do they call your lodge 'The Nine Sisters', Grandpapa?" Benny wonders.

"After the nine Greek Muses, lad. Our members are accomplished in the Arts. I shall teach you the names of the Muses at supper."

Darkness has fallen when the carriage suddenly comes to a stop next to a streetlamp. Benny looks out and reads a street sign as *'Rue Le Pic'*.

The driver calls down and advises Franklin in French, "This is your stop". The coachman jumps down and opens the doors for Franklin and the boys.

Franklin points down *'Rue Le Pic'*, which resembles little more than a dark alley. "The address we seek is down that lane, I believe," he tells the driver in French.

"This is as far as I go," the driver replies firmly. He lowers a lighted lantern down to Franklin. "Take this with you."

"Vous êtes très gentil," Franklin tells the driver, accepting the lantern.

The coachman climbs back up to his seat atop the carriage and it clatters on, soon vanishing from sight.

351

Franklin holds the lantern aloft and peers down '*Rue Le Pic*'.

"Where are we going?" Temple asks nervously, looking down the narrow lane.

"I am to enter by the back door so as not to be seen," Franklin explains. "Come."

He and the boys start down the wet, trash-lined alley.

Benny looks around and holds his nose. "What a stink!" he exclaims.

"You've not been to London," Franklin smirks.

Within a few yards, a large, oily rat emerges from behind a rubbish bin and darts across the boys' path. They both jump back with a shriek.

Temple's eyes are wide with fear. "My God! Did you see that?!"

"What, you've never seen a rat?" Franklin replies calmly.

"Not with a cat in its mouth!" Temple clarifies, breathing heavily.

"We are in France, my boy. Everybody eats well."

Franklin spies a door down the way adorned with a hieroglyphic symbol. "There it is!" he calls to the boys. He goes to the door and raps on it three times with his signet ring. He hears the 'click' of a key turning in the lock, and the door groans open a crack.

The doorman looks out warily. *"Oui?"* he asks in a gravelly voice.

"Franklin here."

"We have been expecting you." The rusted iron hinges of the door screech as it opens wider. I am Claude. I will assist you." Claude pats Benny on his head. "We rarely see young people here. The little one is to partake, *non?*"

"Yes," Franklin replies. *"Oui."*

Claude leads Franklin and the boys to a backstage area.

A performance is about to begin. Musicians tune their instruments, dancers practice their steps, and stagehands arrange set pieces and properties. Participants sit at candlelit dressing tables, applying make-up and adjusting costumes.

Claude grips Temple's elbow and directs him to the side of the stage. "You may view the ceremony there, from behind the curtain," he says.

Temple peers into the great hall of the Lodge. The décor seems poised between worlds. Ionic Greek columns support the ceiling, while the architrave is painted with symbols and figures from the tombs of the Pharaohs. Walls are draped with miles of black fabric. Stout candles burn in the bronze hands of Roman statuary. A large human eye painted on the domed ceiling gazes down on the scene as though rendering judgement.

Members mill about greeting one another, chattering in French. All are men, most between the ages of fifty and eighty. They are elegantly dressed, some wear satin capes draped over their shoulders. Temple is surprised to see Henri Brillon in the gathering, standing next to Monsieur de Chaumont.

Temple looks to his right backstage and sees Claude helping his grandfather and Benny into long white robes.

A trumpet sounds and the hall goes quiet. Temple parts the curtain and sees the members quickly take their seats. Flutes, chimes and percussion begin to play haunting music. A stage curtain opens and nine pretty boys, costumed as the Greek Muses, descend from the stage. The members roar their approval. The boys carry baskets, toss flower petals, and dance gracefully through the hall. They toy with and tease their audience as they dance. Members reach out to touch the dancers, but the boys escape the probing hands and vanish through hidden doors.

There is an explosion of light at the head of the hall and the curtain opens to reveal a large black pyramid. A light glows at its apex. Four young African men, wearing only loincloths, stand next to the pyramid. A drumbeat grows and the Africans slowly rotate the pyramid. It opens to reveal the Grand Master of the Lodge, a snowy-haired gentleman of about seventy. He is dressed in a dark blue robe and wears a mask over his eyes. The Africans escort the Grand Master to the floor of the hall and disappear. The members greet their leader with thunderous applause.

The Grand Master raises his hand. "Have the Petitioners prepared their Candidate?" he inquires in French.

Four men, robed in black, step down from the stage. "Yes, Grand Master, he is prepared!" they shout.

"Then, dispensing with the ordinary proofs, bring him to me!" the Grand Master orders.

A hush falls over the hall as two men, robed in white, appear on stage. A third figure robed in white, a frail old man, stands between them. He shuffles forward as the trio makes its way down the steps. When they reach the floor, the old man raises his head. It is Voltaire.

A cry goes up from the members. Voltaire's escorts bring the gaunt old man before the Grand Master and his Petitioners.

The Grand Master quiets the crowd with a raised hand. "Messieurs! We welcome into our sacred rite a man who surpasses all in the world of Arts and Letters," he shouts. "The Father of the Enlightenment! The Conscience of the Nation! I present to you François-Marie Arouet… VOLTAIRE!"

The room erupts in cheering and applause, until the Grand Master pleads for quiet. He continues with the ceremony. "Dear Brother, the greatest day of this Lodge will be marked by your admission to the mysteries of our order. After receiving the rapturous applause of the nation, you come to receive a crown less brilliant, yet of solace to heart and soul!" The Grand Master places a crown of laurel leaves on Voltaire's head, to more cheers from the audience.

The Grand Master speaks in English. "Tonight, we also have in our presence, a Brother whose reputation as a scientist and philosopher is unmatched among mortals! He has seized the very fire from heaven and tamed it!"

There is an explosion of light on the stage. "I present to you our Brother, Dr. Benjamin Franklin!" the Grand Master shouts.

Two robed Petitioners escort Franklin and Benny down the steps and into the presence of the Grand Master. The members cheer and applaud. Franklin extends his hand to Voltaire. They shake hands, smiling warmly at each other.

A cry of "Non! Non! Embrace in the French fashion!" arises from the members.

Franklin and Voltaire concede. They embrace and kiss one another on both cheeks. The members stamp their boots on the plank floor, raising a thunderous noise.

Voltaire clings to Franklin's arm and speaks in a breathless, heavily accented English. "I give my benediction to the illustrious and wise Dr. Franklin, the man of America to be most respected," he says. Voltaire places his hand on the Benny's head. "To your grandson, I pronounce only these words: God and Liberty!" The members applaud wildly.

Franklin assumes a dramatic stance. "And I shall walk henceforth in bliss, having been touched by the God Apollo! Vive la France! Vive Voltaire!" he cries over ecstatic applause.

Voltaire's eyes close and he collapses into Franklin's arms. The cheering of the crowd is replaced by a collective gasp.

Franklin holds Voltaire in his arms for a long moment. Petitioners come to his aid, fanning the old man's head. Voltaire opens his eyes and stands unsteadily, with his hand to his forehead. He smiles at Franklin. The members cheer wildly.

Behind the curtain, Temple has made up his mind that one day he will try his hand at acting. Music plays briefly, and a poet is introduced, who commences to read from his works - in Polish. Temple is relieved when his grandfather finds him and ushers him and Benny out the front door, where they must hail a hackney carriage to take them home.

CONNECTICUT   SEPTEMBER 1778

William awakens from a nap when he hears a key turn in the lock of his cell door. He sits up on his cot. Although it is a hot day in late summer and the air is humid and close, he covers his naked torso with his blanket.

The door is pushed open, and William is surprised to see Governor Trumbull enter, flanked by two sentries. "Hello, Franklin," Trumbull says, covering his mouth with a kerchief at the stench of the place.

"Governor?" William croaks in a weak voice.

"Can you stand up?" Trumbull asks.

William places his feet on the floor and stands, bracing himself against the brick wall.

Trumbull is shocked by the decline in William's appearance. He is skeletal, has lost hair and teeth, and is in dire need of a bath. "Get dressed. It's time to go. We have both had enough."

A puzzled look comes over William's gaunt face. "Go? Where?"

"You are going to New York... An exchange of prisoners. I struck a good bargain: six men freed in exchange for only you."

William weaves on his feet and steadies himself against the wall at the news. "I... I..."

"I have done it for your father's sake," Trumbull says candidly. First, you will come to my house and clean up and put on some decent clothes. We'll have a farewell meal together."

Each of the two sentries takes one of William's arms, guiding him out of the cell.

William looks back into his home of the past many months. "What about my things?" he asks, pointing to a stack of books and a small pile of personal effects neatly arranged in a corner.

"Leave them." Trumbull replies. "Let's go."

They do not speak again until they reach the prison yard, where William is blinded by the afternoon sun. He has had little exercise and walks with difficulty. "When will I be able to see my wife?" he asks the Governor.

"Your wife is dead. I am very sorry," Trumbull replies.

William swoons. The sentries catch him as he falls. They lower him onto his knees on the ground. William moans a deep, mournful sound. Trumbull stops and shakes his head. "The poor man. Help him to get up."

The sentries struggle to get William on his feet again. They drag him across the prison yard to the prison gates, where the Governor's carriage is waiting.

Paris

The wind had picked up earlier in the day and now blows steadily through the treetops in the wood surrounding the Tuileries Gardens. It is not yet cold enough for snow, but soon will be.

Edward Bancroft is out for a stroll on this blustery evening. The long silk scarf he has wrapped about his neck and tossed over his shoulder flaps in the wind. He is alone in the park until he crosses the path of another gentleman, who appears to be out for an evening's walk as well. This second man has a full crop of white hair, a pinkish complexion, and wears a long, woolen coat. He stops Bancroft and, speaking in English, asks him for the time.

Bancroft takes out his pocket watch and tells the gentleman it is eight forty-five.

The gentleman thanks Bancroft and comments, in a distinctly British accent, on the cold wind, which is whipping fallen leaves around his fine leather boots.

Bancroft looks about, then produces a portfolio from inside his coat and hands it to the Englishman. "I copied the most pertinent sections of the treaties when the grandson wasn't looking over my shoulder," Bancroft says stealthily.

"Excellent. Most helpful, thank you," the Englishman smiles. He nods toward a park bench on the edge of the wood. "Let's sit for a moment."

He and Bancroft walk to the bench and sit down. The Englishman takes an envelope from his pocket and hands it to Bancroft. It is stuffed with bank notes. Bancroft scans them, then tucks the envelope into his own coat pocket.

"The treaties were signed with the French King's assent," Bancroft clarifies.

The Englishman flips through the pages of the portfolio. "I assumed so," he says.

"Franklin has made no mention to Arthur Lee or Mr. Deane of your visit to him."

"I thought not."

"What did you discuss with him?" Bancroft asks brazenly.

The Englishman removes a small pipe from his vest pocket. "I offered the Colonies a speedy conclusion to the hostilities and unfettered independence. Franklin seemed indifferent. He said it was a pity I hadn't come sooner."

"He was right. He surmised the forest would devour General Burgoyne. He *did* tell Vergennes of your visit, however."

"The treacherous bastard... of course he did! And now it's come to this. We are at war."

Bancroft and the Englishman lean back against the park bench for a few moments, not speaking.

"I feel a chill," the Englishman says and gets up from the bench. He lifts his coat collar and strolls on without a 'farewell,' while attempting to light his pipe in the brisk wind. Bancroft takes the envelope out of his pocket and thumbs more closely through the bank notes inside.

Paris

A wooden sign hanging over the entry door of *Restaurant Tante Louise* creaks as it swings back and forth in the wind. Inside the café, candles glow on the few tables still occupied by diners finishing a meal. A waiter wearing a long white apron glides efficiently among them, pouring wine and clearing plates.

Silas Deane and a prosperous-looking gentleman of about fifty years of age are seated at a table in a corner of the restaurant. The two men have eaten their suppers, but their plates have yet to be cleared. Deane raises his wine glass in a toast. "To friendship," he offers, with a smile.

"Santé," says the other gentleman, returning the smile.

"What is the hour?" Deane asks.

The gentleman looks at his pocket watch. "It is eight forty-five," he replies in French.

"They'll be putting up the chairs soon," Deane observes.

"Yes," the gentleman concurs. "We must get back to business. When will Turgot release funds from the Royal Treasury?" he inquires.

"The first tranche has already gone to Franklin's accounts. We will begin placing orders for weapons in a few days."

"You will be able to direct a share of your business to my factories?"

Deane dips a crust of bread into a bit of sauce left on his plate. "A generous share, but your contracts must appear to be competitive," he warns.

"That is a matter easily arranged with my business associates," the gentleman assures him. Deane looks around the restaurant, then continues in a hushed tone. "There is also the question of my compensation," he says.

The gentleman takes a sip of wine. "What do you propose?"

"Your complete discretion?" Deane replies, his brows furrowed.

"*Mais, bien sur.* Of course," the gentleman replies with a grin on his face. He raises his glass. "As you say, Silas, '*to friendship*'!"

DEAR BEN

Paris   1778

Early the next morning, fallen leaves whirl about the stone courtyard of Maison Valentois, as the butler and a houseman load trunks and travel bags into a grand horse-drawn carriage. A passenger is already seated inside the coach, but the man's face is shadowed and cannot be clearly seen.

The front door of the house swings open, and Franklin appears on the top step with his grandson, Benny. Franklin's cashmere robe blows open and closed in the wind. Benny's hair is carefully combed, and he is attired in a woolen suit and cloak, with polished leather shoes on his feet. Mr. Rags is tucked snugly under his arm.

"It is time to go, son," Franklin says.

Benny looks up at him with red-rimmed eyes. "But I don't want to go, Grandpapa," he pleads.

Franklin attempts to escort Benny to the waiting carriage, but Benny digs in his heels, as he has done in protest for the past several days. He had even tried running away a few days before, and managed to flee as far as the Brillon chateau, where Madame Brillon's cook took him in, fed him lunch, and walked him back home.

"But you *must* go," Franklin insists. "I have enrolled you in a fine Protestant school in Switzerland."

"I want to stay here with you, Grandpapa!"

Franklin attempts cajoling the boy. "You will soon make friends, and Temple and I will visit often. And you will come to us for holidays, Christmas and so forth." He places his hands on Benny's shoulders. "Come, my boy. Monsieur Philibert has kindly agreed to escort you all the way to Geneva. We mustn't keep him waiting."

Benny relents and walks, haltingly, with his grandfather to the waiting carriage.

Monsieur Philibert leans out of the carriage to greet his charge. He is extremely thin, with hooded dark eyes looking out from a face badly scarred by the ravages of smallpox. The brim of his hat casts a shadow over a sharp, beak-like nose. "Bonjour, Benny," he says in a screechy voice.

Benny recoils at the sight of the man and grips his grandfather's arm tightly.

Franklin pries Benny off his arm and waves a greeting to Monsieur Philibert. "I know that you and Monsieur Philibert will become great friends. You will practice your French and learn a bit of German along the way. He prefers not to speak English, you see. Come, now, be my brave little lad…"

Benny, his shoulders slumped, reluctantly boards the carriage. He slides into a seat next to a window, as far from Monsieur Philibert as he can manage.

Franklin gives a signal to the driver and the carriage jerks to a start. Benny looks out the window of the coach as it rolls through the gates and onto the street. He wipes tears from his eyes and waves Mr. Rags's little arm, shouting 'good-bye' through the open window. Franklin blows Benny a kiss, turns, and walks back to the house, holding his robe closed against the brisk wind.

Passy

A few evenings later, Franklin and Madame Brillon are seated at a small table in the library, dining by candlelight. A maid places entrées before them on the intimate table, which is covered in white Belgian linen.

"*Merci*, Marie," Madame Brillon says, without looking up.

Marie fills their glasses with wine.

Franklin studies the room and Monsieur Brillon's collections of leather-bound books, porcelains, and landscape paintings while the servant attends to them. Monsieur Brillon's ormolu desk sits at an angle in the corner of the room, with a Louis XV leather armchair sitting behind it. Fine tapestries hang on three walls and are lighted by sparking crystal chandeliers. Franklin looks at the gleaming walnut herringbone floor beneath his feet.

"I hope you do not mind a simple *'diner a deux'* tonight, Papa," Madame Brillon says, looking at Franklin.

"I prefer it," Franklin replies, thinking the room itself is a feast for the eyes.

Madame Brillon wears a silk dress with a scooped neck and high waistline in the style of the ancient Romans. She wears little jewelry, and her hair is worn up and off her neck. She is another treat for Franklin's eyes. "Where is Henri?" he inquires.

"He and Mademoiselle d'Armond have gone to visit the Baron de Jamac in the Dordogne," she replies.

The maid gives a little curtsey and leaves the room.

Madame Brillon tastes her entrée of crayfish in cream sauce. "Temple is otherwise occupied?"

"He dines with Blanchette and Marcel Caillot."

"Ah, the actor and his wife. They are famously Bohemian, as is their neighbor, Catherine Helvetius. Are you acquainted with her?"

"Should I be?"

"She is a rich and beautiful widow."

"Then, I must meet her!"

Madame Brillon sets down her fork and dabs her lips with her serviette. "I am cross with you, Papa," she says, toying with a gold chain on her wrist. "Very cross that you have sent poor little Benny off to Switzerland."

"I couldn't have him on his knees at Mass every morning. He is a Presbyterian, after all," Franklin tells her.

"Presbyterian! That is precisely why my Sophie spurns Temple, although she adores him." Madame Brillon sips her wine.

"He looks forward to Sophie's piano lessons," Franklin chuckles.

"Piano lessons! Temple has yet to find middle 'C'," Madame Brillon retorts. She stabs at her shrimp. "Has Henri told you that he witnessed Benny's benediction by Voltaire at the Nine Sisters Lodge?"

"I haven't seen Henri."

"Henri said Voltaire was overcome with emotion and fell into your arms. Many thought the great poet had expired."

"All part of the performance. The lusty old boy had a nip at my crotch while he was at it." Franklin twirls the wine in his wine glass.

Madame Brillon looks at him with a wry smile. "Voltaire wished to know what makes the famous Dr. Franklin so famous?"

"Come sit on my lap and I will remind you!" Franklin proposes, grinning.

The butler shuffles into the room, carrying their main course on a platter. He sets the platter on a console and begins to slice the '*entrecote*'.

Madame Brillon puts her finger to her lips to 'shush' Franklin.

Franklin raises his glass to her. "Think about my offer," he says.

She arranges stray hairs on the back of her neck.

CHAPTER THIRTY-EIGHT

The Phoenix

FRANKLIN'S BEDROOM, PHILADELPHIA   1790

Franklin wonders if Bobby has heard a word he has said for the past several minutes. He raises his head and sees Bobby standing at his desk with a rag in his hand, polishing a crystal letter opener - a gift from the Comte de Vergennes. "You still awake, Bobby, or are you sleepwalking?" he calls out in a scratchy voice.

"I am awake, yes, sir."

Franklin feels a stabbing pain in his gut as he pulls himself up to a sitting position. He leans back against the wooden headboard.

"The dust blow in here so fast I can't hardly keep up," Bobby says, sounding frustrated.

Franklin studies his right hand in the flickering light of the candle burning on the table next to his bed. "Our hands tell our stories, Bobby," he sighs. "One needn't gaze in a looking glass to see a reflection of our struggles. All is plain to see in our hands."

Bobby turns his own hand back and forth and shrugs his shoulders. "I suppose that is so."

"The last time I saw my son, his hands were as soft as marshmallow and as white as a lily."

Bobby picks up an agate paperweight and wipes it with his cloth. "Whatever happened to Mr. William?" he inquires.

"William..." Franklin takes a sip of Madeira from the teacup on his night table. "William arose from the ashes of his imprisonment like the Egyptian Phoenix. He was soon made head of the Board of Loyalists up in New York."

NORTHERN NEW YORK   FEBRUARY 1779

    A sentry in British uniform rests on his haunches over a charcoal fire burning in a brazier next to a small carriage house. He warms his hands, rubs them together, then stuffs them in the pockets of his greatcoat. Affixed to the carriage house is the split rail entry gate of a winding drive, which leads to a weather-beaten frame house of modest size. Smoke rises from a dilapidated brick chimney at one end of the house.
    The sentry knows there are some important men meeting inside the house and that tomorrow, they may meet in another location, as they are loyal to the King and hunted by the Colonial Militia. He picks up his rifle when he hears a rider approach on the snow-covered lane. A Redcoat rides up and dismounts his horse. He and the sentry salute one another.
    "I come to see Governor Franklin," the Redcoat reports.
    "And what is your business with the Governor, soldier?"
    "I carry a message for him from Colonel Gibbs."
    "You may proceed," the sentry consents, and unlatches the rickety driveway gate. The Redcoat re-mounts his horse and rides on.

    Inside the house, a committee of seven men are seated at a long pine table. A fire burns in the fireplace, but not brightly enough to warm the room and the men have not removed their coats. Maps of the surrounding area are tacked to the walls.
    William Franklin stands next to the hearth, addressing the group. He has gained weight since his release from prison, sports new false teeth, and wears a fine suit of clothes under his greatcoat. "It is time we took the fight to the enemy," he says in a clear voice. "The rebels have built fortifications surrounding us, penning us in. We hide and cower here like a bunch of old women!"
    A committee member, a stout man in middle age, pounds the table. "He is right! Meanwhile, they sting like wasps! Burning our farms, poisoning our wells, and laying waste to our commerce!"
    William continues. "I say we order our troops to wipe out the Militia strongholds, one by one. If not, we face extinction!"

A younger man at the table raises his hand. "There is danger in spreading the few British troops we have at our disposal too thin," he warns. "Who will defend the city?"

"We will divert the rebels' attention... force them to play a defensive game," William argues.

A knock at the door, it unlatches and swings open.

William considers hiding in the kitchen for a moment.

The Redcoat enters and salutes the men gathered at the table. "I have a message from Colonel Gibbs for Governor Franklin," he announces. "Is he here?"

After a pause: "I am Franklin," William says, looking relieved.

The courier hands an envelope to William.

William opens the envelope and studies the letter inside. He looks up with a broad smile. "Splendid! Gibbs has captured a rebel artillery unit at Albany, including its commander, a Captain Ruddy!"

"Colonel Gibbs awaits your reply, sir," the Redcoat says.

"Tell the Colonel to hang Captain Ruddy. I shall write an order directing him to do so." William sits at the table and picks up a pen and paper.

The committee members look at each other with eyes wide. "Surely you will want this Captain Ruddy brought to us for trial first," one of the men pleads.

"Why bother?" William says dismissively.

When finished writing, he folds the paper and hands it to the Redcoat. "Tell Colonel Gibbs, if he doesn't have a gallows handy, a sturdy oak will do. We shall make an example of the bastard!"

"Yes, sir," the Redcoat says, stuffing the envelope into his coat pocket. He hurries out the front door, slamming it closed behind him.

"Well, then," William goes on, "we were speaking of taking out the rebel encampments."

Passy

Franklin has walked for some time on this moonlit night in early April. He is attired in evening wear, with a cape fastened over his shoulders. He walks unsteadily after a long evening of cards, conversation, and fine wines at the chateau of a neighbor a half-mile away. He arrives at the side garden entrance of the Brillon mansion and is pleased to find the gate unlocked. He fumbles with the latch and the gate creaks and swings open. He sniffs at the sweet scent of night blooming jasmine as he crosses the garden to the terrace outside Madame Brillon's bedroom. He reaches the French doors opening onto her suite of rooms. The curtains are pulled closed, but a light still burns inside. Franklin taps lightly on the glass with his fingertip. He hears a dog bark. "Hélène!" he whispers.

Inside the bedroom, Madame Brillon lies in her bed reading by the light of an oil lamp. Floral linen side panels hang from the frame of her cozy four-poster bed. Her little terrier, Maxie, is curled up next to her. She hears another tap at the French doors. Maxie growls. Madame Brillon rises at the disturbance, throws a robe over her nightgown, and scurries to the doors in her bare feet. She parts the curtains a few inches and sees Franklin. She unlocks the doors and opens them a crack.

"Papa!" she whispers. "Are you crazy? Are you aware of the hour?"

Maxie jumps off the bed, prances across the room, and sniffs at Franklin through the narrow opening in the doors.

"I've brought you something," he grins.

Madame Brillon has let her hair down and it spills onto her shoulders. She brushes it to one side with her hand. "You have been drinking," she scolds.

"A little," he confesses. "Are you alone?"

"No. I heard Henri come home and close his door perhaps one hour ago. You had better go, Papa. He might hear you and be very cross," she warns.

Down a nearby hallway, Henri Brillon sits up in bed, reading by candlelight. He hears something and cocks an ear. He opens the drawer in the bedside table next to him and removes a dagger. Rising from his bed, he finds his robe, throws it on, and slides into his slippers.

On the terrace outside Madame Brillon's bedroom, Franklin is persistent. "I will only be a moment," he pleads.

"All right, then," she concedes. "But you must be quiet!"

Franklin squeezes through the opening in the doors. Madame Brillon and Maxie return to her bed and snuggle in. She is propped up against a pile of goose down pillows.

Franklin sits on the edge of the bed. He takes a silk-covered box from his coat pocket and hands it to Madame Brillon. "*Pour vous,*" he says.

She opens the box and lifts out a string of pearls. "How lovely! For me? *Vraiment?*"

she gushes as she holds the string up to the light.

The pearls glow in the lamplight as if ignited from within.

She looks at him with a sweet smile. "They are perfect! What a wonderful shade! Such an extravagance, Papa."

"A mere memento," Franklin says humbly.

Suddenly, the bedroom door flies open, banging against the wall behind it. Franklin and Madame Brillon look up with a start and turn to see Henri standing in the doorway. A lighted candle flickers in a silver holder in his hand. He steps into the room and sets the candle on a commode. He ties his silk brocade robe closed tightly around his waist.

"I thought I heard voices," he says frostily.

Startled, Franklin and Madame Brillon freeze in place, their mouths agape.

"And what brings the illustrious Dr. Franklin to my house in the middle of the night?" Henri inquires, moving closer to the bed.

"I was passing by," Franklin explains, with a guilty look on his face.

Henri considers Franklin suspiciously. "A curious route to your house through my garden, *non?*" He looks at his wife. "And what are you holding there, my dear? Would those be pearls?"

Madame Brillon nods.

"Did you find them under your pillow? A fairy left them? A foreign fairy, perhaps?"

Franklin clears his throat. "They were such a good buy in a shop in Paris, I could not resist them as a little gift for 'Hélène.'"

"*Un bon marché?*" Henri exclaims. "With diamonds on the clasp? Quite expensive, I should think. *Très cher.* A grand gesture for your friend, 'Hélène.'"

Franklin looks toward the terrace. "Well, I should be going…"

Henri paces to and fro. "I am not a small man, Franklin. When you kiss my wife, I kiss you. When I find you in her bed, I am not so amused."

"It only stands to reason," Franklin concurs. "He is *on* the bed, not in it, Henri," Madame Brillon argues.

Henri glares at his wife, "No matter." He forces a smile. "Since we are together, let us lift a glass to the recent alliance between your country and our King." He opens the door of the commode behind him, takes out a decanter of liqueur and three small glasses, and fills them.

Franklin rises from the bed. "I really should be going," he says anxiously.

"Sit, Franklin, sit," Henri commands. Franklin sits back down on the edge of the bed.

Henri serves a glass to his wife and to Franklin, then raises his own glass. "To our distinguished friend and his great achievement!" he offers, sounding civil. "*A votre santé!*"

Franklin and Madame Brillon smile nervously and raise their glasses, joining in the toast.

Henri goes to the French doors and looks out pensively. "I must say it has been remarkable having you as a neighbor, Benjamin. The comings and goings at all hours…"

Franklin sips his Courvoisier. "I hope I haven't made too great a disturbance."

Henri turns to his wife again. "What would you say, *ma cherie?* Have you been disturbed?" he asks innocently.

"*Non. Pas du tout,*" she replies, looking at the string of pearls in her hand.

Henri removes the menacing-looking dagger from the pocket of his robe and lays it on the commode. "It seems I will not need my *poignard* after all. I thought there was an intruder in the house."

An awkward moment passes as Henri studies the two on the bed.

"But then, there was an intruder, was there not?" he reconsiders, after a pause.

Henri places his glass on top of the commode and picks up the candleholder.

"So, I will leave you to do… whatever it is you do. There is more cognac in the bottle, if you like. *Bonne nuit.*" Henri turns and leaves the room, pulling the door closed sharply behind him.

Madame Brillon looks at Franklin with a wary smile.

Henri returns to his bedchamber, places the candle on a bureau, removes his robe and slippers, and snuffs out the flame of the candle. He fluffs his pillows and climbs into bed. Mademoiselle d'Armond lies on the other side of the bed, wrapped in a satin quilt.

She raises herself onto one elbow. *"Qu'est-ce que c'est, Henri?"* "What was it?"

"Rien, ma cherie. C'est rien. Dormez-vous." "Nothing, my dear. Nothing. Go to sleep."

He blows out the candle on his bedside table and lies back on his bed, studying the deepening shadows on the ceiling above him.

PART EIGHT

The Homecoming

CHAPTER THIRTY-NINE

His Majesty

FRANKLIN HOUSE   1790

"What we need is another good rain," Sally Bache says tersely, as she parts the parlor curtains a few inches and looks out to the street.

Outside, a group of neighbors, three ladies and two men, stand under a streetlamp quietly chatting. The women wear bonnets and are wrapped in woolen shawls. The men wear long cloaks and wide-brimmed hats.

Sally clings to the heavy linen drapery. "Might shoo those damn people away. They're out there waitin' on Papa to die. Puts me on edge!"

She turns back to the parlor, where Polly reclines with one arm thrown over the back of a settee and Thomas Jefferson is slumped in an easy chair. His frock coat is draped over the back of the chair. Both have a glass of wine in hand.

"Well, he is not going to give them the satisfaction." Sally sighs heavily. "Not tonight, anyway."

"Perhaps they're waiting to see Secretary Jefferson leave," Polly offers.

"And leave I must," Jefferson says, setting his wine glass on the table next to him. He sits upright in his chair. "I am so much more comfortable here than at my lodgings in town. I have been such a bother!"

"Not at all," Polly argues.

Sally peers out the window again. "Who is that strange woman across the street?" she wonders, clinging to the curtain. "She's looking at this house." Polly gets up from the settee and goes to the next window. Curious, she parts the curtains and looks out. "I don't see anybody," she says.

"She was there a second ago," Sally says curtly.

Polly resumes her supine position on the settee. "Tell us more about your time in Paris with Papa, Mr. Jefferson."

Sally pulls the curtain closed abruptly and walks unsteadily to the center table. She drops into a chair and picks up her wine glass. "Paris? I'll tell you about Paris!" She refills her glass from the open bottle on the table. "While Papa was over there dancin' with that fancy Queen at Versailles, Richard and me and little Billy were hiding from General Howe out in the country, like everybody else."

Sally leans back in her chair, gazing at the ceiling, thinking of a time she would rather have forgotten. "Until General Howe gave up on Philadelphia and moved on, that is. No use occupying a ghost town, I guess."

Franklin House, Philadelphia   1778

Richard Bache tries the front door of the house on Market Street and finds it unlocked. He opens the door and views a scene of desolation. He, Sally and five-year-old Billy enter the parlor, then the sitting room, both of which have been stripped of rugs and furnishings. Curtains hang in tatters at the windows. They wander from room to room with mouths agape. Billy kicks trash and food scraps out of their path as they walk. Paint that hasn't faded shows the outlines of pictures that once hung on the walls. Empty spirits bottles lie strewn in the corners of the rooms. Richard holds Billy's hand as they enter the library, where they find empty shelves, once laden with an extensive and valuable collection of books. The Baches were able to spirit some of them away before the British occupation, but many volumes were left behind. Obscene writing is scrawled on the walls. Richard covers Billy's eyes with his hands.

"He can't read, Richard," Sally reminds him.

In the dining room, china cabinets built into the corners of the room have been torn out, and a brass chandelier and wall sconces have been pulled down and carried away.

The bedrooms upstairs are also barren, with a few filthy blankets scattered on the floors. Sally points to bleached stains on the wooden planks. "Look, Richard. Those pigs didn't even bother to use a pot. Animals!"

"Jesus, Sal, they took everything!"

"I can see that, Richard," she replies. "But they left a message for my father, didn't they?"

Palace of Versailles　　　　　　　　　　March 1778

"Vive Franklin! Vive la Liberté! Vive Franklin!" the crowd screams as Franklin's coach-and-four rolls through the gilded gates into the courtyard of the palace. Hundreds of Parisians of all ages have gathered to greet Franklin's arrival. They cheer, wave flags, and toss flowers in the path of the coach. Many in the crowd wear patched and ragged clothing, but their mood today is light and matches the bright, sunny morning.

Franklin leans out the window and smiles and waves to the crowd as his carriage clatters across the cobbled courtyard to a side entrance on the ground floor of the palace. Franklin's fellow passengers, Arthur Lee and Silas Deane, look at each other warily. The coach comes to a stop, the coachman jumps down and opens Franklin's door. He steps out, wearing a plain brown velvet suit, with white silk stockings covering his legs from his knees to his black leather shoes. His head is bare.

The crowd surrounds Franklin, and many reach out to touch him. He shakes dozens of hands, calling "*Bonjour, bonjour!*" as he moves from one admirer to the next.

Lee and Deane view the demonstration of esteem from inside the coach. "We are of no consequence here," Deane observes grumpily, shrinking back in his seat.

"Because *he* has made it so," Lee concurs. "We are ignored as he shamelessly nurtures his fame and bathes in the glow of it. He doesn't even answer my letters."

The coachman opens their doors and Lee and Deane step down. They wear their best suits, brocade waistcoats and linen shirts trimmed with ruffles. They are soon approached by peddlers offering ceremonial swords and satin sashes for sale.

"You must buy, Monsieur," one of the vendors pleads with Deane. "C'est de rigueur to wear in the palace!" Lee and Deane both buy swords and merit sashes of dubious meaning and don them. Franklin declines the vendors' offers.

Sentries hold back the throng and escort the Americans to the diplomatic entrance of the palace, where they are met by a page who shows them in. As directed, they follow the page up a long flight of stone stairs to an anteroom at the top. Jacques Turgot and the Comte de Vergennes are there to greet Franklin and his colleagues, as a footman carrying a golden salver offers the men glasses of white wine.

After a few minutes of chatter, Vergennes looks at his pocket watch. "Drink up, gentlemen," he says. "It is time."

They return their wine glasses to the footman's tray and follow the Minister out of the room. He shows them to a broad, high-ceilinged corridor leading to the royal apartments. Lee and Deane gape at the ornate gilded console tables, *objets d'art* and glorious paintings lining the walls. They study the polished *'parquet de Versailles'* floors beneath their feet, which seem to go on for miles.

The men come to a pair of tall, carved and gilded doors. Vergennes taps lightly. A butler opens the door. He bows to Vergennes and ushers him and his guests into the bedchamber of the King.

Lee and Deane are awestruck by the splendor of the suite's décor. A four-poster bed draped in plush velvet and trimmed with golden fringe and tassels, rises in the center of the room, almost to the lofty ceiling. The bed is raised on a dais and surrounded by a silver-leaf railing, designed to keep supplicants at a distance from the person of the King. Ostrich plumes adorn the corners of the bed's pelmet. Wall panels upholstered in silk damask and lavishly trimmed with ornate gilded moldings, match silk curtains pooling onto the floor.

Their first glimpse of the King is not as expected. Louis XVI kneels in prayer on a kneeler at the far end of the room. A simple crucifix hangs on the wall above him. He wears a robe over his nightshirt, as though he has just risen from his bed. His dark, curly hair falls to his shoulders. He has plain silk slippers on his feet. The five men stand silently for what seems an eternity, until the King makes the sign of the cross, rises and turns to them. He glides smoothly across the floor toward them, as if by levitation. The King approaches Vergennes. He and Turgot bow.

"Your Majesty," Vergennes says. "We bring you the American Commissioners. Dr. Franklin, Monsieur Dean, Monsieur Lee."

The handsome young King looks each man up and down. Lee feels faint.

Franklin lowers his head. "Your Majesty," he whispers.

Louis assumes a noble stance. He speaks in English with a heavy accent. "I am pleased, Dr. Franklin, that my people have taken you into their hearts."

Franklin bows again, with his right hand over his heart.

"It is my hope that the alliance we have signed will be for the good of both our nations. You may assure your Congress of my friendship," the King says.

"Your Majesty can count on the gratitude of the Congress and our faithful adherence to the tenets of that treaty," Franklin replies smoothly.

The King smiles. *"Bon. Je suis bien content."* He looks at Vergennes and nods.

With that, the audience has come to an end.

Turgot, Vergennes and Franklin back slowly out of the King's presence. Lee and Deane follow, their swords swinging clumsily. The butler holds a door open, and the five men leave the room. The doors close solidly behind them with the 'click' of a slide bolt.

Silas Deane cannot contain his excitement. "How can one possibly describe such a magnificent suite?" he asks Vergennes.

"You have not seen the Queen's bedchamber," Vergennes advises. Turgot and Franklin walk a few steps behind the other men. Turgot taps Franklin's arm, urging him to hold back. They stop walking.

"Franklin… I have a word of caution for you. We fear you have a spy in your midst," Turgot whispers.

Franklin looks concerned. "Do you? I do?"

"The British have learned too soon of the contents of our treaty," Turgot confides. "They plan to recall their Ambassador."

"How do you know this?" Franklin asks.

"We have spies," Turgot admits.

"I suspect I am surrounded by spies, Your Excellency. My *Valet de Chambre* is likely among them. I will be on my guard."

"Monsieur Lee has told Vergennes that he suspects your grandson of indiscretion."

Franklin's face reddens. "Temple? That is impossible!"

"His father is a known informant, is he not?"

"His father is in New York. Monsieur Lee has a sick mind."

"Well, keep your eyes and ears open," Turgot warns. His expression lightens as they resume walking. "In the meantime, Dr. Franklin, you must partake of certain pleasures, one of the greatest of which is the company of my good friend, Catherine Helvetius. She wishes to meet you."

"And I her," Franklin says brightly.

Turgot pats Franklin on his hand. "Good. Her house is not far distant from you. She is at home on Tuesdays. I will escort you there to dinner three weeks hence. Two o'clock." They pick up their pace and catch up with the others.

Passy   1778

It is early afternoon as Franklin reclines in a copper bathtub behind a privacy screen in a corner of his bedroom. He hums a tune and scrubs a raised leg with a large, soapy sponge. A light knock at the door, and eighteen-year-old Temple enters, holding a packet of envelopes.

He speaks through the screen. "Grandfather?"

"Temple! Have you seen my valet? I need more hot water."

"No, sir, but I have come with the post."

"You may leave it on my desk in the library."

"There is a letter here from Mrs. Stevenson," Temple advises.

"Is there? Read it to me, son."

Temple walks around the screen and sets the stack of mail on a side table. He smooths his blonde hair, which is tousled from the breeze outside.

Franklin watches him open an envelope with interest. "I haven't heard a word from Margaret in nearly two years."

Temple reads from the letter as Franklin continues to bathe.

"*'Dear Ben, I enclose a letter from Bishop Shipley, whose servant came 'round asking how to post it to you, so I write to the American Mission in Paris.'*"

"Dear old Shipley. I began writing my memoirs while at his house. Go on, lad."

Temple continues reading: "*'Pray do tell my dear Temple to write to Mrs. Noon, who craves news of him.'*"

"Make a note of that, my boy." Franklin says.

"*'Send my love to Mr. and Mrs. Bache as well. Your old friend, Billy Strahan, goes to the spa at Bath much for his health of late.'*" Temple frowns, "That's not good news, is it?"

Franklin stretches to reach around and wash his back with the sponge. "No. Not good."

Temple glances at the next lines of the letter and looks at his grandfather. "The next bit is quite personal, Grandfather. You may want to read it privately."

"Blather... Read on, son."

Temple reads the next lines of the letter: "*'All your other friends are well, except for myself, as I am out of sorts and low in spirits. But I hope my Dearest Friend will raise them by writing to say that he has forgiven my failings and shall soon return.'* Shall I go on?"

Franklin conceals a smile. "Yes, yes. Go on..."

"*'Oh, my Dear Sir, I shall rejoice at that happy day. My prayers and best wishes attend you. Your sincere friend and servant, Peggy.'*"

Franklin splashes water onto his back. "*Peggy*? She would never allow me to call her that. Well, time heals even the deepest wounds."

Temple folds the letter and returns it to the envelope. "Why don't you invite Aunt Margaret to come visit us here in Passy? I would love to see her."

Franklin looks up at Temple. "Come over here? There would be complications. I shall think about it."

Auteuil, France   1778

It is just after two o'clock on a Tuesday in early April, when Franklin and Jacques Turgot step down from Turgot's carriage and follow a stone path to the Helvetius chateau. The path meanders through an unkempt apple orchard. The trees are in bloom, dropping fragrant white blossoms as the afternoon breeze stirs the branches.

Turgot is dressed formally for daytime, while Franklin wears a plain blue velvet suit. His head is bare. Franklin points out a row of stone monuments standing under the apple trees.

"Madame's dogs are buried there," Turgot explains.

Franklin lags behind to study the grave markers for a minute, then scurries to rejoin Turgot on the path. They walk into a messy farmyard, where chickens scratch about in tall grass. Two over-fed black spaniels appear to greet the men and sniff at their ankles, before loping off toward the gardens.

Franklin's eye follows the dogs to a stone bench under an arbor, where a handsome young priest sits reading a book. He wears a cassock and domed black hat with a wide brim tilted back on his head. The priest pets the dogs. "Who is the cleric?" Franklin inquires.

"An Abbe from the monastery a few miles away," Turgot explains. "The Abbot supplies Madame with a reliable supply of male company. One or two of them live here… to say Mass in the morning, of course."

Franklin and Turgot approach a run-down villa looming ahead. Franklin counts three turrets and ten chimneys, a few of which lean precariously and are propped up by iron rods. Dormers pierce the mossy slate roof. Chipped and peeling white stucco reveals a brick and stone structure beneath it. Green iron shutters hanging askew suggest the once lovely house has suffered years of neglect.

Franklin stops and looks up at the building with his hands on his hips. "It has seen better days, hasn't it?" he ventures.

Turgot nods and smiles. "Like Madame, her outer beauty fades. Inside, she will surprise you. There is nothing shabby to be found there. Come."

Franklin steps into something and wipes his shoe on the grass. "Merde!" he exclaims.

"Very likely," Turgot concurs.

They knock on the front door with a rusted iron knocker. A silver-haired butler opens the door and invites them inside.

Turgot is right. The generous foyer into which they are shown is surprising in its refinement. The oval room is papered above a wainscoting with a hand-painted bucolic scene. A round center table and cabinets set in niches in the walls are provincial pieces, painted white. The chandelier hanging over the table is in the Russian style.

"Madame est dans le salon, Monsieur Turgot," the butler says, leading the way.

Franklin discovers that the décor of the salon is also bright and pleasing. Furnishings are in the simpler style of the present reign and are upholstered in shades of beige brocade. Curtains of apricot-colored silk frame tall windows. Artifacts on tables are restrained and compete with arrangements of cut flowers from the garden. Paintings on the walls depict a serene country life.

A dozen or more guests of various ages mingle and chat in French. The men stand, while most of the ladies are seated on chairs and settees. Two footmen serve canapés from silver salvers and fill glasses with wine. Franklin glances about the room, looking for his hostess. Turgot gestures across the room, where Catherine Helvetius stands, speaking with a middle-aged gentleman in a tailcoat, who barely matches her in height. They study a silver-framed portrait of a man which hangs on the wall before them.

Madame Helvetius is still beautiful and shapely at fifty-nine, if unkempt. She wears her parchment-colored hair up, with a straw hat perched atop her head. Stray strands of hair fall across her face. A tattered net stole is wrapped about her shoulders. Her feet are bare.

Franklin and Turgot approach and overhear her conversation.

"I am not certain, Jean, that you have made a perfect likeness," she says in French to the gentleman in tails. "But you *have* captured the spirit of the man."

"I shall take that as a compliment," the gentleman replies.

Madame Helvetius sees Turgot out of the corner of her eye and whirls around. "Ah! And here we have Turgot, who arrives with our guest of honor!" she says in heavily accented English. She extends her hand to Franklin, who bends to kiss it.

"It is my pleasure," he says.

"Dr. Franklin! You must meet Jean-Honore Fragonard, the painter. He has just completed this portrait of my late husband, Claude." She points to the picture on the wall.

"It is also a pleasure to meet you, Monsieur Fragonard," Franklin bows his head and extends his hand. The two men shake hands.

"Alas, my dearest Claude left us too soon. He died five years ago," Madame explains.

"I am very sorry," Franklin offers.

She turns back to the painting. "Perhaps you find the picture ephemeral, but Claude was devoted to the arts. He founded the Masonic Lodge of which you are a member, Dr. Franklin. He retired from business at a young age."

"I have followed a similar path, but learned that politics was my calling," Franklin says.

"Claude was only fifty-five when he surrendered… but he lived life to the fullest!"

"Life is short, but art lives long!" Franklin replies, accepting a glass of wine from a passing footman.

Madame looks at Franklin with a glint of admiration in her eyes. "Well, said," she concurs.

Franklin sips his wine. "Many people, Madame, die at twenty-five, but are not buried until they are seventy-five."

Madame Helvetius takes hold of Franklin's arm. "Jacques! Why have you been keeping this wise man from us? You will sit next to me at dinner, Dr. Franklin!"

French doors in the dining room are open to the garden and frame a view of a riot of yellow forsythia in full bloom. Madame's party has grown to eighteen guests seated at a long table, which is draped in white linens. Although not yet dark outside, candles glow in a pair of crystal chandeliers and in silver candelabra on the table. Three footmen, in uniforms of gray satin, serve the diners. Fine wines flow freely, and conversation, largely in French, is lively.

Madame Helvetius is seated mid-table, with Franklin on her right and Monsieur Fragonard on her left. She has a small dog in her lap and one lying across her bare feet. "So, I say again, that hardship is not foreign to me."

"How is that so, Madame?" Fragonard inquires.

"My mother and father both died of the White Plague when I was a child. I was sent to a convent, where I worked like a slave for the nuns."

Franklin looks puzzled. "White Plague?" he says.

"In their lungs, you know," she clarifies.

"Ah. Consumption," Franklin sighs.

Madame Helvetius continues: "I was eventually rescued from the convent by my kindly aunt, Camille, who brought me to Paris to live with her. From her, I learned to embrace the unexpected."

"She gave you a marvelous gift," Franklin says, taking a bite of the *asperges* on his plate.

"Yes," Madame agrees. "In Paris, I met Claude, who married me and made me rich." She feeds tidbits from her dinner plate to the little dogs. "But what good is it now? I am an old lady with a receding hairline."

"Your beauty, Madame, is sublime," Franklin remarks. He taps his own forehead. "And receding hairlines are all the fashion these days!" he offers.

Madame Helvetius laughs heartily and throws her arm around Franklin's shoulder. She calls to Turgot, who is seated across from her and to her left. "Turgot! You have been a naughty boy in keeping this charming man to yourself so long!"

Passy

It nears ten o'clock as Franklin and Turgot stroll down a road winding along the bank of the Seine. Turgot's carriage and driver follow at a discreet distance behind them. Quite drunk, Franklin and Turgot harmonize to a French tune they had been singing earlier in the evening. They were among the stragglers gathered around the piano in the music room, warbling and drinking the last of Madame's sauterne, until someone noticed that she had gone to bed. They weave as they walk, occasionally catching each other's arm for support.

"I am smitten, Turgot. Deeply and madly in love, I tell you!" Franklin confesses.

"You must get in the queue. I am at the head of it!"

Franklin leans against a lamp post. "She is *fantastique!*"

"Well, don't raise your hopes too high," Turgot advises, leaning a shoulder on the opposite side of the post. A moment later, his tone changes. "Since you are in a gay mood, I must share a rumor with you."

Franklin looks around the lamp post. "Don't go ruining my fantasy."

"There has been talk of irregularities in Monsieur Deane's procurement procedures," Turgot confides.

"What have you heard?"

Turgot steps around the post to face Franklin. "It is said there are bribes being paid, large commissions changing hands. If the King were to learn of it…"

"You may tell His Majesty that Mr. Deane has been recalled by the Congress. John Adams is on his way over here to replace him."

"Do you know this… John Adams?"

"Well, I've slept with him," Franklin grins.

CHAPTER FORTY

Her Majesty

Passy 1780

John Adams walks briskly along an avenue of grand townhouses. It is late April and magnolia trees lining the street are in bloom, their gentle beauty in contrast to a grim expression on Adams's face. He is stocky, dressed in business attire, with a trim gray wig on his head. He looks at his pocket watch. It is well past noon, and he has missed his lunch, which adds to his dark mood.

Shortly, he comes to the sandstone walls and massive entry gates of Maison Valentois. Adams is fortunate: the gates are open. He enters the cobbled courtyard, crosses it and bangs sharply on the front door with its iron knocker.

After a minute, the butler opens the door a crack. *"Oui, monsieur?"*

"I am John Adams, with the American mission in Paris. I have come to see Dr. Franklin."

The butler looks apologetically at Adams. *"Je regret, Monsieur Adams, mais Dr. Franklin dort maintenant."*

Adams's face reddens. "He is sleeping? It is after one o'clock!" Adams pushes open the door and brushes past the butler. "Show me to his room. We have business to discuss."

The butler shrugs his shoulders and leads Adams down a long hallway to Franklin's suite of rooms. He taps lightly on the door. "Dr. Franklin? You have a visitor," he calls softly through the door. Adams shoves the butler aside. "Oh, get out of my way!" He raps loudly on the bedroom door, using his signet ring. "Franklin! It's John," he shouts. "Get up, you old reprobate. I'm coming in!"

The butler retreats down the hallway as Adams bursts into Franklin's bedroom. The curtains are drawn closed, and the room is dark. Franklin lies in his four-poster bed, covered with a fluffy quilt. He wears a sleeping mask, which he raises to get a look at the invader.

"Have you no shame, man?" Adams scolds. "Are you aware of the hour? It's the middle of the day!"

Franklin raises himself onto one elbow. "Must you intrude on my privacy? You are disturbing my rest."

Adams pushes the curtains aside and daylight floods the room. "Who's in that bed with you?" he asks.

Franklin reluctantly rises from the bed. "Only Miss Gout, robbing me of my sleep, as usual." He wears a night shirt, walks with a limp to a screen in the corner of the room, and steps behind it.

"You were to meet with me and Arthur Lee this morning. Had you forgotten?"

"No. I got in too late last night," Franklin replies from behind the screen. "Ow! Ow! Damn! Damn!"

Adams looks concerned. "What is it, man?" he asks, moving toward the screen.

"I'm trying to pee," Franklin cries. "The stones hurt like the devil this morning!"

"Your life of dissipation will be the death of you," Adams remarks. He steps back when he hears water trickle into the chamber pot. "The sooner we die, John, the longer we shall be immortal," Franklin retorts.

"I can see the audit Congress has requested of Silas Deane's books will not get done if *I* don't do it. Lee tells me the only appointment you are on time for is dinner."

Franklin steps out from behind the screen. "When in Rome, John..."

Adams huffs and sits on the arm of a French chair next to the window.

Franklin splashes water on his face from a porcelain bowl on a commode. "I have a meeting with Vergennes this evening. I will be expected to drink, then dine, then play whist, then drink some more, and perhaps to play chess, etcetera. Which is what I did last night, which is why I am still abed, which is how it is done in this country, John. These men are *not* farmers."

Adams folds his arms. "I am in bed by nine o'clock at night, without fail. Nothing keeps me from it."

"Which explains your foul mood," Franklin says, running a brush and comb through his hair. "You must be lonely."

"I am not lonely!" Adams says, sounding cross. "My days are full, and I am weary by nightfall. We live on opposite schedules you and I… I during the day, and you at night."

"As all things in nature, a perfect arrangement." Franklin goes to a wardrobe, opens it, and pulls out a shirt. "A lady friend is coming for lunch. Why don't you join us?" He points to a bell sitting on a bedside table. "Ring for my valet, would you, John? Go wait in the library for twenty minutes. Study your French."

Adams gets up from the chair and rings the bell furiously.

A little later, Franklin and Adams are seated at a table on a paved terrace set in a lush, walled garden. They are surrounded by a boxwood hedge grown as tall as a man can reach. They have coffee cups before them and are engaged in spirited conversation. Franklin's linen shirt is open at the neck, and he wears monogrammed slippers on his feet. He squints in the brilliant sunlight. The table is set with service for three.

Franklin drinks his coffee. "You may speak freely out here, John. Inside, the walls have ears."

"You have surrounded yourself with every luxury, haven't you?" Adams chides.

A pretty young maid, wearing a frilly white apron and matching cap on her head, crunches along the gravel walk to the terrace. She places bread, butter and a plate of pâté on the table. She smiles coquettishly at the two men, makes a polite curtsey, then turns and retreats to the kitchen.

Adams follows the girl with his eyes. "The soubrette comes with the package, or is she an added charge? I am loathe to think of the cost of all this," he moans.

"Then don't," Franklin advises. He offers the plate of pâté to Adams. "I wish to tell you of my progress with Vergennes with regard to funding General Washington's army."

"If you could favor me and Mr. Lee with a few hours during the daytime, when business *should* be conducted, we would be better informed."

Franklin points to the sun blazing overhead. "What do you call that, John?"

The butler appears and pours each man a glass of white wine and sets the bottle on the table.

"I have requested a loan of an additional twenty million livres from the King, which he is considering." Adams shakes his head as the butler leaves the terrace. "What about men? Arms? Ships? Our need is urgent, and I am not afraid to speak bluntly with the French."

Franklin slathers pâté on a piece of bread. "Arthur was of the same mind, and got nowhere," he argues. "I have *not* told him that Admiral de Grasse is assembling an armada in the West Indies which will sail north at the appropriate time. You must not tell him either. Arthur's poison pen will leak the news to the British, albeit inadvertently."

Adams furrows his brows. "Do you accuse him of disloyalty?"

"No... but *somebody* in our midst is a songbird," Franklin offers candidly as he takes a bite of bread and pâté.

Adams looks into Franklin's eyes over the rim of his goblet and sips his wine.

At that moment, they hear a woman singing on the other side of the hedge. She sings a Scottish country air, a favorite of Franklin's, in a clear soprano voice.

They both cock an ear. The sound of her voice moves closer to them.

Franklin raises a finger. "She is here," he whispers.

Madame Brillon enters the garden through an arbor of white roses. She wears a long white dress and carries a white parasol in her hand. She raises the hem of her dress to keep it from dragging on the ground. Her wide-brimmed hat is trimmed with flowers and satin ribbons.

Adams is astonished by the vision.

Madame Brillon finishes her song and smiles radiantly, making a small curtsey.

Franklin stands and applauds. Adams joins him. "Hélène! Meet my colleague and old friend, John Adams," Franklin beckons.

She sets her parasol on a garden bench and offers her hand to Adams, who bends to kiss it.

"*Enchanté,*" he says.

Madame Brillon turns to Franklin. "How charming! He speaks French!"

"You have just heard the extent of it. Come join us, *ma Cherie,*" Franklin says, pulling out her chair.

She takes her place at the table, arranging the full skirt of her gown around her. "Papa has shown me a copy of your Declaration of Independence. As I recall, Monsieur Adams, your signature appears there."

"That it does," he confirms.

"How very brave of you. Now you must win your little war with the English, or you will be hanged, *n'est-ce pas?*"

Adams swallows hard. "I was just sharing words to that effect with Dr. Franklin," he says meekly.

Franklin pours wine in Madame Brillon's goblet. "Mr. Adams fears that I move too slowly in my deliberations with the Palace."

"The Palace will move only at its pleasure, Monsieur Adams," she says, lifting her wine glass. "*Santé.*"

The butler enters the garden with the maid following behind. The maid carries a tray of food, which she sets on an iron console table. The butler serves Franklin and his guests cold cuts of meat and *salade verte.*

"Cher Papa moves, however, with reckless speed in scattering his favors among the ladies of Passy," Madame Brillon adds. Franklin feigns a hurt expression. "Do I stand accused of infidelity?"

Madame Brillon cuts a piece of *jambon.* "My friendship does not diminish, mind you, but I shall be sterner toward your faults." She turns to Adams. "You must understand, Monsieur Adams, that I am Papa's confessor."

"Are you? Then you must be a busy woman!"

Franklin takes a forkful of salad. "I suggest that just as your piano playing can be enjoyed by a multitude, chère Hélène, I may see many women in concert."

The butler fills Franklin's glass. Adams shakes his head and covers his glass with his hand when offered more wine.

"Papa's gaiety and gallantry cause all women to love him," Madame Brillon explains.

"So he, in turn, loves them all. As Guardian of his soul, I object to his sinful ways!"

Franklin sips his wine. "Rest assured that I will never find a woman I can love as tenderly as I love you."

The butler and maid both exit the garden.

Madame Brillon smiles and waves her fork at Adams. "Do you see? Once again, Papa's brilliant diplomacy conquers."

Adams pushes back from the table. "Well, I should be on my way. I have business to attend to and you have private matters to discuss."

"Oh, do stay put, John," Franklin insists. "You haven't eaten a thing and Cook's *tarte abricot* is not to be missed." He turns to Madame Brillon. "Hélène, let us drink to my old friend and new colleague." Franklin raises his glass. "To John Adams! A true patriot!"

Madame Brillon lifts her glass. *"A votre santé, Monsieur Adams!"* Adams returns the compliment with a cold smile, pulls his chair closer to the table, and takes a bite of *'poulet'*.

Gloversville, New York   1780

A cool morning mist hovers over a clearing in a dense wood, where a British military post of modest proportions has been established. A Union Jack is tacked up between two slender trees. Soldiers squat outside their tents, heating tea kettles over fires of sticks gathered in the undergrowth a few steps away. They are barefooted and have not yet shaved or combed their hair. Some will bathe later in a clear, icy creek that runs through the woods a few paces from the edge of the clearing.

The company was awakened earlier by hammering and sawing as makeshift gallows were constructed at the southern boundary of the camp, barely out of sight. Soldiers going about their business in the commons prefer not to look in that direction. They know what is coming.

Captain Charles Ruddy, a fair-haired man in his twenties, stands next to the steps leading to the rope and noose. He wears the uniform of the Colonial Militia and had been captured in a skirmish with

DEAR BEN

Redcoats near Albany a few weeks earlier. Ruddy's hands are tied behind his back, and he has a look of defiant terror on his face.

Two British officers watch as a soldier secures a blindfold over Ruddy's eyes. A chaplain, recruited for the sad occasion from a local church, looks on. He grips a Bible with both hands. One of the officers had arrived in camp just the day before. "What was Captain Ruddy's offence? Was it so heinous that we take the young man's life?" he inquires.

The other officer nods his head. "Aye. He led repeated attacks on our positions, as well as against civilians. Quite a nuisance, he was. Governor Franklin himself ordered Captain Ruddy's execution."

The newly arrived officer looks deeply troubled. "But, this is not the way of English law… to hang a man without trial."

"There is no law during time of war," the first officer argues.

The chaplain approaches Ruddy and opens his Bible. "I have the Good Book here, son. Kiss the Book and ye shall be received into heaven forthwith, your sins forgiven," he says gently.

"You kiss the Good Book, you bloody traitor," Ruddy screams. "And bend down and kiss my arse while you're at it!"

The chaplain steps back, clasping the Bible against his chest like a shield of armor.

PALACE OF VERSAILLES   1780

The Hall of Mirrors is aglow with candlelit chandeliers and girandoles resting on gilded console tables. They are reflected to infinity. A few courtiers look out the windows toward the gardens, where torchlight illuminates a *'jet d'eau'*, spewing water high into the air.

Card tables and games of chance have been set up in the nearby Salon de Paix, where an evening of gambling is underway. An oval portrait of Louis XV looks down from its position over a marble fireplace, as though surveying the scene. Heavenly paintings of nobility cavorting with cherubs decorate the arched ceiling panels overhead.

The room is crowded with courtiers seated at tables, playing cards, some of them high stakes games. Others hover over the baccarat tables, watching the action. Women drift about in hoop-skirted gowns, adorned with sparkling jewelry, and topped with towering coiffures.

A string quartet plays music by Salieri, the Court composer of the Emperor of Austria, the Queen's brother. Footmen wander the room with salvers of drinks and hors d'oeuvres.

Queen Marie Antoinette was at the tables early, a few minutes before ten o'clock. She arrived with little fanfare to join her friend, the Duchesse de la Rochefoucauld, for an evening of cards and conversation. The twenty-three-year-old Queen wears a sky-blue silk gown, trimmed with lace and velvet ribbons. The aigrette on her head sprouts abundant plumage. A diamond the size of a hen's egg hanging at her cleavage, enhances the Queen's remarkably beautiful face.

The Duchesse is nearly as dazzling in a gray satin gown, with a wide ruby and diamond choker on her neck. Her girlish voice belies her thirty-five years.

The banker at their table pushes a stack of gold coins toward the Queen, adding to a sizeable stash already before her. "Ah, Duchesse, I am sad to take so much from you," the Queen remarks in French. "But last night you were the big winner."

"Think nothing of it, Your Majesty," the Duchesse replies sweetly. "Tonight, you have the cards."

"Such is life," says the Queen. "Just when we least expect it, we are knocked from our perch!"

"Yes, that is so," the Duchesse, smiles. "We must always keep one eye on where the cat is!"

They both laugh and continue their game. The Queen sees Franklin strolling their way. He wears his blue velvet suit, black low-heeled pumps, and a fur cap on his head.

The Queen calls out to him in English. "Dr. Franklin! You have been hiding from me! Come join us."

Franklin approaches the table, doffs his cap, and bows from the waist. "Your Majesty."

"Have you met the Duchesse de la Rochefoucauld?" The Queen turns to her companion. "This is the famous Dr. Franklin."

The Duchesse smiles and holds out a jewel-laden hand.

"A pleasure, Your Grace," Franklin says, kissing her hand.

"You might consider," the Queen says to the Duchesse, "by Dr. Franklin's attire, that he left his mule and plow in my courtyard… But we have grown quite fond of the dear man!"

Franklin bows to the Queen again. "I am honored to hear that."

"He and my husband conspire to separate the English King from his colonies in America," the Queen explains to the Duchesse.

"His Majesty, ever the most benevolent of princes, has come to the aid of our oppressed people, Your Grace," Franklin adds.

"Well put, Dr. Franklin." The Queen looks about the room. "Your friend, our Foreign Minister, is looking for you. He is here somewhere…"

"I am loathe to part company with such beauty, but I shall excuse myself to seek him out. Ma'am, Your Grace…" Franklin bows to the Queen as he backs away from the table. Their banker steps forward and deals the Queen and the Duchesse another hand of cards.

Franklin sees Vergennes coming from the Hall of Mirrors. He is dressed in evening wear and carries a glass of champagne.

"There you are Franklin! You need a drink." He points to Franklin's fur cap. "And perhaps some water for your *chapeau*." Vergennes takes a glass of wine from a footman passing by and hands it to Franklin.

"Ah, *merci*," Franklin says. "His Majesty will be pleased," he offers. "*Her* Majesty is winning at cards tonight."

Vergennes' expression sours. "His Majesty is *not* pleased," he says.

"Oh? Why not, may I inquire?"

Vergennes looks across the Salon de Paix. "Let us go where we can talk privately." He leads Franklin through the crowd of courtiers and out of the room, snatching a bottle of champagne from a footman as they go.

They walk down a broad corridor to a small salon facing the gardens. They are alone in the room. Vergennes motions for Franklin to sit in a gilded chair. He sets the champagne bottle on a bronze side table.

"His Majesty's displeasure with your envoy, Monsieur Adams, has reached boiling point," Vergennes says, candidly.

"Oh?" Franklin takes a sip of champagne.

"Adams writes a barrage of letters accusing His Majesty of being parsimonious in our efforts on your behalf. The King is furious."

"I was not aware, Your Grace, of any such letters."

"How can that be?" Vergennes asks.

"I live on terms of civility with Adams, not intimacy," Franklin clarifies.

Vergennes paces the floor. "His Majesty does not require Monsieur Adams to direct his attention to the interests of the United States."

Franklin looks chastised. "I offer my deepest apologies to you, and to His Majesty," he says.

Vergennes picks up the bottle from the table and refills Franklin's glass. "Matters have come to a delicate pass. We do not wish to entertain Monsieur Adams's solicitations any longer."

"I will speak with Adams, and I shall inform the Congress of his impudent behavior."

Vergennes fills his own glass and sits in a chair opposite Franklin. "Good. The sooner you do so, the better."

Franklin's expression brightens. "Shall I also inform the Congress that we have secured the loan I requested?"

"You ask for twenty-five, but the treasury can only manage six million at this time," Vergennes replies in a stern voice.

"I'll take it," Franklin says.

CHAPTER FORTY-ONE

The Thespian

Passy   1780

Franklin is seated at his desk in the study at Maison Valentois, leafing through a stack of papers. The doors are open, affording him a view of the foyer. He sees Temple walk quickly past.

Franklin sets down his teacup. "Temple?" he calls out.

Temple stops near the front door. "Yes, Grandfather?"

"Where are you rushing off to?"

"Rehearsal," he replies, without looking back.

Franklin rises from his chair and stands behind his desk. "Rehearsal? Come here, lad."

Temple sighs and walks back to the doorway to the study.

"What sort of rehearsal? Come in here, son."

Temple enters the study. "It's a play, with the Caillots, our neighbors down the way. I have a part... just for fun." He displays a rolled-up script he has pressed under his arm.

Franklin looks surprised. "A play? In French? In a theatre?"

"A new English play, by a Mr. Sheridan. The Caillots have fitted out a small theatre in their barn. Marcel is an actor, you know. You must come see it!"

"Indeed I must," Franklin marvels.

Temple turns and hurries across the foyer. "*À bientôt,*" he calls over his shoulder and dashes out the door. He brushes past the butler, who is standing on the steps outside, speaking with a lady visitor.

"Is Dr. Franklin expecting you, Mrs. Asgill?" the butler inquires.

The woman is dressed in English garments of fine quality. She is in her mid-forties and her fair hair is carefully coiffed, worn up and off her neck. She wears a light woolen cloak draped over her shoulders.

She appears agitated. "No, sir, he is not, but I need to speak with him most urgently," she says.

After a pause, the butler says, "*Attendez-vous ici pour un moment, s'il vous plaît.* Wait here." He enters the house, leaving Mrs. Asgill on the steps, looking anxious.

The butler taps on the study door and approaches Franklin. "There is a woman outside who says she has come from London on urgent business. She wishes to speak with you."

Franklin looks up from his papers. "London? She is likely an assassin. Show her in, then."

Moments later, the butler crosses the foyer with Mrs. Asgill following close behind. She clutches her handbag tightly against her breast.

Franklin stands as she is shown into the study. He offers his hand, and they shake hands.

Mrs. Asgill sighs before she speaks. "I am so grateful to you for seeing me, Dr. Franklin!" she says.

"And you are…?"

"Evelyn Asgill. Mrs. Gilbert Asgill. I have come about my son, Charles."

"I regret, madam, that I have no commissions in our army to offer your son at this time." Mrs. Asgill reaches into her handbag. Franklin winces, then looks relieved when she produces an envelope. "Charles is a captain in the British army. I have a letter here from Lord Shelburne which explains our dilemma. I believe His Lordship to be a friend of yours."

She hands the letter to Franklin. "Yes, a very good friend." He gestures to the chair opposite him. "Please sit down, Mrs. Asgill." Franklin opens and reads the letter.

She leans forward. "He asks, and it is my prayer, that you will intercede on my son's behalf with General Washington."

Franklin points to the letter. "It appears that Washington holds your son hostage."

Her eyes well up with tears. "Yes. He threatens to hang Charles as revenge for the hanging of an American boy… a Captain Ruddy."

"Such is war, Mrs. Asgill," Franklin says, shaking his head. "Shelburne says Ruddy was condemned by Loyalists in New York."

She takes a kerchief from her handbag and dabs at her eyes. "The British military then tried and acquitted the soldiers who did the black deed. Now General Washington demands that the man who ordered Ruddy's hanging be handed over to him, or my Charlie will be the next to hang."

Franklin looks at her sympathetically. "I wish I could help you, but your contest is with the British authorities. Lord Shelburne should speak with the military in New York… and quickly. I will write a reply to that effect." He takes a piece of writing paper from a desk drawer.

Mrs. Asgill looks disappointed. "If that is the best we can do… Charles is my only child," she says, replacing the kerchief in her handbag.

"I know it is heartbreaking to lose a son. Believe me, I know," Franklin shares as he writes the note to Shelburne.

"Lord Shelburne thought it indelicate to say so, but we know who the man was who ordered Captain Ruddy's hanging."

Franklin looks up. "You do?"

"It was your son, Governor William Franklin."

Franklin pales. "Was it?" he says after a long pause. "Then I shall advise Shelburne in no uncertain terms to deliver the murderer." He picks up his pen and writes.

PASSY   1780

One evening about three weeks later, a string of carriages lines the drive of a villa on the outskirts of Passy. A wooden barn stands at the end of the drive behind a white stucco house. Laughter and applause can be heard coming from inside the barn. A hand-painted sign over the sliding door of the barn reads, '*THEATRE CAILLOT*'. A sign next to the door says: '*Ce soir: "The School for Scandal" - une Comedie en Anglais, par Sheridan*'.

Inside, the barn has been converted to a theatre, with a proscenium stage at one end and a pair of rusted iron chandeliers hanging overhead. An audience of friends and neighbors are seated on wooden benches and in garden chairs facing the stage. Franklin is seated in the front row, with Catherine Helvetius next to him. John Adams sits a few seats away and one row behind. Jacques Turgot has reluctantly taken a seat next to Adams, who has recently returned from a jaunt to the Dutch capital, having been briefly banished by the French. A performance is underway. Temple is on stage, wearing a suit with wide satin lapels and a starched shirt with a stiff stand-up collar. He has sideburns and a mustache glued to his face and sports a monocle. Blanchette Caillot stands near him. She is shapely and pretty, and her rosy complexion is enhanced by a generous application of rouge. She wears a hoop-skirted dress and a wig of long blonde curls on her head. She uses a fan she carries to coquettish effect as she speaks her lines.

BLANCHETTE

"We shall have the whole affair in the newspapers with the names of the parties involved before I have dropped the story at a dozen country houses!"

The audience laughs. Marcel Caillot, her husband, wears a gray wig and makeup to appear much older than his thirty-six years. He speaks his line as an 'aside'.

MARCEL

"You have heard, I suppose, of Lady Teazel and Mr. Surface… and Sir Peter's discovery…"

Temple delivers his lines with an affected British accent.

TEMPLE

"Of the <u>strangest</u> piece of business to be sure!"

MARCEL

"Now, I don't pity Sir Peter at all. He was so extravagant!"

In the audience, Catherine Helvetius smiles and places her hand on Franklin's knee. He, in turn, places his hand on hers, then slides it up to his thigh. Adams sees the move and raises an eyebrow.

BLANCHETTE

"Why, 'twas with Charles that Lady Teazle was detected!"

TEMPLE

"No such thing. Mr. Surface is the gallant!"

Franklin leans closer and whispers to Catherine. "That's my boy up there. Isn't he good?"

Catherine kisses her forefinger and places it on Franklin's cheek.

TEMPLE

"I tell you, I have it from one..."
MARCEL
"Who had it from one who had it..."
BLANCHETTE
"From one immediately... but here comes Lady Sneerwell. Perhaps she knows the whole affair!"

Blanchette fans herself madly, pointing to the side curtains. A figure behind the curtain pokes and fumbles at the fabric, as if unable to find her way onto the stage. The audience chuckles.

Franklin leans close to Catherine again. "Friday next, I plan to propose marriage to you," he whispers.

She is taken aback for a moment, then whispers to Franklin: "Friday next I shall hide in the country for an extended stay." She pats his hand and extricates hers from his. The figure behind the curtain springs onto the stage. It is Jacques de Chaumont, costumed as Lady Sneerwell. He wears a fussy gown, exaggerated make-up, and a red wig piled high with curls. He carriers a lorgnette, which is in constant motion.

The audience roars with laughter. De Chaumont acknowledges the welcome with a deep curtsey, from which he has difficulty in rising. He composes himself and tiptoes to center stage.
LADY SNEERWELL
"So, my dear Mrs. Candour, there's the sad affair of our friend, Teazle."
BLANCHETTE
"Aye, my dear friend, who could have thought it?"

De Chaumont steps close to the footlights, delivering his line directly to the audience.
LADY SNEERWELL
"Well, there is no trusting appearances, tho' indeed she was always too lively for me!"

The audience laughs and cheers. Franklin looks at Catherine, pondering her unexpected reply.

John Adams sits motionless and stone-faced next to Turgot, who applauds the comedy.

New York   August 1781

William Franklin maneuvers his way hurriedly in the darkness across a wharf at New York Harbor. The wharf is piled high with crates and barrels of goods bound for England. William carries a valise and looks over his shoulder occasionally as he goes, as though he might be followed. His trunk and travel bags are stacked on a cart pushed along by an elderly porter following just behind him. William urges the aging fellow to make haste.

They approach a ship being made ready to sail. Moonlight reveals the ship's name on its stern: *'Amity, Portsmouth.'* Stevedores load the last of the ship's cargo into its hold. The First Mate, a man wearing a white uniform, waits on the dock next to the ship's gangplank.

He spots William approaching and calls out to him, "There you are, Governor! I was about to give up on ye!"

William, short of breath, calls ahead to the First Mate, "I do apologize. So many last things to attend to!"

He reaches the ship, and he and the Officer shake hands. "We sail with the tide shortly," the First Mate says. "Captain will have you on English shores and out of harm's way in no time. Hurry aboard, then."

William follows the First Mate aboard the ship. He looks over his shoulder anxiously as he treads up the gangplank.

Yorktown, Virginia   October 1781

British General Charles Cornwallis pulls his greatcoat closed against the early morning chill. He stands on the parapet of a military fortress captured earlier by his troops. A tattered Union Jack flies above his head, flapping in the wind. The battle he observes from his vantagepoint rages on, as it has day and night for the past two weeks. He is half deaf from the sound of it: a ceaseless bombardment of canon and artillery fire by seventeen thousand combined American and French troops, versus his nine thousand British soldiers.

He had prepared for General Washington's onslaught by ordering the construction of ten redoubts, fortifications dug into the ground, from which his men could pick off the invaders. Cornwallis had goaded Washington to attack, thinking his defenses strong enough to decimate the Colonial Army as they charged across the field toward his earthworks.

But what a man imagines and what transpires are sometimes two different things.

Cornwallis hadn't planned on five thousand heavily armed French troops landing to the north of him and joining Washington, or on Lafayette's legions to the south, who blocked his retreat by land, or on the twenty-nine ships of Admiral de Grasse's fleet which sailed from the West Indies to plug the entrance to Chesapeake Bay, preventing a retreat by sea. Furthermore, he hadn't foreseen the failure of his compatriot, General Clinton, to send British troops south from New York to come to his aid, as was promised.

Shot and shells blaze over his head, pounding the British defensive positions. A few soldiers crouched near him in the battlements of the fortress return what fire they dare. Cornwallis looks through his field glasses again and sees the stomach-churning sight of hundreds of young men of both armies lying still on the battlefield. A few of the wounded attempt to crawl out from the line of fire.

He hears the sound of boots on the stone stairway up to the parapet. His adjutant, Townsend, appears at the top of the steps.

Short of breath, the adjutant salutes him. "General, sir!"

"Keep your head down, Townsend! Have you taken the measure of our supplies? What can you report?"

"Very low, sir… Another day or two, at best. And I have bad news: redoubt no. 9 has been taken in an attack of the enemy using only their bayonets!"

Cornwallis pales and is silent for a moment. "Dear God. Send a drummer out, lad. I won't lead my boys to a slaughterhouse."

Townsend salutes the General, turns and hurries back down the stairs.

Cornwallis raises his field glasses again and sees a lone drummer emerge from the fortress and march toward the field of battle. He soon realizes the drummer cannot be heard over the roar of canon fire. He commands a soldier near him to lower the tattered Union Jack atop the parapet and raise a white flag in its place. The guns go silent.

Early the next morning, a lone drummer on foot precedes Cornwallis, who is on horseback, leading a column of bedraggled

British soldiers who march behind him. They pass through a gauntlet of American troops on one side and French soldiers on the other. All is quiet, but for the sad beating of the drum and occasional catcalls from the French soldiers. The silence seems deafening after days of constant bombardment. Suddenly, the long and bitterly fought war has come to an end.

Windsor, England   November 1781

King George III and John Penn are seated on a wooden bench in a pine-paneled Finnish bath in the King's private apartments at Windsor Castle. A narrow window high on a wall admits daylight into the hot, steamy room. The two men are naked, but for towels spread across their laps. Their skin has taken on a rosy hue and they perspire profusely.

"I am finished, I tell you, Penn, finished," the King says in a strident tone. "I shall order the 'stuffed shirts' to Paris to commence negotiations. I have surrendered two armies… That is quite enough."

As the King speaks, Penn ogles Ingrid, a buxom young Swedish woman, who is naked from the waist up. She stands on the limestone floor of the sauna, beating the King's back with a cedar bough.

"What of all the Negro slaves who ran from their masters to join your army? Will they be welcomed here?" Penn inquires.

Ingrid stops her assault on the King and pours a ladle of water over river rocks piled atop an iron stove. The hot rocks sizzle and send up a cloud of steam. She moves from the King to Penn and goes to work on him with the cedar branches. Penn bends down to better take the blows.

"Most of them are dead the poor beggars, mowed down by Washington's artillery," the King replies. "Cornwallis sent them out on the front lines, you see."

"My family has lost everything out there," Penn says, sounding distressed.

The King glares at him. "*You?* What about *me?*" He turns to the Swedish woman. "Beat him, Ingrid. Beat him hard, like the Finns do!"

CHAPTER FORTY-TWO

Surrender

Passy

Bright moonlight washes over the manicured garden outside Blanchette Caillot's bedroom. A pair of French doors are open, affording a view into the room, where a dozen candles flicker. An oil lamp burns on table next to the bed, which is unmade. Most of the bedcovers have fallen to the floor. Half-filled glasses of wine sit on the night tables.

Blanchette and Temple lie on her bed, both naked, making love. Temple raises himself onto one elbow and admires her beauty. He caresses her tenderly, running a fingertip through a forelock of her hair, over her breasts and down to her stomach.

Marcel Caillot stands concealed behind a Coromandel screen in the corner of the room. He watches the lovers and their lovemaking with keen interest.

Passy   March 1782

Two horse-drawn landau carriages ride through the gates and clatter into the stone courtyard of the Maison Valentois. When they come to a stop, the coachmen jump down from their boxes and open the doors for four British diplomats, who step out and survey their surroundings. They appear to be impressed by the grandeur of Franklin's residence. The diplomats wear velvet frockcoats, black leather shoes with fancy buckles on the toes, and tricorn hats atop trim gray wigs. Leather portfolios are tucked under their arms. Two male secretaries follow the diplomats out of the carriages. They carry satchels filled with papers and wear somber expressions on their faces, in keeping with their dark suits.

Franklin's butler waits at the open front door of the mansion to greet the visitors. He has been expecting them.

A few minutes later, Franklin and the diplomats are seated around a mahogany table in the dining room, with Franklin at its head. All have stacks of papers laid out before them. After some patter about a rough crossing of the Channel, the British secretaries settle into their seats at the end of the long table opposite Temple and Bancroft, who are to record the proceedings. A maid pours tea and serves biscuits to Franklin's company, before withdrawing.

The British delegation is led by Richard Oswald, a portly, balding gentleman of seventy years. He is seated on Franklin's right. He has been appointed emissary by Franklin's old friend, Lord Shelburne, the Colonial Secretary. Perhaps a good omen, Franklin thinks.

Oswald strikes a conciliatory tone in his opening remarks: "Lord Shelburne sends his very warmest regards to you, Dr. Franklin. He is pleased the conflict between our two countries has ended and looks forward to resuming your friendship."

Franklin returns Oswald's smile. "As do I. Please extend my fondest greetings to His Lordship."

Oswald gestures down the table. "We are surprised, Dr. Franklin, to see that you have only your secretaries with you today."

"I am alone for the time being. Mr. Lee has sailed home and Mr. Adams is in The Hague on business. I speak, however, with the authority of the Congress, and in concert with the French Foreign Secretary."

Oswald maintains a pleasant tone of voice. "Would it not be more efficient, Dr. Franklin, if we were to conclude our business *without* the French, with whom I will speak separately?"

Franklin speaks through a thin smile. "Our talks today, Mr. Osborne, are only preliminary and I will consult with our French allies throughout these negotiations."

Osborne stiffens. "Must you defer to Vergennes at every turn, when certain matters, such as the disposition of Gibraltar, pertain only to the French King and King George, and do not concern you?"

Franklin's smile vanishes. "Let us be clear. I *confer* with the French ministers, Mr. Oswald. I do not *defer* to them." Franklin reaches for a bell on the table. Care for more tea?"

Oswald shakes his head, 'no'.

Franklin sets the bell aside and points to a document spread in front of him. "Now, let us consider the matter of reparations for the damage done to our towns by the British troops during the past six years. I have an estimate here of the cost of that devastation."

A middle-aged diplomat seated across from Osborne raises his finger. "What of reparation for Loyalist property destroyed by your militias?"

"There will be none," Franklin replies firmly. "On the other hand, if Britain were to cede Canada to the United States, I believe the ledger would be nicely balanced," he offers pleasantly.

The British diplomats look at each other aghast.

Osborn is wide-eyed. "You can't be serious!"

"You may wish to consider the idea overnight," Franklin suggests. "So, let us move on to other matters: national boundaries, navigation rights, fishing rights, and so on."

Osborne grips the arms of his chair firmly, as if expecting the room to move.

Franklin's bedroom   1790

Bobby is on his knees at the hearth, sweeping up ashes that have blown in from the fireplace.

Franklin sets his empty teacup on the bedside table. "I was not *entirely* truthful with either the French or the British, but such is the way of diplomacy."

Bobby looks over his shoulder. "I heard you say somethin' like that before."

"I was much laid up with gout those days; but did what work I could. Adams returned to Paris and John Jay came to help with negotiations, and he did so brilliantly. A treaty with the English King was concluded without the consent of the French. Vergennes was incensed. I wrote to him, attempting to calm the waters."

MICHAEL KOSKI

Palace of Versailles — December 1782

The Comte de Vergennes is seated at the grand marquetry and ormolu desk in his office. He holds a demitasse cup in his left hand and looks over a letter he holds in his right. King Louis XVI slumps in an armchair nearby. The collar of his shirt is open, and his cravat lies on the side table next to him. His legs are crossed and a woven silk slipper dangles from his toes. He holds a glass of wine in his hand, looks out the French doors, watching gardeners sweep a dusting of snow from the walkways under a hazy afternoon sun, then turns to Vergennes. "So, what does Dr. Franklin have to say for himself?" he inquires in French.

"I have a translation of his letter in English, Your Majesty. Shall I read it so?"

"Oui. S'il te plaît." The King sips his wine.

Vergennes reads in English from the letter: "*In not consulting you before the agreement was signed, we have been guilty of neglecting a point of etiquette. But, as this was not from want of respect for our King, whom we all love and honor, we hope that it will be excused...*"

Vergennes looks up from the letter and sees a slight smile on the King's face.

"*'And that the great work, which has hitherto been so happily conducted, is so nearly brought to perfection, and is so glorious to his reign, will not be ruined by a single indiscretion of ours.*"

The King shakes his head. "The old conjurer charms the birds to fall from the trees. What comes next?"

Vergennes points to a paragraph in the letter. "He begs for additional funds."

"But of course, he does!" The King drinks the last of his wine and sets the glass down on the table. He gathers up his cravat and his slipper, which has fallen to the floor. "Tell him '*non*!" He stands and leaves the room.

Passy — Summer 1783

Franklin is alone in the morning room adjacent to the kitchens of Maison Valentois, enjoying a Parisian newspaper and a late breakfast of boiled eggs, sugar buns and tea. The dressing robe he wears is open to the waist, taking advantage of the warm morning. Franklin hears the cook and her *sous-chefs* clanging pots together in the kitchen next door, preparing for the diplomatic luncheon he will host in a few hours' time.

The butler appears in the doorway, carrying a small silver tray bearing a letter envelope.

Franklin looks up. "What is it, Jean?"

"*Pardonnez-moi*, Dr. Franklin. I have an '*express*' for you." He extends the tray to Franklin, who takes the letter from it and looks at the return address.

"From my old friend, Strahan, in London," Franklin observes.

The butler backs out of the room.

Franklin adjusts his spectacles and opens the envelope. As he reads, the color drains from his face. "No, no, no, no…" he moans. "Too soon," he whispers to the empty room. "Much too soon, Margaret." He buries his face in his hands.

A moment later, he hears the clatter of horses and a chaise riding into the courtyard outside. He pulls his robe closed and goes to investigate the disturbance.

Franklin emerges from the front door of the house to greet the unexpected visitor. A door of the carriage flies open and Benny, now a tall, slender thirteen-year-old, jumps out. He runs to his grandfather and hugs him around his waist.

Franklin holds Benny tightly against himself. Tears roll down Franklin's cheeks. "You are one day early, young man," he says, his voice choking. "We expected you on the morrow."

"We left the post road inns at daybreak to save time. We owe the coachmen a few extra gold sovereigns for their trouble, Grandpapa."

"We?" Franklin teases. He places his hands on Benny's shoulders and holds him at arm's length. "My God, look how you've grown!" Franklin wipes away his tears with a kerchief from his pocket.

Benny looks over Franklin's shoulder to see Temple and Blanchette Caillot step out of the house. Blanchette is obviously pregnant.

Temple hurries across the courtyard to embrace his cousin. "Grandfather, we sent the Swiss a little boy and they have exchanged him for this strange man!"

"There seem to have been some changes made around here, as well," Benny laughs, nodding toward Blanchette, who waits on the steps.

Temple grins and slaps Benny on his back. "Indeed, there have been. And I am going to teach you the latest dances and show you how to charm the ladies of this village! We will do many *'grown up'* things together!"

Passy   Spring 1784

A long iron table on the garden terrace has been laid with cheerful faience dishes and pewter goblets for a luncheon party. Small obelisks of ivy adorn the center of the table. It is a warm, sunny day, the hedges surrounding the garden have shed their winter gloom and are lush with bright green leaves.

Franklin is seated at the center of the table, with John Adams, in a rare, jovial mood, seated at the head of the table. Benny is seated opposite Adams. Sophie Brillon is on Benny's right, then Polly Hewson's two children, a thirteen-year-old boy and a girl of eleven years. Madame Helvetius sits next to Franklin, Marcel Caillot next to her. He passes a basket of bread to his wife, Blanchette, who holds an infant wrapped in a blanket in one arm. Polly, who is sitting next to Blanchette, is attentive to the baby, as is Temple, who is seated next to Polly. Jacques de Chaumont is also at the table. All are enjoying plates of *salade au poulet*.

Two footmen attending the table are dressed comfortably in a celebration of the warm day and the happy occasion. Wine is poured freely, and conversation is animated, as Franklin tells stories and Adams contradicts him good-naturedly. Madame's two little dogs run about under the table, pestering guests for scraps of food.

Franklin's bedroom   1790

Bobby rests the broom and dustpan in a corner near the fireplace and wipes his hands with a rag. "I don't mean no disrespect, Dr. Ben, but if your work was so 'glorious to his reign', like in that letter, why is that King in jail now?"

"A sensible question," Franklin concedes. "We had all but emptied the Royal Treasury and the King was unable to pay his soldiers. He was abandoned. Anything left in that bottle?"

Bobby takes the bottle of Madeira from the dresser top and pours a little into Franklin's teacup.

"We knew not what was coming," Franklin says, lifting the cup to his lips. "So, we briefly enjoyed a time of peace. Jefferson agreed to come to Paris at last, and relieve me of my duties, and I was content to enjoy my retirement surrounded by family and friends. Benny returned from exile in Switzerland, and Polly came from London to visit, as her husband, Dr. Hewson, had died, sadly, not long after Margaret's passing."

Franklin sips his wine and sets the cup down on the table. "The actress, Blanchette Caillot, joined our little entourage, as she had borne Temple a son. Monsieur Caillot appeared not to mind… perhaps he preferred his own sex. It was, Bobby, the time of my most perfect happiness."

Passy   Summer 1784

Madame Brillon's boudoir is aglow with flickering candles massed on her dresser and on a walnut bureau. The candles have burned low, the hour is late. French doors are open to the garden outside, where crickets chirp and the air is heavy with the scent of honeysuckle and night blooming jasmine.

Madame reclines in her tub, bathing. Her ebony hair is pinned up and held in place by a satin ribbon. She washes the nape of her neck with a large sea sponge.

Franklin and Thomas Jefferson are seated on stools on either side of a wide plank stretched across the tub. They play a game of chess by candlelight. Three wine glasses sit on the plank. Franklin picks up his glass and sips as he contemplates his next move.

Jefferson sounds frustrated. "Hurry up, Ben. It's going to be daylight before we know it." He refills his glass from a wine bottle resting on the floor next to him.

Franklin doesn't look up. "Don't rush me. Have you ever thought, Thomas, about how many millions of candles would be saved if we all arose one hour earlier in the summertime?"

"I live on a farm. We're up early enough," Jefferson retorts. "Where did you say Monsieur Brillon was tonight? I should like to have met your husband."

Madame rinses out her sponge. "He is in the country with his lady friend, at Marouatte Castle."

Franklin moves a rook.

Madame Brillon reaches for her wine glass, exposing a snow-white breast, which she covers demurely with soap suds. "You have made a stupid move, Papa."

"You were supposed to give me a signal with your toe," Franklin replies. He breaks wind loudly.

"Papa, you blow the candles out!" Madame scolds.

Jefferson looks at Franklin wide-eyed. "Jesus, Ben, did you fart?"

Franklin nods. "You will be happy to learn, Thomas, I have written a paper on flatulence which I have sent to the Academy in Brussels."

"You jest."

"I suggested that since we are known to produce a prodigious quantity of gas, and are repressed from releasing it, a study of the problem would be of great use to mankind."

Jefferson studies the game board. "Fascinating."

"Just as eating a few sprigs of asparagus transforms the odor of our pee-pee, an addition to our roasts and sauces could be found to do the trick."

Jefferson shakes his head. "I rode out here to hear a treatise on farting?"

Madame Brillon sinks down to her chin in the bath water. "To think, Monsieur Jefferson, the fate of your infant nation has rested in this man's hands!"

Franklin conceals a grin behind his wine glass. "Imagine how conversation will flow much more freely at the dinner table if we are not preoccupied with the task of holding in a hefty fart!"

Madame covers her bosoms with soap suds. "Do you read Montaigne, Monsieur Jefferson? He is much better for your mind than Papa's silly treatise."

"I do, but I struggle with the French," Jefferson admits, averting his gaze from a parting of Madame's soap bubbles.

"You have a way with words. I have read your 'Declaration of Independence'. It is a masterwork."

A young maid quietly enters the room. She carries a large kettle and pours steaming water into the foot of the bathtub. She curtsies and retreats.

Jefferson's eyes follow the maid's shapely figure as she leaves the room. "Ben had a hand in the writing, you know."

"You truly believe all men are equals?" Madame Brillon inquires, stirring her bath water with her foot. "The ploughman? The Count?"

"In the eyes of the Creator, yes," Jefferson replies.

"A revolutionary idea… a notion that might send one to the Bastille," she warns." Now," Madame Brillon continues, "You gentlemen must leave me. Go walk in the garden. I will join you in the library for a brandy." She rings a bell on a table next to the tub.

"Why don't I climb in with you?" Franklin suggests cheerily. "Let's make my 'little boy' fat and jolly!"

"You must fatten your 'little boy' at somebody else's table!" Madame Brillon snaps. She waves her sponge in Jefferson's direction. "You see? Papa is too greedy for a married woman."

The maid reappears, holding a large, white Turkish towel.

Franklin stands, with his wine glass in hand. "We have been banished, Thomas, as Venus rises from the sea! Let us repair to the kitchen, where Cook has hidden the crème puffs. Bring the bottle."

The maid holds up the towel to conceal Madame Brillon from the men as she rises from the tub.

Minutes later, Franklin and Jefferson stroll through the fragrant garden. They both carry a glass of wine and listen to Madame Brillon singing as she dries herself.

They catch up on some business matters.

Franklin looks at Jefferson earnestly. "It's imperative we show our gratitude to Louis now if we are to be trusted in Europe. Adams doesn't see that."

"He is insanely jealous of you. I want to read you something he wrote." Jefferson sits on a garden bench and takes a paper from his coat pocket. He holds it up to the light of a garden torch. "Listen to this: *'The history of our Revolution will be one continued lie from one end to the other. It will be said that Dr. Franklin's electrical rod smote the Earth and out sprung General Washington, etc., etc.'* He goes on…"

Franklin sits next to Jefferson on the bench. "'Tis an ugly thing to be envious of another man's rod, is it not? Well, John must be relieved you have come to replace me on the Commission."

"Nobody can replace you, Ben. I am merely your successor."

Franklin's eyes mist over.

Jefferson folds the paper and returns it to his pocket. "You have an admirable situation here, cuckolding old Monsieur Brillon. Why not stay?"

Franklin looks at him wistfully. "I have often thought, Thomas, of staying here among these people I love. Alas, it is time to go, 'though I dread the voyage. The sail over nearly demolished me. Benny longs to see his mother and the Congress has denied Temple a position with our Embassy here. Once again, my enemies prevail." After a moment, he continues: "When I get home, I intend to free my slaves."

Jefferson looks at Franklin incredulously. "Fine, but I wouldn't talk about it."

"What about you? You own hundreds of slaves."

"The system is abhorrent and won't outlive me," Jefferson replies, glancing at his pocket watch.

"Do you consider your *slaves* to be your equal?"

"One of them has a key to my bedchamber. Is that equal in your eyes?"

Franklin pauses. "Touché," he says.

Jefferson kicks at a few pebbles in the gravel walkway beneath his feet. "I've heard from William," he confides. "He earnestly hopes to see you when you cross the Channel."

A dark look crosses Franklin's face. He gets up from the bench. "And what, pray tell, would I say to a dead man?"

Jefferson looks up at him. "There is a time for peacemaking, Ben… a time for forgiveness."

"Jesus, I am not!" Franklin retorts. "William slithered out of Washington's grasp, let him stay under his rock!"

DEAR BEN

Franklin's face brightens and he offers an arm to Jefferson. "Come, my friend. Allow me to escort you to the kitchen, where a divine *'choux au crème'* awaits."

Jefferson rises from the bench and takes Franklin's arm.

CHAPTER FORTY-THREE

The Road to Calais

Franklin House, Philadelphia   April 1790

The clock on the landing above the parlor chimes the half-hour.

Sally slumps in a wing chair, with the back of her hand resting on her forehead. She listens to the conversation with her eyes closed.

Jefferson stands at the center table, filling his wine glass. "I was there the morning he left. All of Passy turned out to see him off. The mood was somber, eerily silent, but for the sound of a few ladies' sniffles."

Sally opens her eyes. "What was there to cry about, for Lord's sake?"

"Shall I continue?" Jefferson asks.

"Oh, yes," Polly urges.

"The Queen had sent her own carriage to carry Ben to the port in relative comfort. Her coachmen were to wait at Calais until they had word he had crossed the Channel safely and did not wish to return to France." Jefferson sips his wine. "Most extraordinary."

Passy   July 1785

Dozens of friends and neighbors have gathered in the courtyard of Maison Valentois to bid *'adieu'* to Franklin and to see him and the boys off on their journey to the port at Calais. Jefferson is among those who have come to wish them 'farewell'. He touches Madame Brillon's shoulder tenderly, as she wipes a tear from her eye with a lace kerchief.

Marcel and Blanchette Caillot stand next to Madame Brillon. Monsieur Caillot consoles his wife, who is weeping profusely.

The front door of the villa opens, and two footmen emerge, carrying the last of Franklin's hand baggage. They take it to a magnificent coach-and-four which bears the Royal insignia and stands waiting outside the gates of the villa.

A hush falls over the crowd as Franklin appears on the steps, followed by Temple and Benny. Franklin descends the stairs gingerly with the aid of a cane. He places a hand on his heart, moved by the large turnout. The crowd parts to make way for him and the boys as they walk about, shaking hands and kissing the cheeks of favorite friends. Benny finds it odd that Madame Helvetius in nowhere to be seen.

"I shall miss you, *'mes amis*!" Franklin repeats over and over. When he comes to Madame Brillon, he hugs her and holds her close to him for a long moment.

She slips an envelope into the breast pocket of his frockcoat.

After a time, Franklin and the boys board the Royal coach, the doors are closed, and it rolls forward. An entourage runs after the carriage for several yards, waving kerchiefs and calling out, *'adieu! adieu!'* and shouting *'Au revoir, cher Dr. Franklin!'* as the coach picks up speed. When it turns a corner and vanishes from sight, Franklin's friends turn and head back toward the villa, many of them walking arm-in-arm.

An hour or so later, the Royal coach clatters majestically along the highway toward the seaport. Temple and Benny survey the countryside, saying little. A tattered-looking Mr. Rags is tucked in a corner of the seat next to Benny, both of them happy to be going home. Franklin's eyes are still puffy, as he swims in nine years of blissful memories.

Temple breaks the silence. "We should have stayed, Grandfather."

Franklin ponders the comment. "We had to give back Monsieur Chaumont his house *sometime*."

Temple has no response and looks out the window. A minute later, he looks at his grandfather again. "We left too much behind," he says, with a note of pain in his voice.

Franklin smiles at Temple. "A family tradition," he replies.

Temple turns once more to the passing view.

Franklin retrieves Madame Brillon's letter from his pocket and sniffs its perfume. He holds the envelope close to his chest.

The carriage rolls on. The soothing rocking motion of the chaise lulls Benny and Temple to sleep. They nap in the tufted velvet seat opposite Franklin, with their legs stretched out, their eyes closed and heads touching.

Franklin holds out Madame Brillon's letter and opens it.

PASSY

An evening or two earlier, Madame Brillon had been seated at the writing table in her study. She wears a pink silk robe trimmed with ivory lace, and her hair down and falling onto her shoulders. A glass of champagne rests near her right hand, a sliver of *'gateau'* lies on a Limoges plate next to it. She dips her quill into an inkwell and writes:

'Cher Papa, my heart was so heavy when I last saw you, I feared another such moment would add to my misery without proving the tender love I have devoted to you forever.'

She considers her words for a minute, then continues:

'If it pleases you to remember the woman who loved you most, think of me. My heart was not meant to be separated from yours, but it shall not be. Speak to it and it shall answer you.'

She reads what she has written and folds the letter. She takes a vial of perfume from a drawer, pulls out the stopper, touches her forefinger to the bottle, and runs it across the letter. The envelope is addressed simply, *'Dr. Franklin'*.

Madame turns down the lamp on her desk and sits in the nearly dark room, sipping her champagne.

ROAD TO CALAIS

Franklin reads the letter, reads it again, and returns it to its envelope. He places the envelope in his valise before reaching into a picnic basket on the seat beside him and taking out a bottle of claret. He pours himself some wine and sits back in his seat. He looks with admiration at the young men sleeping across from him, raises his glass in a silent toast to his boys, and takes a drink. A moment later, he hears a disturbance outside and looks out the window.

A rider on horseback has overtaken the Royal coach and rides alongside, shouting to the Queen's coachmen. The carriage slows, then stops, with the horses making a ruckus. A few more words are exchanged in French, then the rider on horseback dismounts and hands an envelope up to one of the coachmen. The rider remounts his horse and rides off in the direction of Paris, whence he came.

Franklin opens his window and leans out. "What is it, driver?" he shouts.

"*Une lettre pour vous, Dr. Franklin.*"

The coachman jumps down and hands Franklin an envelope through the open window, then climbs back up to his seat on the *barouche* box and raises his whip to the horses. The carriage lurches forward, with the horses' hooves striking the stone pavement once again.

Relieved, Franklin leans back in his seat.

The boys sit up and shake off sleep. "What is it, Grandfather?" Temple asks.

Franklin holds up the envelope. "An express, you might say… It's from Madame Helvetius!" He takes the letter out of the envelope and smooths the paper on his knee.

"What does she want?" Temple inquires.

Franklin reads aloud from the letter:

'*Come back to us, dear friend, come back to us. You will make our lives happier, and we shall make you happy.*' It appears she would have us turn around!"

Benny yawns and stretches. "Why didn't you marry that lady, Grandpapa?"

"I tried, but she wouldn't have me. She seems to have changed her mind. Ah, well… too late now, eh?"

Franklin retrieves the bottle of claret from the basket and hands it to Temple. "Time for a drink, lads. It will be twilight soon. I'm one or two ahead of you!"

SOUTHAMPTON, ENGLAND   JULY 1785

Charlie Benson, the driver of the drayage wagon which transported Franklin's belongings to the port at Calais, had sailed with the Franklin party across the Channel. Charlie is a broadly built man with wiry salt-and-pepper hair and a ready smile, albeit through a jumble of badly stained teeth. He is an experienced dockhand and had been up that morning before land was sighted, preparing to unload his charge of crates and trunks. With the help of two young stevedores, he now inventories Franklin's possessions piled on the wharf in Southampton.

After a leisurely breakfast, Franklin and his boys disembark the schooner. Temple grips his grandfather's elbow and helps him down the stairs from the ship.

Franklin spies Charlie standing a few feet away and calls to him, "You will see to it that our chattels are loaded onto the packet boat sailing for Boston the day after tomorrow, will you, my man?"

"Aye, sir, I will do that for ye," Charlie confirms.

Franklin takes a gold coin from his pocket. "It has been a pleasure crossing the Channel with you, Charlie." He places the coin in Charlie's hand. "Give this to the wife, *not* the barmaid, eh, Charlie?"

Charlie smiles broadly with his crooked teeth. "Very kind of ye, and a pint is the farthest thing from my mind, ye can be sure!"

Franklin hails a passing hackney carriage, then another. Charlie and the stevedores load a few overnight bags into the carriages as directed. "Take my boys to the White Deer Inn," Franklin instructs the driver of the first carriage. He hands his satchel to Temple. "You and Benny go on ahead. I have an errand to run."

Franklin clambers into the second carriage, throws his valise on the seat, and hands the driver a piece of paper. "Do you know this place?" he inquires.

"Aye, sir, 't isn't terrible far," the driver replies. He whips the horse and the hackney jolts forward.

The driver turns onto an unpaved road heading south along the seacoast. Franklin observes the land rising gently as the carriage rumbles along. The road narrows and becomes more rutted as they go, giving Franklin an unwelcome jostling. They travel through a shady copse of birch trees, then emerge into bright sunlight and fields of wavering wildflowers and purple thistle.

They have not driven for long when the hackney pulls to a stop. The driver points to a stone mile-marker and a path leading up a knoll on the left side of the road. "That be your spot, sir. *Lover's Leap*', it's called."

"Why is that?" Franklin inquires, looking up the path with some trepidation.

The driver opens Franklin's door. "'Tis quite a long drop to the sea on the other side. A romantic notion, you see..."

"Ah..." Franklin removes some papers from his valise, tucks them into a coat pocket, and steps out of the carriage. "Wait for me here. I shan't be long." He crosses the road and climbs up the trail with the aid of his walking stick.

Atop the hill, William stands in the shade of a gnarled oak tree, looking out to sea through a spyglass. He glances at his pocket watch, looks through the glass again, and surveys the ships at anchor in the bay. He is smartly dressed in a dark suit, his gray hair pulled back into a ponytail and held with a black ribbon. A strong breeze off the ocean ruffles the tails of his frockcoat and the silk scarf he wears about his neck. He looks at his pocket watch again.

William doesn't see or hear Franklin reach the summit and approach him from behind. "Hallo, William," he calls out.

Surprised, William turns to see Franklin. "Father! You startled me!"

Franklin walks back and forth a few steps. "I am looking to see if you hold a pistol behind your back. It would seem a natural progression of events if you were to shoot me."

William smiles weakly. "You honor me by coming to meet me, as you are now honored everywhere. I thought you might enjoy this quiet spot... the lovely view of the sea."

"I have seen quite enough of the sea, having crossed it several times," Franklin responds coolly.

William extends his hand. "I offer you my friendship, Father."

Franklin looks at the outstretched hand, hesitates, and shakes hands. Hearing the sound of leaves rustling in the tree above him, he walks to the edge of the point and looks over the precipice. "How many young lovers have entered eternity from this spot, one wonders?" He turns back to William. "Would you know the answer?"

William shakes his head.

"But, how could you?" Franklin smooths a few wisps of his thinning hair blown by the wind as he steps back. "I offer my condolences for the loss of your wife, Elizabeth," he says. "She was a good woman."

"Thank you." William steps closer to his father, measuring his words. "I have lived with the hope that we may revive our affectionate relations, now that the unhappy contest between America and Britain has concluded."

"Unhappy? The 'contest' was unhappy only for the British. They lost," Franklin snaps. He lowers himself onto a stone bench beneath the tree, his hands resting atop his walking stick.

"I may have made an error of judgement that I cannot rectify," William admits.

"A very *grave* error," Franklin concurs.

"I believe, Father, that were those circumstances to occur again, my conduct would be exactly similar."

"I had no doubt that I would find myself deserted in my old age by my only son. Nothing has ever hurt me so deeply," Franklin says bitterly.

"It was a matter of conscience," William explains.

Franklin raises his voice. "*Conscience*? To take up arms against me? In a cause wherein my good name, my fortune, and my very life were at stake? And what of poor Captain Ruddy? Are you not ashamed?"

William looks away from his father. "I saw it as my duty…"

Franklin cuts him off. "This is a disagreeable subject. Let us get down to business." Franklin stands, lays his cane on the bench, and takes papers from his coat pocket. He hands the papers to William and gestures to the bench. "Sit down."

William sits, unfolds the papers, and scans them. A look of shock crosses his face.

Franklin continues. "I will summarize those documents for you. I have offset your debt to me with your properties and accounts in New York. Your son, Temple, has purchased your farm and chattels in New

Jersey for the sum of one pound. You will find a record of those proceedings among the papers you hold in your hands."

"Am I to be left with *nothing?*" William gasps. "Have I no say in this business?"

"You may wish to apply to the British authorities for restitution," Franklin says as he walks around the bench. "You have, therefore, no need to return to America and risk being hanged as a traitor. You may live out your days here… *quietly.*"

William looks ashen. "Am I never to see my son again?"

"I cannot forbid Temple from visiting you, but I shall discourage it."

William fights back tears. "I pray the Creator is more forthcoming in His forgiveness than are you!"

Franklin regards his son with both contempt and pity. "The French have a saying: *'Tout comprendre c'est tout pardonner'*. 'To understand everything is to forgive all'. Unfortunately, I do *not* understand." After a moment, Franklin sighs, "Well, I must be on my way. There is a party in my honor at the Inn tonight, and tomorrow the captain is hosting a *'bon voyage'* dinner for me and a few friends aboard ship." He turns and walks to the trailhead.

William follows for a few steps, tugs at the tails of Franklin's coat, and drops to his knees. "Please, father! Don't do this!" he cries.

Franklin stops. "For Lord's sake, William, get up. You make a fool of yourself. I bid you *'adieu'*."

William hears the 'click' of his father's walking stick striking against the stones as he descends the trail. Franklin's eyes glisten when he reaches the road and climbs into the waiting hackney carriage.

"To the village, then, sir?" the driver inquires.

"Yes, please." Franklin takes a kerchief from his pocket and wipes a tear from his eye. "Have you any sons, driver?" he asks, as the carriage rolls forward.

"Yes, sir. Three boys."

"I have lost two of my own. Pray that is not your fate."

"I will do that, sir," the driver says.

"Don't spare the whip, man," Franklin calls to him. "I am in need of a drink and there's one in it for ye, as well, if ye make good speed."

"Like the wind, sir. Like the wind."

CHAPTER FORTY-FOUR

Au Revoir

Passy   July 1785

Leaves are wet with morning dew as Madame Brillon parts a pair of French doors and steps into the garden outside her bedroom. The sun has just risen above the horizon and the sky has yet to take on color. But it is a warm morning, Madame Brillon wears only a satin negligée and walks in her bare feet. Strands of her ebony hair fall from the chignon she wears at the nape of her neck. She stops at a bed of dahlias, examines a bloom, and leans close to savor its aroma.

Her husband, Henri, approaches her from behind. He says nothing, but places his hands on her shoulders. She turns, and sees that he, too, has not yet dressed for the day. He wears a cashmere robe wrapped around him and monogrammed slippers on his feet.

"Have you had your coffee, darling?" he inquires in French. "Shall I bring it to you here?"

Madame Brillon shakes her head, *"Non, merci."*

"Perhaps a cup of tea? Shall I ring for your *'bonne de chambre*?"

She shakes her head again. "I miss him, Henri. What am I to do?"

Henri is taken aback by her comment. He holds her gaze for a moment. "We have each other, Anne-Louise. We are still together."

"What of 'Hélène'? Whom does she have?"

"She has *me*. I am perhaps not an immortal, but I am here." Henri pulls her close to him and holds her in an embrace. She smiles and rests her head on his shoulder.

DEAR BEN

Southampton   July 1785

Billy Strahan and Sir John Pringle are among the dozen men attending the Captain's farewell dinner for Franklin aboard his ship, *The Iris*, which is to sail with the tide early the next morning. Bishop Shipley, another old friend, has surprised Franklin and ridden over from his parish in Devonshire. A jovial man, he wears the collar of a cleric and looks to be in his mid-seventies.

Oil lamps mounted on pine-paneled walls and candles in glass shades resting on the long, plank table light the dining saloon to a warm, golden glow. Two stewards circle the table, serving platters of roasted meats and pouring wine from flagons of claret. Dinner guests help themselves to baskets of bread and crocks of butter in the center of the table.

Franklin strains to finish telling a story above the din of his boisterous friends, who are laughing and shouting across the table to one another. He taps his wine glass sharply with a knife to regain their attention. "And then," he says in full voice. "And then, I saw two old salts on deck coiling a long, heavy rope."

Sir John 'shusses' the table with a finger to his lips. "Let Ben finish his story, dammit," he slurs.

Franklin resumes his storytelling: "So, one sailor says to the other, '*I can't wait to get to the end of this damn rope!*'"

Temple, seated across from Franklin, teases, "I can't wait to get to the end of this story!" Franklin laughs and tosses a bread roll at Temple, then continues: "The other mate says, '*I have bad news! Somebody's cut off the other end!*'"

His guests groan and laugh in equal measure.

A smile leaves Franklin's face and he turns to Strahan in a moment of quiet. "I wish she had waited for me, Billy. I would like to have at least said 'farewell'."

Strahan is caught off-guard by the remark. "You speak of Margaret Stevenson? She died peacefully, Ben. In her sleep."

Sir John concurs. "Margaret's heart gave out. She felt no pain."

"So much is lost," Franklin says, wistfully. After a pause, his smile returns, and he slaps the table. "Well, let's talk of something more cheerful! I have decided to embark on a building project when I get

---

421

home. I am going to add a new wing to my house, and there will be room for all of ye to come visit and stay as long as ye like!"

Bishop Shipley raises his glass. "Let us drink to a joyful and raucous reunion in Philadelphia!"

The other guests shout an affirmation, raise their glasses, and join in the toast.

While the cheering subsides, Franklin studies the face of his old pal, Strahan, which is haggard and gray, even in the glow of candlelight. Strahan's frame is gaunt, his hands thin and boney. He will not last the year.

Shipboard

The ship navigates through a dense fog. A dog barks at dawn, awakening Franklin.

He arises from his bunk, wraps a robe around himself, and parts the curtains to look out the window, where the first light of day is breaking. He turns and looks across the large cabin and sees Temple and Benny fast asleep on their bunks. Franklin realizes his friends had slipped ashore while he slept, and that he and the boys are miles out to sea. His head is heavy. 'How much did I have to drink?' he ponders.

Franklin emerges from his cabin, which is located on deck, aft. The wind is fair, the sails are full, but the fog can be cut with a knife. He walks forward with the aid of his stick, thumping along on the wooden planks.

Franklin sees the Commander of the Watch standing ahead of him, wearing his white uniform. The Commander calls to a lookout in the crow's nest. "Look out well before ye, lad!" he shouts up to the rigging.

The lookout is a boy of twelve years or so in age, his voice not yet changed. He holds a spyglass and calls back in his boyish soprano, "Aye, aye, sir!"

Franklin reaches the quarterdeck, where a midshipman in uniform rings a brass bell, a warning to other vessels sailing through the thick fog. A distant ship's bell rings an answer, signaling it is sailing the same course as *The Iris*.

DEAR BEN

A small terrier runs up to Franklin, barks a greeting, and jumps up on Franklin's legs. He pets the Captain's dog, known aboard as a good ratter. Her barking also helps announce *The Iris's* location to ships in close proximity.

Franklin walks forward to the prow of the ship and peers out to sea.

Try as he may, he cannot conjure up what lies ahead.

PART NINE

The Prodigal

CHAPTER FORTY-FIVE

On Broad Shoulders

Philadelphia   1786

Benjamin Franklin stands in the waning light of a late summer evening, looking over the framework of an addition to his house on Market Street. He leans on his cane with one hand and holds a glass of wine in the other. Seth Harris, a skilled joiner, and his crew of carpenters, have made remarkable progress since receiving Franklin's sketchy plans earlier in the summer. They have already raised the structure to its full three-story height, and Harris hopes to have the building enclosed before cold weather intervenes.

Franklin cranes his eighty-year-old neck to admire the stout timbers, straight and true, as they stand silhouetted against a slate blue sky. He hears footsteps on the walk and turns to see his neighbor, Melba Perkins, approaching. She is on her way home from the farmers' market on Broad Street and carries a burlap shopping bag in each hand. A nice enough woman, even if a trifle inquisitive, Franklin considers. She always had a mince pie for Deborah at Christmas time, during those long years Franklin lived overseas, he recalls. He notices Melba has added pounds to her girth in recent years, but her features remain crisp, her hazel eyes bright.

She stops a few feet from Franklin. "That's quite some works you got goin' on there, Ben," she says.

"Hello, Melba. 'Tis a fine entertainment for me."

"My husband ain't entertained by all the noise."

"I shall instruct the builders to hammer quietly." Melba sets down her market bags. She lifts the front of her hat and stuffs a curl of her graying blonde hair under the brim. "What's it going to be?" she inquires.

"There will be a library for some four thousand volumes on the second floor and a dining room to seat twenty-four on the ground floor," Franklin boasts.

"You got that many friends?"

Franklin sips his wine. "General Washington has promised to come and inaugurate the new table, now being manufactured up in New York, I will have you know."

"Washington? My, my... Well, don't get too big for your breeches."

Franklin offers his glass of wine to her. "Care for a tipple? 'Tis a fine Madeira..."

Melba shakes her head. "Lord, no. What would Ephraim say?"

Franklin points to an upper story. "And, there will be a new suite of rooms for me on the third floor. That is so you can't peer into my bedroom window," he teases.

Melba laughs and flutters her eyelashes "You old fool. I got a ladder!" She picks up her shopping bags and goes on her way, the heels of her boots clicking along on the pavement.

Franklin's bedroom   1790

Bobby takes a log from a basket next to the fireplace and lays it on the grate. He crouches down on the hearth, watching the log catch fire. He stirs the coals under the log with an iron poker. The fire crackles and sparks rise up the blackened brick chimney. The glow of the fire is reflected in Bobby's face and lively eyes, both warm shades of brown. He hears Franklin cough a deep, hoarse cough. Bobby stands and turns to see him at the window near the bed, wrapped in a blanket. Franklin leans on the sill of the very window he had imagined with Melba Perkins four years earlier. He peers out to the street through panes of glass glistening with rain.

Bobby brushes dirt from the log off his hands. "What you doin' outta that bed, Dr. Ben? You 'sposed to be *in* it," he scolds. "That cough don't sound too good."

DEAR BEN

Franklin pulls the blanket closed tightly about himself. "I was thinking of the day General Washington arrived in town for the meeting of the former Colonies in 1787. Do you remember?"

Bobby places his hands on the old man's shoulders and guides him gently toward the bed. "Yes, sir, I remember. We *heard* the General before we seen 'im."

"Yes," Franklin says as he shuffles along in his slippers toward the bed. "It was a grand occasion. Light another candle, would you, Bobby? The light in here is fading."

Philadelphia   May 1787

Hundreds of Philadelphians line the banks of the Schuylkill River and the pier at the foot of Market Street on a warm, sunny morning. They have come to witness the spectacle of four wooden barges, decorated with flags and draped with bunting, crossing the choppy river. The red and blue cloth flaps noisily in a stiff breeze. The crowd roars when General George Washington comes into view, riding on the back of his chestnut charger on the leading barge. He is accompanied by a squadron of foot soldiers, wearing uniforms of the Continental Army. The General, looking fit at fifty-five, sits erect on his splendid mount, which is sixteen hands tall.

A military band playing a march on the second barge can barely be heard over the peal of church bells, booming canons, rifle fire, and the din of the crowd. Companies of uniformed men on horseback ride on the third and fourth barges, swaying on their mounts as the river rises and falls.

The excited throng gives Washington a hero's welcome as he lands and disembarks the barge. They shout words of thanks and praise for his victories over the British. Women toss flowers in his path, men fire rifles into the air, dogs bark and encircle the prancing horses.

A woman in the crowd reaches out and touches Washington's leg. "You should be our king!" she calls up to him. He scowls and pretends not to hear her.

The Franklin mansion has been electric with anticipation since early morning. Four of the Bache children, ages seven to fourteen years, have taken positions hanging precariously out of second-story windows, for a good view of the coming parade. Temple and Benny lean out their bedroom windows on the third floor, and Bobby watches from the dormer window of his garret.

The front door of the house opens, and Sally and Richard Bache step out, both dressed in their Sunday finest. Sally fusses with strands of her hair that stubbornly refuse to stay in place and blow in the wind. They look down Market Street, straining for a glimpse of the parade they can hear but not yet see.

A few minutes later, Washington appears, with the boisterous crowd from the wharf following close behind. He rides up to the Franklin house, tips his bicorne hat, and dismounts. Richard steps forward to shake hands with the General, while a nervous Sally makes a polite curtsey. The crowd cheers as the front door opens again and Franklin, aided by his walking stick, emerges from the house. "I am going to catch hell from my neighbor, Perkins, over all this hubbub!" he shouts.

Washington tilts back his head and laughs.

Franklin invites Washington into the house and leads him to his stately new dining room. They take seats at the gleaming mahogany table, recently arrived from a cabinet maker in New York. Franklin sits in a Queen Anne-style armchair at the head, with Washington on his right. Their places are laid with English silver and Irish linens. They hear the band outside strike up another march and the noisy parade of citizens and soldiers regroups and moves on.

Franklin makes an attempt to stand. "You should sit here… And get used to the Chairman's seat at the conference."

"Nay, nay." Washington urges Franklin to remain seated. "The delegates will certainly elect you to the chair."

A tap at the door, and Jake, graying at the temples and regal in a butler's uniform, enters. He goes to a keg on a sideboard and pours ale into two silver tankards. He serves the two men, bows at the waist, turns and leaves the room.

Franklin shakes his head. "I am too old and too lame for such a task." He lifts his tankard. "This fine stout, by the way, was sent to me by a friend in England. I am pleased to share it with you today. To friendship and good fortune!"

"To friendship," Washington concurs, and sips his ale. After a pause, "I don't foresee any benefit coming of this meeting, do you? There are too many regional issues dividing us. Perhaps each state should go its own way." Franklin wipes foam from the ale off his lips with a serviette. "Our differences are a challenge, but not insurmountable. Besides, I am not certain the states could survive independently. They would forever be at risk from threats from the great European powers."

Washington sips his ale and considers Franklin's remark.

Aggie taps at the door and enters the room carrying a tray bearing luncheon plates and an imposing cake. She rests the tray on a sideboard and places plates of cold meats, biscuits, and cheeses before the men, then sets the cake on the table.

Franklin smiles. "Aggie, please tell our guest about the special dessert you have made for us."

"Yes, sir. I calls it a 'Washington cake'," she says shyly, placing her hands in the pockets of her crisp, white apron. "Three layers with lemon crème filling and chocolate on top."

Washington claps his hands together. "Splendid, Aggie! Splendid."

Aggie makes a little curtsey, beaming proudly. She picks up the silver tray and leaves the room, gently closing the door behind her.

Franklin picks up his knife and fork. "I am convinced, General, that we need a strong central government to unite us, if we are to remain free. The present Articles of Confederation are not up to the task. The question is: who will be sovereign? A man of the people, or a figure fashioned after the English monarch? There are those who would place you on the throne."

"I have heard of such nonsense." Washington takes a bite of ham, chewing carefully with his wooden teeth. "I am comforted that you will be there to guide us."

Franklin looks at Washington with downcast eyes. "I am afraid I won't be there. My health is too poor. My gout is so painful at times that I dare not walk to the State House, and my stones are so bad I cannot bear the jostling of a carriage any longer."

Washington lays down his fork. "Damn it, Ben, I will get you there somehow, even if I have to carry you!"

Franklin is touched by Washington's determination, and begins to think about what he might wear to the coming conference.

PHILADELPHIA   1787

A gray haze hangs in the late morning sky. A crowd of well-wishers, wilted by the hot and humid summer day, lines Franklin's path to the Georgian-style government building. They shout greetings as Franklin passes by, seated in a sedan chair held aloft by the strong arms of four burly prisoners borrowed from the city jail for the occasion. The prisoners gently lower the chair onto the cobbled street at the entrance to the State House. Franklin steps out to cheers from the crowd. He waves a greeting and walks slowly and painfully into the hall, aided by his walking stick.

Inside the hall, fifty-five delegates, all male, have taken their seats at thirteen round tables. Aged twenty-six to Franklin's eighty-one-years, they fan themselves with paper fans against the oppressive heat. They have removed their coats, cravats are undone. George Washington is seated at a table on the dais at the head of the room.

Franklin sits with four members of the Pennsylvania delegation. He appears to sleep. His head is tipped back, his eyes are closed and his mouth agape.

Alexander Hamilton stands on the floor in front of Washington, addressing the assembly in his strident voice. He is diminutive and has an admirable face, despite a somewhat haughty expression. He paces to and fro, stabbing at the air with his finger for emphasis. "I believe the British system of government forms the best model this world has ever produced!"

Jeers rise up from several delegates, but Hamilton carries on defiantly. "The voice of the people has been said to be akin to the Voice of God, but that is, in fact, not true!" he argues.

A delegate seated at the table next to Franklin, looks at the old man and nudges the associate sitting next to him. "Look there," he whispers. "The Great Philosopher sleeps like a common man... with his mouth open, catching flies."

His neighbor nods in agreement. "How he sleeps through Hamilton's harangue, is beyond me."

Franklin opens his eyes and slides upright in his chair. He finds his pen and jots down a note, as though Hamilton's words have caught his attention.

Hamilton is undeterred by his rude and restless audience. "Give, therefore, to the upper classes a distinct, permanent share of the government!" he carries on. "They will check the unsteadiness of the common people and, because they gain no advantage in change for the sake of change, will ever maintain good government!"

A few delegates stand and applaud the speech, while catcalls arise from others as Hamilton returns to his seat.

Franklin rises to his feet with the aid of his cane and addresses the chair. "May I speak, Mr. Chairman?"

Washington gives his consent. "You may, Dr. Franklin."

Franklin clears his throat. "My colleague's oratory was impressive for its sincerity, especially for a poor immigrant lad from the Island of Nevis. I am a poor boy from Boston, but I do not share Mr. Hamilton's faith in the aristocracy," Franklin says, arousing laughter from the delegates. "A French lady friend of mine once said to me, '*men will always make kings*', as Mr. Hamilton now proposes. I believe the age of kings has passed, having witnessed the depravity and corruption of the English Court during my years of service there."

Delegates lean forward and strain to hear Franklin's elderly voice.

"The diversity of opinion among us turns on two points: if proportional representation takes place, small states contend their liberties are in danger. If equal votes take its place, the large states worry their *money* will be in danger."

A delegate across the room half-rises from his chair. "Speak up, Ben! We can't hear ye!" he calls in Franklin's direction.

Franklin attempts to raise his voice. "'Though I prefer a unicameral legislature, I move that we revisit the proposal made by Mr. Sherman of Connecticut for two houses: one elected by the people, based on population, and an upper chamber with an equal number of members appointed by each state."

A delegate near Franklin jumps to his feet. "I second the motion!" he shouts.

The room erupts in cheers and shouting. Washington stands, pounding his gavel to restore order.

Franklin House   1787

On afternoons when the Congress is not in session, Franklin is pleased to invite delegates to join him on his new dining room terrace for tea or a glass of sherry. The shade of his leafy mulberry tree provides a welcome respite from the sweltering heat of the meeting hall in the State House. Shirtsleeves are encouraged, cravats and hats forbidden. The delegates gathered around his table often speak of things other than their morning at the Convention. They share local gossip, discuss the rising price of land, bemoan a mother-in-law's lingering illness.

On this hot summer day, three-year-old Richard Bache, Jr. sits contentedly on his grandfather's lap. He is shirtless, wears short pants, his feet are bare, and his right thumb is in his mouth.

Rufus King, a delegate from Massachusetts, sips sherry and leans back in his chair. He brings the conversation back around to the business at hand. "I still say, Ben, your motion saved our convention," he offers.

"Here, here!" Mr. Gilman of New Hampshire concurs, raising his glass.

Franklin attempts, unsuccessfully, to extricate young Richard's thumb from the boy's mouth. "You give me too much credit, gentlemen. I merely brought your attention back to the idea proposed by Roger Sherman of Connecticut."

Jacob Brown, a representative from Delaware, pours himself another glass of sherry. "There is still much work to do. Let us pray it will be in harmony and with cool heads."

Sally and Aggie emerge from the house carrying trays bearing a tea service. Sally wears a cotton summer dress, Aggie a long white apron and white cap on her head. Sally greets the men at the table with whom she is familiar. "Good afternoon, Mr. Morris, Mr. Ingersoll, Mr. Wilson." Aggie walks behind Sally, helping her to pour tea and serve cake to Franklin's guests.

Franklin feeds his grandson a bite of cake, as he picks up the thread of Mr. Brown's conversation. "Indeed. The issue of slavery has yet to be broached, and how they are to be counted in the lower house." He turns to James Wilson, who is seated on his right. "What say you, James?"

"Why not as they were for the Articles, which allowed owners to count three-fifths of their slaves as population?" he suggests.

Franklin nods toward Aggie, who calmly goes about her business. "Is a black man in this country forever to be worth only three fifths of a white man? Is my servant equal to only three-fifths of my daughter? The idea troubles me."

There is a murmuring around the table until Pierce Butler, a gray-eyed gentleman from South Carolina, clasps his hands behind his head. "You northerners will never understand our southern way of life," he drawls, looking up to the sky. "Three-fifths or one-half or one-quarter… That is an issue best left to us to decide."

Abraham Baldwin of Georgia, who has spent the past half-hour swatting flies with a folded newspaper, concurs. "And this is not the place or the time," he adds, stirring milk into his tea.

All are silent as they watch Sally and Aggie finish their service and retreat into the house.

Franklin searches his memory for an amusing story to lighten the mood around the table.

Philadelphia   September 1787

As he has every day of the past summer, George Washington will preside over the Constitutional Convention in the State House, from his seat at a table on the dais. Representatives from the member states mill about the floor of the hot and stuffy hall, chatting and fanning themselves with paper fans.

"Oyez! Oyez! Oyez!" the Sergeant-at-Arms shouts, and Washington pounds his gavel, calling the meeting to order. When the men have taken their seats, Washington looks toward the Pennsylvania delegation. "Dr. Franklin, you wished to address the Assembly?"

Franklin stands with the aid of his cane. "I thank the Chairman," he says. "Now we have the completed document before us, as well as a 'concluding endorsement' as outlined by my colleague, Gouverneur

Morris, to consider for signature." And, after a pause, "I am reminded of another French lady friend of mine..."

Franklin hears tittering from several delegates. He removes his spectacles, surveys the room and grins. "I had more than *one* French lady friend, as you may well know." He replaces his spectacles on his nose as the Assembly erupts in laughter.

Franklin continues as the laughter subsides. "She, while arguing with her sister one day, announced, *'I don't know how it is, sister, but I meet with nobody but myself that is always in the right!'*" The delegates laugh again.

Franklin waits for the laughter to die down. "I confess there are parts of this Constitution of which I do not approve, but I am not sure I shall *never* approve them. I ask another of my colleagues, James Wilson, to read my remarks so you can better hear." Franklin resumes his seat and hands his notes to Wilson, who stands and reads from them in a strong, baritone voice: "*Sir, I agree to this Constitution with all its faults, if they are such. I think it will astonish our enemies, who are waiting to hear that our councils are confounded like those of the builders of Babel. Thus, I consent to this Constitution, Sir, because I expect no better, and because I am not sure it is not the best.*"

The Assembly applauds wildly.

"*I hope, therefore,*" Wilson concludes, "*that for the sake of posterity, we shall act heartily and unanimously.*" A cheer arises from the delegates as Wilson turns to Franklin and shakes his hand.

Franklin House   1790

A light rain continues to fall. Jefferson's horses and carriage have moved from the mews to the glistening street in front of the house, preparing for Jefferson's departure. The horses are restless, their hooves swipe at the paving stones of the street. Jefferson's coachman and driver stand next to the carriage, gossiping with a group of five neighbors who are huddled under umbrellas next to a streetlamp, maintaining their vigil.

Moses Hayes, a close neighbor, lights his pipe and helps the young coachman to light his. "Where does Secretary Jefferson travel to next?" he inquires.

"We ride on to New York to meet with the President in a day or two," the coachman replies, pulling up the collar of his greatcoat.

Two women nod their approval. One of them points to the front door of the house. "Well, then, he's got to come out of there *sometime*," she chirps.

The other lady looks up to the third floor, where a light still burns in a window.

Franklin's bedroom

Bobby settles Franklin onto the edge of his bed. He removes Franklin's slippers and helps him to lie back, nestling pillows under his head. The skin on the old man's forehead appears translucent in the candlelight.

Franklin's voice is thin and raspy. "We've come to the end of my story, Bobby."

"Oh, I hope not," Bobby says sadly. "I enjoy it so far."

Franklin points across the room. "Look in my desk drawer. You will find an envelope there with your name on it."

Bobby goes to the desk and opens the drawer, locates the envelope, and opens it. His eyes widen. "They's money in here! A lot of money!" he declares as he thumbs through a wad of bank notes.

"To get you started. You must go now, while I'm still alive," Franklin wheezes. "Sally may have another idea."

"I can't leave you like this, Dr. Ben."

"All will be well. The lady will come for me soon. Time for you to go... Write your own story."

Bobby stuffs the envelope in his jacket pocket and offers his hand to Franklin.

Franklin holds Bobby's hand in both of his for a long moment. "Godspeed, my boy."

On the walk outside, the neighbors and coachmen stop their chatter when the front door opens and Jefferson emerges from the house. Polly and Sally stand just inside the entry hall, avoiding the rainfall.

"Thank you, ladies," Jefferson says, doffing his leather hat to them. "You have been more than kind. I will come by tomorrow and collect my maps from Dr. Franklin."

Sally and Polly wave to Jefferson and retreat inside, closing the door behind them.

"Any news, Mr. Secretary?" Moses Hayes inquires.

"He's doing just fine. You folks might as well go home and get into your warm beds," Jefferson reassures them. He doffs his hat, climbs into the carriage, and the coachman closes his door. The driver lashes the horses and the carriage jolts to a start. It rolls into the rainy night, swirling a fog that has settled on the street as it goes.

Sally sinks into a chair at the center table in the parlor and empties the wine bottle into her glass. "Well, that went well," she mumbles to herself.

Polly tidies up, collecting glasses and plates on a tray. "He is such a charming man! I hated to see him leave," she says.

Sally looks at Polly with daggers. "Charming? All that talk about how the French *'venerated'* my father nettled me no end! My mother didn't *'venerate'* him. She died of loneliness... All those years away..."

"Your mother died of a stroke," Polly reminds her.

"*Your* mother killed my mother! She knew what was going on over there," Sally hisses, with venom in her voice.

Polly ignores the cruel gibe and carries the tray into the hallway. "I'll put these things in the kitchen and go look in on Papa."

"He is *not* your Papa!" Sally calls after her, and takes another sip of wine. "Tell him I'll be up in a minute."

Temple and Benny are on horseback, riding slowly along an unpaved, muddy road on their way back to town. Their coat collars are raised and their hats pulled down against the persistent rain. Darkness separates them.

After several minutes, Temple calls to Benny: "Did I ever tell you what became of my son?"

"No, you didn't," Benny replies, surprised by Temple's choice of subjects. "I recall that you had a child..."

"With Blanchette... You know... the actress."

"Yes, you cad, I remember." And after a pause, "Where is the boy now?" Benny inquires.

"In Paris… dead and buried. He died when he was not yet two. The pox."

"I didn't know… how terribly sad. I am very sorry, Temple."

"Yes…"

The two ride on and do not speak again for a long while.

CHAPTER FORTY-SIX

Stealth

Franklin lies in his bed with his eyes closed and his head settled into a feather pillow. His breathing is thin and irregular. John Adams stands in the shadows nearby, silently observing his old nemesis. He walks closer to the bed and whispers: "Franklin... Ben..."

"I thought you left, Bobby," Franklin says in a raspy voice, without opening his eyes.

Adams leans close to Franklin's ear. "It's me. John. John Adams," he whispers.

Franklin opens his eyes and raises himself onto one elbow. "Jesus, John!" What are you doing here? Turn up the lamp so I can see you."

"I came to say 'good-bye'."

"Where are you going?"

Adams turns up the bedside lamp. "I am told you haven't much time."

"No, not much time. I have always had a distaste for the end of things, but one's own finale is inescapable. How'd you get in? You weren't announced."

"Through the terrace. I wasn't seen." After a beat: "I wish to make amends. I'm sorry I called you a sodomite that night up in New York."

Franklin coughs deeply and takes a kerchief from the night table. There is blood on the cloth when he lays it back on the table. "'Twas a *pederast* you called me, but no need to apologize now."

Adams looks out the window. "You know, I never would have bothered to vilify an ordinary man, to say unkind things..."

"All in the past, John. Why don't you sit down?" Adams sits down in the chair next to the bed. "I loved you for all you did for this country. I still do."

Franklin sits upright, with considerable effort. "Coming from an honest man, I take that as a compliment." He props a pillow behind his back. "You have recently returned from service in England as Ambassador. How'd you like it over there?"

Adams smiles. "The King was very kind to me." His smile is fleeting. "I still think that had you paid more attention to business whilst we were in France, we could have taken Canada from the British."

"You will be President someday. Why don't you invade and see what happens?" Franklin points to a bedside table. "Hand me that cup, will you?"

Adams hands Franklin the teacup. "Do you think I will... be President?"

"I have no doubt."

"Have you any regrets, Ben?" Adams inquires.

Franklin takes a sip of wine. "I regret losing both my sons, and I envy you yours."

Adams nods his head in sympathy. "Well, I shall leave you to rest. I will slip away quietly, the way I came in." He rises from his chair.

"And I shall soon *'slip away quietly'* the way *I* came in... and lie next to Deborah and succor the worms." Franklin lies back down on the bed.

"The earth will not consume you," Adams says.

Franklin furrows his brows. "What? Are my remains to be spat out of the ground like spoilt meat?"

"'Tis heaven that will." Franklin's eyes glisten.

"I bid you *'adieu, mon ami',*" Adams offers quietly.

"Your French still stinks, Adams," Franklin says, his voice cracking.

Adams pats Franklin's shoulder, turns down the bedside lamp as he found it, and leaves the room, without making a sound.

Polly climbs the narrow back stairway from the kitchen to the third floor. She wears an apron over her Paris gown and carries a small tea tray. She arrives at Franklin's bedroom, taps lightly, and opens the door. She finds Franklin reclining on his bed, his eyes closed. She sets the tray on the dresser. "I've brought you some nice hot tea, Papa," she says cheerily. "How are you feeling?"

Franklin opens his eyes. "Never worse. 'Tis laudanum I need, child, not tea." He points to the dresser. "On the chest there, next to your tray."

Polly turns up the lamp on the bedside table and touches Franklin's forehead. "Your fever is up. I don't like that." She goes to the dresser and wets a cloth in a basin.

"Did you see Adams just now?" Franklin inquires.

Polly squeezes water out of the cloth. "I saw no-one."

"He must have gone down the back stairs."

"I came up the back stairs," she says. "You were dreaming." Polly wipes Franklin's brow with the cloth. "You will feel better in the morning, you'll see," she says.

"I won't be here in the morning." Polly wipes his brow again and replaces the cloth on the edge of the basin. "Shall we say a prayer, Papa? One longs to feel close to the Lord at a time like this."

Franklin shakes his head. "I do not fear the journey, Pigeon. I have read the New Testament five or six times. Paul tells us our bodies are like *'tents in the desert'*, a temporary home for the soul. When the tent is destroyed, we go to a more substantial dwelling made ready by the Creator. That may be so…"

"I can't bear the thought, Papa." Polly finds the laudanum and prepares it in a glass.

"Tell me, did she ever speak of me? At the end, did she mention my name?"

"Mama? You *were* her end." Polly stirs the laudanum. "She loved you most ardently. Without hope of spending the remainder of her life with you, she was wretched indeed."

"By the time I could return, she was gone."

"Polly sits on the edge of the bed. "Mama deeply regretted passing those letters on to you."

Franklin raises himself onto his elbow. "She spoke of the 'Hutchinson letters'?"

Polly helps him drink the mixture of opium and alcohol. "They were, in fact, copies. The Queen kept the originals."

"They were given to her by the Queen?"

"Charlotte thought her husband was going mad. She manipulated events as best she could, but not well enough, it turned out."

"No, not well enough."

Polly smooths Franklin's brow with her forefinger. He closes his eyes contentedly. "Did Margaret tell you that I suspected your father was an agent for the French?"

"So thought the French. In truth, he was Mama's entrée to St. James's."

Franklin's eyes open wide. "Dangerous business…"

Polly gets up and replaces the glass on the dresser. "Yes. He was poisoned. By whom, Mama never knew." Polly steps to the window and looks out. "There are still a few people down there in the street," she observes. She turns to look at Franklin. "I always knew Temple was a Franklin. I wasn't sure if you were, or William was, the father."

"Had *I* been, your mother wouldn't have allowed the boy in the house."

"I sorted that out eventually. I feared him, you know… William, I mean."

"He can do you no harm now," Franklin consoles her.

She points toward the far corner of the room. "Sometimes, I awaken in the night, and I can hear him. Just there… in the darkness… breathing."

Franklin raises his head. "Dear child."

"Where is Bobby?" Polly asks brightly.

"In the mews. He's riding out tonight. I have freed him."

Polly is stunned by then news for a moment. "Bless you! I must say 'good-bye' to him!" Polly touches Franklin's hand and hurries to the door.

"Polly?" Franklin calls after her. "Did she ever forgive me?"

Polly hesitates in the doorway and smiles mischievously. "Did you fly that famous kite?" she asks, before dashing down the stairs.

Jake's sleep has been interrupted. He is in his undershirt and pulls the braces on his breeches up over his shoulders. The rain has let up for the moment and he helps Bobby to saddle up his horse, one of Franklin's fine quarter horses, and to secure his travel bags. He affixes a scabbard to the saddle to hold Bobby's firearm, also a gift from Franklin.

"This horse is fast, Bobby. He ain't real friendly, though. I hope he don't throw ya," Jake warns.

"I has ridden Major a few times. We'll do just fine."

Polly crosses the drive, wrapping her cloak around her. "Must you leave in the dark like this?" she calls to Bobby.

"Dr. Ben afraid Missus Bache send the Marshall after me if she hear about it," he replies.

"Where will you go?"

"Ohio, Ma'am. I got family out there. How about you? You goin' home to England now?"

"No, I shall stay here and help out, if I can. Well, God bless you, Bobby. Do write to me. Let me know where you are and how you are. Do you promise?"

"I will do that, Miss Polly."

"Do you have a weapon?"

Bobby displays his rifle. "Yes, Ma'am."

"Do you know how to use it?"

"I killed a rooster once," Bobby grins.

Polly takes a paper from her apron pocket and hands it to Bobby. "If anybody stops you, show him this letter. You are on business for Dr. Franklin." She stands on her tip-toes and gives him a peck on his cheek. "Farewell, Bobby." Bobby stuffs the paper into a saddle bag and mounts his horse. He closes his coat and adjusts the brim of his hat. He offers a wave, takes the reins, and with his boots pressed to Major's flank, rides off into the night.

Polly and Jake look after Bobby and stand quietly next to one another.

"Will you be leaving as well?" she asks, after a minute.

"No, Ma'am. Me an' Aggie, we don't know nothin' else."

"Mm," she says, nodding her head. She slips her arm through Jake's. "I'll walk you home."

Sally opens Franklin's bedroom door and walks brusquely into the room. She sees her father lying in his bed with his eyes closed. She places the back of her hand on his forehead. "Papa?" she says.

Franklin opens his eyes. "Hello, Sal," he whispers. "Has Jefferson gone?"

"Yes, he left a few minutes ago. You're feverish again." She takes the cloth from the basin and wipes Franklin's forehead. "I thought Polly was with you."

"She was just here. Have the boys come home yet?"

"No, Papa, not yet. Those devils." Sally sees the cameo portrait of Margaret Stevenson lying on the side table. She picks it up, looks at it, and turns it face down as she replaces it on the table. "Where has Bobby gone?"

"I sent him on an errand."

"An errand? Where to?"

"Ohio."

Sally looks at Franklin blankly, then tosses the cloth into the basin on the dresser.

"I'll be right back," she says, as she bustles out of the room.

A clock in a church belfry a few blocks away begins to strike eleven.

Sally wraps a shawl about her shoulders and hurries out the kitchen door, slamming the door behind her. She meets Temple and Benny while crossing the lawn. They are unsteady on their feet as they approach her. "It's about time you two showed up!" she snarls.

Benny points toward the kitchen. "Anything to eat in there, Ma?" he slurs.

"Cold chicken in the larder," she snaps. "Your grandfather has been asking for you all night. Go say 'good-night' to him before he falls asleep again. Go!" Sally commands and continues on her way.

CHAPTER FORTY-SEVEN

The Late Hour

The clock on the landing two flights below Franklin's bedroom begins to strike eleven. He is pleased that his daughter has left him in peace. He reaches for the teacup on the night table next to his bed and takes a sip of Madeira. He rests his eyes again. A few moments later, he grips his abdomen, his face twisted in pain. He moans, a deep animal sound.

The pain subsides. He hears a woman's voice singing softly. He opens his eyes again and sees Madame Brillon seated in a chair near his bed. She studies an object she holds in her hand.

"Hélène?" he whispers.

"*Oui, c'est moi, cher Papa.*"

"Is it time?" he asks.

"*Oui,* dear Ben, this is the hour."

He manages to raise himself up onto his elbow. "What do you hold in your hand?"

She holds up the cameo portrait of Mrs. Stevenson. "Who is this lady?" she inquires.

"Margaret, my friend in England."

"She is very pretty," Madame Brillon concedes.

"She is gone now."

"Who loved you more?"

"You did, Hélène, you did," he replies.

"Then we shall dance. Come." She extends her hand. Franklin takes her hand and rises from the bed. She leads him into the room's shadows, where they enter an elegant salon. It is the ballroom of the Brillon mansion at Passy, with its gleaming parquet floors, mirrored walls, and chandeliers overhead aglow with candlelight. French doors are open to the terrace, silk curtains blow in and out on a gentle breeze. Franklin smells jasmine and chamomile.

An orchestra plays, filling the salon with a romantic sound. Franklin and Madame Brillon dance. They both appear younger. He is dapper in evening wear. She is more beautiful than ever, wearing a billowing white silk gown and glittering jewels.

The respite from the storm is brief and rain pelts down as Sally crosses the yard toward the stables. She meets Polly returning from her walk with Jake. They face each other in the muddy drive, pulling their shawls closed around themselves. Their hair soon becomes matted, raindrops run down their foreheads.

Sally's grim expression is illuminated by a yard lamp in the alleyway between outbuildings. She stands with her legs spread apart. "That was my property you just kissed 'good-bye'!" she screams, wiping water out of her eyes with her hand.

Polly attempts to step around her. "No man is another man's property," she replies calmly.

Sally blocks her way. "He won't get far. Ten miles and he'll turn back."

"I wouldn't be so sure."

Sally digs in her heels. "Papa has lost his fekkin' mind. He wants me to get rid of Aggie and Jake and everybody else. I won't do it."

"It is your father's dying wish, Sal," Polly reasons. She begins to walk on, but Sally grabs her arm. "What am I supposed to do for help? Tell me that! I've got a useless, philandering drunk for a husband!"

"*I* would like to stay and help you," Polly offers.

"Help me? You and your mother have been nothing but trouble for me all my life."

"My mother never meant you any harm," Polly argues.

An icy smile crosses Sally's face. "Maybe not, but she was still a whore!"

Polly slaps Sally across the face. "How dare you!" she screeches.

Sally brings a hand to her burning cheek. "You… bitch!" she yells, as she slaps Polly's face roundly with her free hand.

Polly grabs Sally's shoulders and gives her a push. Sally loses her balance and falls, landing flat on her back in the mud.

Sally takes a moment to recover her wind. She sits up and begins to sob. "Papa walked you down the aisle and gave you away at your wedding, but he couldn't be bothered to come to mine!" she wails.

Polly places her hands on her hips. "All right, then! He loved my mother! He loved *your* mother! He loved Hélène Brillon. He may have loved *William's mother*! Your father loved a lot of women. But… he loved *you* most of all."

"You're a liar!"

"You have always been his favorite, Sal."

Sally wipes her nose with her wet shawl. "That's not true."

"'Tis." Polly looks at the pitiful, drenched woman sitting in the mud and reaches out to her. "Come. Get up. I'll make us some hot coffee." Sally regards Polly's hand for a long moment before taking it in hers. Polly pulls her up to a standing position. Without another word, the two women collect themselves as best they can, turn, and walk toward the house.

Temple and Benny stand next to the kitchen table, gnawing on pieces of cold chicken.

Benny tosses his chicken bone into a sieve in the sink. "Let's go say *'hallo'* to Grandpapa."

Temple takes another bite and pitches the last of his chicken into the sieve.

Benny goes to the back stairwell. "C'mon! I'll race you up!"

Temple accepts the challenge, and they race each other up the three flights of stairs in the dark, their boots pounding on the wooden treads. They try to block each other's progress on the way up, and are laughing when they reach the hallway outside Franklin's room.

"Hush, now," Temple cautions. "He may be sleeping." He taps lightly on the door frame and opens the door. They walk on tip-toes into the room.

They find Franklin lying on his bed. His eyes are open, his breathing is labored.

Benny pulls a stool up to the bed. He sits down and takes Franklin's hand in his.

DEAR BEN

A window near the bed rattles in the wind. Rain outside runs in rivulets down the panes of glass. Temple goes to the window and closes it tightly.

"Grandfather? Can you hear me?" Benny asks in a whisper.

After a moment, Franklin's breathing stops. Benny gasps.

Temple lays his head on Franklin's chest, then stands and shakes his head. "He's gone, Benny. You had best go get your mother." Benny's eyes fill with tears. He rises and walks toward the door.

"Wait," Temple says. "Let's do what he would want us to do."

"What?" Benny asks through his tears.

"Close his eyes."

Benny nods. They close Franklin's eyes. Benny kisses the old man's parchment-like forehead and turns down the lamp on the table next to the bed.

"I'll stay here with Grandfather," Temple offers.

Benny walks out of the room. Temple sits in the chair next to the bed, with his hands folded in his lap. He looks at Franklin's lifeless figure, bathed in the flickering light of the candles on the dresser.

He cocks an ear and looks into the shadows at the far end of the room. He listens.

"Is someone there?" he says out loud. He doesn't move a muscle. "Bobby, is that you?"

He thinks to himself, *"The way this big house creaks in the wind, a person can hear voices… things that aren't there, sometimes."* He snuffs out the candles.

Downstairs, in the street, a few hearty souls remain huddled under umbrellas in the wind and rain.

Melba Perkins has rejoined the group after fixing a late supper for her husband. "I put Ephraim to bed," she tells the others. Alfred Singer, a merchant who lives above his shop on Chestnut Street, retrieves a silver flask from his pocket and hands it to Melba. She takes a drink. "Very kind, Alfred," she says and passes the flask to the neighbor standing next to her. Melba places her hands in her coat pockets and looks up at the third floor of the house. She sees the light go out in Franklin's bedroom. It is suddenly dark. "Oh dear," she says, pointing to his windows.

Mr. Singer places his hand on Melba's shoulder. "He must have left us…"

She pats his hand. "I didn't want to read about it in the newspaper," Melba says. She turns away and walks toward home.

Eastern Pennsylvania   April 1790

Bobby makes camp several yards away from the road heading east out of Philadelphia, as he has for the past few nights. The rain has stopped, but he is exhausted and the muddy, rutted trail is not easy to navigate in the dark. He dismounts and leads his horse into a thicket of aspen trees. He follows the sound of water to a running brook and finds a clearing next to it. He tethers Major to a tree, goes to the brook, fills his hat with water, and offers it to the horse. He spreads a blanket on the ground, then feeds Major from a saddlebag. He settles down on the blanket with a crust of bread and a piece of dried sausage. He takes a drink of whiskey from a flask in his coat pocket, pulls the blanket around himself, lies back and observes the stars peeking through the trees overhead. Bobby jolts upright when he hears two men on horseback on the road nearby. They speak loudly to one another as they ride. He picks up his rifle and sits motionless. The riders' voices fade as they pass by. He puts down the rifle, lies back again and before long, sleeps.

First light breaks. Bobby lies on the ground, wrapped in his blanket. His flask is at his side. Major is grazing on tall grass near the brook. A twig snaps. Bobby is awakened by the sound and raises his head. He looks in the direction of the noise and sees an Indian scout, perhaps sixteen years old, naked but for a loincloth and squatting on his haunches at the edge of the clearing. The young brave snaps another twig between his fingers and waits for Bobby's reaction. Startled, Bobby sits up and reaches for his rifle. It is gone. The Indian has it. He picks up the rifle and aims it at Bobby. Bobby shrinks in terror and holds his hands up in the air. The young brave grins, turns and sprints into the woods, taking the rifle with him.

PHILADELPHIA   1790

Few have stayed home on this cool, gray April morning. They line the streets to observe the procession or walk with two thousand other citizens of the town behind a horse-drawn hearse, which carries Franklin's body to the cemetery. The simple wooden casket inside the hearse is covered with garden flowers. The parade is nearly silent, but for the steady march of mourners, the clatter of the wheels of the hearse, and the 'clip-clop' of the horses' hooves on the cobbled pavement. The crowd is solemn, quiet, all are dressed in black. Couples hold hands as they walk. Many women weep, dabbing their eyes with kerchiefs, Melba Perkins among them.

A dozen clergymen of all faiths lead the procession, locked arm-in-arm as they walk. Seven of the clergy are Protestants of various sects; two are Roman Catholic priests. A Rabbi and a Muslim Mullah have joined them.

The Bache family walks behind the clergymen. Richard, Sally, Benny and Eliza are first, Billy and Louis, the youngest, follow. Polly and her two children, Tom and Eliza Hewson, walk just behind them. Aggie and Jake walk a few paces behind the Hewsons, looking dignified, but weary, in their mourning attire. All the family wear somber expressions on their faces, their eyes are puffy and red-rimmed.

A lone church bell tolls a few mournful notes repeatedly in the distance, as it has all morning.

CHAPTER FORTY-EIGHT

The Solicitor

Ohio, Northwest Territory

A small farmhouse is set well back from the unpaved road that fronts it. A narrow, washboard drive winds from the road through a grassy field to the two-story house, which appears quite new, but unfinished and in need of a coat of paint. Lights glow in the kitchen and in an upstairs window. A grassy area behind the house leads to a modest barn. An ample kitchen garden snuggles up to the barn. Beyond it, twenty acres of plowed fields of maize and wheat are bordered by a stand of oak and pine. A pair of wolves, hunting for a kill, howl in the dark depths of the forest.

Inside the house, Ellen Carter carries an oil lamp as she climbs a narrow, wooden stairway. Bobby follows close behind, with his pack over his shoulder. A brown and white hound dog wags his tail enthusiastically as he follows them.

"How'd you find your way to us, Bobby?" Ellen inquires as she reaches the landing at the top of the stairs.

"Dr. Ben taught me about the North Star. I followed the stars."

She shows Bobby into a tiny bedroom. A single bed, a small dresser with a wash basin atop it, and a narrow wardrobe cabinet more than fill the space. The dog crowds his way into the room, his tail still wagging and his tongue hanging out. Ellen sets the lamp on the dresser and fusses with a sheet nailed up on the window, which suffices for curtains. "I hope this will do for you, Bobby," she says apologetically. "It's kind of cramped." Bobby throws his brown leather pack on the bed. "This will do just fine. It's nicer than I had at home."

"Home?"

"At the Franklin home."

"Oh." She wipes dust off the dresser with the hem of her apron, which is nearly as long as the printed house dress she wears under it. "So much to do around the farm, I don't get much time for makin' curtains and such."

"It's fine, Ellen," Bobby assures her. "Very comfortable."

"Well, make yourself at home." She slaps her thigh. "Come on, Sparky. Let's leave the man in peace," she commands the dog. Ellen leaves the room with the dog following on the heels of her boots. "Supper's on the table in a half-hour," she calls back as she descends the stairs.

Later that night, Bobby and his cousin, Jonas, are seated at the kitchen table after the evening meal. An open bottle of whiskey sits on the table between them and they each have a drink in hand. The seventeen-year-old Carter son, James, sits across the table, studying a schoolbook. Sparky sits on the floor next to James, waiting for a scrap of food to fall.

Rachel, thirteen years of age, helps her mother to clear the table and wash the dishes in a tin basin in the wooden sink. Ellen may not have time for sewing, but the house is clean and well-ordered, Bobby considers. Everything is in its place, as in Aggie's kitchen back home.

Bobby takes a sip of his drink. "I feel real bad 'bout losin' my rifle that way. Dr. Franklin give it to me. It was a fine piece."

Jonas shakes his head. "You are a very lucky man you didn't lose your life."

James looks up from his book and chuckles. "Or your horse!"

"How'd that Indian sneak up on me like that?"

"You wouldn't hear an army of Chippewa sneak up on you," Jonas explains in his gentle, low voice. "We stay out of the woods after dark in this country."

Ellen sets a plate of cookies on the table. Bobby thinks her a handsome woman, graceful in her movements, almost feline. But there is a hard edge to her, something simmering just under the surface. James helps himself to a cookie and gives a piece of it to the dog.

Ellen returns to the sink cabinet and leans against it, facing Bobby with her arms folded. "I still say it's just like a white man to pitch you out in the middle of the night, and say he's doin' you a favor!" she declares in a brittle tone.

Bobby is taken aback by her comment. "Wasn't like that, Ellen. Dr. Ben afraid Mrs. Bache won't let me go after he gone. He *did* pass away later that night. I hear'd about it when I get near Johnstown." Bobby reaches for the whiskey bottle and pours himself another glass. He offers the bottle to Jonas, who shakes his head, 'no'.

Bobby glances at his cousin's muscular torso, on display through his unbuttoned shirt. Jonas's strong arms are chiseled by years of strenuous farm work. "I been a house man all my life, but I try my best to help you around here," Bobby offers. "You gonna have to teach me."

Jonas smiles and reaches for a cookie. "I'm glad you came, Cousin. I can use your help. I still got plenty of land to clear. We'll get those pretty hands a' yours roughed up soon enough. I hope you like gettin' up early!" Bobby, curious, leans his elbows on the table and rests his head in his hands. "How'd you get your hands on a piece o' land like this?" he inquires.

"Put the kettle on, Rachel," Jonas calls to his daughter. He turns to Bobby. "Old Mr. Lamb bought a hundred acres from the Congress when the English handed over the Territory after the Treaty of Paris in 1783. When he died, Mrs. Lamb didn't want it, and passed it on to me and Ellen. She set us free at the same time."

Bobby sits up in his chair. "Dr. Franklin tol' me he signed that Treaty of Paris."

Rachel, a dish towel draped over her shoulder, places a teacup before her father and joins them at the table. "Was Dr. Franklin really the most famous man in the whole world, Uncle Bobby?"

"I reckon so, Rachel," Bobby replies. "But fame don't do you no good when you gone." He turns to Jonas. "Is it safe for black folk around here?" he asks.

Ellen places a stack of plates in a cupboard. "It ain't safe for black folk anywhere," she cries over her shoulder.

Jonas takes a small pipe from his pocket and looks for his tobacco pouch. "Slavery is prohibited in the Territory, but a clause in the charter allows slave-owners in other states to come and seize fugitives an' haul 'em back to the plantations."

James looks up from his schoolbook again. "Nobody bothers us here, Uncle Bobby."

"Not yet," Ellen snaps.

A long summer day has cooled as evening falls, but the air is still heavy and humid. Bobby and Rachel are seated in rustic chairs on the covered porch after supper. They listen to the sound of crickets chirping in the fields and an owl 'hooting' in the rafters of the barn. A breeze has picked up, providing relief from the stuffy air in the house. Sparky meanders out the open kitchen door to join them and curls up at Rachel's feet.

Bobby is happy to sit and rest after a day in the fields. His cotton shirt is stained with rings of perspiration. Rachel's summer frock looks cool and fresh in contrast to his mud-caked overalls.

A glass of whiskey rests on the floorboards next to Bobby's feet. He struggles to read a letter he holds in his hands by the light of an oil lamp resting on a small table between them.

Rachel swats a mosquito that has landed on her neck. "Who is that letter from, Uncle Bobby?" she inquires.

"From Miss Polly. You know, the English lady I tol' you about. I sent her this address, like I promised."

Rachel tugs her skirt down over her knees as defense against the mosquitoes. "Is Miss Polly still with the Baches?"

"Seems so. Her writin' is so fancy, I'm havin' trouble readin' it. Care to help me?"

Rachel takes the letter from Bobby and begins to read. "Miss Polly is telling you about Dr. Franklin's funeral. *It was a sight to behold. Philadelphia has never seen anything like it. Thousands of people came to say 'farewell' to the Great Man.*"

Bobby nods his head. "I ain't surprised," he murmurs.

Rachel continues reading from the letter. "*'A few days later,'* she says, *'I joined the family in the solicitor's office for the reading of Papa's will.'*"

"Ain't it nice they include Miss Polly?" Bobby comments and takes a drink of his whiskey.

Philadelphia 1790

A sign over the door of the office on Chestnut Street reads: *'Edward Hessel, Esquire. Attorney-at-law.'*

Inside the office, Richard Bache, Sally, Benny, Temple and Polly are seated at a long oak table. All are dressed in Sunday attire as they listen to Mr. Hessel speak from his seat at the head of the table. Sally notices that Hessel's head seems to rest on the stiff collar of his shirt without the benefit of a neck. She rearranges the folds of her skirt as he drones on about their responsibilities as heirs of his long-time client, Dr. Franklin. Sally's face suggests that she would tell the lawyer to speed up, if she dared.

Mr. Hessel turns pages, reading from a document spread on the table before him. At length, he gets to an item of interest: "*'To my beloved daughter, Sarah, known as Sally, I hereby bequeath my mansion house and other properties on Market Street in Philadelphia, known as Franklin Court, including all outbuildings, save that building which houses the print shop of my grandson, Benjamin Bache, known as Benny, which I hereby bequeath to him.'*"

Sally breathes a sigh of relief. She and Richard hold hands and smile at each other. Benny, too, looks pleased.

Hessel continues reading. "There is one caveat, however, written into the bequest, which states: *'Providing my man, Bobby, is forever freed of servitude.'*" Mr. Hessel looks toward the Baches. "Has this man been granted his freedom? I trust he is a slave?"

"Oh, he's gone, all right," Sally says tartly, glaring at Polly.

"Very good," Hessel says. "Let us continue. *'I leave also to my daughter, Sarah, the diamond brooch given to me by King Louis XVI of France, provided she promises to never sell or dismantle it for purposes of personal decoration.'*"

Sally looks smug. "I have that piece locked up in a safe place."

"Good, good," Hessel says. "*'To my grandson, Temple Franklin, I leave my rental properties in Philadelphia, listed herein, as well as my personal papers, my memoir, my silver and gold, and any cash monies on hand at the time of my death.'*"

Temple and Benny smile at one another and shake hands.

Hessel proceeds to read from the will: "*'To Polly Stevenson Hewson, I bequeath the silver and crystal inkwell set which rests on my desk in my library, as a memento of our many long years of friendship.'*"

Sally lets out a cackle, then covers her mouth with her hands. Polly appears unmoved, her expression stoic. She looks down at her hands folded in her lap.

Hessel goes on: "*'To my son, William Franklin, I leave my claim to lands in Nova Scotia, granted to me in 1766 by the King of England.'*"

Richard turns to his wife. "Those claims are worthless today," he remarks candidly.

Sally smiles wickedly. "Looks like Papa put you and my brother in the same boat, eh, Polly?"

Polly rises from her chair, stands proudly, and smiles at the attorney. "Thank you, Mr. Hessel," she says, and leaves the office.

OHIO

Rachel lowers the letter, folds it, and hands it back to Bobby. "Why would he do such a nasty thing to Polly, Uncle Bobby?"

Bobby takes another sip of his drink. "Dr. Ben gave her somethin' he couldn't give to Miss Sally."

"What? The inkwell?"

"Think about it, child."

"He loved Miss Polly?"

"That's it. He gave her his love."

PHILADELPHIA

Sally is short of breath as she reaches the top of the stairway leading to a shop on the second floor of a building on Mills Street. A sign over to the door reads: '*Boyce and Goldman, Estate Jewelers.*' She rings a bell hanging next to the door, and a minute or two later, a 'peep' door opens at eye level. A man's icy blue eyes look out at her. The sturdy shop door is unlatched, swings open, and is quickly closed behind her and latched again after she enters. The blue eyes belong to Mr. Boyce, a tall man with thinning blonde hair and an agreeable demeanor. "I have been expecting you, Mrs. Bache," he says, and leads Sally to a stool at a work table. "What have you brought us?" he inquires.

Sally takes a small velvet bag, closed with a silk draw cord, from the pocket of her coat. She carefully removes the Louis XVI brooch from it.

Boyce's eyes widen. He lays the brooch on a cloth, takes an ocular glass from a drawer in the table, brings it to his eye, and examines the cameo closely. "The stones are of very high caliber…finest quality," he says eagerly. "Flawless, I would say."

"Of course they are. Consider the source, Mr. Boyce. Now… will they buy me and my husband passage to Europe?"

"I should think to Europe and back, several times," Boyce replies. "This is, however, a treasure of historical significance. It merits a place in a museum, Mrs. Bache, to be kept for posterity." He gingerly hands the brooch back to Sally.

She slides the precious cameo back into the velvet bag. "I don't much care to keep pictures around of people I never met. What can you give me for it?"

Boyce hesitates a moment. "Allow me to consult with Mr. Goldman. He is setting a stone in the back room. May I take the brooch to him for a look?"

Sally passes the velvet bag across the table to Mr. Boyce. "I suppose so, but don't forget where it came from."

He offers to help her off with her cloak. "Make yourself comfortable, Mrs. Bache," he says. He picks up the velvet bag and goes to the back of the shop.

Sally unties her bonnet and lays it on the work table. She hopes Goldman will make her a generous offer before she changes her mind.

OHIO   1792

Bobby likes to sit at the kitchen table in the afternoon, looking out the window, watching late summer dissolve into autumn. Hay has been cut and stored in the barn, crops harvested, and fields plowed during long days of back-breaking work. Soon, dry and twisted remains of cornstalks will be dusted with snow, then buried in it. Winter will set in… it will pass slowly.

Rachel and James have their studies to occupy their time. Ellen has housework, as well as sewing, mending and knitting to keep her busy. She will spend countless hours pickling the bounty of her garden in crocks in the larder. She will store root vegetables in bins in the cellar, and she will make preserves of fruit and honey.

Even on the coldest days, Bobby tries to be up and out of the house at dawn. After a visit to the outhouse, he trudges through the snow to the barn to milk the two Guernsey cows, Ida and Martha. The task is made easier by a nip of spirits to warm him in the cold, drafty barn. He keeps a bottle hidden in Martha's stall for that purpose. On milder days, Jonas can be found in his workshop in the barn, repairing plows and sharpening knives.

Some evenings, when Rachel isn't studying or helping her mother, she reads to her uncle from one of her history books, which he relishes. Occasionally, Bobby and Jonas play cards, or there are parlor games. Every night, Bobby has a few drinks. Candles are snuffed out by nine o'clock.

Spring arrives unexpectedly. The rains come, snow melts and recedes, exposing patches of bright green grass in the backyard. Days grow longer, fields are plowed and planted again. The work is hard, but Bobby knows he is lucky to have landed on his feet with this family. The weather is warm and pleasant by early June, then hot and humid in July and August. Bobby enjoys a drink in the evenings on the covered porch. The mosquitoes are a nuisance, but he likes to sit up at night, by himself, after Rachel has gone to bed.

He thinks about his life in Philadelphia. Bobby misses the big house on Market Street, the excitement of famous and powerful men coming to call. He misses Dr. Franklin, more than he can say.

On a morning in mid-summer, Bobby lies on his bed, sprawled face down on top of the blankets. A rooster crows, first light breaks through the bedsheet covering his window. He reaches for his pocket watch on a side table, looks at the time, then jumps up from the bed, goes to the basin on the dresser and splashes water on his face. He doesn't want to be late, again. He dresses quickly, slips a small flask into his back pocket and hurries down the stairs.

Bobby treads along a grassy path between plowed fields to the edge of the wood, where he and Jonas have been digging up tree stumps for the past few days. Jonas has harnessed the mule and tied him with ropes to a large stump.

"Get over here and start digging, cousin," Jonas calls as Bobby approaches.

Bobby picks up a shovel and starts digging under the stump, with great effort.

Jonas yells at the mule, pleading with him to move forward. "'At's it, Elmer! Pull! Move, move! Get-a-goin' now!" The tree stump begins to slide out of the ground. "Good work, Elmer!" Jonas looks at Bobby. "You keep digging, Cousin. We'll get the bastard out yet!"

By the time the sun is high overhead, men and mule have extracted three massive stumps from the earth. Both men's shirts are soaked with perspiration.

Ellen approaches along the path with a basket on her arm. She spreads a cloth on a tree stump and produces refreshments from the basket. She arranges sandwiches and a jar of lemonade on the cloth. "Jonas! High time you give that poor beast a rest," she shouts.

Bobby leans on his shovel. "What about me?" he inquires.

"That's who I'm talkin' about!" she grins.

Port of Philadelphia   1792

A three-masted schooner in the harbor makes ready to set sail. Deckhands shout from one end of the ship to the other, manning the ropes as they prepare to raise the jib and foresail. Longshoremen finish loading the cargo of goods and supplies into the hold, while others help porters carry the last of the passengers' trunks and baggage aboard the ship. The purser, a middle-aged gentleman in a crisp white uniform, greets Sally and Richard Bache at the gangplank. Richard carries a valise, Sally a hat box. The smell of the sea has already made Sally feel queasy.

"I had the honor, Mrs. Bache," the purser tells Sally proudly, "of serving your illustrious father on his last crossing from Southampton."

"Did you?" Sally says, trying to watch her step on the plank.

"Yes. I have arranged the very same cabin for you. 'Tis our finest and most spacious accommodation."

"That is very kind of you sir," Richard chimes in.

The purser takes Sally's hatbox from her. "Dr. Franklin had planned to sail with a Mrs. Hewson, but she was unable to join him. He was terribly disappointed."

A dark look crosses Sally's face.

"My wife fears the sea, a trait inherited from her mother," Richard reveals. "She wouldn't be taking this voyage but for an abiding desire to see her brother in London."

"Then, I shall ask the captain to order up the smoothest possible crossing for you, Mr. Bache," the purser offers cheerily.

AT SEA

As the purser promised, the voyage has been tranquil for the past fortnight, and Sally's mood has lightened. The Baches find themselves seated in the dining saloon on a Saturday evening with six other passengers assigned to their round, oak table. Among the four men at the table are a mustachioed Southern gentleman, who introduced himself earlier as Gabriel Pierce, and a Reverend Gage, who wears the collar of a cleric and a perpetually stern expression on his face. A large, bowed window near their table affords a view of a breathtaking sunset.

"Look there, everybody," Sally gushes, pointing to the window with her fork. "The sea is on fire... all ablaze as far as you can see. Red, purple, orange..."

Her fellow diners look out the window and nod their heads, murmuring in agreement at the remarkable beauty of the sunset. A din of conversation and laugher comes from passengers seated at tables nearby. Four stewards, young men wearing long white aprons, whirl about the tables gracefully, serving the diners.

Sally takes a sip of claret. "I must say that I am pleased and surprised by the victuals on board. They are really quite good."

The lady across the table from her raises her wine glass. "We're only two weeks out, my dear. It's downhill from here on."

A woman on Sally's left leans close to her. "I have meant to say that you must be proud of your legacy, Mrs. Bache. Your father was a great man."

Sally turns to her neighbor. "Every man has his foibles, ye can be sure."

Richard directs a question to the Southerner. "Do you have business in England, Mr. Pierce?"

Pierce leans back in his chair as a steward serves his supper. "I am a grower of rice and cotton near Beaufort in South Carolina, and I have partners in London. I am largely retired now… my sons have taken over the business. I can't help but notice you speak with an English accent yourself, Mr. Bache."

"I was born and raised in that country," Richard replies.

Pierce smooths back his silver forelock and turns to Sally. "I held your father in great esteem, Mrs. Bache, until he presented his Abolition Petition to the Congress. It would have eviscerated our plantation way of life," he says in a velvety voice.

"You are an advocate of the present system of slavery, Mr. Pierce?" questions a rosy-cheeked, portly man across the table from Pierce.

"I am, sir. I own two hundred slaves," Pierce replies, and smiles warmly. "Please, call me 'Gabe'."

"How many slaves did you lose to General Cornwallis during the war, *Gabe*?" inquires a young man seated around the table from Pierce, in a taunting tone of voice.

"None, sir," Pierce tells him. "I keep dogs that will tear apart a man on the run. It sets an example for others." He raises his glass to the young man. "To your good health," he drawls.

Another steward appears with a carafe of claret and refills wine glasses.

A lady to Sally's left passes the breadbasket to her. "I think it is immoral to keep people against their will," she declares.

Reverend Gage pulls himself up in his chair. "Ye can be sure, Madam, there will be a reckoning on the Last Day for those who have kept men in bondage," he warns.

The portly man signals the wine steward to fill his glass. "The Bible says: *'Thou shalt not covet thy neighbor's manservant'*, this in reference to a man's slave, not his paid retainer. I sympathize with Gabe's predicament. No *white* man would pick cotton or plant rice. The work is too hard."

Pierce picks up his knife and fork. "You are quite right, sir." He turns to face the preacher. "And, Padre, as I do not believe in an afterlife, I will not be in attendance for your *'reckoning'*. If this boat goes down, that will be the end of us," he says and cuts into his roast meat.

Sally's face goes pale. She gasps and reaches for her wine glass.

Richard gently pats the back of Sally's hand. "Dr. Franklin predicted a day when all slaves would be emancipated by dictate of the Congress, Mr. Pierce." Pierce furrows his bushy, silver brows. "The South will have its way on the question, Mr. Bache, or it will go its *own* way, I can assure you."

Later that night, the ship sails into a tempest and rough seas.

Ohio

Bobby and Rachel are seated on the covered porch on a very warm summer evening. It is still daylight. Bobby holds a glass of whiskey in one hand and fans himself with a paper fan with the other. Sparky lies on his back between them, with his paws in the air, cooling himself.

Rachel sips from a glass of lemonade as she reads from the Bible: "*'The man who walks in the dark knows not where he is going. Put your trust in the Light whilst you have it, so that you may become the Sons of Light.'*"

"My mama loved that part," Bobby says.

"What does it mean?" Rachel asks.

"It mean always do right, honey, and you will see Jesus when Judgement Day come," Bobby explains.

They both look up at the sound of horses in the drive from the road to the house. Rachel and Bobby go quiet as they watch four white men ride into the yard. The men carry rifles and have knives in scabbards at their waists. They are young men. Their hair is straggly and worn long. Sparky rolls over, growls, then barks at the intruders. Rachel shushes the dog and closes her Bible. One of the riders dismounts and walks toward them. He is unshaven and his clothing looks dirty and unkempt, as though he has been on the road for several days.

Rachel leans close to Bobby as the man approaches. "I've seen him before," she whispers.

The man stands a few feet from the porch. "Carter at home?" he inquires in a gravelly voice.

"I believe so, sir," Bobby replies.

"You believe, or you know?" the man snarls. "I'd like to talk to him."

"Go get your papa," Bobby says to Rachel. "Take Sparky inside."

Rachel rises from her chair and leads the dog into the house.

"You a runaway, boy?" the man inquires.

"No, sir, I's a free man."

"You can prove it?"

"Yes sir," Bobby replies nervously, not knowing how.

Jonas steps out of the kitchen and onto the porch, pulling up the braces on his breeches. The other three riders dismount and walk toward the house. They hold their rifles at their sides.

"Evenin', Mr. Ellsworth. What can I do for you?" Jonas inquires, keeping calm.

Ellen looks out the kitchen window, then jerks the curtains closed.

"We heard you had a colored man helpin' out here. We ain't gonna have no depot for runaways in these parts," Ellsworth snorts.

"Bobby ain't a runaway. He's my cousin," Jonas explains. "He was Ben Franklin's man. Franklin set him free." Jonas steps down off the porch.

"I hear'd 'Old Lightnin' Rod' turned Negre lover at the end!" one of the other riders calls out.

Ellsworth takes a step closer to Jonas. "If the Carolina Militia come out here and rounds up fugitives, they'll burn us out while they's at it. We ain't gonna have that."

Jonas smells alcohol on Ellsworth's breath. "No, sir, we don't want that. No, sir."

"You own this land, Carter?"

"Yes, sir, I have title, free and clear," Jonas says firmly.

"Well, we aim to keep an eye on you." Ellsworth takes another step toward Jonas. "You keep that black nose a' yours clean, eh Carter?"

Jonas fumes, but politely replies, "Yes, sir."

Ellsworth spits on the ground and saunters back to his horse. "You mind what I say, you hear?" he yells to Jonas over his shoulder.

"I hear you, sir."

Ellsworth mounts his horse. "C'mon, boys," he says to the others.

Bobby and Jonas watch as the four white men ride off in a cloud of dust.

DEAR BEN

Bobby takes a drink of whiskey with a shaking hand.

Jonas heaves a sigh. "Don't know about Ellsworth, but I'd wager them other demons are bounty hunters. They'll be back."

"Maybe I should go…"

"Over my dead black body."

CHAPTER FORTY-NINE

A Portrait

LONDON

Lights glow in the tall windows of a red-brick Georgian residence on a street of stately homes, a short distance from the Thames. Trees in front of the three-story Franklin house are beginning to turn to color; leaves float down and flutter past the front door, which is painted white to a high gloss.

Inside, dinner is underway in the sedate dining room. A crystal chandelier and candles flickering in silver candelabra shimmer in the room's walnut paneling. Sparkling crystal and Chinese porcelains grace the table atop crisp, white linens. Wine flows freely and conversation is spirited; it is a long overdue reunion with family from America.

William Franklin, sixty-four, sits in a high-backed chair at the head of the table. His hair is mostly silver now, still worn pulled back into a ponytail and caught with a ribbon. He looks distinguished in a quilted silk frockcoat, with stand-up collar and turned-back cuffs lined in black velvet. He wears monogramed pumps on his feet.

His wife, Mary, sits at the bottom of the table. She is a handsome woman, more than a decade William's junior. Her features are sharp, her skin tends toward olive, her eyes are dark and deep-set. Mary's younger sister, Anne, is seated next to Mary. She is a brunette like her older sister, but her features are softer, her skin pale and lightly freckled on her high cheek bones.

The Baches are seated mid-table, opposite one another. Sally has purchased a new gown from a London dressmaker for the evening; she is almost pretty in pale blue silk trimmed with white ruffles at the neck. She has powdered her cheeks and added a touch of color to her lips. Her husband, Richard, wears his best black suit for the occasion. Two footmen wait on the table, serving rib-roast, late summer vegetables and trimmings. Sally has never enjoyed such opulence in a private home. Richard wonders how William can afford it.

The silk brocade of Mary's dress rustles as she raises her wine glass in Sally's direction. "It is truly wonderful that you came all this way to see us," she says. "Did you enjoy the crossing?"

"Not one minute of it," Sally replies curtly. "I see why Papa had boils on his butt and other ailments."

Anne looks across the table at Sally. "Since you have not been before, I would be pleased to show you the sights of London!" she offers brightly.

"By 'sights', my dear, Anne means the dress shops and hat-makers," Mary clarifies.

The footmen begin to clear the diners' plates. Not quite finished, Sally grips her plate with two hands. "I've done enough shopping already. When can we meet the King and Queen?"

Anne and Mary smile at each other painfully.

"That would not be possible, I am afraid. I have not had an invitation to the Palace since Father signed the Treaty of Paris," William explains.

A white-haired butler in tailcoat enters with a carafe of wine and moves around the table, refilling the glasses.

"That is a pity," Sally says with a sigh and takes a last bite of her roast meat.

"Nor has William received a pay packet from the Royals. Perhaps you can find room for my husband in your import business, Mr. Bache. We are using my inheritance at a fast pace."

Astonished by Mary's candor, Richard looks at her over his wine glass.

William scowls at his wife. After a moment, "I tell you what, let's ride to the spa at Bath. All the nobles visit Bath to take the waters. Heaven knows whom we might meet," he says, on a hopeful note.

"Sally longs to have her portrait painted whilst we are here," Richard confides.

William slaps his hand on the table. "Then you shall, my dear! And I know just the man to do it."

A maid wearing a frilly white apron and a white cap on her head enters from the kitchen. She carries plates of pudding and serves the Baches first. William pushes back from the table. "Richard, let's you and I go into my study for a cognac after supper. We can talk about how we will make right the shameful disgrace of my father's will. We can concoct a plan…"

Sally drops her cake-laden fork on her plate with a clatter. She wipes her mouth with her serviette. "Disgrace? What disgrace, Billy?"

"I know you will want to share your ill-gotten riches with me and Mary," William replies innocently.

Sally looks at him with disbelief in her eyes. "Ill-gotten?"

William reaches for his wine glass. "Father's properties should have come to me, his first-born son, as is the custom. Primogeniture, you know."

Sally's face turns red. "Share? Share? I am not giving you a goddam penny! I have no intention of paying you for the bad choices you made!" She empties her wine glass, stands and throws her napkin on the table. "I'm going to bed," she declares.

"Temple should at least give back William's farm in New Jersey," Mary says in a reasonable tone.

Richard drains his wine glass. "Temple sold the farm, Mary. Too late now."

"Are you coming, Richard?" Sally demands sharply. She pushes her chair out of her way and leaves the table, her voluminous silk skirt rustling as she goes.

Richard raises his upturned hands, smiles at his hostess, and rises from his chair. "If you will please excuse me…"

Later that evening, Sally and Richard lie in the four-poster bed in an upstairs guest room. Candles burn on tables on both sides of the bed. Sally studies the intricate design of the plasterwork on the ceiling high above her. Richard lies with a book open on his chest, his eyes are closed. Sally wears a flannel bonnet on her head.

"You awake?" she asks.

"No," Richard replies.

"I am sorry we came over here."

"I was sorry we came over here *before* we came over here. You know I have never gotten on well with your brother."

"He has gone raving mad. Share? The man must think I'm a simpleton!"

"Don't you see? He's running out of Mary's money. I will go to the ships' broker in the morning and arrange passage for us on an earlier packet boat," Richard volunteers.

"What about my portrait?" Sally pouts.

"In the meantime, I shall find us an artist with a quick brush… and you can keep your clothes on for the sitting. Let us hope the paint dries before we sail!" Richard teases.

Sally smiles, leans over and pecks Richard on the cheek.

Richard places his book on the night table. He reaches over and lifts the bonnet off Sally's head and tosses it on the floor. Her hair falls down onto her cheeks. Richard rolls on top of her, kissing her on the lips.

"Stop now," Sally protests in a whisper. "They might hear us!"

Richard blows out Sally's candle. "You may rest assured of it," he tells her.

Philadelphia   1792

Temple crosses a leafy, brick courtyard off Market Street and approaches a storefront. A sign leaning in the window reads: '*Aurora Newspaper printed here. B. Bache, prop.*' He pushes open the door and enters the noisy print shop, wrinkling his nose as he confronts the combined odors of ink, fresh newsprint, and the grease of the press machinery.

When his eyes adjust to the light, he sees Miriam, Benny's wife, talking with two pressmen, looking over a sheet of newsprint. She and Temple have exchanged few words since he stood up for Benny at their wedding the previous year. Temple surmises (correctly) she may consider him to be a bad influence on her husband.

"Hallo, Miriam," he calls to her.

Miriam turns to the handsome cousin and regards his attire. He is dressed in smart travelling clothes and carries a leather valise. She gives him a weak smile. "Going somewhere?" she inquires.

"Could be," he replies. "Is Benny in?"

"Benny! Temple's here!" she calls to the back of the shop.

Benny emerges a moment later, wiping grease from his hands on his printer's apron.

"'Morning, Temple," he says with a pleasant smile. "And why are we so honored?"

Miriam, a petite red-headed Irish beauty, stands with her arms folded awaiting Temple's reply.

"Let's step outside," Temple suggests.

"Ye can say what ye have to say right here," Miriam snaps.

Benny places his hand on Miriam's shoulder and gives her a gentle nudge. "Leave us for a minute," he urges.

She shakes her head and goes back to the pressmen.

Temple waits until she is out of earshot. "I do wish you would change your mind," he says earnestly. "Think of the fun we had together those last years in Paris."

"You had more fun than I did," Benny replies.

Temple turns on the charm. "I know you would *adore* London, old friend. It's the most fascinating city in the world. My father will introduce us to all the grandees!"

"I never knew your father, and I would just as soon keep it that way. I've got my work here… and the newspaper to get out. We have to keep a watch on President Washington, or he'll crown himself Emperor for life."

"Your parents will sail home from London soon," Temple reminds Benny.

"There's another good reason to stay here. Mother and Miriam scratch like two cats in a crate. I hope you will have a splendid time… and pray you hurry back." He offers Temple his hand. "I shall miss you."

"And I you, Cousin," Temple says, shaking Benny's hand.

Miriam watches the two men embrace and hug each other tightly. She wouldn't be unhappy if Temple were to take a *very* long journey.

DEAR BEN

Philadelphia   1793

Polly Hewson's new house is smaller than she is used to, but it suits her fine. The parlor is compact and simply furnished, with a settee on one wall and two comfortable chairs flanking it. A pair of brass candlesticks rests on a mahogany chest to light the room at night. A stack of unread books sits next to the candlesticks. A fireplace opposite the settee warms her on cool evenings. The beamed, whitewashed ceiling is only two feet above her head, but adds to a cozy feeling, or so she determined when she rented the place from Mr. McLeod, Ben Franklin's former neighbor on Market Street.

Her writing table is set in the bow window facing the street. One day soon, she plans to buy a bolt of fabric and run up some curtains for the window, with the help of her daughter, Eliza, who lives upstairs and is clever with needle and thread. Polly enjoys the view and often spends long hours at the table writing to friends and family back home in England. Today, she writes to her friend, Bobby, in Ohio.

She sips from her teacup and considers what she has written: 'Hello, Bobby. I thought you should have the news that the Baches have moved to a farm on the Delaware River. They sold all the properties on Market Street, so are well set for the rest of their lives. I have taken my own little house in town, as Sally and I never did see eye-to-eye.'

Ohio

On a warm evening two weeks later, Bobby and Rachel are seated in the bent willow chairs on the covered porch. Sparky is curled up next to Bobby's bare feet. Polly's letter lies open on Rachel's lap. Bobby strokes the dog's head and gazes over the fields to the tall trees beyond, which sway hypnotically in the wind. "I can't see Mr. Richard workin' no farm, no how, but I suppose he don't have to now," Bobby speculates.

"I suppose not," Rachel concurs. "Polly says her son, Tom, and Willie Bache have both gone to England to study medicine. Tommy wants to be a doctor, like his father was, she says."

"Ain't that somethin'? A doctor!"

Rachel picks up the letter and resumes reading: "*'Temple, ever the dandy, also left for London last year to live with his father and his new wife.'*"

Bobby shakes his head. "I sure am glad Dr. Ben ain't here to know 'bout it, is all I can say."

"Polly wonders if Mr. Temple will make something of himself over there. *'On a sad note,'* she writes, *'the King and Queen of France were executed last year by the Rebels.'* Oh, my…"

"I am glad Dr. Ben ain't here to know 'bout that one, too."

Rachel considers the news for a minute, then continues reading. "*'I am content here for the moment, but long to return home to England soon. I hope you love your new life on the farm. Your friend, Polly Hewson.'* It is so nice Miss Polly writes to you, Uncle Bobby."

Bobby stares at the empty glass in his hand. "Yeah. Keeps me close to the family that way."

Later that night, Bobby is about to climb into bed when he hears the 'whinny' of a horse on the road out front of the house. He snuffs out the candle burning next to his bed, pulls back the bedsheet covering his window, and looks out. He sees two white men on horseback, stopped on the road. One of the men, a young clean-shaven man, had been with Ellsworth when he dropped in on Jonas many months ago. Bobby doesn't recognize the other man, who is stocky, sports a full beard, and carries a lighted torch in his hand. They speak with one another as they look toward the house. Bobby's stomach knots up. After a few minutes, the bearded man throws the torch onto the road. It flares when it hits the dirt, sparks shoot up, then it flames out. The men laugh and ride on. Bobby feels his heart pounding in his chest. He closes the curtain, jumps into bed, and pulls the covers over himself.

He hears voices through the wall from Jonas and Ellen's room next door. Ellen sounds agitated. Jonas speaks to her in a calming voice. They, too, have seen the night visitors.

CHAPTER FIFTY

A Reunion

OXFORDSHIRE, ENGLAND　　　　　　　　　　1793

Temple and his stepsister, Anne, walk hand-in-hand along the edge of a crystal-clear stream. It is a soft spring day under a cloudless sky. Leaves on the trees above them and tall grass edging the stream are tender shades of green.

Anne leans her head on Temple's upper arm. "I am happy here in these lovely green fields, away from the city," she says, smiling sweetly.

"Then we shall stay!" Temple says brightly. "I could teach French at the University."

He stops, picks up a stone, and skims it across the water.

"How perfect!" Anne concludes. "We will live in a cozy cottage in the village with a bookshop across the road. I shall sit in a comfy chair next to a roaring fire and read volume after volume I have longed to read."

Temple holds both her hands in his. "Then I shall submit my credentials to the Provost of Magdalene College first thing in the morning!"

Anne looks into Temple's eyes. "There *will* be children, won't there?" she asks.

"Of course there will be children. At least a dozen!"

"I would miss my sister, Mary, though, if we were to move away. She has looked after me since my husband died so suddenly."

Temple caresses Anne's face with the backs of his fingertips. "It is time you get on with your new life with me." He pulls her close to him and kisses her on the lips.

LONDON 1793

Six months have passed since Anne's visit to Oxford with Temple. She enters the sitting room of the Franklin townhouse and lowers herself into an easy chair next to the fireplace. A crackling fire in the hearth is inviting and warming. Her expression is placid, her complexion rosy and radiant; she appears to be several months' pregnant. She opens a sewing box next to the chair and takes out her needles and yarn. A garment she has been knitting for several weeks is beginning to take shape.

She looks up when she hears her brother-in-law's raised voice coming from his study, where he and Temple retired for a chat a few minutes earlier. The door to the study slams shut with a loud 'bang'. Anne returns to her knitting.

Behind the closed door, William crosses the room to the fireplace. He has a brandy glass in his hand. He places his other hand on the mantel and gazes into the fire. "Of course, you will marry Anne!" he insists.

Temple is seated in a wing chair next to the fire, smoking a cigar. "I most certainly will not!" he retorts.

William looks at his son. "Do you not see the disgrace of it, Temple? It's too much of a comedy! You, the bastard son of a bastard son, now has an illegitimate child after having sired a son with a neighbor's wife! People will be sniggering behind your back. It's ruinous!"

"*A family tradition*', Grandfather would have said. I can't marry Anne. The woman clings to me like a dog in heat! I cannot bear it. She would be a burden to me as I make my way in business."

William refills his brandy glass from a decanter on a sideboard. "You *haven't* any business. If you were to marry Anne, my wife would help you get started. Think about that, son."

Temple looks up at his father. "I have wondered... is that why you married her? For her money?"

William sips his brandy. "I didn't marry her for her beauty," he concedes with a wry smile.

Ohio

Shortly after sunrise, Ellen raps on Bobby's bedroom door. She doesn't hear him stirring and peeks in the room. She finds Bobby fast asleep, sprawled on his bed, face down, still in his breeches from the day before.

"Bobby!" she calls to him, opening the door wider.

Bobby raises his head. His throat is parched and his tongue thick. He reaches for a glass of water on the table next to the bed.

"You're late again! Jonas is gonna be hoppin' mad."

"What time is it?" he croaks.

"Time to get on with your chores! I know the pay ain't much, but you gotta show up!" she says, sounding cross.

Bobby sits up on the edge of the bed. Ellen points to an empty whiskey bottle on the dresser. "Looks like you drank your dinner again. It's no good, Bobby… just plain no good." She turns to leave, shaking her head. She turns back and takes a letter from her apron pocket. "This come for you in the post yesterday… from Mrs. Bache." Ellen throws the letter onto the bed and pulls the door closed sharply behind her as she leaves.

Delaware River   1795

Sally, with a basket on her arm, wraps her shawl about her as she makes her way from the chicken coop to a low-slung farmhouse sitting on a rise above the river. She passes a rowboat tied to a rickety dock protruding into the water. She can't quite see the far end of the dock in an early morning fog, which has settled on the river. She crosses a patch of wild grasses growing between the house and the river and climbs the wooden steps to the porch, which runs the length of the house.

Sally goes to the kitchen and places the basket of eggs she carries on a sideboard. She hangs her shawl on a peg by the door and sits at the kitchen table. She picks up her pen and resumes writing a letter she had begun earlier that morning: *'We are settled in our new home on a farm in Delaware. Richard calls himself 'a gentleman farmer'.'*

Aggie enters the kitchen and makes Sally a cup of tea and sets it before her. Aggie may move more slowly than she did in Philadelphia, but her eyes are still bright, and her pretty face is unlined but for a few wrinkles about her eyes.

Sally nods her thanks and continues writing: *'We grow only a kitchen garden and have one cow and raise a few chickens.'*

She takes a sip of tea. *'Our journey to England was interesting. I had my picture painted, which cost a fortune, but I look like an old washer woman. I thought you would want to know that Polly Hewson died a few weeks ago. She was only fifty-six, about as much as we can expect from this life, I guess. Her daughter, Eliza, was with her.'*

Philadelphia   1795

Eliza Hewson, twenty-two years old, dressed in mourning attire, stands next to a freshly dug grave in a churchyard. A preacher, wearing a cassock and stole, stands next to her, reading a burial service from a Book of Prayer. They are alone, but for two sextons who let out ropes as they lower a wooden casket into the grave. Eliza wipes a cascade of tears from her cheeks with her kerchief.

"Ashes to ashes, dust to dust..." the cleric intones, concluding the brief service. He picks up a handful of dirt and throws it onto the casket. He bids Eliza do the same. She shakes her head, 'no', and backs away from the grave site.

Eliza walks unsteadily through teetering stone markers toward the entrance gate on Maple Street. A headstone catches her eye. It has been cleared of lichen and a crock of wildflowers rests on the grass at its base. She reads the inscription carved into the face of the stone. *'Aquila Rose, poet. B.1695, D.1723.'* "My, such a short life," she muses aloud.

Eliza continues on the gravel path toward the gate, thinking, *'And such a funny name. I wonder who he was?'*

Ohio

Bobby sits on the edge of his bed, reading Sally's letter. His mouth quivers as he reads: *'She was buried at the Community Church. None of her friends showed up for the ceremony, I am told. Strange, eh? Well, take care of yourself. By the way, Eliza plans to stay over here.'*

Bobby folds the letter and places it in the top drawer of his dresser. He takes a deep breath, looks in the mirror and regards the puffy eyes he sees looking back at him with disdain. He splashes water on his face from the basin atop his dresser.

Delaware River   1797

John Adams and his secretary, Lawrence, wait on the porch of the Bache farmhouse. Both wear business attire and the secretary carries a large leather valise. Lawrence, a thin and wiry young fellow, towers over his employer, in contrast to Adams's ample girth and modest stature. The manner in which Lawrence fusses with the kerchief spilling from the breast pocket of his frockcoat suggests a soft and effeminate nature, also a contrast to Adams's gruff persona. Adams looks at his pocket watch impatiently. Lawrence sighs and sits down on a willow armchair. He crosses his legs tightly and places the valise on his lap.

Inside the farmhouse, Richard is seated in an armchair in his study reading a recent copy of the '*Aurora*' newspaper.

Aggie finds Sally sitting in an easy chair in the parlor, darning a pair of stockings. "You have a visitor, Ma'am," she advises.

"Who is it?" Sally inquires, not looking up from her chore.

"Mr. Adams, Ma'am."

Sally looks up at Aggie. "John Adams?"

"Yes, Ma'am, that same gentleman Dr. Ben didn't care for so much."

"Aggie! Mr. Adams is the President of the United States now! Show him in, for Lord's sake!"

"Yes, Ma'am."

Aggie hurries to the front door and finds Adams pacing the floorboards of the porch. "Missus Bache say, '*Come in, for Lord's sake!*'" she calls to him.

Minutes later, after a cordial greeting, Sally, Richard, John Adams and Lawrence are gathered around the dining table. Lawrence takes newspapers from his valise, opens them, and spreads them on the table. Aggie moves around the table, serving tea and biscuits.

"I have come out of respect for your late father, Mrs. Bache, who would have been outraged by the vicious attacks your son has mounted against me in his newspaper," Adams advises.

Sally and Richard scan the articles in the papers as pointed out by Lawrence. Richard stands to get a better look at a particular piece.

"I had no idea, Mr. President, that our Benny was up to such misconduct. Our boy *does* have a sharp tongue at times, I will grant you that," Sally offers in an apologetic tone.

Richard indicates a column of print. "I am aware that Benny opposes your Federalist policies, Mr. President… building a bigger army, goading France into a war, and the like. He's a Jefferson man. I don't find that offensive."

Adams glares at Richard.

Lawrence points to a front page of the '*Aurora*'. "Look here, sir. Your son refers to the President as '*old, querulous, bald, blind, crippled, toothless Adams!*' That is not very agreeable, is it?" he huffs.

Aggie hides a smile as she leaves the room with her tea tray under her arm.

"Certainly not called for," Sally agrees. "I will have a talk with him."

"To disparage my high office so, is seditious!" Adams fumes.

Richard resumes his seat and takes a sip of tea. "Benny's grandfather taught him that a printer has a responsibility to present both sides of an argument to his readers," he says. "Dr. Franklin believed truth would out-match evil in the end. As an Anti-Federalist, it would appear my son feels a need to speak out. What is the harm in that?"

A sour expression crosses Adams's face. "I see that I will find no satisfaction here, but I assure you I will find it in Congress and in the courts!" He nods to Sally. "Thank you for your hospitality." Adams stands and steps back from the table. "Come, Lawrence!" he calls over his shoulder as he leaves the room. Lawrence gathers up the newspapers on the table. He stuffs them back into his valise, mutters a "harrumph," and follows Adams out the front door.

Early one morning a few months later, Jake drags the old carriage out of the barn, sweeps the dust off it and polishes it. He readies two horses for the five-hour journey to Philadelphia, as Mrs. Bache had instructed him the previous evening. Aggie places a basket of refreshments on a seat in the coach, along with a woolen blanket to ward off any chill.

Mrs. Bache appears on the front porch, satchel in hand, shortly after sunrise. Jake thinks her attire unusual for a long ride and on the dusty, potholed road north. She wears a silk dress with a gauzy white shawl draped over her shoulders. A creation from a fancy hat-maker in London is perched on top of her head. Jake senses trouble as he takes Sally's bag and opens the door to the carriage. Her mood has been dark since the President's visit, and plain foul since a message arrived from one of Benny's friends in Philadelphia a few days ago.

"Let's go, then," Sally says tersely, without so much as a 'good morning'.

After several hours, with only one brief stop at a coaching inn, they arrive at their destination in Philadelphia. Jake jumps down to open Sally's door, but she has already stepped out and onto the street.

"You coming with me?" she inquires, smoothing her skirt.

"I thought I'd like to stay right here, Ma'am."

Sally nods her head. "Suit yourself."

Jake watches her totter over the cobbles to the entry of a three-story row house. The house is that of a prosperous man, of pinkish-red brick, with tall parlor windows and a front door painted glossy blue. Ivory curtains are tied back in most of the windows on all three floors. Sally climbs the front steps and pulls the bell cord next to the door. She adjusts her shawl as she waits.

A moment later, Benny's maid, Sigrid, shows Sally into the entry hall and takes her wrap from her. Sally declines to surrender her hat. Sigrid is not more than seventeen, a fair-haired, hefty German girl.

"I received word from a friend of my son that he is unwell."

"He is in a real bad way, Mrs. Bache," Ingrid whispers in her German accent.

"Where is he?" Sally inquires anxiously.

Ingrid points to the stairway. "Upstairs… in his room."

Miriam steps into the foyer from the back of the house. She looks as though she has had little sleep in recent days; her eyes are dark and hollow. "Mother! It is so good of you to come!" she exclaims, attempting to peck Sally on the cheek.

Sally retreats from Miriam's kiss. "So, what seems to be wrong with my son?" she asks. "I must tell you that President Adams paid a visit to Benny's father and me. He spoke in the most threatening terms about Benny."

"It's the fever, Mrs. Bache. Benny has the Yellow Fever," Miriam replies, with fear in her weary eyes.

"Why didn't you send for me?" Sally growls, and brushes past Miriam. She hikes up her skirt and hurries up the stairs.

Miriam follows her. "The doctor has just left him. He's resting now," she calls after her mother-in-law.

Miriam places a kerchief over her mouth as she follows Sally into the bedroom, where Benny lies in a four-poster bed. The curtains are drawn closed and the room is quite dark, but for the embers of a recent fire glowing in a fireplace on the wall opposite the bed.

"Why is it so goddamn dark in here?" Sally barks as she goes to the windows and pulls the curtains back. Afternoon sunlight floods the room. Sally steps close to the bed, and sees that her son is jaundiced, weak and soaking with perspiration.

"Benny, it's Mama," she whispers in his ear.

Benny appears to not hear her. Delirious, he rolls his head from side to side.

"You should have called for me!" Sally hisses at Miriam. She looks from a bandage wrapped around Benny's arm to an enameled pan half-filled with blood sitting on the floor next to the bed. "What's this about?" she demands to know.

Miriam lowers the cloth over her mouth. "The doctor has been bleeding him."

Sally pulls a chair next to the bed and touches Benny's forehead with the back of her hand. "He's hot as blazes! What have you done besides bleed him?"

"Dr. Rush has been purging him. The bad humors are evacuated out the bowels that way, or so he says."

"You stupid woman!" Sally fires back. "He has hardly any pulse! We have got to get him into a cold bath. Fetch Sigrid to help us make a tub ready." Sally points to the doorway. "Hurry! Go!" she shrieks.

Miriam scurries out of the room, as ordered. "Sigrid! Come, quickly!" she yells down the stairway. Sally opens the window and sees

Jake leaning against the carriage, smoking his pipe. "Jake!" she calls down to him. "We need your help!"

He hears her and looks up to the window.

"Take the carriage around to the mews. We're going to be here a while," she yells.

Jake nods his head. He knew in the morning that something wasn't quite right.

London   1798

A gilded sign over the doorway of a shop in Soho reads, '*The Splendid, Fine Coffees. Est. 1757*'. William and Temple are seated at a table in the bowed front window of the coffee house. Dark green walls behind them are covered with framed etchings of the establishment's artistic and celebrated clientele.

William stirs sugar into his cup. "If you go to Paris now, I fear I will never see you again," he says earnestly.

"Nonsense," Temple argues. "Benny's passing was a sign I should get on with my life…

Go back to the place where I was happy, whilst I'm still able." Temple leans across the table. "Benny was only twenty-nine, Father!"

"Truly tragic," William concedes. "The Fever does not discriminate. It takes all ages. At least poor Benny escaped Adams's wrath and a prison sentence. There were rumors of a charge of *treason*." William sips his coffee. "You *do* plan to take Anne and your daughter with you, do you not?" Temple lifts his cup. "I may send for them eventually. First, I will stay with the Caillots… get my bearings again. You *will* look after little Elizabeth, won't you Father?"

William furrows his brows. "I will, if you marry Anne before you leave."

Temple sips his coffee. "I will *never* marry Anne."

William looks into his son's defiant eyes and can hear his own father, sniggering from 'The Beyond'.

Ohio   1799

Bobby and James Carter, now a strapping nineteen-year-old, walk toward the farmhouse on a warm afternoon in autumn. Both carry a scythe and are at the end of a long day in the fields. Their shirts are stained with perspiration. They see Jonas and Ellsworth step out of the barn and into the sunlight. A man stands next to his horse in the drive, waiting for Ellsworth.

Bobby grabs James's arm and pulls him behind an apple tree. They wait there and watch. After a few minutes of chatter with Jonas, Ellsworth joins his companion and they mount their horses and ride off toward the road. Bobby and James emerge from their hiding place.

"What did those men want, Pa?" James calls to his father.

Jonas slides the barn door closed. "They're after two boys on the run from a master in Virginia. Seems they come in this direction. I let Ellsworth look around the barn, like he asked."

Bobby shakes his head. "One 'a these days, that Ellsworth is gonna snatch me outta that field yonder and sell me to pick cotton down South," he predicts, pointing toward stalks of maize, swaying in the afternoon breeze.

James holds his scythe in a menacing pose. "They would have to get past me, first, Uncle Bobby!"

Bobby grins and tousles the hair on the back of James's head.

Later that evening, Ellen crosses the yard from the house to the barn, carrying a milk pail. She slides the big door open a few feet and enters the barn. She sets the pail next to the ladder to the hayloft.

She looks up to the loft and clears her throat. "Ahem! I am leavin' some food here for you. You boys get movin' before daylight. Stay away from the roads. Cross the creek a few times so's the dogs lose your scent. Keep on heading north."

Up in the loft, two African American boys, fifteen or sixteen years old, huddle behind a wooden partition. They are partially covered with dried hay. Their shirts are ragged and dirty. They listen to Ellen with wide eyes, but don't move or make a sound. One of them holds a knife in his hand. The long blade of it gleams in a shaft of moonlight that peeks through a gap in the wall boards.

DEAR BEN

"There's two 'a my son's shirts hangin' on the line behind the house. Take 'em when you go. Listen to me now: you boys be on your way at first light. My husband will kill me if he finds out I been helpin' you!"

Ellen goes out the barn door, sliding it closed behind her, and scurries across the yard to the house.

Bobby has trouble sleeping that night. He's had a few drinks, but they are not helping him get to sleep. A candle still burns on the table next to his bed well after dark. His door is ajar. He hears Jonas snoring in the room next door. Bobby sits up and looks at a letter lying on the table. It is from Mr. Bache and had arrived in the post the previous day, but Bobby hadn't gotten around to reading it. Mr. Bache's hand reminded him of Dr. Ben's books in the Greek language.

Bobby hears a noise from downstairs. Somebody was attempting to jimmy open the kitchen window. He sits up in bed, swings around, and plants his feet on the floor. His heart races. Bobby remembers latching the window himself and turning the key in the kitchen door to lock it securely. The noise stops. He hears footsteps leaving the covered porch.

He blows out his candle and pulls back the sheet covering his window a few inches and sees two dark figures bounding through the tall grass between the house and the road. Are they men? Boys? He can't be sure, but they both carry a cloth of some kind in their hands. One of them holds a long knife. The figures sprint across the road and disappear into the woods on the other side.

Agitated, Bobby relights his candle, rises from the bed and takes a drink from the whiskey bottle on his dresser. He picks up Bache's letter and tiptoes out of his room and down the hall to Rachel's bedroom. He sees a light under her door and taps lightly. A moment later, Rachel opens her door. She is barefooted and wears a flannel night gown. An oil lamp burns on the table next to her bed and she holds a book in her hand.

"I couldn't sleep," Bobby whispers.

"I can't either," Rachel whispers and opens the door wider, inviting Bobby in. She jumps back into her bed and Bobby sits in a spindle-back chair next to it. "I think I saw those runaways that your Pa was talkin' about. They musta been hidin' behind the barn or somethin'."

"You think so?"

"They gone now." Bobby hands Rachel the letter. "Can you help me read this, honey? Mr. Bache's handwritin' so bad…"

"Sure." Rachel takes the letter out of the envelope, unfolds it, and begins to read. "*Dear Bobby, The past couple of years have been real hard on Mrs. Bache. We lost our boy, Benny, and Aggie and Jake passed away within three months of each other. We are lost without them. Here we are, two lonely old folks looking after each other.*" Rachel lowers the letter. "Kinda sad, isn't it?"

Bobby nods his head and sits up in his chair.

"'*The children visit sometimes, but don't stay long. They have their own busy lives many miles away, so we live here quietly.*" Rachel and Bobby catch each other's gaze. After a moment, Rachel returns to the letter. "*I do enjoy fishing, and Sally reads and tends to her chickens, so the days pass. Sometimes, I can't see anything ahead for us, but who's to say?*" Rachel re-folds the letter. "I know what you're thinking," she says.

The next evening, Bobby saddles his horse and secures his travel bags. A bracing wind whistles through the rafters of the barn. Rachel walks into the barn and stands a few feet away from Bobby, watching. Sparky sits near Bobby's feet.

After a minute or two, Rachel hands Bobby a rifle she has concealed behind her back. "Take this, Uncle Bobby. It's old… Pa won't miss it."

Bobby grins and accepts the firearm from her, and inserts it into a scabbard attached to his saddle. He caresses her face with his hand. "I will miss you, child. You are a' angel from heaven, you know."

She smiles and holds Bobby's hand close to her cheek for a moment.

Bobby leads his horse out of the barn into the gathering dusk.

A scattering of brilliant stars has begun to sparkle overhead. He puts on his hat, pulls his jacket closed, mounts his horse, and rides down the drive to the road. The dog, tail wagging, runs alongside Bobby's horse as far as the road, then turns back and lumbers toward Rachel. She stands next to the barn with her arms folded across her chest, her long skirt blowing in the breeze. She watches Bobby until he disappears.

A few nights later, Bobby plods along a narrow country lane in a light rain. He pulls down the rim of his hat and raises his coat collar, sinking his head into his coat, turtle-like. After a time, he dismounts and leads his horse to shelter in the woods near the road. They both take water from a brook running through a clearing in the trees. He tethers his horse, spreads his coat on the ground, sits down and leans against the trunk of a stout elm. He wraps himself in a blanket, and listens.

An owl high in a nearby tree hoots, swoops down into the clearing at lightning speed, and scoops up a small critter with its talons. Bobby can hear the rush of the great bird's wings as it flies off with its prey. Rain patters on the leaves above him and drips onto his blanket. A hungry wolf howls in the woods. Bobby rolls onto his side, with one hand on his rifle, and sleeps.

Delaware

Richard Bache decided to try his luck fishing for brown trout earlier in the morning than is usual. He stands at the end of the dock below the farmhouse, with his fishing pole in hand and his creel on the dock next to him. He hears a fish jump for an insect, but he can't see it for the fog rising from the river and swirling about his feet like smoke. He hears another fish jump and casts his line into the river, moving his rod left and right, hoping for a bite.

He hears a horse ride from the road onto the drive to the farm. *'Odd,'* he thinks. He isn't expecting company. As the visitor rides closer, the fog parts and eddies behind his horse. Richard recognizes the man: it is Bobby, Ben Franklin's servant. "*I'll be damned!*" he says, under his breath.

When he nears the dock, Bobby dismounts and tethers his horse to a rail.

"Hallo, Mr. Bache," he calls. Bobby's boots stomp along the wooden planks of the dock as he approaches Richard, who lays down his pole and walks to meet Bobby half-way.

"Bobby! What a surprise!"

Richard wipes the remains of fish bait onto his trousers and offers Bobby his hand. The two men shake hands warmly. Bobby is surprised by the silver hair peeking out from under Richard's hat.

"Are you on your way somewhere?" Richard inquires.

Bobby shakes his head. "I got your letter. I was hopin' you might have some work for me," he confides.

Richard studies Bobby without speaking for a moment, then: "You should talk to Sally," he says, pointing up a rise toward a weathered board-and-batten barn. "She's up there feeding her chickens."

Bobby tips his hat to Mr. Bache, then turns and walks up the hill toward the barn.

He meets Sally walking from the chicken coop with a basket on her arm. When she sees him, she stops, sets the basket on the ground, wipes her hands on her calico skirt, and pulls a shawl draped over her shoulders closed tightly around her.

"Well, well," Sally says, placing her hands on her hips. "I didn't think you'd get ten miles and you have been gone near ten years."

Bobby shrugs his shoulders. He fights back the tears welling up in his eyes.

"You just passing by?" she inquires, fussing with a strand of hair falling over her eyes.

"No, Ma'am. I thought I might like to stay," Bobby says, his voice cracking.

Sally regards him quietly for a long moment. "Well, then, we had better go get your room ready," she offers, and picks up her basket.

As she passes by him, Bobby attempts to take the basket from her.

Sally pulls the basket away from him. "I can carry my own damn eggs," she says curtly.

She leads Bobby down the slope toward the river and the house. As he follows her up the steps and onto the porch, the treads feel secure and steady under his feet. He feels safe.

EPILOGUE

Bobby lived the rest of his days with the Baches, as a free man. William never saw his son again. He and Mary raised Temple's daughter as their own. William outlived Mary by several years, and died a pauper in London in 1814, at the age of 86. He was next in line to win the 'Tontine', which was worth a considerable fortune.

Polly's daughter, Eliza, remained in America and raised a happy family in Philadelphia, as did Polly's son, Tom, who returned from England to practice medicine.

The Franklin mansion on Market Street was demolished in 1812.

Temple married an English woman a few months before he died in Paris in 1823, aged 61. His wife took Franklin's papers to London afterwards. They were later found being used for patterns in a tailor's shop.

Life, like a drama,

should finish handsomely.

Benj Franklin

ACKNOWLEDGMENTS

I was challenged by my friend and neighbor, the actor David Huddleston, ("The Big Lebowski") to write a Franklin play for him. He had played Benjamin Franklin in the musical, "1776," on Broadway and loved the role. David and his wife, casting director Sarah Koeppe, were pleased with an early reading of the play and I was off on "A Long Day's Journey Into Franklin." Unfortunately, David did not live to see the work completed.

I later approached Hollywood script consultant Kathie Fong Yoneda, telling her, "I have this play…" "You need Rocaberti," Kathie said, sending me to the 2018 Rocaberti Writers' Retreat in Angouleme, France. Claire Terry, Founder/Director of Rocaberti, had faith in my project and urged me to study under the brilliant Joan Lane ("The King's Speech") the following year.

Meanwhile, the stage play evolved into a movie for television. Playwright and script consultant, Theo Salter, gave me invaluable notes on an early draft of the "Dear Ben" teleplay, helping shape the script for my second retreat at Marouette Castle. Thank you, Theo.

Under Ms. Lane's tutelage, "Dear Ben" morphed to a nine-episode mini-series for television. A teacher of writing and editor extraordinaire, she urged me to go on to write a book based upon the mini-series. I was happy to oblige, with her looking over my shoulder.

Both teleplay and book are largely fictional, but based on historical records. Research associate Laurel Reisinger was always at the ready with historical tidbits needed to fill the gaps and to move the narrative along. (As well as supplying a few great lines of dialogue.)

A note of gratitude as well to playwright and author Kay Eldredge, who provided her very thoughtful and spot-on insights after looking over an early draft of "Dear Ben."

Thanks, also, to Debra Engle of Story Summit Writer's School for her friendship and advice.

Early readers of bits and pieces of "Dear Ben" are my heroes; they did the heavy lifting. Among them are: Jeannie Walla, Dr. Sue Laudert, Tanya Binford, Betty Sullivan, Rick Erdenberg, Jon Jahr, Whitney Stewart, and Tom Hockins. English friends Lady Caroline Wrey and her family, as well as Charles and Hilary Barker, have been endlessly patient with readings and performances. Troupers, all of them.

Special thanks to Al Reisinger for his guidance and support of the "Dear Ben" project, after reading only one scene.

Of course, I think of David Huddleston. If I hadn't seen David for a while and then caught him at the mailbox, I might ask him, "How are you?" "Very talented," he always replied, which he certainly was.

"DEAR BEN"
BIBLIOGRAPHY

THE FOLLOWING BOOKS INFORMED AND INSPIRED THE "DEAR BEN" STORY

- **"The Autobiography of Benjamin Franklin"**
  Intro by Andrew S. Trees
  Barnes & Noble 2005

- **"The First American, The Life and Times of Benjamin Franklin"**
  H. W. Brands Doubleday/Random House 2000

- **"Benjamin Franklin, An American Life"**
  Walter Isaacson
  Simon and Schuster 2003

- **"Young Benjamin Franklin, The Birth of Ingenuity"**
  Nick Bunker
  Knopf 2018

- **"Benjamin Franklin"**
  Carl Van Doren
  Viking Press

- **"The Real Benjamin Franklin"**
  Part I
  Andrew Allison
  National Center for Constitutional Studies 2009

- **"The Real Benjamin Franklin"**
  Part II

- **"Timeless Treasures from Benjamin Franklin"**
  Prepared by W. Cleon Skousen and Richard M. Maxfield

- **"The Papers of Benjamin Franklin"**
  Frank Donovan
  Apollo Editions 1962

- "The Age of Reason" and
  "The Age of Voltaire"
  Will and Ariel Durant
  Simon and Schuster

- "Famous Last Words"
  Ray Robinson
  Workman Press 2003

- "Immortal Last Words"
  Terry Breverton Quercus
  Publishing 2010

- "His Excellency George
  Washington"
  Joseph J. Ellis
  Knopf 2004

- "Alexander Hamilton,
  A Life"
  Willard Sterne Randall
  Harper Collins 2003

- "Twilight at Monticello;
  The Final Years of
  Thomas Jefferson"
  Alan Pell Crawford
  Random House 2008

- "The School for Scandal"
  Play by R.B. Sheridan
  Gutenberg.org

- "History of Art"
  H.W. Janson
  Abrams, Inc 1964

Important Articles

- "Speaking American,
  A History of English
  in the U.S."
  Richard W. Bailey

- "Ben Franklin's
  Dangerous Liaisons"
  William Econberger
  Chicago Tribune, May 6, 1990

- "Street Lighting in
  Paris Around 1800"
  Google Search

- "A Bit About Voltaire"
  Quotations Book Online.com

- "What led Benjamin Franklin
  to live estranged from his wife
  for nearly two decades."
  The Smithsonian Magazine.com
  181964400

- "Glenda Jackson on
  Shakespeare"
  New York Times,
  March 31, 2019

- "The House that
  Franklin Built"
  Antiques and Fine Art
  Page Talbott, PhD.

Additional Online Sources

- "Sarah F. Bache (Sally): History of American Women"
  Wikipedia

- "Temple's grave, women, and children."
  The Friends of Franklin.
  Re: Temple Franklin
  Martin Mangold

- "Thomas Jefferson's Monticello"
  Monticello Archives online

- "Benjamin F. Bache (Benny), Journalist"
  Wikipedia

- "Letter to Benjamin Franklin from Margaret Stevenson"
  April 24, 1775
  Founders Online

- "Covent Garden Market Moves Out"
  Ann Bransford

- "Covent Garden History"
  Coventgardenmemories.org.uk

- "Virginia Plantations, Colonial Life"
  Historyisfun.org

- "South Carolina Plantations"
  scencyclopedia.org

- "Dogs at Sea"
  The Mary Rose Museum, Portsmouth

- Letter from Charles F. Barker

- "Benjamin Franklin's 200 Synonyms for 'Drunk'"
  Mentalfloss.com

- "William Franklin's Imprisonment"
  New England Historical Society

- "Muzzleloaders"
  Popularmechanics.com/weapons

- "Smoking: History of London's Lost Tobacco Houses"
  Telegraph.co.uk

- "The Tontine"
  Thomas B. Costair

- "White's Club"
  Wikipedia.org

- "Black's Club"
  Wikipedia.org

- "Lincoln's Inn Fields"
  Wikipedia.org

Additional Online Sources, continued

- "Lord Rockingham – 2nd Marquess" Wikipedia.org

- "Carlton House, History and Décor" Wikepedia.org

- "Leicester House" Wikipedia.org

- "Signers of the Constitution; Concluding Endorsement" Gouverneur Morris Wikipedia.org

- "Valley Forge" History.com/topics/amrev/vf and U.S. History.org/march/phl/vfand Mt. Vernon.org/library/digital history

- "Nine Sisters Masonic Lodge" freemasonry.network

- "Masonry in the World Famous Lodge of the Nine Sisters" Freemasons for dummies.blogspoke

- "Franklin Papers in the Library of Congress" Collections/benjaminfranklin/pages

- "Franklin Quotations" fiedu/bf.famquotes

- "Benjamin Franklin in the American Revolution" Smithsonian Magazine.com 87199988

- "Letter from Benjamin Franklin to the Comte de Vergennes" April 15, 1782 and July 10, 1780 Founders Online

- "Letter from Madame Brillon to Benjamin Franklin" June 9, 1778 Founders Online

- "Ambassador to France" Benjamin Franklin Historical Society

- "History of European Royalty from 1650" Letter from Jon Jahr

- "The Quarter Horse and Hobby Horse" International Museum of the Horse

- "George III and Equerries" Our American Revolution.org

Additional Online Sources, continued

- "How to be an
  18th Century Gentleman"
  Pinterest

- "Libraries Acquire Franklin's
  Formative First Publication";
  An Elegy on the
  Death of Aquila Rose
  The Pennsylvania Gazette

- "Symptoms of Small Pox"
  The Cleveland Clinic on line

- "French Monuments, EU"
  French Gardens in April

- "Yorktown"
  History.com

- "Epidemics in 1700's America"
  National Institute of Health

- "History of T. B.
  (White Plague)"
  PHBMED.gov

- "Bathing in the 18th Century"
  Dr. Jerry Hedrick
  Blogspot.com

- "History of the Cuckoo Clock"
  Google Search

- "History of the Queens's Chapel"
  royalchapelsavoy.org

- "How Did the Traditon of
  Christmas Trees Start"
  Britannica.com Amy Tikkanen

- "Map of 1752"
  Philadelphia – Facts,
  Early History, on line

- "Vintage Wine Bottles"
  Steven Hannegan, on line

- "Small Arms From
  1700 – 1799"
  Kentucky Rifle, mfg.in
  Pennsylvania in 1730

"DEAR BEN" REVIEWS

"'Dear Ben' is brilliantly well-written, really colorful and evocative. I can picture it being a huge success as a TV series, providing a sumptuous period piece on a really interesting topic. The characters were all very human, and many of them endearing, which made it a real page-turner, for I found I cared what happened to them all."
Sophie Cox, former reader for Oxford University Press.

"'Dear Ben' is just delightful. Such a great window on to the man."
See-Saw Films, London.

"'Dear Ben'" is so interesting and enjoyable. This is a great work... It was a pleasure to read.
Fran Hampton, Wichita Friends' Book Club

Michael Koski's fictional adaptation of the life of Benjamin Franklin brings a new perspective to this storied American statesman. Koski's descriptions are not only poignant and insightful, but often amusing. I so enjoyed this book and highly recommend it.
Mary Kachoyeanos, author of "Zoe"

I was fascinated to learn about Franklin's relationships with his family, including his common-law wife, Deborah, and his son, William, about whom little has been written. "Dear Ben" confirms Franklin's reputation as a ladies' man!
Dr. Sue Laudert

I just read the excerpt from "Dear Ben" and LOVED it...A fascinating scene with great characterizations and realistic dialogue. Great stuff!
Jeannie Walla, Singer/actress, Aspen

ABOUT THE AUTHOR

Michael Koski is a graduate of the UCLA Department of Theatre Arts. He has written ad copy, commercials, and made many short films, including "Eye Music" for the Frank Lloyd Wright Foundation. He wrote and directed the soap, "Edge of Ajax" for television in Aspen, Colorado. As corporate vice-president, he designed advertising, events, and public relations for Design Center South in Laguna Niguel, California.

He lives in Palm Springs, California, where he is a residential interior designer. His projects have included a guest house for the Kingdom of Saudi Arabia, as well as interiors for fine homes in several states. He is presently working on projects in Palm Springs, Rancho Mirage, Orange County, and Scottsdale, Arizona. See michaelkoskidesign.com for more information.